Wiesław Myśliwski

A Treatise on Shelling Beans

Translated from the Polish by Bill Johnston

archipelago books

Archipelago Books
232 3rd Street #A111
Brooklyn, NY 11215
www.archipelagobooks.org

Distributed by Random House
www.randomhouse.com

Library of Congress Cataloging-in-Publication Data
Mysliwski, Wieslaw.
[Traktat o łuskaniu fasoli. English]
A treatise on shelling beans / by Wieslaw Mysliwski ;
translated from the Polish by Bill Johnston. – First Archipelago Books edition.
Originally published in Polish as Traktat o łuskaniu fasoli.
ISBN 978-1-935744-90-0
I. Title.
PG7172.Y8T7313 2013
891.8'5373—dc23   2013010328

Cover art: Paul Klee

The publication of *A Treatise On Shelling Beans* was made possible with
generous support from Lannan Foundation, the National Endowment for the Arts,
and the New York State Council on the Arts, a state agency.

This publication has been funded by the Book Institute –
the © POLAND Translation Program.

Printed in the United States of America

A Treatise on Shelling Beans

1

You're here to buy beans, sir? From me? I mean, you can get beans in a store, any store. But please, come on in. Don't let the dogs scare you. They'll just sniff at you a bit. Whenever anyone visits for the first time they have to sniff them. For my benefit. I didn't teach them that, they just do it of their own accord. Dogs are as much of a puzzle as people. Do you have a dog? You ought to get one. You can learn a lot from a dog. All right, sit, Rex, sit, Paws. Knock it off.

Out of curiosity, how did you find the place? I'm not that easy to find. Especially now, in the off-season. There isn't even anyone around to ask. You saw for yourself, there's not a living soul in the cabins. They're all long gone. Not many people even know I live here. And here you come asking about beans. It's true, I do grow some beans, but only enough for my own needs, which are pretty modest. Like with everything else. Carrots, beets, onions, garlic, parsnip, just so I have a little. And truth be told, I don't even like beans that much. I mean, I'll eat them, because I'll eat almost anything. But I'm not wild about them. Once in a while I'll make bean soup or bean stew, but not that often. And dogs don't eat beans.

Back in the day, sure, a lot of people grew beans around here. Because as you might know, at one time beans used to take the place of meat. And when you work as hard as the folks hereabouts would work, from dawn till nighttime, you need your meat. Not to mention that the shopkeepers often used to come out here to stock up on beans. Not beans alone, but that's what they'd buy most of. That's right, during the war, when there was a village here. At that time, in the towns people were starving, as you know. Almost every day the locals would drive out to the station in their horse and cart to pick them up. The station's a couple of miles away. Then afterwards they'd drive them back with what they'd bought. It was around this time of year, late fall, that they'd come most often. Or in any case more of them would come about now, when the harvest was all done. They'd take all the beans that anyone had had time to shell, down to the last bean. Often the pods hadn't even dried out properly but already people would be shelling away in all the houses so as to finish in time. Whole families would be shelling together. From early morning till late at night. Sometimes you'd go outside at midnight and there'd still be a light in a window here and there. Especially when there'd been a good crop. Because beans are like everything else, sometimes they grow well, other times not. It has to be a good year weather-wise. Beans don't like too much sun. When there's too much sun there's not enough rain, and they get parched. Whereas if there's too much rain, they rot before they can grow. Even so, it can be a good weather year but still every other pod will be empty or the beans'll be bad. And no one knows why. Simple thing like beans, but they have their secrets.

Did you used to come out here back then, as a shopkeeper? No, I think I'd have recognized you. I knew almost all the people that used to come to buy beans. We grew a lot of beans, and all kinds of merchants would come buy them. Ever since I was a kid I've had a good memory for faces. And everyone knows that what you remember in your childhood, you remember for good. Course, you'd have been young back then, and dressed differently. In those days the shopkeepers would wear any old clothes, however rich or poor they were, they'd dress down so as not to draw attention to themselves. In the trains they'd be searched, have their belongings confiscated. Shopkeepers was just our name for them. While now I see you're wearing an overcoat, hat, scarf. I used to have a brown felt hat like that, and a coat like yours. And I'd wear a scarf, silk or cashmere. I liked to dress well.

But why don't you take your coat off? Hang it on the back of the door, there's a hook there. And please, sit yourself down. Either on a chair or on a bench, as you prefer. I'll just finish this nameplate, I'm almost done. It wouldn't take me so long, but my hands aren't what they used to be. No, it's rheumatism. Though it's better than it used to be. I can do almost anything. I just can't play the saxophone. That's right, I used to play. But aside from that, anything. Even repainting these nameplates, as you see. And that needs concentration in your hands also. The worst is with the smallest letters. If the brush slips you have to wipe the whole letter off with benzine and start over.

Why did I think you maybe used to come here as a shopkeeper? Well, you just appeared out of nowhere wanting to buy beans. You must have known people used to grow beans around here and you thought they still did. People often think, what could possibly have changed in a place where they've grown beans since forever. But how did you manage to hold on to the conviction that there are timeless places like that? That I can't understand. Didn't you know that places like to mislead us? Everything misleads us, it's true. But places more than anything. If it weren't for these nameplates I myself wouldn't know that this was the place.

You've never been here before? Not even as a shopkeeper back then? Then I'm sorry I took you for one. Evidently I've been sitting too long staring at these nameplates. What are they? First and last names, dates, God rest their souls. Every year at this time I take them from the gravestones and repaint them. It's pretty time-consuming. The first name and last name alone's a lot of letters. And I have to mind every letter so the deceased won't think I repainted his nameplate any old how because, for instance, he was from the other side of the river. Folks here were always divided into this side and the other side of the river. When people can be divided by something they always will be. It doesn't have to be a river.

Why do I think the dead have thoughts? Because we don't know that they don't. What do we know? Sometimes, after only two or three letters, especially the littlest ones, my eyes hurt and my hand starts to shake, and I have to break off. You need a lot of patience with those dead letters. I barely finish one lot when the paint starts peeling on the ones I did last year. It comes off faster in the woods. It's damp there, you only get sunlight in the clearings, so I'm always having to repaint. If I didn't do it, by now you wouldn't know whose nameplate was whose. I've tried different kinds of paints, including foreign ones. They all peel. You don't know any kind of paint that doesn't peel? You're right. It's not in anyone's interest that something should be permanent. Especially paint. Things are always being painted over with something else.

That I don't know. Maybe someone used to repaint them before, though not for long probably, because I could barely read what was written on them. Whoever it was must have decided that either way no one can be guaranteed anything in perpetuity in this world, so they just stopped. Plus there are the costs, the paint alone, then the brushes, labor. It's just as well I used to know everyone in these parts. Even so, I still had to scour my memory in some cases. It was worst with the children. Some of them I felt I was only now christening.

This here is Zenon Kuźdżał. I'm almost done with him. He was the youngest of the Kuźdżałs. Neighbors. Here on this side, a bit further into the woods. That was why they only had a fence on the side where the road was, the other three sides were woods, so they'd say they had no need of a fence. The woods are the best fence you can have. What danger could come from the woods? Who could come to the house through the woods? At most some animal. So they set snares and traps in their yard. Often their own chickens and geese and ducks would get caught if they forgot to remove the traps during the day. Though in the evening they never could count up all those chickens and ducks and what have you properly. And every evening they'd suspect their neighbors.

They only ever let the neighbors in through the wicket gate on the road. The wicket gate was in one side of the main gateway, and the gateway wasn't just an ordinary gateway. It was twice as high as the fence, and it had a shingled roof and two figures on either side. I don't remember which particular saints they were. The fence itself was tall. The tallest person in the village was Uncle Jan, and he couldn't touch the top even when he went up on tiptoe and stretched out his hand. A rattle hung on the wicket gate, you had to rattle it and someone would come down from the house and let you in. But try getting in through the woods and right away they'd be coming at you with crowbars, sicking their dogs on you. You'd have to go back to the wicket gate and shake the rattle.

You wouldn't have gotten any beans from them, though, because they were all carvers. The grandfather made carvings, he was old as the hills, he had cataracts but if you could have seen him carving away you'd never have believed he couldn't see. How he did it I have no idea. Maybe he made his hands look? His three grandsons, Stach, Mietek, and Zenek, they were all carvers. All strapping guys, though you'd never see them out with young ladies. You only ever saw them carving. The only one who wasn't a carver was their father. He'd cut blocks of wood for them to make their carvings out of, rough-hew them. He probably would have made carvings as well but he was missing these three fingers here on this hand, they were blown off in the war before the last war. But he somehow managed with chopping and hewing. Word was the great-grandfather had been a carver, and the great-great-grandfather, and there was no telling how far back in time you'd have to go with those carver ancestors, because from what they said everyone in their family had made carvings since time immemorial. Even on Sundays, after the service or high mass they'd come back from church and right away they'd start carving what they'd heard from the Gospel so as not to forget it. They had plans to carve the whole Gospel, because as the grandfather put it, the world was the way God described it, not the way people saw it.

Their whole yard was littered with those carvings of theirs, they stood them all the way up into the woods. They went further and further. That may have been another reason they didn't build a fence on the side of the woods. You couldn't turn a wagon round in their yard, you had to back up. When they'd lead the cows out to pasture they had to mind they didn't knock the carvings over. Cats would lie about on them sunning themselves. Sometimes their dog would start yapping out of the blue, they'd rush out of the house thinking someone must have come in from the woods, but it would turn out the dog was only barking at one of the carvings. Just as well he was on a short leash. Mrs. Kużdżał would go out to throw grain down for her poultry and people would laugh and say she was feeding the carvings, because they were getting bigger and bigger.

They weren't regular carvings like you might imagine. I can see you're a decent height yourself, but those carvings were way bigger than either you or me. "The Last Supper," for instance, when they started carving that they made a clearing in the woods. The table alone was like several of these tables of mine, the benches were several times the size of my benches. And even so, the apostles were sitting so close to each other that it seemed there wasn't any room for Jesus. He was squashed between one apostle who stood with a glass in his outstretched hand, and another one who was already asleep with his head on the table, and he was a lot smaller than the others. If they'd all stood up next to one another he wouldn't even have come up to their waists. He was already wearing his crown of thorns, and he seemed worried about something; his head rested on his hand. From the other side of the table another one of the apostles was reaching out toward the crown of thorns as if he wanted to lift it off his head because it was too soon for it, but he couldn't reach it. On the table there were pitchers of wine, and each one of them, I don't own anything to compare with it. That big jug over there, or that bucket, they'd be too small. As for the bread, I don't recall ever seeing such huge loaves being baked anywhere. And back then people would bake loaves that weighed over twenty pounds. They were going to add a roof over the scene, but they didn't manage to.

I couldn't tell you what those carvings were worth. Back then I was simply afraid of them. But can fear be a measure for carvings? Especially when you're the age I was then. When mother sent me over there on some errand, to ask about something or borrow something, I'd tell her they didn't have any or that nobody had been home. Did you shake the rattle? I did, but no one came out. Actually I don't think she believed me, because a short while later she'd send over one of my sisters, Jagoda or Leonka, but she'd do it so I wouldn't see.

You never heard of them trying to sell any of their carvings. Who would they have sold them to? Take them to market? What an idea. And who would come all the way out here to the village to buy carvings? People came for foodstuffs, like I said, beans, flour, kasha. Though one time the grandfather, that's right, the blind one, he went to ask the priest for permission to put one or two of the carvings up in the church. But the priest wouldn't allow it because none of them had gone to any school to learn to carve.

Sometimes I'd have dreams about those carvings. I'd jerk awake in the middle of the night with a shout, bathed in sweat. Mother would think I was coming down with something. I'd have to drink herbs and eat honey because I was afraid to tell her it was the carvings. I don't know why. Maybe I was afraid that I was afraid. And of carvings on top of everything. Every fear has different levels, as you know. One kind of fear tears you from your sleep, another kind makes you fall asleep. And yet another kind . . . But there's no point talking about it. The carvings are gone, the Kużdżałs are gone. Besides, I actually liked honey, though the herbs made me scrunch up my face. But mother would stand over me, drink it all up, it'll do you good.

Do you like herbs? Then you're like me. But I bet you like honey? I'll give you a jar to take with you. At least you won't be mad at yourself for making a wasted trip. I have my own, not store-bought. Here at the edge of the woods, maybe you noticed, there's a handful of hives, they're mine. There aren't that many of them but when it's a good year I get oodles of honey. I couldn't eat it all myself. I've got some from a couple of years ago, the best kind is when it's left to stand awhile. When someone does a favor for me I'll thank them with honey if they won't let me pay them. Or like now, in the off-season, whenever anyone comes to visit they won't leave without a jar of honey. Or if someone has a name day party in one of the cabins, I'll go wish them all the best and at least take a jar of honey as a gift. Or where there are children, I always remember children even without any special occasion. Children ought to eat honey.

But honey's best when it's drunk. How? You put a teaspoon of honey in half a glass of lukewarm water. Let it stand till the next morning. Squeeze in a half or a quarter of lemon, stir it, and drink it on an empty stomach at least half an hour before breakfast. If it's too cold, add just a dash of hot water. It's pure goodness. Good for your heart, for rheumatism. Honey's good for everything. It'll keep you from catching cold. When I was young and I worked on building sites, one time we roomed at the house of this one beekeeper and he taught me all that. But back then who gave a thought to drinking honey? There was never the time. And if you were going to drink anything it would be vodka. In those days vodka was the best for everything, not honey.

What kind do you prefer, heather or honey-dew? The honey-dew is from conifers, not deciduous trees, it's virtually black, it's much better. In that case I'll give you a jar of each. My favorite is buckwheat honey. There used to be a guy here grew a lot of buckwheat. Three days ago I repainted his nameplate. The buckwheat hadn't even begun to flower and already he'd be putting up hives in it. I used to go watch him collecting honey from those hives of his. He'd be wearing a hood with a net over his face, and I'd just be there. And you won't believe it, but I never got stung by a bee. They'd land on me, but they never did a thing. He couldn't get over it. You're a strange kid, that you are. I'm the beekeeper here . . . Go bring a pot. And he'd pour me some honey straight from the hive.

These days, who'd grow buckwheat around here, and where? You saw for yourself, there's the lake they made, the cabins around the lake, and the woods. The woods were always there. They're the only thing that was there then and is here now. Except that the woods were mostly on this side. Now they've spread to the other side, where the fields used to be. If you don't hold woods back they'll grow everywhere, into your yard. They overgrew where the farmyards used to be. When I say the other side, I mean the other side of the Rutka. The Rutka?

That was the river that used to run through here, I told you how it split the village in two. How could they have made an artificial lake if there hadn't been a river? The name comes from *ruta*, rue, not from *ruda,* iron ore. Do you know what rue is? You're not the only one. Here in the cabins hardly anyone knows anything about herbs. At most mint, chamomile. They don't know their trees, can't tell an oak from a beech. Not to even mention hornbeams, sycamores. They can't tell rye from wheat, wheat from barley. They call it all grain. I wonder if they'd even recognize millet. I don't see many people growing millet these days.

Rue was used to treat different illnesses, on its own or with other herbs. They used it for eyes, for nerves, cuts and bruises, to prevent infection. You could drink it or make a compress. It could break spells. And most important of all, young women wove their garlands out of rue. It was like a magnet for young men. A lot of it grew around here, maybe that's where the Rutka got its name? You can't imagine what that river was like. It wasn't especially big, rivers that run through villages never are. It came down a broad valley where there were meadows, then after the valley the fields began. It was wider at some points, narrower in others. In some places, when it hadn't rained for a long time you could get across by stepping from one rock to another. When you stood at the edge of the valley and the sun would come out from behind the clouds, it looked like the Rutka was flowing across the entire width of the valley. Course, there were times it actually was that wide, when the ice melted, or when it just kept raining and raining. At those times you wouldn't believe it was the same Rutka, it was so wild. It didn't just cover the valley, the fields flooded as well. Anyone that lived close to the river had to move to higher ground. At those times people swore revenge on the Rutka, they wept over it. But then the waters would fall and it'd go back to being calm and good-natured. It would flow in its leisurely way. You could throw a stick into the water and walk alongside on the bank to see who was faster, you or the Rutka. Even if you only walked slowly, you'd always win. It twisted and turned, and in the places where it meandered it got overgrown with sweet rush, bulrushes, water lilies, white lotuses. When it all bloomed you can't imagine what it was like. Or if you could only have heard the nightingales in May.

It wasn't all shallow. Most places it was shallow. But it had its deep moments too. One of them was the deepest of all. People went there to drown themselves. Mostly young folks, when their parents wouldn't agree to them getting married. They said most of the ones that had drowned there, it was for that reason. That people had always gone there to drown themselves, because that was where it was deepest. Though they did it for different reasons. And not just young people. Though they didn't always choose drowning, some people hung themselves. And the Rutka just flowed on.

You might find it hard to believe, but to me it seemed the biggest river on earth. I was even convinced that all rivers were called Rutka and that they all came from the Rutka, like from a single mother. I'd already started at school but I still couldn't believe there were much bigger rivers in the world, and that they each had their own name.

We had a boat. Sometimes I'd drag it into the densest rushes, everyone would be calling me, mother, father, but I wouldn't answer. I'd just lie there in the bottom of the boat feeling like I was nowhere at all. And if you were to ask me whether I'd ever been happy, it was only ever then. You'd rather not ask me that? I understand. Or I'd take the boat out into the middle of the stream, lie down in it and float and float, and the river would carry me. What do you think, do rivers like that disappear? I really don't know. Sometimes I go and stand down by the lake and look out there wondering where it must flow now. And you know, one time I managed to make out one of its banks. Which one? To know that, I'd have to have known which one I was standing on.

I couldn't tell you where it came from or where it finished up. Back then no one went that far. It was scary to walk such a distance, the woods in these parts stretch on and on. Nowadays I don't go walking that far either, because why would I. Besides, you go into the woods on this side or the other, and right by the edge you have everything you could need. Blueberries, wild strawberries, blackberries, mushrooms. Not at this time of year, of course. You're too late for that. Now there's only cranberries. But you'd need to wait till the frosts set in, because they mostly grow in the bogs. The bogs aren't far from here. I could give you a jug, you could go pick yourself some. Cranberries are delicious with pâté. Especially when you add pears as well, and if it's pâté made from hare.

I don't go picking. I don't have time, I have to mind things here. Now for example, in the off-season, aside from me and the dogs, there's not a soul here. Once in a while someone'll come by to check on their cabin. Though in fact they don't need to. Everyone knows that it'll all be OK. It couldn't not be, because I'm here looking after things. They've had many an opportunity to see that for themselves. But I've no right to stop them if they want to come and see what's what. They belong to them. But that's usually in the morning. This time of day no one's likely to show up. At this time nothing happens. And dusk is starting to fall a lot earlier. A month ago I wouldn't have needed to turn on the lights. I could see the letters perfectly well, even the tiniest ones. And I wouldn't have needed my glasses. Whereas now, like you saw, it's dusk, and there isn't even the faintest ripple on the lake. You'd be forgiven for thinking the water had hardened into solid ground. Especially on a day like today, when there's no wind, someone might imagine they could cross from one shore to the other without getting their feet wet.

So you're staying in Mr. Robert's cabin? I don't think you arrived in the night, I would have heard you. I didn't sleep at all in the night, I'd have heard. In the night the faintest sound carries across the lake. I only got to sleep in the morning. The dawn was already starting to break, I looked out the window, but you weren't there then. After that I dropped off, I don't even know when. The fog held you up on the way? We didn't have any fog here. True, in the fall you get fog that's so dense you can barely drive through it. You're driving along and all of a sudden there's this white wall.

When I was still living abroad, one time in the fall, round about this time of year, I decided to come for a visit. In fall, when no one would be here. And I stayed in Mr. Robert's cabin, like you. Mr. Robert had told me where to find the key. Under the deck, hanging on a nail in the beam. That's where you found it too? There you go. Before that I'd only ever been here once, one Sunday during the season. Mr. Robert and I arrived together then. This time Mr. Robert couldn't make it. Of course I could have the use of his cabin, he said when I phoned him, but unfortunately he wouldn't be able to join me. He told me where things would be, and where I'd find the key.

The sun had already set by the time I crossed the border. I figured I'd arrive in the night and maybe even get a decent night's sleep. As long as I was on the highway everything went OK, it was a starry night, the moon was out, I could see clearly. But I turned off onto a side road, then onto another, and the fog started. To begin with it was sparse, and it only appeared here and there, I'd just drive through strips of mist lying in places across the road. My fog lamps worked just fine. I was even driving pretty fast for the time of day. But with every mile the strips of mist grew thicker. After a bit, it seemed like barriers of fog were starting to rise up in the road. You could only see anything in the towns, where there were lights. But as I'd leave each town I'd find myself in even thicker fog. It got denser and denser. The fog was in front of me, on top of me, to the sides, behind. It was like the world had gone away and there was only fog. I tried turning on all the lights I had, but nothing did any good. I was well aware that full beams are the worst in a situation like that. You turn them on and immediately you have a white screen in front of you. You can only use your sidelights and fog lamps. Best of all is if someone's with you in the car, they can crack the door open and watch the road surface, tell the guy at the wheel which way to go. But I was on my own. On top of that, there were no other cars either in front of me or behind. Because you can agree with another driver to take turns at leading, him for a bit, then you for a bit. In fog, the best way to know where to go is to follow someone else's red tail lights. At moments I almost lost confidence in whether I was even on the road, I was scared I'd drive into the ditch or hit a road sign or a tree. Honestly, I'd never driven in fog that bad before. Every now and then I'd stop and get out to take a breather. I'd stretch a bit, climb back in and drive on.

All of a sudden I see these strange faint little lights along the sides of the road. What could it be? To start off they were only here and there. But you could see they were in people's windows, even though the windows themselves were barely visible, let alone the houses, which were no more than faint outlines in the fog. I guessed I must be driving through some town, especially since there were more and more of the lights, they came closer together, and soon they formed a shining chain on either side of the road so it was like driving down a kind of avenue. Well, I wasn't exactly driving, more like inching along. The fog in front of me was still as dense as before.

Then, out of the blue two figures emerged from the fog right in front of the hood. It looked like two men. I didn't have time to hit the horn, I just slammed on the brakes. I broke out in a sweat and my heart pounded so loud it almost made the car shake. I was convinced they'd go for me, start hammering on the car windows, pull the door open, start calling me all kinds of names. And they'd have been right, because what of it that they'd been walking in the middle of the road? But can you imagine, they didn't even notice the car. I think they were arguing, I could hear hoarse raised voices. They were waving their arms, pushing at one another. It looked like on top of everything else I was about to witness a scrap in the middle of all the fog.

I wound the window down a bit and turned the radio up to the max. There was some booming music playing, I thought maybe they'd hear and get out of the way. Not a bit of it. They stood there swaying every which way, then all at once they threw their arms around one another, hugged affectionately, and kissed each other on the cheek. They were so drunk they each had to take turns holding the other guy up when he started to slip to the ground.

In the end I sounded the horn once and twice, and to my surprise they patted each other's arm and one moved to one side of the road, one to the other. My foot was already poised over the gas pedal when they suddenly came back and started hugging each other again. And this time they stayed there, holding on to each other and rocking, as if they'd vowed that they'd never part, they'd simply lie down and sleep where they were, on the road. But luckily they put their arms around each other and set off into the fog, taking up the whole width of the road. I crawled after them, hoping I might be able to get around them when one of them pulled the other to one side of the road. But whenever one of them pulled his companion toward one side, the second man would pull him back the other way. They zigzagged forward, plus they'd come to a halt every so often, clapping each other on the back, shaking the other guy or tugging at his hand. And I had to stop with them.

At a certain moment a gateway loomed up out of the fog over the road. Actually, it shone there. A chain of faint little lights, like the ones in the windows, marked it out from the roadside on one side. The lights climbed up then broke off in the middle over the roadway, probably the bulbs in the other half were burned out or there'd been a short circuit. On the half that was lit up, one word could be seen: Welcome. The message for sure was longer, but the other half of it had gone out.

They stopped in the gateway. They weren't hugging anymore, or shaking one another, or slapping each other on the back. They just shook hands, and I started to hope that maybe they'd finally go their separate ways. They couldn't let go of each other's hands, as if they weren't sure they could stand on their own two feet. In the end, though, they managed to pull apart, and one disappeared on one side of the road, the other one on the other.

I breathed a sigh of relief. But I didn't move off right away. I got out of the car and stood there for a while to calm down. The chill of the fog did me good. Only then did I get back in the car and move off very slowly. I'd gone maybe a few dozen yards, and here they appeared out of the fog again, in the middle of the road. I didn't know what to do. I pulled up. But they must have noticed the car, because they turned around clumsily to face me, still arm in arm. I rolled the window down and leaned out.

"Good evening, gentlemen. Do you think you could . . . ?"

They gestured as if to tell me they'd get out of the road right away. And in fact, a moment later they staggered forward. I decided to wait a while. I found some music on the radio and listened for a bit before I set off again. I drove with my heart in my mouth, my eyes peeled, worried they might loom up yet again out of the fog in the middle of the road. You may find it hard to believe, but it was like I'd grown attached to them. I'd even begun to miss them.

The lights came to an end and I sped up a little. A few miles further on I suddenly felt so tired that when I saw a lighted sign saying "Inn" I decided to stop.

The place was quiet and the owner polite. He advised me against driving in the fog. Fog like this, you've no business driving in it. Get some sleep, some rest, let the fog clear. Our rooms are comfy, reasonable. Would you like something hot to eat? We can make it right away. Will you have a beer? These days you can get any kind of beer you want. Imported even. Or would you prefer something a little stronger? We'll have a room ready for you in no time. We've had a busy day today.

"What were all those lights in the windows? And the gateway?" I asked without thinking. "Was it because of the fog?"

He gave me a distrustful look.

"Where are you from?"

"I live abroad."

It was only then he softened:

"There was a procession with a holy picture."

But you know, I didn't sleep a wink all night. I was even weighing up whether I should keep going or turn back. You got a decent night's sleep, though, right? Because when I woke up, or rather when the dogs woke me, and I glanced out the window a couple of times, there was still no sign of you. The car was there so I gathered someone must have arrived. I only wondered who it could possibly be this time of year, in the fall. Especially as it was a different car, no one around here has a car like that. What kind is it? Thought so. I used to have one of those. Went like greased lightning. And never a problem. I'd take off from the lights and be half way down the street before the other drivers had even moved. I'd step on it and the thing would almost leap under me. Hardly anyone ever overtook me on the open road. I liked to drive fast. Drive fast, live fast. I used to think that if I lived fast, life would last shorter. Was I afraid? Of what? It was no big deal. There really isn't that much of a reason to respect life. My life at least. Oh yes, I got plenty of speeding tickets. One time my license was suspended for a year. Accidents? Can anyone drive without having accidents? Just like you can't live without having accidents. Once I broke my leg, right here, in this place. Once I had a broken collar bone, once three ribs, another time I had a concussion. One time they had to cut me out of the car. But can you imagine it, I was all in one piece. Just a few scrapes and bruises, nothing more. I was lucky? Perhaps. Though I don't know what luck is. It was only when I came down with rheumatism that I didn't drive at all for three years. Then after that I drove much slower.

What's your license plate number? I didn't see it, and I have to note it down. I write down every car that comes here. Not just the number. Make, model, color. Not the owners of the cabins. I've had their cars written down from the beginning. Except when someone gets a new car. But otherwise I already have them all. During the season all kinds of friends of the different owners come to visit. Often I have them show me their auto registration document, and I check to see whether the car has any dings or scratches. You can never be sure with friends. He's a friend, but he could turn out to be anyone. And you can't count on witnesses if something were to happen. Ten witnesses and there'll be ten colors, ten makes and ten different models, not to mention all the license plate numbers. I don't trust witnesses. I even write down when they arrive and the time they leave. I have a separate notebook for cars. I've a different one for the cabins, who and when, for how long, how many people. And a third one for other business. You can't keep proper order with just one notebook.

I didn't realize at first that you were staying in Mr. Robert's cabin. It was only when you opened the curtains. Could it be Mr. Robert? I thought to myself. I couldn't believe it. It's been such a long while since he was last here, but here he is after all this time, how about that. It must have been after midday when you came out, right? You stood on the deck, took a look around and it was then that I saw it wasn't Mr. Robert. Though not right away. You're the same height as him and you're both slim. Also, your hat was covering your face. The dogs started pawing at the door to be let out, and that was when I knew it wasn't Mr. Robert. But I wouldn't let them out on their own with a stranger. I decided to wait till you came over to my place, you'd tell me who you are, why you're here, how long for.

What puzzled me the most was how you knew where to find the key. Aside from Mr. Robert and me, no one knows it's on a nail in the beam under the deck. I even thought you must be a close friend of Mr. Robert, so all the more I won't go over there, especially with the dogs, asking you questions and checking on you like with other visitors. You're sure to come see me, tell me what's going on with Mr. Robert, where he's living, how he's doing. I once tried to find out where on earth he'd moved to, but even his closest neighbors on the same floor didn't know. He didn't leave a forwarding address with anyone. He sends me the money regularly. In an envelope, not by money order. But he never even includes a note, just money folded in a blank sheet of paper. And the postmark's so faint I can never read where it's from. He must have a friend at the post office. If it's not from him, who could it be from? Why would some stranger keep sending me money? I don't get it. He might at least visit just once. To see how things are here. Or at the very least send me his address so I can write and tell him everything's fine. The cabin's still there. I'm looking after it. So he needn't worry.

I look after all of the cabins, so I look after his also. I sometimes go inside as well, make sure everything's all right. Air the place out, dust, make repairs if I see something's broken. That's not part of my duties, but since I have the keys I see to it all. That's right, I have keys to all the cabins. Soon as they all leave I go around, check the cabins one by one, make sure the doors and windows are shut and locked, because you never know. When something needs fixing I make a note, then over the fall or winter I see to it. There's always something needs repairing after the season. I can't just leave it. I can't stand to see when something's broken. It hurts to look at it. If only it were just those kind of things. Sometimes I'll go into a cabin and it's like they fled the place in panic. The refrigerator's still running, the TV's playing. The stove is on, water's not been shut off, bed's unmade. One time I went into one of the cabins and there was an iron plugged in, standing on a blanket on the table, and the blanket was smoking. A moment later and the whole place would have gone up in flames. The neighboring cabins as well, because it was a windy day. Ever since that time with the iron I watch for when they move out.

Sometimes they even leave unfinished food on their plates. Dirty dishes. Empty bottles and beer cans on the table, empty vodka glasses, trash cans over-flowing, used tampons or condoms on the floor. Someone just took it off and dropped it. It's partly my fault, I've gotten them all used to the fact that I see to everything. But I couldn't do otherwise. I won't deny that there are some cabins it's a pleasure to go into. Sometimes I'll even sit down and listen awhile. What to? You can hear all kinds of things if you're inclined to listen.

Usually, twice during the day and at least once in the night, I do the rounds of all the cabins on both sides of the lake. Early morning, soon as the sun's up I check all the windows and doors in every cabin, make sure nothing's been smashed or broken into. If something doesn't look right I'll go peek inside. Actually, the dogs are always the first to sense when something's amiss. They run around each cabin and they give a short bark to say everything's fine. Then they run to the next one. If there's something wrong they wait for me, barking like there's no tomorrow.

And again in the evening. At that time I look in on every cabin, turn the lights on. Inside, on the deck. I leave the lights on and move to the next one. Cabin after cabin, it all gets brighter and brighter as I go. It's like a chain of lights round the lake. The whole place glows, as if the lake was shining, and the sky above it, and the woods. You have no idea how much the dogs love it then. I'd never have imagined dogs could enjoy something so much. Most of the time they're real quiet, alert, they don't bark unless they have a reason. They never howl like some dogs do. Not even to the moon. Or one time someone died in one of the cabins, not even then. Unless they're imagining something to themselves, when that's the case there doesn't even need to be anything happening. You wouldn't believe what they're capable of imagining. So maybe when all those lights are lit, they imagine it's their paradise? I mean, dogs don't have to see paradise as a flowering garden that contains everything there is. All that matters to them is that there aren't any people. What about me? Maybe they think I'm the one that looks after paradise for them.

Then we go back to the first cabin and switch off all the lights in each one in turn. What is it that you found surprising? About the dogs' paradise? Well if you ask me, human beings are the worst creatures for dogs. I have my reasons for saying that. Rex there, I found him in the woods. He'd been tied to a tree with a steel cord. I probably wouldn't have even noticed him, I was staring at the ground looking for wild strawberries, then all of a sudden I heard something whimpering like a child. It never even occurred to me it could be a dog. With a deer for instance, when it's caught in a trap and dying, when you hear it you know right away it's a deer. I've found dying deer like that once in a while. But this time it sounded like a kid. I stood still and held my breath. Could someone's child have gotten lost in the woods? It must have been tiny, because only tiny ones whimper that way. Except that a baby couldn't have made its way into the woods on its own. The sound stopped. I looked around, couldn't see anything. I went back to looking for wild strawberries. Then a moment later I hear the whimpering again. It's faint as anything, but I can hear it. I have good ears. There was this warehouse keeper used to teach me the saxophone, he'd always say, you've a long way to go with your playing, but you've got a good pair of ears. Just keep at it.

I started wondering which of the people in the cabins could have a newborn baby. Let me tell you, nothing could surprise me anymore, even if someone had left a baby in the woods. I started checking one bush after another, all the nearby trees. All at once I see him, Rex, under a beech tree. He must have smelled me and whined, even though he was half dead. You should know that the sense of smell is the last thing to go in a dog. When he saw me he even tried to get up from the ground. But he didn't have the strength. Then he whimpered again like a baby. Are you going to make it or not, I started wondering. If not I'll have to bring a spade and bury you. One more grave in the woods won't make any difference. I repaint everyone's nameplates, I can do yours too. That was when I gave him the name Rex. Here lies Rex. May he rest in peace just the same. I won't put a cross up for you, though you deserve a cross after what you've been through. He tried again to get up. He scratched at the earth with his claws and looked at me like he was begging me not to leave him there.

So I put my hands under his belly and stood him up. I thought to myself, if he can stand upright maybe he'll pull through. I didn't believe he'd be able to. And guess what, he stayed on his feet. Skin and bone. He was getting verminous. His neck was all bloody from the cord, and vermin had gotten into the wound. Into his eyes. Bloody foam was coming from his mouth. He swayed and he trembled, but he stayed on his feet. All right then, come on, I said, let's try and live. I untied the cord from his neck and I urged him, come on, take one step and you'll be able to walk. The first step is the most important. He did take one step, but then he collapsed. What was I to do? I picked him up and carried him. But my arms began to get tired. You can see what a huge animal he is, even though then he didn't weigh half what he does now. I wished I'd had my penknife with me, I could have cut a few branches, made a stretcher and pulled him behind me somehow or other. Luckily I was wearing a jacket. I took it off, took off my shirt, tied them together, fastened them with the cord, put him into the whole thing, sat down, and somehow hoisted him onto my back, then I managed to struggle to my feet. And that was how I brought him home.

After that I asked around at the cabins whether anyone had lost a dog. No one had. I fed him up, brought him back to health, you see what he's like now.

The only thing that made me think was that the folks from one of the cabins left immediately afterwards and they didn't come back the next season, then they sold their cabin. It's belonged to someone else for a good few years now, but whenever we do our rounds Rex always lies down outside that cabin, by the door to the deck. I always have to take him away from there, the new owner can't understand why this dog always has to pick his doorway.

The other one, Paws, I saved him from drowning. One evening, it was also late autumn, the off-season, I was listening to music. When I listen to music I usually leave the lights off. All of a sudden I thought I heard someone driving up to the far shore of the lake in a car. You see, I can be listening to music and still hear everything. I went outside, didn't see any lights, I thought I'd been mistaken. Then I heard a faint thud like a trunk being shut. Who on earth could it be at that time? Being so quiet, without lights? I thought, I'll go see. And I snuck over there, stepping softly so whoever it was wouldn't hear me coming and drive away. I was still some ways away when I recognized him. It was a guy from one of the cabins.

"What are you doing here?" I asked him.

"Nothing really," he said evasively. "I just came to pick up some stuff from my place, I didn't mean to wake you up. Your lights were off, I figured you must be asleep."

"I wasn't asleep." Then I hear a squealing sound. I look around, and in the dark I see what looks like a sack. And something's clearly moving inside it. "What's with the sack?" I ask.

"I took a few rocks," he says. "I've got a yard at home. It looks nice when you put rocks around the flower beds, so my wife asked me while I'm here . . ."

"Rocks," I say, "and they're moving and squealing?"

In fact there were also rocks in the sack, but he couldn't explain the movement and the squealing. In the end he couldn't keep it up:

"Forgive me. It's a little dog, a puppy. I came here to drown it. I bought it for my grandson. He was crazy about having a dog. But he doesn't want it anymore."

Ever since then, whenever he comes here he always brings something for my dogs. Dog chow, or canned dog food with beef or turkey or salmon. And not just during the season, in the off-season as well, he often visits in the winter and brings them something. I tell him he needn't bother, they have plenty to eat. All he'll do is spoil them. But one time he says to me:

"You saved my soul."

I was taken aback – all he'd been intending to do was drown a dog, and here he was talking about his soul. All the more because if you ask me, these days the soul is a commodity like anything else. You can buy it and sell it, and the prices aren't high. Maybe it was always that way. I read in some book that centuries ago someone said the human soul is a piece of bread. Do you think bread could have been so very expensive back then? If so, it's hardly surprising things are the way they are. Sorry for asking, but I imagine you must know what a human soul might cost these days, even just thinking about my dogs here. Or the graves in the woods.

You didn't know there were graves in the woods? I was convinced you'd gone into the woods to look for them. I even wondered how you knew about them. Could Mr. Robert have told you? He let you stay in his cabin, said where to find the key, so maybe he told you about the graves as well. That was why I didn't want to bother you. It's always awkward to go ask someone who they are, why they're here, how long for. Some folks I have to ask to show ID, because not everyone can be taken at their word. Or I even ask to see written permission that they can stay in someone's cabin, especially if I've never seen them here before. But since it's Mr. Robert . . .

Tell me at least how his health is. You don't know Mr. Robert? Really? I bet you just don't want to let on. Mr. Robert must have told you to say that. I was even thinking he must have sent you to let me know what's going on with him. I thought maybe he's ill and he couldn't make it himself. So I waited till you'd had a good night's sleep and came to see me. But you went off into the woods. To begin with I thought you'd gone for a walk, to relax a bit after the drive, get some fresh forest air, but that you'd be back soon. I kept looking out the window,

I even went outside a couple of times and stood there, but there was no sign of you. Everything started to get dark, the lake, the cabins, the woods. Soon it'd be night, then how would you find your way back? I was worried. It's your first time here, you don't know the woods, you could get lost. I'd have to take the dogs out and go looking for you. I turned a light on just in case, thinking that the light might lead you back. You saw it? There you are. It's not hard to get lost out there, especially this time of year, in the fall. Right now nothing is what it is.

I almost got lost there myself. Yeah, that time the fog held me up on the way. It was all quiet and deserted, and just like you I went into the woods to find where the graves are. That was basically why I'd come in the first place. I didn't know exactly where they were, only that they were in the woods. When Mr. Robert told me about them, he just waved toward the woods in general, as if to say, over that way. But the woods go on and on, where are you supposed to start? And if they were at least together, but no, they're all over the place. I walked about the whole day, I don't even remember how many of them I found that day. I didn't notice it had started to get dark. Especially because the darkness doesn't come all at once, as you know. For a long time you think you can see fine. And since you can see . . . I knew the woods, so I somehow managed to find my way back in the dark. But imagine this, it was only when I came out by the lake that I no longer knew where I was. On this shore or the other one. I remembered which direction the Rutka flowed, but now it seemed to me it was the opposite. The cabins could just about be made out in the darkness, but which one was Mr. Robert's, I couldn't have said. So I just stood there, I was completely unable to get my bearings. I even started to doubt whether it was me standing where I was standing.

All of a sudden, I saw a tiny light in the distance. At first it was ever so faint. I thought someone must be walking, lighting their way with a flashlight. But I didn't know how I could call to them, whether they'd hear me at that distance, since I myself didn't know where I was. All at once the light grew brighter, it stopped moving, and it came much closer. It was like I was standing on this side of the Rutka and it was shining on the other side. At that moment you know what I thought? That they must be shelling beans at our place. And imagine this, they actually were.

Bean shelling always began with a light. Mother would wash the dishes after dinner, sweep up, then till dusk she'd disappear between the bed and the dresser with a rosary in her hands. Grandmother usually dozed off. Granddad would go out into the yard to check that everything was in its place. It was like everyone was waiting for the dusk, when we were going to shell beans. Father would sit on the bench by the window and smoke one cigarette after another, and stare out the window like he was expecting someone. Dusk gradually crept in everywhere, and he would just keep staring and staring out the window. You might have thought it was the dusk he was watching. But can you ever tell what a person's staring at? You think they're staring at one thing or another, but they may be staring inside themselves. People have things to look at inside themselves, that's for sure. But perhaps he was also staring at the dusk as it settled in. What could have been so interesting about the dusk? Let me tell you, I often stare myself as dusk is falling, and at those times, I wonder whether it's the same dusk my father used to stare at. That means something. From time to time he'd sort of accompany his staring with a running commentary:

"The days are really getting shorter. They really are. There's barely room for people in them. They're hardly over, and here it's night. Why does there have to be so much night? What's it for?" And as he put out yet another cigarette he'd turn to mother and say: "Light the lamp."

Mother would get up from her rosary. She'd take the lamp down from the nail on the wall and check there was enough kerosene in it for the shelling. Sometimes she asked father:

"Should I top it up?"

To which he would usually say:

"Sure." And he'd never fail to remind her to trim the wick, because it was probably burned hard, or to clean the glass because it had gotten sooty the day before.

He didn't need to. Mother would have done those things anyway. Getting the lamp ready was like the crowning moment of the day for her. A kind of thanksgiving even, that the day had been gotten through. So she put all of her care into those preparations, as if surviving the next day depended on it. When she brought the match to the wick her hand would tremble and her face would be intent. After she put the glass back on the lamp she'd keep watching to make sure the flame caught. Only then would she turn the wick up a little. Her eyes behind their wire-rimmed glasses were lit up from underneath, and her expression would show she couldn't quite believe that the miracle of light had happened by her own hand.

You may not believe me, but I couldn't wait for the moment when mother would light the lamp. As soon as it started to get dark outside, I'd beg her: "Light the lamp, Mama, light the lamp." I can't explain it, but I wanted the light in our window to be the first one in the village. Father would hold her back, say it's still too early, we can still see each other. Grandfather and grandmother would agree, they'd say it was a waste of kerosene. Uncle Jan would get up for a drink of water, which perhaps meant he had no need of light in general. And in my mother's eyes there'd be a sort of indulgent smile as if she understood why I was so anxious for her to light the lamp.

Whenever she'd reach for the lamp on its nail on the wall, I'd rush out of the house, run down to the Rutka and wait there till the miracle of light by mother's hand appeared in our window. When the first light in the whole village came on in our window, it was like the first light in the entire world. Let me tell you, the first light is completely different than when there are already lights here and there, in all the other windows, in all the other houses. It shines differently, and it's immaterial whether it comes from a kerosene lamp or an electric bulb. It can be faint, like from a kerosene lamp, but you still have the impression it's not just shining. It's alive. Because the way I see it, there are living lights and dead lights. The kind that only shine, and the kind that remember. Ones that repel you, and ones that invite you. Ones that see, and ones that don't know you. Ones that it's all the same to them who they're shining for, and ones that know who they shine for. Ones that however bright they shine, they're still blind. And ones that even if they're barely glowing, still they can see all the way to the end of life. They'd break through any darkness. The deepest shadows will surrender to them. For them there are no boundaries, there's no time or space. They're capable of summoning the most ancient memory, however eroded it is, even if a person's been cut off from it. I don't know if you agree, but in my view memory is like light that's streaming toward us from a long-dead star. Or even just from a kerosene lamp. Except it's not always able to reach us during our lifetime. It depends how far it has to travel and how far away from it we are. Because those two things aren't the same. Actually, it may be that everything in general is memory. The whole of this world of ours ever since it's existed. Including the two of us here, these dogs. Whose memory? That I don't know.

In any case, when I saw the light I knew right away where I was. The more so because when we shelled beans in our house, mother would always turn up the lamp to almost the full wick. Before she did it she'd always remember to ask father whether she should make the flame bigger. Though she knew full well he'd say: "Yes, turn it up. It'd be fine like it is for everyone else, but for your eyes it needs to be brighter." Then she'd spread a canvas sheet on the floor, put a stool in the middle of it, stand the lamp on the stool, and father would go bring the bundles of beans.

So when I saw the light get brighter and come to a stop, I knew mother had put it on the stool and father had gone to fetch the beans. Though I paused a moment outside the door, because I didn't know what to say when I went in. So many years had passed, no one expects you anymore, what should I say, what had I come for? I kept weighing it up, whether to go in or not, and what I should say when I crossed the threshold. As you know, crossing the threshold is the hardest part. In the end I thought to myself, it's best if I just go right on in and ask whether they might have any beans for sale.

They were all sitting in the circle of the kerosene lamp, father, mother, granddad, grandmother, my two sisters Jagoda and Leonka, and Uncle Jan, who was still living. He was the only one who got up when I came in, he went to get a drink of water. He drank a lot of water before he died. The rest of them, the bean pods were motionless in their hands. I stood beyond the circle of light, just inside the door, while they sat in the ring made by the light, I could see them all clearly. But no one smiled or showed surprise or even frowned. They looked at me, but their eyes already seemed dead, it's just there hadn't been anyone to close their eyelids. It was only the pods in their hands that showed they were shelling beans. And they didn't know me.

Did you want a lot in the way of beans? That much I think I might have. Though they're unshelled. But if you helped me we could shell them. You've never shelled beans before? It's not so hard. I'll show you. After a couple of pods you'll figure it out. I'll go fetch some.

2

So did you come here of your own accord, or did someone send you? Well, I don't know who it could have been. I thought maybe it was Mr. Robert. But you keep saying you don't know Mr. Robert. I just wonder in that case how you knew where to find the key to his cabin.

No, not like that. See here, watch my hands. You hold the pod in your left hand, not flat, like this, then with your right hand you split it open with your thumb and your index finger. Then you put your thumb inside and slide it down to the bottom. See, all the beans pop out. You try. Wait a minute, I'll find you a better pod. Here, this one's even and it's nice and dry. That's it, use your thumb. There you go. You see it's not so hard. The next one'll be easier. And every one after that will be easier still. You just need to keep your thumb straight, with the nail pointing forward. The thumb's the most important thing in shelling beans. Like a hammer when you're putting in a nail, or a pair of pliers when you need to pull one out. When we'd shell beans grandfather would often say the thumb ought to be the finger of God. The left thumb's also important for playing the saxophone, it operates the octave key.

Of course we did, the children took part in the shelling as well. Ever since we were tiny. They started to teach us how to shell beans even before we could properly hold our drinking cup by the handles. They usually put Jagoda by grandmother, Leonka would sit by mother, and me, I was the youngest, I'd be between mom and grandmother. The drier pods were too hard for us, so mother or grandmother would take our hands in theirs and shell the beans with our fingers, and use our thumbs to slide the beans out. So it looked like we'd done it ourselves.

I have to admit, when I was a child I hated shelling beans. My sisters too, they were older than me but they hated it as well. We'd always try to get out of it. My sisters would usually say that one of them had a headache or a stomachache. For me, I came up with different methods. One time, I cut my thumb right here with a piece of broken glass. Then later, when we started school in the order of age – first Jagoda, then Leonka, then me – we'd usually use our homework as an excuse, we had to study for tomorrow, we had a whole ton to do. It wouldn't get done if we were shelling beans. My mother's heart would always soften right away when we mentioned homework. You go get your schoolwork done, we'll manage here on our own. On the subject of schoolwork grandmother would always mention God, she'd say if God wasn't going to allow something, no amount of studying would help. Uncle Jan would usually just get up and go get a glass of water, so it was hard to figure out whether he was for homework or for shelling beans. Father, on the other hand, he would say that shelling beans was one of the lessons we should be learning:

"And not just any lesson. It's one of the most important ones. Not just math or Polish. It's a lesson to last you your whole life long. Math and Polish, all that'll vanish from their heads anyway sooner or later. And when they're left on their own it's not math and Polish they'll be drawn to. No sir."

Grandfather would usually refer to the war, because he liked to use the war to make his point. Once he told a story about how a long long time ago, so long that his own grandfather had told the story, there'd been a war and the family was shelling beans. All of a sudden there's a hammering at the door. "Open up!" It's soldiers. Their eyes are all bloodshot, their faces are twisted in fury.

They would have killed everyone dead just like that. But when they saw that everyone was shelling beans they put their rifles in the corner, unfastened their swords, had stools brought for them, and they sat down and started shelling beans with everyone else.

As for Mr. Robert, I can't say I knew him that well either. For some reason we never were able to open up to one another. We never went to the informal *ty*, even though we'd known each other for years. He had a store in the city, he sold souvenirs . . . What sort? I couldn't tell you, I was never there. The one thing I can say is that in the letters he wrote me he'd always make fun of those souvenirs. He'd say that he himself would never in a million years buy the kinds of things he sold. And that if souvenirs like those were supposed to help you remember, it was better not to remember at all.

The first time I met him we were abroad. One evening a group of men and women came into the place where I played in the band. It was a Monday, and on Mondays there were usually free tables. Other days you'd have to make a reservation ahead of time. Though we'd still play every evening, even if there was only one table occupied.

They took two tables close to the little stage. I might not have noticed them, but I heard them speaking Polish. They were acting in a deliberately nonchalant way, as if they were trying to draw attention to themselves. They talked loudly from one table to the other, and I heard that they were part of a bus tour. They spent a long time looking through the menu and equally loudly discussing the prices. At the more expensive items they'd say, look how much this is! Wait a minute, how much is that in Polish money? Good grief! Back home you could live for a month on that. Not to mention if you ate in a cheap cafeteria. But being at a place like this in a foreign country, it'll be a tale to tell. Instead of just endless castles, cathedrals, museums, scenic views. Come on, let's order the most expensive thing. What if we don't like it? At that price we'll have to. And maybe some vodka too. Why? We have our own. Well, at least one shot each to kick off. I mean, we're going to need glasses anyway, right? We have our own glasses as well. But what if someone sees? What's there to see? Vodka looks the same wherever you are.

They called the waiter, and each of them in turn ordered by pointing at the menu. And it was all the costliest items, the waiter bent double under the weight of all the prices. There was something impetuous in that scramble for the most expensive dishes, and at the same time it was disarming. But I had no intention of talking to them. I avoided those kinds of meetings.

There was a break. When the next set was about to start, one of the Polish group – Mr. Robert, as it later transpired – got up from his table. He came up to the band and started saying something in a mixture of words, but no one could understand him. I couldn't decide whether to let on or not. He was trying to request a tango and he was asking how much a request like that would be. They understood the tango part, but not the bit about how much it would cost. Whether I liked it or not I spoke up, I said we'd play a tango, and it wouldn't cost anything.

"You speak Polish?" He immediately held out his hand. "Robert's the name."

But I already had the mouthpiece between my lips so I didn't reciprocate. We started up the tango. He went to each of their two tables in turn and said something, pointing at me. The people at both tables began watching me with a smile. He asked one of the women to dance. He didn't lead her into the middle of the dance floor; instead they danced as close as possible to the band, as if he didn't want to lose sight of me. He held her close, the way you do in a tango, and he kept smiling at me over her head as if we were good friends. I was mad at myself, I knew he wouldn't leave me alone.

And he didn't. During the next break he dragged me over to his table, just for a minute, so he could at least exchange a word or two with a fellow countryman. I didn't let myself get drawn into any toasts to lucky meetings. All the same, from both tables they showered me with questions and I regretted giving myself away when he was trying to ask for the tango. Do you live here permanently? Since when? What brought you here? How did you manage to get a place in a band in a club like this? Was it right away, or did you have to start by washing dishes? So you must have known someone. Normally everyone begins by washing dishes. Even for that you need to have good luck. Then if you're really lucky you might get to wait tables. But this is something else! I bet it's so great living here. Working in a place like this. Dance parties every evening. And they pay a decent wage, not like . . . One of them even asked:

"You can be honest with us. Did you leave for political reasons? Did you escape?"

"No," I said.

"Oh, then I know!" cried one of the women as if she'd finally hit on why I'd found myself there. "I bet it was because of a woman. Well? Was that it?" They crowded in to hear what I'd say.

Another woman, who was sitting at the next table and up till now hadn't asked any questions, gave a sigh and said:

"The things love can make you do."

"The hell with love," Mr. Robert retorted in irritation. "Who can afford love these days. It's all about going to bed, nothing more."

"Don't say that," the woman protested. "Love is the most important thing in life."

Fortunately the other musicians waved to say the break was over. But the matter didn't end there. You might say that was only the beginning. A few days later, a postcard arrived addressed to me at the club, in which Mr. Robert thanked me for an unforgettable evening. He said he was glad to have met me and that he'd write a real letter soon. With no idea of what might come, I wrote a postcard in return to say I'd also enjoyed the evening and I was glad I'd gotten to know him. But you know, it's not good to be too polite. You can never be sure that even with common courtesy you're not setting a trap for yourself. It was just that his postcard had kind of touched an unhealed wound in me. I'd never gotten a postcard from anyone back in Poland before.

Some time later the promised letter arrived. It was long and cordial. He invited me to come take a vacation. He wrote that he had a summer cabin on some lake. All around there were woods. It was secluded, quiet, peaceful, in a word a magical place, as he put it. Even if it was true that some woman had left me, like we'd been saying that evening, in this place I'd be able to forget her. Because here you could forget anything. Here you went back to being a part of nature, without any obligations, without memories. Besides, if it was women I was after, there were any number of them here, and he'd find one who'd be right for me, cheer me up after the other one. Pretty young things, they come here on the weekends, or for their vacation. Some even spend the whole summer here, so there's no need to try very hard even, they fall into your arms of their own accord. You won't be disappointed, especially as you're coming from abroad.

In the next letter, which arrived right on the heels of the first one and was even longer, he invited me to at least come for mushroom picking. They were expecting a big crop that year. He had a battery-driven heating device for drying the mushrooms. Because he was sure I liked picking mushrooms, who doesn't? He loved it. Apart from women, there wasn't much he enjoyed more than picking mushrooms. He'd get crazy jealous when someone else found a boletus and he had nothing, or maybe just some slippery Jack. He'd hope the other person's mushroom was maggoty. But was there any deeper way of experiencing nature? It hurts to even think about what people can be like. Mushroom picking's also the best form of relaxation. You don't think of anything, don't remember a thing, all your attention, all your senses are concentrated on the search for a mushroom. You might say the entire world shrinks to the proportions of that mushroom you're looking for. So if someone wants true relaxation, it's actually better when there aren't that many mushrooms. Him, he said, when he needed to relax he'd head off into the woods even if there weren't any mushrooms. Take his basket and his penknife and go looking.

It would be a source of great pleasure to him if we could do that together. I took a liking to you, he wrote. On that very first evening I had a feeling we could become friends. I value people who I can tell in advance are hard to make out, impossible even. I'd really like you to come. The cabin has all the amenities. Fridge, radio, TV. There's a bathroom with a shower, a water heater, you just need to turn it on and in a short while you have hot running water. Upstairs there are two bedrooms, we won't get in each other's way. If you wanted to bring someone along I can sleep downstairs on the couch. Or I'll take my vacation at a different time and just visit on Saturdays and Sundays. I have a boat, we could go out on the lake. And if you like kayaking, you can borrow the neighbor's kayak. You could even go with his wife. She's good-looking and she likes to go kayaking. He's some director or other, he's had two heart attacks and spends all his time indoors because the sun bothers him. No wonder she gets bored. And the bored ones are always the most willing. You really must come. Write and let me know when.

I wrote back to say thank you for the invitation, but for the moment I wasn't able to take him up on it. As he knew, I played in a band, I wasn't a free agent. And in those kinds of clubs the musicians rarely have much time off. Only when the club is being renovated or redecorated. I thought that would discourage him.

But a short time later he wrote another letter. And it was the same thing all over again. He was inviting me, when would I come. I replied with a postcard saying thank you, I send my best wishes, but let's wait till I have more free time. But he wouldn't take no for an answer. He wrote one letter after another, and in every one he kept repeating his invitation.

In one of the letters he gave me his phone number and asked for mine, saying he often wished he could call me up. I could hardly refuse, but I made a point of saying it was hard to catch me at home. Rehearsals in the morning, gigs in the evening, and life in general kept you busy, as he well knew. He rang on what turned out to be the same day he'd gotten my letter:

"I've been calling and calling since morning. You're right, it's hard to get a hold of you. But there's nothing like the sound of an actual voice. Letters are fine, but they don't speak. There's no comparison with a live voice. Hearing you, it feels like we're meeting again. Have you decided yet when you're going to come visit?"

This went on for years. I would always put off replying to his cards and letters as long as I could. Then I'd apologize, saying it was for this or that reason, I hoped he understood. He understood completely. In the next letter he'd send me an even more enthusiastic invitation. One time he wrote to say he'd gotten a color TV to replace the old black-and-white one in the cabin, he told me what kind, how big of a screen it had. Another time he said something else was new there. And with each letter he painted an ever more vivid picture to convince me to come. While I for my part felt an increasing distrust toward him. To be honest, I even started to be afraid of him, suspecting him of something, though I couldn't have said exactly what. He was trying to drag me into something, that much I was sure of. Or maybe it just seemed that way to me, because distrust toward other people was the defensive wall I'd built around myself.

With every letter he grew more heartfelt, almost poetic, and so open toward the world that it terrified me. In one letter he said, you can't imagine how the smell of sap from the woods fills this place, especially in the early morning. It's a pleasure just to breathe. There are even crayfish in the lake, that's the best proof of how clean the water is. The deer have gotten so comfortable with humans that they come and graze among the cabins. You can even stroke them. One time an owl perched on his windowsill, he wrote. One sultry night he opened the window. When he opened his eyes, there it was, right on the sill. He thought he was dreaming. He got up and shone a flashlight in its eyes, I'm telling you, he wrote, they shone like two diamonds. Another time he was lounging about on the deck and a squirrel came up to him. It stood on its hind legs, and they just stared at each other. He was mad at himself for not having any nuts around. This was the only place I'd be able to see a proper sunrise and sunset. It wasn't at all the same as where I lived, in the city. It might not be the same anywhere else at all. If he didn't have a cabin here he might never have known what sunrises and sunsets really are, what humans have lost for good. Because what can they see in their cities? What can he see from his souvenir shop?

Of course, from all those letters over the years I could easily have figured out where the place was, but it never entered my head that it might be here. Thankfully, after a while he stopped writing so frequently. His letters got shorter and his invitations were less eager, I thought our chance acquaintance would eventually dry up. So all the more I'd no reason to wonder if this might be the place. The whole business had come and gone, the way things often happen. And if he'd been playing some kind of game, maybe he'd finally understood that I wasn't the kind to play along.

By now our correspondence was limited to cards with best wishes and season's greetings. He'd sometimes just scribble a few words in tiny handwriting in the margin to ask if he could hope I'd come visit one day. Or, Think about it, time's passing and more and more plans come to nothing. Soon even the cards stopped coming. What I found worrying, though, was that the phone calls also ceased.

I started to wonder if something might have happened to him. Perhaps I should at least give him a call? I couldn't muster up the courage. But whenever my phone rang, I'd pick up in hopes that it might be him. Previously, I'd never felt like answering his letters and cards, it was always an effort to do so; now, whenever the telephone rang I wanted it to be him. I came up with all kinds of explanations for his silence, despite the fact that I barely knew anything about him. For all the effusiveness of his letters there were never any confidences apart from the fact that he had a cabin by a lake in the woods and a souvenir shop in the city. It was as if he'd set firm boundaries on what he could write to me about. And in fact it was the same with me. Though of course I was supposedly the put-upon one in the relationship.

A year went by, and another. Then out of the blue he wrote me – a long, cordial, enthusiastic letter just like before, filled with the same efforts to entice me out there. You can't imagine what a wonderful crop of mushrooms we have this year, he wrote. Ceps, birch boletes, chanterelles, slippery Jacks, milk-caps, parasols – you name it. Parasols fried up in butter – makes your mouth water. Better than a veal cutlet any day of the week. Or milk-caps with onion in sour cream – delicious. And the best place to find them is where the graves are. No one picks them there. What are they afraid of? It makes no difference to me whether they're from around the graves or not. They're just mushrooms. Who cares what's in the earth underneath? If you started thinking about that you'd have to stop walking, driving, building houses, you couldn't even plow or sow, because the whole world till now is down there. We'd have to fly above the earth or move away from it completely. But where to?

Everyone's picking, drying, preserving, frying. In the evenings there are mushrooms everywhere. Pints, quarts. You can't imagine how much fun it is. Did you ever eat pickled wild mushrooms? They're a real delicacy. There's a woman here who's a dab hand at pickling. Though for pickling, tricholomas are the best. And they'd be right in season if you came for a visit. Please let me know. Come try the pickled ones at least. I talked with her, she'll pickle some for you if you come.

Where the graves are, that struck me. I picked up the phone impulsively to call him and say, I'm on my way. But I put it down again at once. And almost every day from then on I did the same thing. I'd pick up the phone and put it down again, telling myself I'd call the next day. Though each time something seemed to whisper to me that if I didn't do it now I never would. But still I'd put it off till the next day. One time I actually dialed his number, waited till the second ring, then hung up. Another time I even heard his voice:

"Hello? Hello? Goddammit, someone's having trouble getting through again. The hell with these telephones!"

I could barely keep from saying, it's me, Mr. Robert. Then one time I had the day off. I poured myself a glass of brandy and drank it. Then a second, a third. Mr. Robert? It's me. I'm coming. There was a moment of silence, I thought he must just be taken aback. Then I heard a kind of sigh:

"Finally. What made you decide?"

"I couldn't resist those pickled mushrooms, Mr. Robert. I've never had pickled mushrooms."

"I just wish you'd have let me know sooner. I don't know if the woman'll have enough time to do the pickling. I mean, she has to pick them first. I don't even know if there are any tricholomas this time of year."

"Don't worry about that. I was only joking. Sooner or later I had to make up my mind, and I did."

"I'm glad. I understand. I've been inviting you all these years."

Yet I didn't hear in his voice that he was as pleased as I might have expected from all those letters of his, especially the last one.

I arrived at his home towards evening on the Saturday. Because you don't know where the place is, he said over the phone. You wouldn't be able to find it on your own. So Sunday morning we set off together for the lake.

"This is a nice car. Must have cost a pretty penny. Me, I drive a baby Fiat, as you see." His little Fiat was parked outside the building. "I just had the body-work all redone. It was rusting away. And I work like a dog. All day long in the store. I don't even break for lunch. In this country you can never earn any real money. Even selling souvenirs." Then, when we got into my car: "I see you have a stereo as well. You've got all sorts of things." He was so taken with the car that it brought on a whole litany of gripes. In fact, he forgot to give me directions for the lake. It was only when we were already in the woods, on the last stretch, that he suddenly snapped out of it:

"How do you know the way?"

"From your letters, Mr. Robert. And the map."

"You must have looked at an ordinance map, the lake isn't on the regular road maps. Good thing too." A note of doubt sounded in his voice: "From my letters? I don't recall describing the way."

"All these years, there were so many letters, Mr. Robert. You can't remember everything. Me, I tried to learn something from each one of them. It just goes to show how carefully I read them. All the more because for a long time now I've wanted to come visit."

"It's true, I wrote endless letters." He relaxed a little. "You didn't always reply. You'd write back once to every two or three of my letters. And usually only a few lines. Or just a postcard, thanks, greetings, best wishes. I often used to think you weren't interested. That it got on your nerves. Though after all . . ." I could tell he was upset. So I jumped in:

"The thing is, Mr. Robert, I hate writing letters. I'd much sooner call, or even just come, as you see." I gave a laugh.

"You hate it?" He thought for a moment. "But it's like talking with someone, confiding in them. Except on paper."

"That's exactly it – the paper."

"What about the paper?"

"The letter's on paper. All we're doing is leaving unnecessary traces."

"In that case why didn't you let me know I should stop writing to you?"

"You were the only person who wrote to me from here, Mr. Robert."

"How is that possible?"

"Let's drop it."

"We can drop it." He didn't say another word till we reached the lake.

But in his silence I could sense a growing mistrust. When we arrived, all he said was:

"Park the car over there." Whereas he ought to have at least said, Here we are, take a look around. It's like I said in my letters, just like I said. I didn't need to make anything up.

He took our things from the trunk and with a jerk of the head as if to show where his cabin was, he said:

"Come on."

He'd written so much about that cabin of his, yet he didn't even suggest a tour.

"Let's sit out on the deck awhile," he said. "Should I put the parasol up or do you prefer it like this?" He carried out a little wicker table, two wicker armchairs, two cans of beer and a couple of glasses. "See the logo? I bought these glasses that evening, as a souvenir."

"How about that," I said.

"Are you hungry maybe?" he asked. "Fine, then let's just have a drink. I'll make something to eat later."

Something was clearly bothering him. As we drank our beers he hardly said a word, he just mumbled some triviality or other every so often. As for me, I was overcome by a feeling of helplessness in the face of everything that was happening to me. I couldn't think of anything worth saying. So we sat there sipping our beers, and the sun rose and rose, as if it meant to reach the top of the sky and then, instead of starting to drop toward the west, it was intending to keep on rising upwards till it disappeared in the distance, breaking the age-old laws. So that even the sun seemed to have changed from those earlier years when it would set every day beyond the hills that could be seen in the distance. Nothing here looked like itself anymore. The smell of sap did still come from the woods, but I somehow couldn't even believe in the sap. Its scent seemed no more than a faint trace, not as bitter as it should be. Back then it would make your nose wrinkle up and your eyes water, especially when sap was collected from the mature trees. Except that those trees grew only before my eyes, because as I gazed at it all I was looking inside myself. But I wasn't able to retrieve much from my memory. Not even the old course of the Rutka. Maybe because the new lake dominated everything – earth, sky, woods, memory. All the more so because it resounded, it made a din – it fairly shook from all the shouts and cries and squeals and laughter, as if it was showing me how it was able to change the world. Its shores seemed to push deep into the woods. Or perhaps the woods had retreated before it of their own accord, making room for the sunbathing bodies that kept spilling from the cabins and the incoming cars, or emerging from the water. The water in turn was strewn with boats, canoes, floating mattresses, and with heads, heads in colorful caps, that looked as if they were crawling unhurriedly across the surface in every direction, without rhyme or reason. They would disappear only to pop up again a few yards further on, or rise suddenly above the surface of the water as if they were trying to break loose of their bonds. There were multitudes of them. They reminded me of the water lilies, the ones called white lotuses, when they'd bloom in one of the broad bends of the Rutka. In the midst of all this I felt like a thorn able only to inflict pain, because I was evidently incapable of anything else. I decided to leave that same afternoon.

I was just about to let Mr. Robert know when he spoke first, breaking our silence.

"I think I told you in one of my letters that I'm planning to sell this place."

I swear that in fact he'd never mentioned this. Why on earth had he invited me in that case? As a farewell to the cabin?

"Then I'm going to move. Away from here, away from the city, the whole nine yards. I don't yet know when. I'm waiting to find a buyer. There is one guy, but he wants to pay in installments. And you know what that's like. He'll pay the first installment and the second, then after that he'll start making excuses. With installments that's just the way it is, there are always more important things, the payments can wait."

"Maybe I could buy it?" I said jokingly. I immediately regretted the joke. The words had bypassed my will, my intentions – they'd come out by themselves. Especially that at that very moment I'd meant to say to him: I'm sorry, Mr. Robert, but I have to leave today, this afternoon. I've a long drive ahead of me and tomorrow I ought to be at work. I have commitments, you understand.

"You?" He laughed, I didn't have the impression that he'd taken what I said as a joke. "You?" he repeated with a hint of mockery. "That's a good one. You live in a different country, miles and miles away. And here you'd have your summer house. How would that look, you'd drop by for a day or two at the most?"

"Sometimes it's good to visit another country even just for a day or two," I said, blundering ahead as if to spite myself, to spite him for not having understood that it was a joke.

"And you'd visit often? I don't think so. All those letters for so many years and I couldn't get you here. Now you say you'd come often. I don't think so. Exactly how often?"

"It would depend."

"On what?"

"The circumstances."

"What circumstances?"

"All kinds. There's no predicting circumstances."

"The thing is, a cabin like this can't just sit there waiting for circumstances to be right for you. It needs looking after. Aside from the fact that something's always in need of repair. Plus, crime is getting worse. Not a week goes by without a break-in somewhere. We tried forming a neighborhood watch, but then one person would come, another would forget, for the third person something would come up that night. Best of all would be to hire somebody to mind the place, but they'd have to live here." Then after pondering for a moment, calmly now, as if finishing his thought: "And you could only come here maybe once a year..."

"Maybe twice," I said, testing him further, because I couldn't fathom his resistance.

He looked at me dubiously.

"Even twice. But what for? What for?" His voice rose in irritation.

"The same thing everyone comes here for," I said. Though I'm not sure I wasn't testing myself also. "To breath fresh air. Rest up a bit, get away from it all."

"What on earth are you saying?" He shifted angrily in his seat. "Where is there fresh air these days? There's no fresh air, no clean water, nothing. And who's aware of what kind of air they're breathing anyway? They breathe because their organism tells them they have to. And even if you're right, does it really do anyone any good to breathe a little fresh air on Saturday or Sunday? Or even for a month or whatever, on their vacation? None of it helps anyone. You think they come here to rest, to get away from it all?" He pulled the glass of beer abruptly away from his mouth, a little of it splashed onto his shirt. "Don't you see this place has gotten more crowded than an apartment building? In an apartment building, even if it's ten stories or more, I don't have to know anyone. Good morning, good morning, that's it. And not even with everyone, I don't have to talk to the downstairs neighbor, or the person upstairs. A week can go by without seeing the guy next door. If the two of you go out and come back at different times you don't have to see him at all until they carry him out when he's dead. Whereas here, you have to whether you like it or not. The moment you arrive they're all over you like ants. They itch, pinch you, bite you. After a week of vacation I no longer know whether I'm me or someone else. I mean, tell me how many different people can fit inside someone till he stops feeling that he's himself? People, they're like this glass, you can't pour more into it than'll fit. I have a shop in the city, but I know almost the whole city not from there but from here. And if it were only their first and last names, job, address, phone number, that I could handle. I already have a whole drawerful of business cards. So what? They're just lying there lifeless. I don't know how many times I've copied out my address book to at least weed out the ones that have died. But it keeps getting thicker and thicker all the same. Still, even that would be bearable. But that's not what I wanted to say. The point is that here I feel like I'm in an ant's nest, and I mean, who wants to be an ant? They won't spare you in any way. The most intimate things come spilling from them as if they were going to the bathroom. There's no worse place than somewhere where everyone has to be together and it's all during the season. Who's with who, who's against who, who's on top of who, who's underneath who, who does what for what reason, who's hiding one thing or another, who's being given away to who – you hear all different kinds of things. You want illnesses, you got them. So-and-so has one thing, another person has something else, one of them's had something removed, with another one it's some other thing, a third person has something else again. Who's constipated, who has diarrhea, you name it. Even orgasms, you'll find out. One woman has one every time, another one's never had one.

They sit or lie there, sighing away. You have no idea how sound travels around the lake. Plus, the cabins are all close to each other, and if it's a hot day like today all the doors and windows are open, as you see, so it's not just your neighbors you can hear, it's everyone. On the shore you hear what's being said on the water, on the water what they're saying on the shore, everything can be heard somewhere. You can't get away from hearing things. You can't get away from seeing things. However much you want to. It goes into your ears and your eyes of its own volition. And of course no one comes here just to lock themselves away in their cabin. The faintest whisper gets magnified here, the tiniest detail is blown up. Whether you like it or not you have to know every stomach, every belly button, backside, all the veins on their legs, the scars from operations. Your eyes and your ears have nowhere to hide. Even your thoughts become a trash heap for other people's thoughts. And here you're considering . . ."

I didn't recognize him. He was a completely different person than I'd imagined from his letters. Could something have happened to make him change so dramatically? I couldn't for the life of me figure out why he was so hell-bent on turning me off this place. He'd been inviting me, luring me even, all those years, and now I was finally there . . . Aside from anything, he should have realized I was just joking about buying the cabin. But maybe even before, on the way, when we were still in the car, he'd started to suspect that I wasn't the person he'd imagined from my letters either. And the thing with the cabin merely confirmed it for him.

"And here you are considering . . ." he repeated, this time as if only to his own thoughts. "Believe me, when I return home I have to get used to myself all over again from the beginning, collect myself, from all the way back in childhood, from my first words, my first thoughts, my first tears, feel once again that it's me. Here it's like living on a screen. And what's a person without secrets, eh? You tell me." He was practically boiling with anger: "I'm going to sell this place, I swear to God! And move away."

He poured the rest of the beer from the can into his glass and, gazing at the noisy lake in front of us, he fell silent again. I ought to have spoken, he may even have expected it of me. But nothing came to mind aside from saying that I had to leave that afternoon. I decided, though, that it wasn't the right moment to bring it up. So I asked him as if casually:

"So where are those graves where you told me the mushrooms grow the best?"

"You want to go mushroom-picking? Not now though, not now." He jumped up from the table. "Let me fetch another beer. Should I make something to eat? Are you hungry yet? OK, I'll make something later. I brought some grilled chicken, all we need to do is heat it up."

A moment later, returning with fresh cans of beer he stopped halfway:

"See over there? I think she's new. I've not seen her here before. I must find out who she is. That one there. See?" He put the cans on the table, opened them, poured for me and for himself. "You know, that's the only thing keeping me here. If it weren't for that I'd have sold up long ago." He took a mouthful of beer and started looking around again, with completely different eyes it seemed – they glittered, they were almost predatory. From time to time he'd glance at me with something between a smile and a mocking twist of the mouth. "That one over there's not bad either. The one getting into the boat. Her I know. She really likes it, and the things she knows how to do! I'll show you another one also, she lives close by, two cabins away. Except I don't think she's here yet."

I tell you, I was listening to him but I couldn't believe this was Mr. Robert. The same Mr. Robert from all those letters and cards and phone calls. I wondered what was true in him, as I compared what he was saying now with what he'd written me all those years. Maybe nothing at all. But I didn't let it show.

"Or that one over there, check her out. The one walking along the shore. She's even looking our way. That's the only good thing, with all of these irritations here. Because with a woman like that, here it's as if you found her in her natural state. And finding a woman in nature isn't the same as finding her on the street or in a cafe. Ah, nature. It straightens out the most crooked person. What's she wandering around like that for? Oh, there you go, she's lying down. She's going to sunbathe. She can lie in the sun for hours on end. Even at the beginning of summer she'll look like a black woman. To be honest I don't really like it when they're tan like that. Though the tanned ones are a lot easier. They can't bring themselves to let all the torment of lying in the sun go to waste. And obviously they wouldn't go through all of that just for the chumps they're married to. They make those guys go try to lose weight on their boats and canoes. I mean, how long can you put up with one of those oafs? A year, two, then so much for being faithful. It's a good thing the world has set aside all those superstitions and habits and customs. These days no one can afford to have a longer relationship. Everyone's chasing after something, reaching for something, being with some-one else is like having your legs in chains. You have no desire to talk, but here you have to. There's nothing left to talk about, but you've got to talk. True, there are marriages that last till death. But they're relics of the past. Before long you'll be able to visit those kinds of people the way you visit castles and museums and cathedrals. The truth of it is, these days marriage is a corporation. One fails, you start another. Then you do what you can just so as to keep going somehow or other, to make it to the end. This life of ours isn't worth a damn, I'm telling you. All these dreams and hopes we have." His eyes suddenly flashed. "See over there. She just arrived. You know, the one from two cabins away. Wait till you see her in her bathing costume. You won't be able to keep your eyes off her. She sometimes sunbathes topless. Sure, that's reached Poland also. Why wouldn't it. In that respect there aren't any borders, languages, all that nonsense. I'll have to invite her to go boating one of these days. Maybe there'll be an opportunity. I mean, we know each other enough to say hello. But something's holding me back. I'm all set to do it, then I lose my nerve. Maybe to begin with it'd be better just to suggest going berry-picking? The blackberries should be ripe by now. Next Sunday I'll go check in the woods. Though she might not want to do that, because of the thorns. Too bad there aren't any more wild strawberries this year. That's the only thing that keeps me here. I mean you tell me, what do people really get from life? All that effort, the maneuvers, the sleeplessness, the worries, and what do they get? Then you add in the illnesses, other misfortunes, what do they get? Try sitting like that all day long in my shop. With the souvenirs. Ha, ha! I'll sell the shop as well, the hell with it!"

He took a sip of beer. A moment ago his eyes had been glittering, but all of a sudden it was like they'd lost their color and been extinguished. After a moment of silence, in a voice that was just as colorless and extinguished he said:

"And if you knew what happened here once. Unless you're the kind of person that can live anywhere."

"I know, Mr. Robert." I'd decided to finally tell him. I'd come to the conclusion that it wasn't right to keep it a secret. Especially since he'd gotten suspicious of how I knew the way here when we were driving.

"How?" A look of consternation came over him. "Not from my letters, surely? I never wrote you about that. Ever."

"I was born here."

"What do you mean, here?"

"Here."

"Here? What do you mean, here?!" I was taken aback by the vehemence with which he was trying to reject my confession. "Unless you weren't around at that time. No one survived from here. No one."

"Except that as you see, I survived, so to speak. In one sense it wasn't just me, but you, and all these people on the lake – we all survived. All of us who are still alive."

"But back then no one did. No one." He was almost angry. "You see those hills. We lived over there during the war. Then one day, all of a sudden we heard they were burning whole villages around these parts. My mother grabbed me by the hand, I was a kid then, and we ran to the highest hill. Winnica it was called. There was already a crowd up on top. I couldn't make out very much aside from the sea of smoke over the trees. But the grownups saw everything. Burning houses, barns, cattle sheds, frantic animals, people being shot at. At one point my mother picked me up, but I still couldn't see anything beside the smoke. Then she knelt down and told me to do the same, because everyone was kneeling. She told me to cry, because everyone was crying. Except that I felt like laughing. My mother was wearing makeup, and her tears were making dark streaks that rolled down her cheeks. I couldn't help myself. People turned to look at me, and someone said:

'Look at him laughing his head off, and over there people are being killed.'

My mother was embarrassed. She pulled me to my feet and dragged me after her. 'Don't look back.' We walked down from the hill."

"The graves are over that way." He pointed in the direction of the woods. A moment later he said abruptly: "I have to do it . . . Maybe I'll go with the installment guy. Five payments, ten, it's all the same to me."

To tell the truth, when I saw you coming out of Mr. Robert's cabin I thought you might be the guy that was going to pay in installments. Though you must have already paid the last installment. Otherwise you wouldn't have gone into his cabin. How would you have known where to find the key? Not till I have the last installment in my hand, that's what he said back then on the deck.

Oh, he's still alive. Why wouldn't he be? Who else would be sending me money to mind the place. One time I raised the fee for each cabin, and the next envelope that arrived had the new amount. Though I hadn't intended for Mr. Robert to pay more. No one lives in the place, none of his friends ever visit, why should he have to pay extra? The only thing was that last fall the roof started leaking a bit. It began at the end of summer, the leaves were already off the trees and it just kept on raining. The sun was nowhere to be seen all day long. It chucked it down day and night. I don't remember a fall like it. The lake rose all the way up to the closest cabins. Fortunately they're built on concrete pillars, like you saw. I like the rain, but that time it went on way too long. The leak was upstairs, in Mr. Robert's bedroom. I figured I'd wait for the rain to stop then go mend it. But it didn't ease up even for a moment. So I had to do it in the rain. I put some new tarpaper down on a part of the roof. Not long ago I replaced a couple of rotten planks in the deck. I oiled all the locks in the doors, the hinges of the windows, I checked all the outlets and switches and cables. They can just as easily go wrong in an unoccupied cabin. If I'd had his address I would've written to him. I often think of him, please let him know. I know, I know, you said you don't know him. But maybe one day, you can never tell.

The thing that worries me most is how he's doing after his operation. That's right, he was going in for an operation. No, it wasn't then that he told me. It was during my next visit, the one with all the fog I was telling you about before. I didn't see him in person, we just talked on the phone. But he was still living in his old place. As to whether he still had the shop, that I couldn't tell you.

After he moved I made inquiries with his neighbors. They told me he'd first sold the shop, then the apartment. But where he'd moved to, no one knew. Everyone said they didn't really know him that well. And more from the shop than from the neighborhood. In general, though, they didn't see him that often, sometimes just as he was leaving or coming home, good morning, good morning, that was all. He wasn't a big talker.

The guy that bought the shop from him had no idea either. He even seemed to resent it when I asked if he maybe knew anything.

"How should I know? I paid what he was asking. Didn't even haggle. It's a good location. What do you want from me, mister? I don't sell souvenirs. Fruit and veg, like you see. He moved away and now he's gone, that's all there is to it."

It was the same at the lake, no one knew a thing. Some of them hadn't even noticed that his cabin had been standing empty for a couple of seasons already. They raised their eyebrows as if they were surprised he'd stopped coming. Mr. Robert, you say? Wait, what season was that? What season was it? Oh yes, I remember now, you're right. And you say he also left the city?

I called him up before he moved to say I wanted to come for a visit. He didn't seem the least bit pleased.

"Now, in the fall?" His voiced sounded dry, irritated even.

"Is it a bad time for you?"

"No, it's just I wasn't expecting it. You should have come in the summer."

"I couldn't make it in the summer, Mr. Robert. Also, I wanted to see what it's like in the fall."

"Winter's right around the corner. The leaves are almost all off the trees. It'll be snowing before you know it. Why are you so drawn to the place, eh? You might end up regretting it."

I wondered if there was maybe something the matter with him, and I asked:

"How's your health?"

"What you'd expect for my age," he answered tersely. "I have an operation coming up."

"Is it anything serious?"

"That remains to be seen. For the moment I'm waiting for an available bed in the hospital. They've promised me there'll be one. It could even be tomorrow or the next day. They're going to let me know. I already have a bag packed. I wouldn't be able to drive down there with you. I haven't sold the cabin yet. You can stay there."

He told me where to find the key. Under the deck, on a nail in one of the beams. He said I should just put it back there when I left. He told me where to turn the electricity on so I'd have light and hot water. And heating of course, since it was already cold there. Where the bedding was, towels, this and that.

"When do you reckon you'll be back from the hospital?" I asked.

"How should I know?" he retorted almost rudely, as if he wanted to bring the conversation to a close.

"Maybe I could come visit you if you're still . . . ?"

"What for? A hospital's no place for a visit. Besides, I don't like that sort of thing."

"Perhaps I could be of help in some way?"

"You, help me? How do you like that." His tone was so ironic it left a really unpleasant impression.

"Still, I hope we'll meet again some time."

"We already did meet."

Those were his last words.

3

Haven't we met before? But where and when? As I look at you, your face seems somehow familiar. Actually, I thought so the moment you walked in. Though maybe you just look like someone I must have met at some time. I don't know who it could have been. If I could remember who it was I might also remember when and where. I mean, it can happen that people resemble one another, that one person can sometimes be mistaken for someone else. Especially if you were close with someone then you never see them again, you want to meet up with them again even in a stranger. Though when it comes down to it, what difference does it make whether someone looks like somebody else. As the years pass we resemble our own selves less and less. Even our memory isn't always willing to remember us the way we once were. Let alone when it comes to other people.

I often experience that here as well. I know everyone, I have it all written down, who lives in which cabin, but at the beginning of the season when they start arriving, with some of them I have to remind myself all over again whether or not they're the same people. I sometimes wonder, can a human face have changed so very much from one season to the next? True, there are faces that seem in general to escape your memory. With a face like that, you can look at it every day, then it's enough not to see it till the next season and you can't say anymore whether it's new or whether you've seen it before. But there are also faces that you barely catch a glimpse of, and already they're fixed forever in your memory.

Oftentimes I've been walking down some crowded city street, a throng of people, you're constantly bumping into someone or other, and I might be seeing nothing at all, none of the buildings, advertisements, shop windows, cars, and people's faces are just flashing by for a brief second, then suddenly amid all those glimpses there's one face, why this particular one I couldn't say, but it bores into my memory and remains there for good. Actually I carry inside me an infinite number of those faces that were conceived in those short flashes, as it were. I don't know whose they are, I don't know where or when, I don't know anything about them. But they live in me. Their thoughts, their expressions, their paleness, their sorrows, grimaces, bitternesses – it all lives in me, fixed as if in a photograph. Except that these aren't regular photographs where once someone's captured, they stay that way forever. Then years later they themselves may not even recognize that it's them. And even if they know it's them, they're not able to believe it. No – in the photographs taken by my memory, even from a passing glance, over the years all those faces develop wrinkles and furrows, their eyelids begin to droop. So if someone used to have big wide eyes, for example, now they're narrowed to slits. Someone else would smile and show a row of even white teeth, now all they have left is their open mouth. Frankly, they ought not to smile any more. Or a beautiful woman, it was her beauty that struck me in the flash of seeing her face, and now you wouldn't want to meet her. I've known a number of beautiful women and let me tell you, whenever my memory brings back their image to me, I wonder whether beautiful women shouldn't die before their time.

But who on earth am I, what right do I have to them, to these faces that happen to be fixed in my memory and are with me as if my life were their life too? I feel as if those faces have left their stamp on me inside. I try to put them out of my mind, without success. I sometimes even have the impression that they themselves are asking me not to forget them. I tell you, it's not easy living with so many faces inside yourself, not knowing anything about them.

Though occasionally the opposite also happens. For example, I'll have been traveling by train, sitting opposite someone, and as often happens on a train, we couldn't help talking a bit with one another, and I can remember the day and date and the time the train departed, what its arrival time was, he got out and I continued on and I even thought about him later, but I couldn't recall his face. So you and I may have traveled one time in the same train, in the same compartment, we could have talked, I could have thought about you afterwards, and now for some reason I can't recall your face aside from the fact that it seems familiar. Maybe we were on a plane together, or a ship. So you don't remember me either?

No, I don't mind. You had no reason to pay any attention to me. Why would you? Memory has no obligation of reciprocity, you didn't have to notice me. Me, I try and remember this and that if only to maintain order, to try and keep everything neat and tidy. Maybe that'll help me find myself also. Order isn't only what you suppress, it's what you allow. No, it isn't that alone. That may not even be it at all. Sometimes I have the impression that it's something like the flip side of life, where everything has its place and its time, things proceed not just according to their own wishes, and nothing can go beyond the limits imposed by order. I don't know if you'll agree with me on this, but it's order that turns our life into fate. Not to mention that we're merely specks in the order of the world. That's why the world is so incomprehensible to us – because we're nothing more than specks within it. Without order people wouldn't be able to put up with themselves. The world wouldn't be able to put up with itself. Even God, would he be God without order? Though people are the strangest beings in the world, who knows if they aren't even stranger than God. And they refuse to understand that it's better for them to know their place, their time, their limits. I mean, the fact that we're born and we die, that's already a sort of order imposed on us.

I'll be honest with you, even here I wouldn't have taken on the job of minding the place if they hadn't agreed it would stop being the way it was up till then, when anything went. Minding the cabins, that also requires giving something up so as to have something else. I said, fine, I'll do it, but I have to be able to impose order here. Never mind that we're in nature. Ever since people left nature behind, in doing that they agreed to a different kind of order. If they still lived in nature, nature would do the minding. But since it's going to be me . . .

I began by marking out the paths, because people were walking any way their feet took them. They trampled the grass not just in front of the cabins, everywhere you looked it was all trodden down. I had them provide spades, and string to do the laying out. The pegs I made myself. I sketched out where all the paths would be, made a plan for each side of the lake. And can you imagine, they even started objecting to the paths, they said I was restricting their freedom. It made me mad and I said, do they want me to look after the place, yes or no? If so, then we need to get to work. I'm restricting their freedom, can you believe that? And they're not restricting my freedom? Any reciprocal arrangement is a restriction. Not to mention that I didn't come here to look after their cabins. I have my nameplates, that's more than enough for me. Who knows if it isn't actually too much, because there's always too much work for one person. I could easily just live my own life, so long as I have my dogs. Besides, I don't have long to go now. In my spare moments I could go walking in the woods, read, listen to music. That's right, I brought some books. Not too many, but any of them can be reread, you can do that as often as you like. I always liked reading if I only had the time.

Back when I was working on building sites, whenever the site had a library I'd always borrow books. I had to read at least a few pages before I fell asleep. It depended on how tired I was. But even when I was exhausted I had to, otherwise I couldn't get to sleep. Even when I was drunk I had to. I'd read even if I didn't understand what I was reading. Actually, you don't have to understand right away. You can live any amount of life and you don't understand that either. I brought a lot of things, TV, radio, cassette player, video, lots of records. It's all through there in the living room.

I wouldn't have to know all the people here, know who's who, which cabin they're from. But now I do, though I don't need them for anything. I have to remember who and where and when, who gave what to who and all that. I have to give everyone's cabin the once-over after each season. I have to do this and that and the other, but I wouldn't have to do any of it, because I don't have to do anything at all anymore. They go mushrooming then they ask me to come check whether any of the mushrooms they've picked are poisonous. And I have to go, because what would happen if they got poisoned?

I'm restricting their freedom. Like anyone knows what that even means. Or they come to me with all sorts of problems and complaints, and I have to hear them out. It goes without saying that they tattle on each other as well. You can't have all these cabins and all these people without someone telling on someone else. Sometimes I feel like a priest in the confessional. Except that priests teach you how to forget. They forgive your sins and forget them. But I don't forgive anything, and I can't forget either. So who's restricting whose freedom, tell me that.

Freedom. You could say the word itself conceals its own negation. In the same way that despair lurks in the most beautiful illusion. Because if you understand it as freedom from all constraints, then that includes freedom from yourself. After all, people are their own most troublesome constraints. They can be unbearable to themselves. Some of them are too much for themselves. Uncle Jan for instance, the first example that comes to mind. Nothing in particular happened to make him do what he did. What might have happened, in any case what they suspected him of, maybe he could have endured it somehow or other. People have put up with worse. Did he hang himself because he was free? Or because it was the only way he could get free of himself? I'll tell you one thing, free people are unpredictable. Not just to other folks. Above all to themselves.

When I think about it sometimes, I come to the conclusion that freedom is just a word, like lots of similar words. They don't mean what they're supposed to mean, because that isn't possible. They aim too high and end up becoming illusions. Which is hardly surprising, since life is just one long series of illusions. We're guided by illusions, motivated by illusions. Illusions drive us forward, hold us back, determine our goals. We're born out of illusions, and death is just a transition from one illusion into another.

After all, there are words like that that don't have any fixed meaning. Words that can adapt to any of our desires, our dreams, our longings, our thoughts. You might say they're immaterial, words drifting in a universe of other words – that they're words searching for their own meaning, or to put it more precisely, for their own idea. For example eternity, nothingness. Who knows if freedom isn't one of those words. Yet you have to beware of words like that, because they can assume any meaning, any idea. Depending on how ready we are to yield to them, and what we intend to use them for. In my view not even nature is free.

To tell you the truth, it's only the children that keep me here, otherwise I'd have given up this minding business long ago. Yes, I like children. Children may be the only thing I still like. Myself? Why do you ask that? I've no reason to like myself. When they bring their children here, the kids come running to me of their own accord. And whatever they want, I always do it, show them things, explain things. I dig up worms so they can go fishing, put them on their hooks, teach them how to tell one kind of fish from another. Teach them to swim. If they break something I mend it without a word. Sometimes I take a larger or smaller group of them to the woods. With their parents' consent, of course. We learn about the trees, how to tell an oak from a beech, a larch from a spruce. We pick blueberries, wild strawberries, blackberries, or we collect pine cones or acorns. Learn how to tell poisonous mushrooms from edible ones. Sometimes I give them little quizzes so they'll remember things better. When we see a bird I explain to them what kind of bird it is and how not to confuse it with other kinds. If we find a nest I'll tell them what sort of bird lives in it, and what kinds of nests other birds build. Then when they get tired we sit down and I tell them stories. What about? No, not about what once happened here, not that. And I never lead them to where the graves are. They might stop being children, because being a child has nothing to do with how old you are.

I don't have any children of my own. I was married, but I don't have any children. That was why my wife and I split up, because she wanted to have children. I liked my friends' children, though. Whenever I visited I'd always bring them some gift. It pleased me to see how it pleased them. I liked to play with them. But the thought that one of them could be mine would fill me with anxiety. It's the same now, whenever I think that one of the children here could be mine . . .

With adults I know at least that nothing much links me to them anymore. And nothing needs to, aside from the fact that here for example, I look after their cabins and insist on order. Not for its own sake, or even because order makes the looking after easier. No. It's that when there's order around you, it's easier to find order in yourself. When they make a fuss, I can always threaten to stop minding their cabins. I demanded a lights-out time in all the cabins. After all, they come here to rest, it ought to be quiet. Do you think they all got it right away? Not a bit of it. Some of the cabins, they'd deliberately leave their lights on all night long. They only began to catch on when I refused to look after certain cabins. Unless someone had a nameday or some other special occasion, then I'd let them have an extra hour or two, but not all night. I marked out firepits for bonfires, at a distance from the cabins and the woods, close to the water. I've nothing against people grilling sausages, but only up to such and such a time. Then the regulations say they have to douse the fire. I go around and check.

For instance, the cabins didn't have numbers. When someone new came they'd get lost. Or come to me and ask which cabin belonged to so-and-so. I'd have to take them there, because they wouldn't find it even if I gave them directions. I'd even make mistakes myself about who lived in which cabin. You saw for yourself, a lot of the cabins look the same. And in fact pretty much first thing I decided to number all the cabins. Having numbers would make things much easier. You'd think I'd have been given a round of applause. Not on your life. It was nothing but an uphill struggle. To start with, everyone wanted the lowest possible number. Then someone hit on the idea of numbering the cabins in the order they were built. With that kind of arrangement no one would ever have been able to find any cabin. Number one would be over by the woods, say, then number two would be on the far side of the lake. Plus, they'd never be able to agree on whose cabin was built first or second or tenth, because at the beginning the same company put up all the cabins. And not one after another, but depending on who greased the right palms or knew someone in the firm. Then they started discussing which side of the lake the numbering should start from. And they couldn't agree on that either, because the people on this side wanted the numbers to begin here, then to continue on the far side. While the folks over there wanted the opposite.

What would you have done in my place? I wanted them to decide it among themselves, because I reckoned that if they didn't reach an understanding on their own, there'd never be agreement. They'd always be bothered by the numbering, that they didn't live at the number they wanted to live at. Besides, they were their cabins, their numbers. I just said I'd buy the paint, cut out some stencils and paint the numbers on. It almost drove me nuts. I said to them, do you want me to paint the numbers on? Because someone has to. Then in that case they'll begin here and end here. And both sides of the lake together, not separately.

Do you think that was an end of it? No such luck. When it came down to it, no one wanted to have number thirteen because that's unlucky. Except what kind of order is it when one number's missing? Someone could come and be looking for number thirteen. Nothing I could do, I had them draw straws, and it came out that now number thirteen is between number twenty-six and number twenty-seven. But so be it, I guess no order can be perfect.

Another thing, they'd throw their trash out wherever they wanted, they mostly chucked it into the woods. When you went walking there it was an offense to the woods. At one time the woods didn't even have any sticks left. I made them bring trash bags for their trash, then take the bags back to the city to dispose of. Cities are beyond saving anyway. If I ever find even a beer can or a soda bottle or anything, the dogs will sniff out who dropped it, and bring it back to their doorstep.

Then sunbathing, they can't just go sunbathing right away or for as long as they want, there's a warning on the signboards to say they have to do it gradually, and bald people have to wear a cap. One time it happened that someone figured he'd get a full tan on the first day, and we ended up having to call an ambulance.

I made two signboards. I put up two posts, one on each side of the lake, fixed the signboards on the posts, then each season I write what they can and can't do on the boards. Whenever anyone arrives for the first time they have to read what's written there, because every season there's someone new, and also I change some of the wording to make it clearer, so later no one can claim it's ambiguous.

Would you like to see the signboards? They're propped up through there, in the hallway. That's right, I take them down in the off-season. Maybe you could suggest something to add. There's never any end to order. All right, maybe another time, if you come during the season. You'll see for yourself then. I'm thinking of making two more. Actually, there really should be one in front of every cabin. Or even better, everyone should carry a sign like that on their back. That way they couldn't claim they didn't have time to read it.

Why do I do it? Let me ask you, do you know people? I get the impression you sort of don't. Would you be able to turn a blind eye to all these things? And what, just let it all happen? That that's how people are made? Then why were they made at all? They didn't have to be. It's easy enough to imagine a world without people. Why not? You say that in such a case the world would have no imagination? Perhaps our imagination is our misfortune, and by the same token it's the misfortune of the world? Maybe I'm not as strong as you. I can't say, I don't know you. But here at least, in this place, it can't be so. I could be indifferent to all this if I weren't looking after it. But once I took the job on, even though I didn't have to, it became an entirely different matter.

For instance, since last season they're not allowed to take children out into the deep water. They're not my kids, but I couldn't stand to see some father or mother taking a child into deep water to teach them to swim. Don't be scared, don't be scared. That's not how to stop a kid from being afraid. One time a little one nearly drowned. The father accidentally swallowed a mouthful of water, and he let go of the child. Before anyone could have swum out there it would have been all over. Luckily Rex and Paws jumped in and pulled it out.

I've stopped allowing adults just the same, if they're not good swimmers. I was even thinking of requiring everyone to get a swimming certificate. How else can you know if someone really can swim when they say they can. I mean, I can't stand in front of everyone and check. Maybe one day I'll organize races and everyone can show whether they're a good swimmer or not. You can't mess around with water. Water, fire, destiny.

But there's one thing I haven't been able to do anything about. I haven't been able to stop them having fights and beating up on their wives. I say wives, it makes no difference whether it's their wife or not. There are guys that bring a different woman here every season. But I know my boundaries. There's others have someone different with them every weekend. Last time it was an older woman, this time he's with someone much younger. You can't help seeing. Some of them even swap women among the cabins. You can't help noticing that one of them was staying in one cabin and now she's in a different one, then two or three weeks later she's in one of the very furthest ones. I don't pry. It'd never even occur to me to ask one guy or another, So is this your new wife? And I won't listen when other people come and complain about these wives or whatever they are.

One time they came to tell me that in one of the cabins, forgive me for not saying which one, the man was always beating his wife or non-wife. It was always in the middle of the night. And that I should do something about it. But what was I supposed to do? I can't just go there and say, stop beating her. I don't even have the right to say, your wife or your non-wife, whichever it is. Myself, I'd never strike a woman. But how can you explain it to a type like that? What am I to him? I just take care of the place, I let myself be hired. Or if I wanted to write it on the signboards, what am I supposed to write? Beating of wives and non-wives prohibited? There are things that don't belong on signboards.

Then one night I was woken by a shout. Or maybe I wasn't asleep? I jumped out of bed and ran outside, the dogs followed. I couldn't see lights on in any of the cabins. It was quiet as it usually is around here. Maybe I dreamed it, I thought to myself. I sometimes dream something that wakes me up. Even from a deeper sleep. Afterwards I find it hard to believe that I only dreamed it. Like what? I won't tell you, dreams can't be told. When they're told, they stop being a dream. It's like you wanted to tell about God. Would God still exist? Besides, can anything actually be told? Things told are just things told, nothing more. Usually they have little in common with what was or is or will be. They live their own lives. And they don't settle down for good, but instead they keep on moving, growing, getting further and further away from what was or is or will be. Though who knows, maybe in that way they draw closer to the truth?

Try and reach down deep, try if you can to touch the world with the very first thought, that's still untainted by anything. You'll admit then that it's what's told that establishes what was or is or will be, not the other way around; that it fills it out, determines whether it's bound for oblivion or resurrection. And what is told is the only possible eternity. We live in what is told. The world is what is told. That's why it's harder and harder to live. And perhaps only our dreams determine who we are. Perhaps only our dreams are ours.

To be honest, mostly I don't dream that much. Less and less. Plus, when I wake up I don't remember anything. In general I sleep badly. Often I'll be dead beat, but when I go to bed I can't get to sleep. Then if I do, I can't tell if I'm sleeping or not, whether I'm sleeping in a waking state or dreaming of being awake. This doctor that has one of the cabins gave me some foreign sleeping pills, he told me they'd for sure send me to sleep. He sometimes comes and gives me a checkup, listens to me with his stethoscope, checks my blood pressure. I tell him, what for, doc? I don't need to live so very long. What I've already lived is enough. Let's say I take a pill, and I'm sound asleep, and during that time something happens in one of the cabins. If I take a pill the dogs might not even be able to wake me up, and they can't go off and help all on their own. They can't even open the door, I always keep it locked. I've never taken sleeping pills, and I'm not going to start now.

How long have I had trouble sleeping? As long as I can remember. Except it's getting worse and worse. Who knows, it could be that death is already getting me used to not sleeping. They say the closer you get to it, the more you sleep. But with me it's evidently the opposite. I'll die when I stop wanting to sleep at all. Maybe I'll see Death. I'll ask him, why didn't you come for me back then? That way it would all have been over long ago.

So as you can see, I don't even have time to dream. Besides, my dogs protect me from having dreams. I don't know if they don't like it when I have a dream, or whether they don't want dreams to add to my difficulties. Whenever I start having a dream they come up right away and start licking my hands and my face, tugging the blanket off of me, or yelping as if someone was breaking into one of the cabins. Then when they finally manage to wake me up they jump for joy that they've woken me. Something tells me they know about my dreams. Because I sometimes dream something that makes it really hard to even get up afterwards. It's like I'm still wandering about inside the dream, helpless, I can't tell whether it's me or someone in my place. Everything around seems to still be the dream.

In the middle of the night I'll take the dogs and go check up on the cabins, and I have the feeling I'm walking in the dream. The air is like now, in autumn, it's sharp, it pinches your cheeks, or even more in winter, and I can't be certain that I've woken up, or if I'm only dreaming the lake and the cabins and my dogs trotting beside me. And to tell you the whole truth, sometimes I'm not even certain it's my own dream. No, you didn't mishear. I'm not sure if it's my dream, or if someone else is dreaming me. Who? I don't know. If I did . . .

I remember my grandmother used to say that you don't always dream your own dreams. For instance you can dream the dreams of the dead, that they didn't manage to dream in their lifetime. Or the dreams of people who haven't yet come into the world. Not to mention that according to my grandmother dreams can sometimes pass from person to person, house to house, village to village, town to town and so on. Sometimes they can even get lost. One person in some house was supposed to have a particular dream, but actually someone else had it. Someone in the village was supposed to have a dream, but it ended up being dreamed by someone in the town. Someone in this country, but it was dreamed by someone in a distant place. So it's quite possible I'm having someone else's lost dreams, and that's why the dogs sense it right away and wake me up when I'm having that kind of dream.

I should tell you too that my grandmother was known to be an expert on dreams. There wasn't a dream whose meaning she couldn't explain. Not just in the family. Neighbors came from near and far, from both sides of the Rutka. They came from other villages. Old folks, young ones. Unmarried women, wives, Doubting Thomases. They'd seen the world, but they came when one of them had had a dream that was too much for them. And grandmother would explain everybody's dreams. When she explained them, every dream became clear as waking life, as if it were simply something the person had lived through but overlooked. She'd have them provide some small detail, because people don't pay enough attention to details. And that detail would sometimes alter the meaning of the dream from one thing to another, from good to better or from bad to not so bad at all. Or even that the dream was meant to have been dreamed by somebody else, because one detail was from someone else's life.

Every day over breakfast we'd each have to tell her what we'd dreamed about. And it couldn't be that no one had dreamed anything. To sleep through the night and not have any dreams? The only exception was grandfather, who never had any dreams. It's hard to believe, right? Even us children, we always dreamed something. Though according to grandmother our dreams didn't count yet, because we still got our dreams from our mother or father. She'd say that you only grow into your own dreams through suffering.

You can't imagine how many dreams she knew. When we were shelling beans she'd tell one dream after another, as if she was pulling them out of the husks. Dreams that belonged to the living. Dreams dreamed by the dead. The dreams of kings, princes, bishops. I remember one time she told about a king who dreamed that a pearl fell out of his crown. No, she didn't say if he'd actually come to her for an explanation of what the dream meant. But I believed he had, and that he'd brought her the pearl in the palm of his hand. Aside from me, I don't know if anyone else believed it. Grandfather did for sure, because he believed every story grandmother told. Though it made no difference whether anyone believed it or not. When you're listening, especially during bean-shelling, you don't have to believe in what you're listening to. It's enough that you're listening. For me in any case, my heart would stop when grandmother would begin, saying, one time a king had a dream, a prince had a dream, one night a bishop had a dream . . .

Everyone would be enthralled, whether or not they believed it all. It would go so quiet that if it hadn't been fall or winter, you could have heard a fly buzzing. Mother and father, Jagoda, Leonka, even Uncle Jan, who didn't believe in anything anymore. Not to mention grandfather, who would be so intent on listening he'd stop shelling beans. Though the others too, the husks would hang loose in their hands, and the beans would fall much less often onto the canvas sheet. Though father didn't like kings, he used to blame all kinds of misfortunes on kings, so when grandmother started telling about a king he'd sometimes interrupt her:

"What country was he from? You know, the king. A king can't be from just anywhere. Ordinary people can, they have to live wherever they find themselves. But not a king. Where there's a king there has to be a kingdom. If there's no kingdom, even dreams wouldn't want him as king."

Though for the dream it made no difference what country the king was from, and it would often upset Uncle Jan, who was sort of brought back to life from the bean-shelling:

"It's all nonsense, mother. Dreams are nonsense and waking is nonsense. And kings, they were gotten rid of long ago, how could their dreams still be around." After which he'd get up and go drink some water.

Mother, on the other hand, she'd always defend grandmother loyally. For mother no dream was dreamed in vain, whatever it's meaning was, and people should know what it meant. Because it was worse not to know than to know the worst. So grandfather, who believed that all dreams came from God, would praise grandmother's wisdom all the more:

"All those learned folks and ministers and priests, while she never studied at all and yet look what she knows."

And every morning, as we were eating our *Żurek* soup with potatoes, amid the slurping and the clatter of spoons against the tin bowls, when grandmother would ask who had had what dreams and would try to explain them all, grandfather would be so filled with admiration at how clever grandmother was that he'd pause with his spoonful of soup or potatoes halfway to his mouth. At times the soup would spill on the table, or a potato would fall off the spoon, and grandmother would tell him off:

"Don't make such a mess."

But he'd have to give words to his admiration:

"How about that. You wouldn't even know what you'd dreamed about if she hadn't explained it for you. Dreams really are a second life once they're explained to you. But for that you need to be smart, sharp as nails. Smart enough to take you into the next world and beyond."

He never could forgive himself for not having dreams. When he fell asleep it was like he'd died. Then when he woke up it was like he was rising from the dead. But between the falling asleep and the rising from the dead there was a big gap. If he'd ever felt like counting up all those gaps, it would come out that a third of his life he wasn't in the world. He couldn't even dream anything from wartime, though he'd been through four wars in his life. He fought in one of them, got wounded, he had this huge gash from a bayonet in his stomach. But he was fine. Maybe if the bayonet wound had hurt, but it hadn't hurt him a bit, quite the opposite, he'd felt such a surge of strength that he killed the guy that stuck the bayonet in his belly, and the guy's two buddies as well.

When it came to wars, grandfather was just as much an expert on them as grandmother was on dreams. No one was his equal about wars. Wars were the milestones that prevented him from getting lost in his memory, in the world. He stuck to wars like they were familiar paths, whatever he happened to be talking about. When someone else would tell a story, grandfather always asked which war it happened after or before. Grandfather's memory was made up of wars instead of calendars or saints' days. Wars were more important than the seasons, above wars there was only God. According to grandfather, time moved from one war to the next. And in the same way, wars marked out space much more accurately than maps. Everything that happened, happened where there was a war. And everything happened after the last one, before the last one, after the one before it, before the one before it, or before the one even before that. He even remembered that war. He remembered that his father, which is to say my great-grandfather, had fought in it, and he'd been wounded, though in the head, not in the belly. And from great-grandfather's memory he also remembered an earlier war that great-grandfather remembered from the memory of his own father, that is, grandfather's grandfather, and it had a particular name, and that was even before the other one, when neither me nor any of you were in the world, he'd say.

You'd have gotten lost in all those wars if you'd listened to grandfather. He was so meek and helpless in it all. You'd never have imagined he could have been a soldier. All the more that he could have killed someone. He couldn't kill a chicken. He'd put its head on the chopping block, lift the ax and just stand there till someone came out of the house and took the ax from him and brought it down on the chicken's neck. Or he'd grumble about the moles that were digging up the meadow. The damn things wouldn't stop burrowing, pretty soon there wouldn't be a meadow anymore, just endless molehills. He'd go out with a spade, stand over one of the molehills, and even though he knew perfectly well that the mole was frisking about inside, he'd always say that something held him back from driving the blade of the spade into the molehill. Supposedly he was waiting till the mole was sure it was safe, so it'd come closer to the surface. He'd be holding his breath, standing stock still, poised to sink the spade in, and he'd tell himself, now, do it now, but something would hold him back. He would have hit it for sure, the mole was already poking its little snout outside, he would have sliced its head off without any problem, the blade was sharp as a razor, he'd sharpened it specially beforehand. But something stopped him. Evidently the thing that stayed his hand was stronger than he was.

I heard that one time the mole actually came out of the molehill and the two of them just stood there, grandfather and the mole, looking at each other. And grandfather got this feeling as if it weren't a mole he was about to kill. And he said:

"Live on, you're one of God's creations. The meadow'll survive somehow or other."

Grandfather never even got into fights at dances when he was young, though there were fights, there were all kinds of fights, sometimes the whole dance would be fighting among themselves. He never even fought over grandmother, though she was constantly being whisked away to dance. He'd just sit on a bench while grandmother danced. He preferred to just watch her dancing with someone else, rather than fighting over her. No, he was a big man, strong as an ox, when he was young he must have been a strapping guy. It was just that, like I said, he was meek and helpless, as if his own strength made him weak.

"Ah, she'd dance and dance, you wouldn't have known her," he would remember proudly. "When it came to the *oberek*, she'd fly through the air. When I looked at her feet, they wouldn't even be touching the floor. Why should I have been angry? She'd dance her fill, and I knew she'd be mine anyway."

When they got married, grandfather had already been called up to serve in the war. He didn't want the marriage, who knew if he'd come back, he said. But grandmother said that a wife waiting for a husband was different than an engaged woman waiting for her fiancé. And she led grandfather to the altar. Now she was his wife he'd know how to go to war. They'd have a different kind of joy when he came back, because he had to come back. She might curse God if he didn't come back.

And so to stop grandmother having to curse God, grandfather had such a rush of strength when he felt the bayonet in his belly that he killed the man who stuck it in him, along with the guy's two comrades. He remembered them like it was yesterday. The one that stuck him was a skinny guy, short, looked like he was all greatcoat from his neck to the ground, with nothing but a helmet on top. Like he had sleeves instead of arms, and it was the sleeves that stuck the bayonet in grandfather's belly. And he did it right at the moment when grandfather had opened his mouth to say, Let's not kill each other. I have to go back home. And you have to go back home. But he had to kill him. Not even with a bayonet, not with a bullet, but with the great strength he felt inside himself instead of pain. He grabbed hold of the other guy under his helmet and pushed him to the ground. He did the same with his two pals. They even went down on their knees to ask for mercy, but he couldn't stop the strength within him. He grabbed one under the helmet and brought him down, then he did the same with the other one. It was only after he'd killed them that the strength left him. He sat down by the bodies and cried. It was only then that he felt the pain in his belly from the bayonet wound.

But even they wouldn't appear to grandfather in dreams. He'd tell grandmother to explain to him how it was, what it meant. If wars mark off people's lives, they ought to mark off their dreams as well. Had he stopped being a person? Let her explain it to him. But grandmother would usually just lose patience with grandfather:

"Explain what? What do you want me to explain? First you have to have dreams."

Though to tell you the truth, I suspect she must have known the meaning of a gap in the night like that. Perhaps she simply didn't want to make grandfather worry, because she always looked for something comforting in a dream, even if it was a frightening one. With all those dreams she carried inside her, she couldn't have not known. So grandfather held it against her. But he also held it against God for not granting him the grace of dreams, when other people are given great grace. Could it be that He was angry with him for the three men he'd killed? He was God, surely He knew that in wars people kill each other. He ought to understand. So many wars had passed through the world since He created it, and He hadn't stopped a single one with His almighty powers, so why would grandfather's one war and those three killed men be of any importance? Plus, if He ruled the world then He also ruled wars, and grandfather wouldn't have killed without His having willed it. Why was he being punished?

During the bean-shelling, when he started talking about wars it never ended till we ran out of beans. One time, I remember, he told about how he'd met a philosopher. No, it wasn't one of the three men he killed. If it had been one of those, he wouldn't have known he'd killed a philosopher. When you kill someone, no one introduces themselves. Especially when it's one extended line against another, one bayonet against another. And in that war most of the killing was done by bayonet. They'd all jump out from the trenches and rush at each other with a Hurrah! Then they'd go back to their trenches, and between the trenches there'd be a growing mountain of bodies. At times the war would stand in one place for weeks on end, so when they weren't killing each other they'd often even get to know one another. That I can't tell you. You'd have to have asked grandfather. I was a child when I heard all this. And children believe everything. Why would I not have believed it. You've never lived through a war? You're lucky, though I also feel sorry for you. In wartime all kinds of things can happen. War mixes things up, levels them out. Farmers or philosophers, they're all good for dying. So anyone can meet anyone. Where else could a farmer meet a philosopher?

So when they weren't fighting, especially at night, because obviously you can't fight with bayonets at night, and there were days on end when they didn't fight because there were no orders, the men from the two lots of trenches would go out and meet up with each other. They'd sit around among all those bayoneted bodies, share their tobacco and vodka, swap various things, sometimes play cards. Why not? Blackjack, for example, you can play that in the dark. All you need is to take a drag on your cigarette, the tip lights up and you can see your cards. Other times they'd sing songs, sometimes the men on both sides would sing in the same language.

So anyway one time, this was also at night, it was raining on and off, everyone was squatting under their waterproof capes in their trenches. All of a sudden grandfather sees someone leave the enemy trench, stand among the bodies and turn his face up to the sky, as if he was trying to gather all the rain on his face. So grandfather went out there, and turned his face upward into the rain the same way. The other guy asked if grandfather maybe wanted something to eat. Grandfather's belly was rumbling, because they'd even run out of hard tack. So the other man went back to his trench and brought a can. They sat down together, opened the can, and set about eating. With the same bayonets they'd been sticking each other with, of course.

Grandfather was too shy to ask who he was eating with. Besides, what difference did it make? All that mattered was that the other guy had brought the can. And since he was also in uniform, though it was an enemy uniform, there's no way grandfather could have known he was eating with a philosopher. So they sat there eating, leaning towards each other to shelter the can from the rain. The other man didn't say anything. As for grandfather, it was true he liked to talk, though mostly about wars, like I said. But how could he talk about war since they were actually at the war, and they were sitting and eating amid the bodies of men who'd been killed. They did take the casualties away, but only the wounded ones, the dead weren't cleared till the front moved.

So grandfather started singing the praises of the canned food, he said it was really tasty, and not just because his belly had been growling, but in general he liked to say nice things about everything. The day, the night, life, people, God. That's the kind of person he was. So the other man told grandfather to finish off the whole of the rest of the can. Out of gratitude grandfather got to talking about himself. That he'd left a young wife behind at home. That he hoped to go back to her. That he had three cows, two horses, this many acres, some meadowland, some woodland. That he sowed and plowed, day after day. And in the fall and winter they mostly shelled beans, because they planted enough of them so there'd be sufficient for the shelling all fall and winter. They'd all sit down, the lamp would be lit, they'd be shelling beans and telling stories. When he got back he'd tell stories about the war, and about how the two of them had eaten a can of food together.

The other man said he envied grandfather. True, he didn't know how to shell beans, but he'd rather shell beans than do what he did for a living, especially as it didn't serve any purpose for people. So grandfather asked him what he did. The other man introduced himself to grandfather, saying he was a philosopher. He gave his name. Grandfather repeated the name to himself all through the war, so as not to forget it when he got home. He wanted to at least repay the man with his memory, for the can of food he'd shared. Unfortunately though, he forgot. Who do you say that was? Are you sure? Did you know him? It's too bad grandfather's no longer with us, you could have reminded him.

In any case, grandfather could talk forever about wars. And especially during bean-shelling, it was like his memory opened up completely. I don't know if it was the wars that had that power, or whether it was the beans that could open any memory right to the bottom. You actually had the impression that war and beans got along together.

You know, I sometimes wonder whether grandfather really did kill those three men. Maybe he just imagined he'd killed them, hoping that because of that at least they'd appear to him in dreams. It could have been his way of doing something about the fact that he never had dreams. Like I said, in everything he nearly always turned to wars for support. Even when he wanted to offer comfort to himself or other people. He'd always bring up something from one of the wars. Not necessarily the one he'd been in. Sometimes it was another one, a more recent one or an older one, one when he hadn't yet been born.

One time when we were grazing the cows on the meadow, I heard the other boys whispering that Uncle Jan wasn't grandfather's son, because he'd been born too soon after grandfather got back from the war. Though I never noticed grandfather treating his two sons differently in any way. And Uncle Jan never gave any indication he didn't feel like grandfather's son either. When he hung himself, it affected grandfather more than anyone.

"How was he not my son, how?" he kept repeating. Then another time he said: "No one can even imagine their son might hang himself. It's too bad I had that burst of strength back then and didn't let those three guys stick their bayonets in me. Three bayonets, I wouldn't have had to live to see this. Oh, son, son. If you'd at least died in wartime it wouldn't be so sad."

Who knows how it actually was. Grandfather's gone, grandmother's gone, Uncle Jan's gone. At times it seems to me that everyone's gone. Maybe I've gone too? I sometimes try and figure out whether I'm here or not. Except you can't be a witness to yourself. Someone else has to testify on your behalf. People are too easy on themselves. When they can, they protect themselves from themselves. They dodge and twist, anything so they don't have to go further, deeper, to where they have something hidden. Everyone wants to appear to themselves the way they look in their wedding picture. Neatly combed and shaved, in a suit and tie, well-fed and smiling, looking like a decent guy. And as young as possible, of course. And they believe that's them. Though if they really took an honest look . . .

Every wedding photo is a happy one, as you know. Heads close, shoulder to shoulder, like two poppy seeds that found each other in a tub. If you believed in destiny you might think this was a photograph of destiny. But what happens afterwards, that you won't see in any photograph. The camera doesn't exist that can do that job, or the photographer. Maybe one day there will be one, who knows. But so far, all wedding photos are always happy. Think how many happy pictures there are like that hanging in people's homes. Though honestly, I sometimes wonder if happiness can only ever be found in a wedding picture.

There was a wedding photograph in that guy's cabin too. Oh, I never finished the story. So when I got woken in the night by that shout, I decided to go see what was up. It was a dark night, the stars were hidden behind clouds. It was so quiet that my own steps sounded like I don't know how many pairs of feet walking. I could even hear the dogs' footsteps. I went between the cabins, put my ear to various walls, stuck my head in where there was an open window. But everyone was sound asleep, some of them I could hear snoring. I was starting to think I must have dreamed it. Then all of sudden the dogs start pulling me. What is it? But I let them lead me. And by one of the cabins I see a white body. A woman. Naked as the day she was born. I lean down, there's no sign of life. When I shine my flashlight on her face I see it's all bloody.

I picked her up and brought her back to my place. I laid her down through there in the living room and cleaned her up. She had so many bruises that even today, telling you about it makes me mad. I wrapped her in a blanket and held her, because she was shivering all over. I made tea for her but she couldn't drink, her lips were too swollen. I had to feed her the tea on a little spoon, propping her head up with my other hand because she couldn't hold it up by herself. When she opened her eyes she looked semi-conscious. She started to talk, I leaned over her but the only thing I could make out was a frightened whisper:

"Who are you?"

"Get some sleep," I said. "Sleep'll do you good."

But I don't think she slept, because I kept being woken by a sobbing sound through the wall. Or maybe I was just dreaming she was crying through there, and the dream kept waking me up. Early in the morning I went to get her clothes from the guy whose cabin I found her by. To begin with he denied it, swore blind it was nothing to do with him. No way. I mean, I'd often seen his wife. She hadn't come with him this time because she wasn't feeling well. Here, that's our wedding picture, you recognize her, right? He had no idea who the other woman was. Plus he took a sleeping pill last night, he hadn't even heard any shouting. Must have been one of the other cabins, you must be mistaken. I found her outside your cabin, I say. Then someone must have dumped her there out of spite. You ought to know the people that come here, what they get up to, he says, you're the one keeping an eye on it all.

If it hadn't been for the dogs he'd have kept denying it. But the dogs dragged some women's clothes from under the bed, underwear, blouse, skirt, house slippers. And can you imagine, he wasn't at all shamefaced about it. All he did was laugh.

"Come on, buddy, what kind of world are you living in? Don't be so old-fashioned. If you feel so sorry for her you can have her. I was going to get someone else anyway."

He tried to offer me a beer. The dogs had their hackles up, I had to quiet them down, easy Paws, easy Rex. They were only waiting for me to give them a sign.

"Maybe I am old-fashioned," I said. "But if anything like this ever happens again I'll burn this place down. And you'll never know who did it because you'll be inside."

"Keep your nose out of things that aren't your business, mister!" he said, getting angry.

"Everything's my business," I said evenly.

"We pay you to keep an eye on things!"

"Exactly."

4

This time of year, the off-season, one day is pretty much like all the rest. In the morning, like anyone getting up, I wash and I put my clothes on. Though I'll be honest with you, when I think about the fact that the whole world is getting up with me, washing, getting dressed, I sometimes feel like going back to bed and just this once not getting up, or not getting up ever again. It's like some curse hanging over you, making you get out of bed, wash, dress every day. From all that you'd be justified in losing interest in the whole day, even though it's only beginning, losing interest in anything that may or may not happen that day. Now imagine feeling that through your whole life. How many times have we gotten up, washed, gotten dressed – and for what?

It goes without saying that I'm talking about this side of the world, the day that's just beginning. Because on the other side, when we're getting up, washing, dressing, they're undressing and washing and going to bed, which we'll only do at the end of the day, when they'll be doing what we did in the morning. And that's the clearest indication the world is turning and not going anywhere.

I divide the world into two sides, but only for the morning, because by evening there aren't any sides anymore. By evening people are all broken into little pieces, the same everywhere. Whereas in the morning people are still whole.

No, first I have to feed the dogs. They have to get their food on time. Especially in the morning. Even if I couldn't get out of bed they'd still need to be fed. Whether I'm sick or not. They get it once in the morning then a second time in the late afternoon. When it comes time they let me know. They lie down flat and stare at me. When I wake up in the morning they're already lying there staring.

So how can you not get up, however much you don't feel like it or you don't see the point. Their eyes are shining, not because they're starving but because they're certain they're going to get fed. How can you not get up? Let me tell you, these days I couldn't exist without them. I often have the feeling that without them the day would refuse to begin and refuse to end.

After that we go see what's up with the cabins. Then it can be this or that. It varies depending on the day, though it's mostly the same. Sometimes I'll hop in the car and go get some groceries. That's right, I have a car. I have to run errands from time to time. Swing by the post office or the bank once in a while. Other than that I don't go anywhere. I don't have anyone to visit, any place to go, any reason. Plus, there's always something needs doing around here. The laundry, the ironing, the dishes; sweep the place out, tidy up. And even when I don't have any other jobs, there are always the nameplates. They take up a lot of my time. Though I don't work on them every day. Some days my hands work well, other times they hurt. I don't have a regular daily schedule.

I start each day like I don't expect anything of it, that it'll bring what it brings. Though I don't expect it to bring anything. Honestly, keeping an eye on the cabins is the only thing that gives any kind of order to the day. It's only from the cabins that I can see the day isn't standing still.

It's fall now and you'd think the days would be getting shorter and shorter, but for me they get longer and longer. Often, when I wake up in the morning and think that I have to live through till evening, I feel it's like living from birth to death all over again. I don't know if you've ever felt anything like that, but it's as if it's harder and harder to live through the day. No, it's not that it's long.

How shall I put it. Well, like today. It's a day like any other, but at the same time it's the whole of life.

In the evenings I read a bit, or listen to music. No, I hardly ever watch television. The dogs don't like it. When I turn it on their hackles rise and they start growling. So I have to switch it off. Maybe if I played. If you ask me, nothing binds life and death together the way music does. Believe me, I played all my life, I know. That's right, I even have three saxophones, I brought them with me. Soprano, alto, tenor. I played all three. They're through there in the living room. You want to see? Maybe we can take a look later. Let's finish with the beans first. I have a flute as well, and a clarinet. Sometimes I'd play piano too, when someone was needed to step in. But my instrument was the sax. Did I go to school? Depends what you mean by school. By my book I went to several, though I can't say I have any diplomas. But do you need to sit at a desk for years to know how to do something? It's enough that you want to know how to do it. And I wanted to ever since I was a kid.

I started on the harmonica. Got it from my Uncle Jan. One time we were sitting at the edge of the woods, under an oak tree, and uncle was playing. He was really good. He could even play tunes from the operettas. All of sudden an acorn fell on his head.

He stopped playing, looked upwards and said:

"Maybe even from this oak."

"What about the oak?"

"That I'll hang myself," he said. "But for now don't say anything to anyone."

He put the harmonica back to his lips, but he only passed it across them without a sound, then he lost himself in thought. After which he gave me the harmonica and said:

"Here. I won't need it anymore. It'd be a pity for it to go to waste. It was a good one."

I asked him:

"Why don't you want to live?"

"What can I tell you. You wouldn't understand. You should play me something instead."

"I don't know how yet, uncle."

"That doesn't matter. I'll know if you're going to be able to learn."

I started blowing and moving the harmonica back and forth across my lips. I couldn't get the sounds to match up. But uncle evidently heard something:

"You'll be able to play. Just make sure you practice."

And that was how I began. Does that count as the start of school in your eyes? Let's say that was only preschool. Back then they called it nursery school, not preschool. But since that oak tree I started to play. Actually, I was really determined. I played for days on end. I wanted uncle to hear me play before he hanged himself. On the pasture the cows wandered wherever they wanted, but I kept playing. When they sent me out of the house, I ran off into the woods and played there. When it was raining they'd kick me out because they couldn't take my music any longer, so I'd just go stand under the eaves and keep playing. I'd climb trees, go as far up as I could, so they wouldn't be able to reach me and make me come down. I'd get in a boat, drift down the Rutka, and play. I'd even go to the outhouse, latch the door shut, take out my harmonica and play. They couldn't understand how anyone could take so long in the outhouse. Luckily the outhouse was behind the barn and they couldn't hear me playing.

No, Uncle Jan was still alive then. It was like he was waiting to be able to hear me play. One time I saw him sitting under the same oak tree at the edge of the woods and I went up to him.

"Will you listen to me play, uncle?"

"Absolutely." Then, as he listened he said: "I see the harmonica won't be enough for you much longer. When the time comes you should choose the saxophone. No one here has even seen a saxophone, you'll get asked to play all the dances and weddings. Maybe even further, higher. Saxophones are in these days. And a saxophone is the whole wide world. I've got nothing against fiddles, but the fiddle is a Gypsy instrument. You have to have Gypsy blood, a Gypsy soul. Roam like the Gypsies, steal like the Gypsies. A non-Gypsy will never be able to play that way. There are people in the villages play the fiddle, but they're not real musicians. Fiddle and accordion and drums, they get together and they play everything all in the same style. One two three, one two three. They'll never play any differently, that was always how it was here. That was how they lived, how they played, and they'd die that way. One two three, one two three. For it to change, a saxophone has to come along. Maybe when that happens they'll start to dance differently, live differently. One time I went to a dance in the town, in the band there was a saxophone, and I'm telling you . . . Then I saw one just like it on display in a shop window. Next to it there was a fiddle. If I'd had the money, which I didn't, I'd have bought it. I'd have taught myself. You can learn anything if you just set your mind to it. It cost the earth. Much more than the fiddle next to it. I don't know how much you could get for this land of ours . . . I'll leave you my share, maybe that'll be enough. If not, then save up. Perhaps if I'd been younger . . . But you need to be your age to start."

It happened that after the war I found myself in this school. It wasn't an ordinary school. The best proof of this was the fact that the rec room, which took up a whole hut, was crammed with musical instruments. You wouldn't believe what all they had in there. Music school? No, nothing of the sort. But trumpets, flutes, trombones, oboes, bassoons, clarinets, violins, violas, cellos, double basses. There were instruments whose names we only learned from the music teacher, once he was brought in.

There was a saxophone too, an alto. True, it was missing two keys, but you could cover the holes with your fingers and more or less play it.

Some instruments were in even worse shape. Bent, cracked, torn, they had holes from bullets and shrapnel, as if they'd fought in the war too.

But there were also ones that were perfectly fine, or at any rate that all that was needed was to solder something together or fix it back on, or stick on an extra part, or take bits from two or three of them to make one whole one, transfer something from one to another, strings for example, on something else switch out the mouthpiece, and you could play. There were shops there, so you could mess around with little repairs like that.

It turned out some people already knew how to play a little on one instrument or another. But most of them had never touched a musical instrument in their lives. Me for example, all I'd known was uncle's harmonica. But when the music teacher showed up a short while later, he said right away that he'd make us into a band. Apparently that was the pedagogical task the school had assigned him. Fortunately he soon seemed to forget about it.

In general he didn't make much of an effort. It was another thing that I don't know if anyone at all could have made a band out of the ragbag of kids there were at that school. Most of the time he went around half cut, there were days he could barely stand upright. Sometimes he'd fall asleep in class. Or whenever he picked up an instrument to show us how it was played, he'd play and play, often till the end of the lesson.

We also had practice with him in the evenings in the rec room, depending on whether he showed up more or less drunk. If it was more, he'd get all sentimental about one broken instrument or another, ask how someone could have hurt it like that. Barbaric was what it was. An instrument like that suffered the way a person does. Every bullet hole, every snapped string, every chipped neck, was a wound. According to him some of the instruments had ended up in the school by mistake, they ought to have been in a museum.

But it may have been that they were brought from a museum, that they needed to be moved somewhere and it happened to be to our school. I'm sure you remember, back then everything was transported here and there and everywhere, back and forth. Not just instruments. Machinery, animals, people. Furniture, bedding, pots and pans. Sometimes we'd go down to the station and there'd be one goods train after another standing there, each one of them stuffed with all kinds of belongings. You rarely saw a passenger train, just freight trains one after another. Maybe it's like that after every war, that everything goes back to its place, even though the war alters places too, swaps them around, while some places there's no point looking for even, they don't exist anymore.

One time a truck arrived and brought a harp, a harpsichord and a viola da gamba. We didn't know what they were and we asked him, but he started crying. The harp was missing half its strings, the harpsichord only had a few keys left, and the viola da gamba looked like someone had used it for target practice. From that moment on we took a liking to him. Him alone of all the teachers. Even though like I said, usually he was tipsy or straight up drunk.

He always carried a kind of flat bottle. Here in his breast pocket. It never bothered him that he was the teacher, he'd pull it out and take a swig in front of us.

"Sorry boys, I just have to."

All the teachers behaved like they were military, and they treated us like recruits. Aside from him they all wore uniforms without stars but with epaulettes and crossed military straps. Word had it they even carried pistols in their pockets. The students also had uniforms that were a sort of black or dark blue color, and they wore hobnailed boots, side caps, and on the side caps metal insignia with a kind of rising sun in a semicircle of rays. Which, as was explained to us in homeroom, was meant to symbolize a better new world that was rising. And that that new world was ahead of us. We just had to learn to have faith, unbreakable faith. And it was for learning faith that we were here in school.

Aside from that, we learned trades. Bricklayer, plasterer, joiner, roofer, metalworker, millworker, welder, mechanic, electrician, a few others. Everyone could choose what trade they wanted to learn. Though not entirely. In the end it came down to how many places the school had for one trade or another.

We lived in barracks, and we were divided into teams. Each team had a team leader, the oldest and strongest boy, and above him every team had its own homeroom teacher.

To begin with I learned the trumpet a bit and for a year I played reveille in the morning. After reveille we'd get washed and have breakfast – black ersatz coffee, bread and jam. Then it was assembly on the parade ground, standing in line two deep, roll call, orders. Usually a couple of kids getting reported for some wrongdoing. Then off to class, each team to a different room, or to shop. And twice a week we'd be marched off to do physical labor, carrying shovels and pickaxes, singing.

What labor did we do? There was no lack of work to be done. Especially because for several months the front had been situated in the area where the school was. We filled in bunkers and trenches and bomb craters, some of them you can't imagine how huge. You've seen that kind of thing? There you go. We patched roads, at least roughly, so cars could drive there. Or we broke rocks to build more roads. We demolished ruined buildings that were in danger of collapsing. Or bridges over rivers if they were beyond being repaired. We fixed embankments that had been crushed by tanks or dug up to allow trucks and artillery through. The way it always is after a war. Come rain or shine, because as they told us, we needed to be toughened up. In winter too, it goes without saying. We cleared snow from the roads and the railroad tracks.

As far as lessons were concerned, some of the boys had attended underground school during the war. Some had even completed seventh grade. But most couldn't either read or write. Some, even if they'd been able to once, they'd forgotten because of the war. War can make you forget lots of things, not just reading and writing. You can forget yourself. And that's what had happened to them. They didn't know where they were from, what they were called, where they were born, when. They were all just this postwar hodgepodge, like I said, with no homes, no fathers, mothers, and a good few with unclean consciences. Plus we were all different ages, older, younger, including some really young children. Though truth be told, no one was a child anymore. You couldn't be a child however much you longed for your childhood.

So we weren't entirely a school, we were part school, part youthful army. We were held accountable the way you are in the army, and for the slightest offense we'd have to run to some tree way the hell off somewhere, often carrying weights. Or wade into water up to our neck, in full uniform and boots. Or do x number of pushups. Or if it was something worse, lockup with nothing but bread and water. You'd have to report to the teachers, and you didn't say please sir to them like in school, instead you addressed them as citizen teacher, and the commandant was citizen commandant. So we didn't exactly feel like school students. Not many people even wanted to be promoted from one class to another. Though getting promoted didn't make much difference. The people in charge reduced us all to the same level, they probably thought the war had set all of us back to the beginning, so they taught us from the beginning.

Maybe they were right to, because if you'd visited one of our lessons and heard us stammering out answers, or seen the scrawl in our notebooks, I don't know if you could have told who'd had how many years of schooling versus who was just starting. For instance, for several lessons we practiced writing our signatures, because we even made mistakes writing our own names. Besides, reading and writing wasn't the most important thing there.

For a trade, I picked welding. I don't know where I got the idea. I'd never seen anyone welding. I'd only seen iron being forged in a smithy. And once I heard the blacksmith say to someone that he couldn't help with a particular repair, that it would need to be welded. But after a year it turned out there weren't enough welding torches to go around. Plus, the ones they did have kept breaking down. Not to mention that you'd often have to wait forever for a delivery of oxygen cylinders.

So they put me in with the electricians. The school could train any number of electricians, since the electrification of the villages was beginning. Just like when I picked welding I had no idea how welding was done, I also had no idea what electricity was. How could I have? The only light I knew was the sun and oil lamps. Though Uncle Jan had told us that in some cities they even lit the street lamps with electricity. And that in the houses, it was everywhere. When we asked what electricity was, he said it shines much brighter than an oil lamp.

You don't need to add oil, or clean the glass, or trim the wick. There's a switch on the wall, you turn it and the light comes on.

Why did they put me with the electricians and not the bricklayers or the joiners, for instance? Well, when I picked welding I had to pass a test that involved climbing a pole. Because welders often have to work high up. They needed to check whether I could handle heights, or if I'd get dizzy. There was a pole on the playground, with the bark stripped off, it was all slippery from those tests. I shinned up it all the way to the top. I might have gone even higher, but they started shouting from below:

"Come down! There's nothing above the pole! You're done! Come down!"

Because what was a pole like that for me? I used to climb every tree in the woods. The highest poplars along the Rutka. And let me tell you, poplars are the hardest trees to climb. Especially if it's a tall thin one. I'd pull myself up with my arms alone, brace my bare feet against the trunk, without any belt. And since electrician training depended on passing that test, as electricians even more than welders work high up, they decided I could just as well be an electrician as a welder.

Electrician or welder, it was all the same to me. The only thing keeping me in that school was the chance of learning the saxophone. Otherwise I would have run away like others did. Sometimes they'd catch them and make them come back to school, other times they vanished without a trace. Me, they wouldn't have caught me, I knew where I'd need to go.

Almost every evening I went down to the rec room and practiced. We'd come back for example from a whole day filling in trenches, we'd be fit to drop, our eyelids drooping with sleep, sometimes the other boys would collapse on their beds even without washing or eating, but I'd go to the rec room and practice. My hands would be numb from using the shovel, my lips were cracked from thirst, but I had to practice at least a bit. Once in a while the music teacher would come by. He'd sit and listen, taking swigs from that bottle of his. From time to time he'd correct something I was doing, make a suggestion, or offer an excuse, say that if only he weren't drunk. And since the more swigs he took the drunker he got, he'd end up just mumbling after every sip:

"You're a stubborn one, that you are. But music likes the stubborn ones. It may even repay you for it one day. But don't give up. Never give up. It doesn't always repay people, but maybe with you it will. Maybe you'll know that happiness. Sometimes it sucks you in to the point that you lose yourself, you lose the will to live. But maybe you'll be lucky. Don't give up. And it'd be good if one of these days you found a better teacher. One who's not a drunk. A real teacher. Forgive me, son, I just have to. I hope it never happens to you."

He'd sometimes even fall asleep with the bottle in his hand. I'd take it from him and slip it back in the pocket where he always kept it. He'd wake, smile, then go back to sleep. I'd tell him to wake up and go to his room. He lived in the teacher's block. I'd shake him. Or tell him the commandant was coming, so as to scare him into getting up. But he was only afraid of the commandant when he was sober. When he was drunk, even if I managed to wake him by mentioning the commandant, he'd only spit out some cuss word, mumbling as if I'd made him mad. You know where that peasant can put it, son. Sorry.

And he'd go back to sleep. What worked better was the trumpet, or best of all the flute. The flute seemed to reach deepest into his drunkenness. So if the trumpet didn't do the job I'd put it down, pick up the flute and play it right by his ear. Not too loud, of course. After a moment he'd put his pinky finger in his ear and wiggle it, something evidently itched. Then, though his eyes were still closed, a smile would appear on his lips, when it was the flute that is. With the trumpet he'd make a face. Then he'd open one eye and give me a warm look for a moment. Then the other eye, though that one was usually indifferent and ponderous. Sometimes he'd wag his finger at me, but in a well-meaning way.

"You are a stubborn one." Especially because his finger, trembling along with his drunken hand, wasn't exactly threatening. "Don't give up. Don't give up."

And he'd reach into his pocket for the bottle. Often there'd be nothing left in it, but still he'd tip it back and get a last drop.

"You see, son," he'd say, sighing heavily as if at the empty bottle. "You see, I've gone to the dogs. But you, don't you give up."

But in order for him to let me take him back to his room, I'd first have to sit him, drunk as he was, in front of the piano. He would say he just had to play a few bars, then we could go. But it was never just a few bars. There were times he played and played. Despite being drunk, you wouldn't have credited it. The strangest thing was that his hands sobered up completely, you had the feeling they were stroking the keys.

His hands were slim like yours, with long fingers. When I watch you shelling the beans it's like I'm watching his hands on the keyboard. Come on, you must have done this before. You're already better at it than I am. My hands are stiff. You wouldn't have gotten so good so quickly if you hadn't ever done it before. We haven't shelled that much yet, but already you're doing such a good job I can't believe it. Maybe you just forgot? When you haven't done something in years you can forget it, even shelling beans. You can forget anything. But it doesn't take much to remember again. I'd forgotten too. That's why I planted beans, so I could remember once more. Though like I said, I'm not even that fond of beans. I can take them or leave them.

Do you play the piano? No, I was just asking. I can still see those hands of his as he sat drunk at the piano. It was like he himself was intoxicated, then there were his hands living a life of their own on the keyboard, sober as can be. He may have been a great musician, who can know. The fact that he was playing in that pseudo-school of ours was another matter. How many people are there that are in the wrong place? No, he didn't just play the piano. He could play any instrument he picked up. Violin, flute, cello, French horn, anything. Of course, only if he wasn't too inebriated. For me he recommended I concentrate on the violin. He didn't like the saxophone.

"With the saxophone, the most you'll do is play in a dance band. The violin on the other hand, that can take you far, son. You were born to play the violin. I know what I'm talking about."

One time I led him back to his room when he was drunk, I had one arm around his waist holding him up, and I put my head under his arm so his whole weight was leaning on me. He was muttering something into my ear. What I caught of it was:

"The violin, the violin, son. The violin appeals to your heart. The violin appeals to your soul. You're a good kid. You'll be dearer to God with the violin."

"I don't know if God would agree to listen to me play," I said without thinking.

"Don't say that." He stopped me with the entire inertia of his drunken body. "Don't think that. If He listens to anything, it's only the violin. The violin is a divine instrument. He doesn't listen to words anymore, it's beyond Him. There are too many of them. And too many languages. Eternity wouldn't be long enough to listen to all the languages of the world. But the violin is in one language. The violin contains the sounds of all languages, all worlds, this world and the next, life and death. Words are beyond Him, however all-powerful He is."

I don't know, maybe it was helpful advice. But I chose the saxophone. Course, you might ask what help a drunk could be when he couldn't help himself. It may have been that it was against God I chose the sax, since His favorite is the violin. The fact was, God owed me. And him, whenever he'd had a skinful he'd always go on about God.

One time, in front of a full rec room he talked about how building a new world should start not from bricklaying and plastering, or welding or glazing, but from music. And if God had started from music, no new world would even be needed. Someone informed on him to the commandant. The commandant called him in, apparently there was a scene and he threatened the music teacher that if he didn't quit talking about God he'd be sent back where he came from. He was lucky he'd been drunk when he said what he said. Of course they knew he drank. But they had no way of finding another music teacher. He was the only one who'd agreed to work at the school. That was the kind of school it was. They said the instruments had been confiscated from various oppressors, parasites, tyrants, all kinds of bad guys.

I didn't understand who they were referring to. We were told this by our homeroom teacher. Now the instruments were for us, who were the future of a new and better world. Actually, I found it hard to understand anything back then. I was afraid of everything, people, things, words. Whenever I had to talk I'd get stuck on every word. Often I couldn't even get past the first one. The simplest word would hurt, and each one would feel like it wasn't mine.

When everyone in the dormitory had already fallen asleep, I'd put my head under the blanket and quiz myself in a whisper about this or that word, as if I was learning them from scratch, taming them, getting them used to being mine. Once in a while some boy in a nearby bed would wake up, tug at my blanket and ask:

"Hey, what are you talking to yourself for?"

"Hey, wake up, I think you're having a nightmare. You were talking in your sleep."

Sometimes boys in the other beds would wake, they'd wake others up, and one bed after another they'd laugh, make fun of me for talking to myself.

Why did I do it in bed, under the blanket? I couldn't say. Maybe words need warmth when they're being reborn. Because when I landed in that school I was virtually mute. I could already talk a bit, but not much, and all in a jumble. When someone asked me a question, I couldn't give them an answer even if I knew what I was supposed to say. It was only thanks to starting to play music that I gradually got my speech back, and along with it the feeling that I was alive. In any case I stopped stuttering so badly, and I held onto more and more words, and I was less and less afraid of them.

In fact, I was so insatiable that I decided to learn every instrument there was. Even percussion. There wasn't much in the way of percussion instruments. A drum, one snare, a cymbal, a triangle. But when I played them I would some-times feel something twitching inside me, as if a clock were starting to tick that till now had been stopped. In time I came to understand. In my view it's not just music but life itself that's governed by rhythm. When someone loses their sense of rhythm, they lose hope. What are tears, what is despair, if not an absence of rhythm. What is memory if not rhythm.

Though most of all I practiced on the saxophone. And let me tell you, there was something in the saxophone, even though those were only the very beginnings, that when I slung it around my neck, and put the mouthpiece between my lips, and placed my hands around the tube, just by doing that I could feel hope entering into me. Or that's not quite it, it was something deeper, like I was trying to be born all over again. Who knows, maybe there's something of that sort in all instruments. But I could only feel it with the sax. And right then, in school, I made up my mind that one day I'd buy a saxophone. I had to, come what may.

So when I graduated from the school and got a job working on the electrification of the villages, from the very first pay day I began setting money aside for that saxophone. Not a lot to begin with, because I didn't earn a lot. I wasn't a fully-fledged electrician right from the beginning. More of a gopher, as they say. I mostly worked putting up telegraph poles. One team strung the wires up on the poles, the other installed electricity in the houses. It was only later that they let me do other jobs. For example, when a house was built of stone and you had to make grooves in the stone for the wires, I would make the grooves. In the houses it was much better. You could earn a little extra for this or that odd job. Though in those days there weren't that many stone-built houses. Sometimes they'd give you something, a cup of milk and a slice of bread and cheese. Or they'd let you pick an apple or a plum or pear if they had an orchard. Because sometimes our stomachs rumbled from hunger, especially toward the end of the month.

But however hungry a month it was, I had to set something aside for the saxophone. I knew the moment I collected my wages that I'd run out before the end of the month, but I had to put something away for the saxophone. Often I was tempted to borrow a few zlotys from the saxophone. Not for food. For food I wouldn't have dared. But for instance when my shirt was in tatters, or my socks couldn't be darned anymore. Winter would be coming and I could have used some warmer clothes, long johns, a sweater, new shoes. It goes without saying that we worked in the winter too. Just not in severe frosts, we'd only work inside the houses then. But when it was only a bit below freezing we'd go on digging holes for the telegraph poles, breaking the frozen earth with pickaxes.

I kept my money in my mattress, in the straw, wrapped in newspaper. Believe me, a mattress is the best place to hide money. Especially when you changed villages and lodgings the way we did, your mattress was the best place. You slept on your mattress, squashed it with your body, who would have suspected there was money in there. When I added to it from the new month's wages, I'd often have to search the entire mattress to find it.

I really was tempted to borrow some back. I'd take it out, unwrap it, and wrestle with myself that maybe after all I could. I mean, of course I'd return it. Maybe I'd even give it back with interest for however long it was till the next pay day. One time. I swear I'll give it back. Just this once. Nothing'll happen. When all's said and done it's my money, I'm borrowing from myself. It'd be a whole other story if I was borrowing from someone else. I'd be borrowing from myself, so I wouldn't even have to explain if I just took something for a week or a month, because it certainly wouldn't be any longer. Did I really not trust myself to that extent? My own money and I didn't trust myself? Let me at least count how much I've saved. Though I already knew how much. I'd count it every month when I added more. But what was the harm in it, I'd count it, since I wasn't going to borrow anything anyway. True, counting it doesn't make it more, but it cheers you up that at least it hasn't gotten any less.

I'd count it, smooth out any wrinkled notes, sort it into piles of hundreds, five hundreds, thousands, wrap each pile with a single note. Then I'd divide it all up again, but this time not according to denominations but in equal amounts. If I thought there weren't enough piles I'd reduce the size of each amount so there'd be more. You know, there's something in money that when it sucks you in it becomes hard to spend it on anything at all. I even started to worry that later I'd be reluctant to spend the money on a saxophone.

One of the electricians fell from a pole and broke an arm and a leg, and they put me in his place. I became a full electrician even though I hadn't finished my whole training period. So I was earning more, which meant the saxophone was getting closer and closer. They began letting me do overtime and take on private jobs. I wasn't putting up poles anymore, but installing wires on the poles. And you put in the most overtime on those poles. Everything was way behind schedule and a directive came down that things should be hurried along. So there was a lot more overtime to be had. Before the pole was put up you had to fix glass or porcelain insulators on the top. Then you'd go up and string the wires, attaching them to the insulators.

Despite the overtime, there weren't that many volunteers for working on the poles. Most of the guys preferred installing electricity in people's homes. So the lines were behind, they had to catch up with the houses. We'd sometimes be working on the poles right up until dusk. It was another matter that if you weren't used to it, you couldn't stay up on one of those poles for long. Oh no, you'd have spikes on your feet, you could put your weight on them. Have you never seen electricians working up on a pole? The whole planet is covered in those poles. Here, on the lake, the electricity comes from poles. Concrete ones, but back then they were wooden. How can I explain what the spikes looked like. They're like sickles, semicircular, they fasten onto the soles of your boots. You don't know what a sickle is? Never seen one? Way back when, they'd cut the crops with sickles. What does a sickle look like? You know, like a new moon. Plus, you'd have a big belt around your lower back that went around you and the pole. Despite that, you had to have strength in your back and in your legs to go up one pole after another, day after day.

Most of the electricians were older guys, from before the war, some of them were sickly after their wartime experiences, so when they'd climbed one pole, climbed a second, on the third one their legs wouldn't obey them and their lower back would be killing them. When the weather turned colder their hands would be numb. They had gauntlets, but it wasn't the kind of work you could do in gauntlets. And though overtime paid double, they left the pole work to the younger men. They'd make up for it and more when they were installing electricity in the houses. Otherwise they wouldn't have given us the overtime so easily.

Another thing was, most all of them drank. Boy did they ever! In the lodgings, after work, not a day went by. But also at work. Sometimes they'd drink from the early morning. And if they didn't drink it was because they hadn't yet sobered up from the previous day. How could you climb a pole in that state? Whereas for me climbing a pole was nothing, like I said. I could clamber up poles the whole livelong day. I even enjoyed it. And back then I still didn't drink. I was protected from it by the saxophone, I was trying to earn as much as I could and save as much as I could.

Actually, the other guys might not have drunk so much themselves, but in almost every home people made their own moonshine. You could get hold of booze any time of the day or night. You'd just knock on someone's window and they'd hand you the bottle through the window. Not to mention that moonshine was the preferred form of payment. In general you could do anything with moonshine. No one believed in money anymore. The true currency was moonshine. And what else could you do with moonshine but drink it? So they drank.

I have to hand it to them though, despite the fact they drank, they were first-rate electricians. They could do any job, drunk or sober. All the things I learned in school were nothing compared to what I learned from them. You just had to watch closely when they were doing something. And listen real carefully, not miss a single word. Each one of them had his secrets, and sometimes one or another of them would give them away despite themselves. What secrets? You're not an electrician, what would be the point of telling you?

Well, it's not hard to guess. You didn't know what spikes are, what a sickle is. I will tell you one thing, a pro can recognize another pro from two or three words, especially one from the same line of work. I'm not denying that ignorance is also a kind of knowledge. But ignorance won't help you learn the secrets of electricians. When someone doesn't have any trade at all it's hard to understand him even as a person. In any case, when I'd sometimes watch them at work I had the impression that electricity flowed through them the way it does through wiring. There was no problem they couldn't fix. Often there was a shortage of materials, so they'd switch one part from here to there, wrap it in something, solder something or other. For them, nothing was impossible. So later on, when I started working on building sites, I could handle the most difficult installations. For instance I worked on the building of a cold storage plant where all the machinery ran on electricity. I set it all up without a hitch.

The one thing I didn't learn from them was drinking vodka. That wasn't till the building sites. Back then though I never touched a drop, the saxophone meant that much to me. At one of the lodgings I was living with a group of men and every evening they kept trying to persuade me, invite me, and they were heavy drinkers. They even started to accuse me of being a snitch. Because in their eyes, anyone who didn't drink had to be a snitch. Especially a young guy like me. They didn't trust young people. That's understandable. Young people will do anything to get ahead of their elders. Young people are in a hurry. They don't have the patience that comes with experience. They don't realize that either way we're all headed toward the same thing. Young people always think they're going to build a new and better world. All of them. New young people, old young people. And they end up leaving behind the kind of world no one wants to live in. If you ask me, the quicker you outgrow your youth the better it is for the world, really. I was young once and I know. I believed in a new and better world too. Especially since after a war like that it wasn't hard to believe in, because there wasn't anything else to believe in. And few things are easier to believe in than a new and better world.

So it's hardly surprising they'd accuse me of one thing or another, even of informing, since I didn't drink. They didn't know I was saving up for a saxophone. I kept that a total secret. I might have often had a drink with them, but I knew the expectations for when you drank. If I drank a glass I'd have to provide at least one bottle. Plus bread, pickled cucumbers, sausage. And I would regret every least penny. I excused myself by saying I had duodenal ulcers. I didn't actually know what ulcers were, I didn't know what a duodenum was. But one time I went into a compartment in a train calling out, pears, plums, apples, and someone offered some to someone else but the other person refused saying he had duodenal ulcers and he had to stick to a strict diet. As it happened, I looked like I had ulcers. Years later, when I was abroad, it turned out I in fact did.

According to those electricians of mine, however, and not just those ones but other ones I lived with in different lodgings, when I was on the building sites already, vodka was the best medicine for ulcers too. Because why did they not have ulcers? Well, why?

I may surprise you by saying this, but perhaps it wasn't such a bad thing that they drank. Because when they didn't drink they had trouble sleeping. You'd think that when they were exhausted after a long day's work, they ought to have been out like a light. But one of them couldn't get to sleep, another one would wake up all the time, a third one slept such a shallow sleep he couldn't say if he'd been asleep or not. And here it was morning already, time for work. The worst of it is that when you have problems sleeping, all kinds of different thoughts come to you and make it even harder to sleep.

In one village five of us were sharing a place together, all of them older guys, I was the only youngster, and one of the master electricians was also living with us. We called him master even when he wasn't there. Go see the master, ask the master, the master'll know what to do. I don't know if you know how people usually talk about masters behind their back. In any case, they don't call them master.

He didn't talk much, he never let himself get drawn into conversation even over vodka. He liked vodka, why wouldn't he? But getting him to talk was like drawing water from the deepest well. And they were never words that meant anything to you. Maybe to him, but not to others. Yes, no, who knows, maybe, we'll have to think about it. Nothing was definite.

One evening it so happened that they didn't drink. We'd come home late from work. One of them asked, Has anyone got anything? No one did, and no one felt like going to get some. All right then, let's just go to bed. We got into our beds and turned out the light, it went quiet, I began to fall asleep. All at once one of them let out a deep sigh, another one turned on his other side with the whole weight of his body. And then everyone started switching from side to side, straightening the bedding, twisting and turning. The beds were old ones, they creaked with the slightest movement.

The master's bed was by the window. After the light was turned out he would always smoke a last cigarette. He'd also smoke when he woke up in the middle of the night. At those times he'd have to smoke two or three before he could get back to sleep. It was only vodka that put him to sleep right away. Though that also depended on how much he'd had to drink. If it was quite a bit, then right away. If it wasn't much, it was a lot harder for him. At those times he'd smoke and smoke. There was a geranium on the windowsill by his bed and he'd tap the ash into the flowerpot and put his cigarette out in it. He'd always fish the butts out in the morning, and from the number of butts you could tell how he'd slept. And not only that.

It wasn't only a measure of his insomnia. But what did we know, we were just electricians. For us cigarette butts were just cigarette butts. On top of that, you could always smell the smoke in the morning, so we'd sniff and say, boy, the master sure smoked up a storm. So that night he lit up just the same, and one of the guys asked:

"Are you not asleep, master? For some reason I can't get to sleep myself."

Right away, from all the other beds people said they couldn't either.

"That's how it is when you don't have a drink before you go to bed," someone said, and someone else cursed. One of them recollected that somewhere or other the moonshine was stronger than some other place.

And a conversation started up. The master lit up again. He ashed the cigarette in the geranium and the geranium glowed for a second. When he took a drag, his face glowed too. You could see he was lying there with eyes open. But he didn't seem to be listening to what the other men were talking about, because he didn't say a word. Me, I was the youngest so I had no right to speak, I just listened. Besides, what could I have said when for instance they were discussing what each of them would do if he found out his wife was cheating on him. They were all married, whereas I wasn't even thinking about that. Though we didn't know if the master was married. He never spoke about it. But obviously, start thinking about your wife cheating on you and you won't sleep a wink all night. Then the next morning you'll be all fingers and thumbs. But each one of them knew what he'd do. One of them would kill her, another would kick her out of the house, a third one would do some other thing.

Then they started wondering if old guys can still do it, and when a man starts being old as far as that's concerned. You know what I mean. And if he can't, then what keeps him alive? And is it even worth living then? One of them said that God directs life, that people have no right to ask whether it's worth it. So they got on to God. Whether after a war like the last one people should keep believing in God or not. One of them said they should, because it wasn't God that started the war, it was people. Someone else said, fair enough, though if He'd wanted to He could have held people back. Someone else again put in: They say that people pull the trigger, God brings the bullets, so He could have arranged the war so there'd be less misery, less suffering, less death. And they started telling stories of different things they'd seen or heard about. One of them whose brother had been executed by firing squad got so upset that he asked right out whether God even exists. He asked each bed in turn what we thought. Does He? I pretended to be asleep. Eventually he got to the master.

"What do you think, master, does God exist?"

The master had just put out a cigarette in the geranium pot, and he lit another. It was about the fourth since we'd put the light out. The whole time he'd not opened his mouth, it was like he wasn't even listening. We waited intently to see what he'd say, as if it depended on him whether God existed. The one who'd asked him repeated his question.

"What do you say, master? Does He exist or not?"

"Who?" he finally said.

"God."

He didn't answer right away, first he crushed his cigarette out.

"Why are you asking me? Why are you asking them? You don't need to take a vote. You should ask yourself. Me, all I can tell you is that where I was, He wasn't there."

He lit up yet again. Everyone went quiet, no one dared ask any more questions. No one said anything at all to anyone else. A moment later they started falling asleep. Here you could hear a whistling sound, over there someone breathing more loudly. I was wondering if the master was asleep, because no sound came from his bed. But he also hadn't lit another cigarette.

As for me, I couldn't get to sleep. My head was spinning with thoughts from the conversation, because for me all the things they'd been talking about were kind of beyond the bounds of my imagination. And the thing that troubled me the most was where the master could have been, that God wasn't there.

The next day I went to him for advice because the fuses kept blowing when I'd turn on this three-way switch. And I asked him:

"Where were you?"

He gave me a suspicious look.

"I hope you never have to go there." After which he grunted: "Get back to work. You know what you need to do."

As far as the saxophone was concerned, I was managing to put more and more aside every month. I never missed the chance for overtime. In addition, in the evenings or on Sundays there was work on the side. I wouldn't take moonshine in payment, only money. I preferred getting paid less but that it be in cash. I could wait, but let it be cash. In pretty much every village there was always someone wanted us to put in a second switch, a second outlet, and for each switch or outlet you'd have to do the wiring. According to the regulations, which is to say, at the lower cost, they were only allowed one switch and one outlet per room. And hallways, pantries, attics weren't allowed, or anywhere else. The attics you could understand, in most of the houses the attic was under a thatched roof, if there'd been a short circuit the house would have gone up like kindling. But for example, why should you have to walk down the hallway in darkness, groping for the door handle? Or take an oil lamp to the pantry, when there's electricity in the house?

So we'd install things wherever people wanted them. Privately, it goes without saying. If someone wanted it in the hallway, in their pantry, over the front door, say the word and it'll be done. For so and so much. Someone wanted to have an extension out to their cattle shed, why not, that could be done. It was rare, but some people asked for that. In one village someone even wanted us to put in an extension to his barn, because he'd bought an electric motor on the cheap, and he wanted to convert his thresher and winnowing machine to electricity instead of keeping on using the treadmill. We did it. He just had to wait a bit till we were able to siphon off some of the materials from the official allocations. But we also did installations in attics under the thatch if people wanted. You'd wrap the cable in an additional layer of insulating tape, feed it through an insulated tube that was made of metal, but properly lined, and attach it on elevated brackets at the necessary distance from the thatch, along a beam, while the switch would be put in on the chimney flue. And nothing untoward would happen. With private work there were no restrictions. As you know, things that were not possible officially were possible unofficially.

Not everyone was in favor of electricity, though, far from it. Some folks wouldn't even give permission for a pole to be put up outside their house. What, I'm supposed to stare at a pole for the rest of my life? The hell with that! It's my land up to the middle of the road. There were times they came after us with pickaxes, we had to call the police. They wouldn't let us into their homes, they'd drive us off like thieves. Especially because with the houses, they weren't being forced. If someone didn't want electricity, that was their business. How did they explain it? In different ways. That there'd be another war soon, just you wait. And in wartime oil lamps are your best bet. If you run out of kerosene you can burn linseed oil. You just had to plant flax. Of all the different kinds of light, the most reliable were the sun, as long as God was willing, and oil lamps. It doesn't need to be as bright in the night as during the day. It's enough if it's light during the day, nighttime is for sleeping. Were we trying to turn the world upside down? With all these poles and wires? What if the sparrows and the swallows sit on them? They'll get burned to cinders. It'll draw lightning. Sickness too, maybe. The sicknesses we already have are more than enough. You wouldn't earn anything extra from those kinds of people, of course. But in general you didn't do too badly with the private jobs. For millers, for example, before the government took over the mills. In the presbyteries and churches. Though with the priests you could never be sure. They'd always get away with a God bless you.

So one time when I counted up again how much I'd put aside for the saxophone, it seemed like it might actually be enough. I had no idea of the price of a saxophone. I started asking around among the musicians in the villages. They could tell me the price of a harmonica or fiddle or clarinet, but most of them had never even heard of a saxophone. Well, I took one day off and headed for the nearest town. There was a music shop, but they didn't have any saxophones, nor did they know how much one might cost, especially now after the war. So some time later I took myself to another town, a bigger one. They didn't have one either, but they promised to find out how much one might be, they might even try to order one if they could. They'd also ask around privately, maybe someone would have one, because from time to time people brought them instruments to sell. I gave them my name. I wanted to leave a down payment but they wouldn't take it. They said to try back in a month or two. If one came in they'd set it aside.

You have no idea how much each night before I fell asleep I'd imagine hanging that saxophone around my neck, putting the mouthpiece between my lips, running my fingers over the keys. I even decided that when I finally got it, I'd throw a drinking party to celebrate and get drunk myself.

All of a sudden, out of the blue one day, someone heard on the corn cob that there was going to be a change of currency. What's the corn cob? Not the airplane, they also gave that name to the radio speakers that were put in people's homes, only if they wanted of course, where they already had electricity. And the new currency, you know what that was about? Not just that there were going to be different banknotes. It was that with the new ones you could buy three times less. You never heard of a change like that? Where were you then? Though never mind that. In any case, a saxophone was out of the question now. To be honest, I didn't even feel angry. I didn't feel anything at all. The only thing I felt was that I had no reason to go on living. So I decided to hang myself.

That day we were working on a transformer pole. Transformer poles look like giant As. They're made of two poles that come together at the top, while lower down they're reinforced by a linking horizontal crossbeam. I was going to use that beam. The previous day I borrowed a halter from one of the farmers. Towards evening, when I was through with work I put my tools away in the toolbag and dropped it to the ground. I tied one end of the halter to the cross-beam and made a noose in the other end. I put the noose around my neck and I was about to pull my spiked boots clear of the pole when I glanced down at the ground and I saw Uncle Jan. He was standing with his head tipped back, watching what I was doing. No, it wasn't an illusion. I saw him plain as I see you now.

"Don't do it," he said. "I hanged myself, and I don't see any difference."

5

No, I stopped saving up for a saxophone. Besides, pretty soon I starting working on a building site, and when I got my first wages I bought myself a hat. Why a hat? I don't know. Maybe I had to buy something so I wouldn't be tempted to save up for a saxophone again. And maybe it was a hat because when I was still in school I'd made up my mind to buy a hat once I had a saxophone. Saxophone and hat, I used to like to see myself that way when I imagined myself.

They once brought this film to show at the school. There's a big hat shop, a man and a woman come in, his name is Johnny and she's Mary, and the guy wants to buy a hat. He starts trying them on, while Mary sits down in an armchair and buries herself in a magazine. It was the first film I'd ever seen in my life. So when he was trying on all those hats I had the impression that he wasn't trying them on on the screen, but that he was with us in the rec room. Or that we were all in the shop where he was trying on hats.

He tried hat after hat, while Mary, who by the way was a stunner, was sitting in the armchair like I said, her nose in the magazine. She was wearing furs, her legs were crossed, she wore a chic pair of pumps.

I don't know if you'll agree with me on this, but a woman's legs make or break the whole. And as long as she's wearing nice shoes, everything else can even be very plain. Her face can be plain if the legs are OK. But she has to be wearing nice shoes. You rarely see legs like that anymore. Most all women go around in pants, and even if they're in a dress they often wear the kind of shoes that remind you of wartime. Plus, these days hardly any of them can walk the way a woman ought to walk. Have you seen how women walk today? Take a look some time. They jerk their legs, stomp their feet. They're more like soldiers than women. Even here, they're in bathing suits and barefoot but most of them still walk around that way. And not on concrete but on earth, on grass. A movie director abroad once told me he couldn't find an actress to play the part of a princess in a movie. The faces were right but not the walk.

So anyway, Mary was so engrossed in her magazine that she wasn't paying any attention whatsoever to the man. And he kept trying on hats. In each one he would stand longer and longer in front of the mirror, and seemed less and less sure whether he should say, this one might work, or take it off and ask for another one, or study himself in the mirror a bit longer. He'd tried quite a few already, but he evidently didn't like himself in any of them because he kept asking to see something else. And the clerk, he didn't bat an eyelid and just kept bringing one new hat after another. Also, each time he brought a new hat he'd smile and give a half-bow. And even though the man could see himself full length in the mirror, the clerk still went around him with a hand mirror, holding it up to one side then the other, now in front of his face, now from behind so he could see how he looked in the reflection of the hand mirror in the big mirror in front of him. Each time, he'd sing the praises of each hat equally while the man was trying it on:

"Take a look now, sir. And now. Tip it forward a little over the forehead. Tip it back a little. A little to the side, a little this way, a little that way. Perfect, just perfect. It goes ideally with your face, sir. With your forehead, your eyes, eyebrows, and so on. Perfect."

In retrospect I'm sure it must have been a comedy. But at the time it didn't make me laugh in the slightest. Every hat that Johnny took off and handed back to the clerk was a personal loss for me. Evidently laughter doesn't depend on what you see and hear. Laughter is people's ability to protect themselves from the world, from themselves. To deprive them of that ability is to make them defenseless. And that's how I was. I simply didn't know how to laugh. It even seemed strange to me that anyone could ever laugh at anything. Most of us who'd found ourselves in that school were the same. Though not all of us, it goes without saying. Some of them were able to laugh even when they were in lockup.

So at the film, some boys were laughing their heads off. But it wasn't just laughing. Behind the laughter you could sense a growing rage, a resentment. With every hat the man tried on, amid the laughter there were oaths, insults directed at him, at the clerk, and above all at Mary, for losing herself in her magazine and not helping the man. She was just sitting there like me or you. If she'd at least have raised her eyes, said he looked good or didn't, that that one was worse, the other one was better. Then she could have gone back to her reading.

The rec room was packed, you can imagine what was going on. The moment the guy didn't like himself in one of the hats there were shouts, whistles, stamping of feet. It was getting louder and louder, more and more bitter, especially because it made no impression on him at all. He even hesitated a tad longer before saying no to this one after all, for some reason or other. The clerk continued to bend in a half-bow, with the same smile on his face, agreeing with the man.

"You're absolutely right, sir. It really is a little too dark. Really is a little too light. The shade isn't quite right. The style isn't quite right. The brim's a little too wide. With your face, this hat isn't quite right. Never mind. Let's see what else there is."

By this point the room was in uproar. To be honest I was even starting to be a bit afraid. Meanwhile the clerk was going off and bringing a new hat, with the same hope that for sure the man would like this one.

The whole countertop was piled high with the hats he'd tried on, since the clerk set all the hats there in a heap so the man wouldn't have to wait too long.

If I hadn't seen it with my own eyes I'd never have been able to imagine so many hats in one place. And all for the head of some guy named Johnny. If he'd at least have been someone. But he was no one in particular. He was just like you or me. I mean I'm sorry, I'm not trying to insult you, but the clerk wouldn't have known who you are if you'd gone in and said you wanted to buy a hat. All the more if it had been me. Though you he might have recognized. Hat shop clerks are smart people. I knew a guy like that.

In any case, in all that crowded rec room no one knew who Johnny was. We hadn't an inkling. Unless the clerk knew. Or it came out at the end of the film. After he tried on the umpteenth hat it occurred to me that a hat isn't such an ordinary thing, though it's just a covering for your head. The film went on and on, and this guy was choosing and choosing, it couldn't have been an ordinary thing.

One time they brought this fellow to the school who pulled a rabbit out of a hat. At some point the rabbit ran away and started scurrying all around the rec room, we all chased after it. That time too the room was filled to bursting, we had a heck of a job catching it. It was white as can be, an angora, it was trembling all over it was so afraid, even though it knew how to vanish then appear again, one moment it was in the hat, the next it was gone. Or maybe it was the hat that had this power, such a notion came to me even then.

In the end, the rec room kind of began to take over the job of Mary, who was indifferent to the whole business, and when the man tried on a new hat everyone would jump to their feet and try to persuade him to buy that one, the one he was trying on right now. Then, when he finally decided against that one and asked to see another, they'd yell at the clerk and tell him not to bring the guy any more hats, let him buy that one. That one or none at all.

But the clerk wanted the man to buy at least something, and bowing the whole time, with the same smile he'd bring him another hat. At that moment, as if in retaliation for the disappointment he'd caused the room, the choicest obscenities were heaped on both of them. I'd be embarrassed to repeat them.

It was like they were throwing stones at both of them. You such-and-such, buy the thing or . . . ! And a lot worse. You this and that, stop bringing him hats! He should buy the one he's got on right now! Kick his ass out of the store! You know what he can do with that mirror! Son of a . . . ! It was like they got themselves all riled up with cursing, because when the man asked to see another hat, their shouts would get even wilder.

The rec room was low, like you'd expect in a hut. The whole place was shaking, walls, windows, ceiling, it felt like it was about to fall apart. The screen hung down from the ceiling and covered about three fourths of the wall, while the projector stood against the opposite wall behind us. The older boys, along with some of the teachers, were sitting on benches along the side walls, while the rest of us were on the floor. The stream of light from the projector passed right over our heads. For some kids the shouting and whistling and curses weren't enough, they had to also jump up from the floor into the beam of light, waving their arms as if they were trying to knock the hat off the man's head as he was trying it on, and knock the next one out of the clerk's hands when he brought it.

I don't know if you can imagine all this. It was a storm, a tempest, not laughter. The teachers were shouting, Calm down! calm down! It made no impression. Actually, they may already have been afraid. Especially because the older boys sitting among them on the benches had also gotten to their feet, they were standing in the beam of light right by the screen blocking the clerk's way back to the man.

"Where do you think you're going?!"

But the clerk would pass right through them like he was walking through mist, give the man the new hat and take back the one that once again he'd decided against. In the end they turned on Mary. You so-and-so, put the magazine down! Tell him to buy the one he's trying on! Stop crossing your legs! Move it! Kick him on the backside, on the shin, in the balls! I won't repeat any more of it. At one point it looked like they were going to invade the screen, trash the shop, beat up the clerk and the man, and maybe rip Mary's furs off, tear off her dress and take her by force. Especially because there were people who'd been sent to the school for doing exactly that.

The teachers were still trying to calm everyone down. We'll stop the film! You're criminals, not children, the lot of you! You'll all get written up tomorrow! You'll pay for this! That just set everyone going even more. It was only thanks to the clerk that it didn't end badly. He was the only one who kept his cool and with the same bow, the same smile kept handing the man one hat after another. But the man, whichever one he put on, he would look in the mirror without a trace of goodwill towards himself. Sometimes it was like he was overcome by doubt about one hat or another. Sometimes he'd study himself more closely in the mirror, as if he himself no longer believed it was him standing at the mirror in a hat. And a several moments it looked like he was finally about to say resignedly, maybe this one.

And who knows why, because in the opinion of the rec room he didn't look good in that particular one, a view that was expressed in a swelling wave of whistles and shouts and stamping. He looks like a scarecrow! Like a beggar! He looks like . . . ! All this slowly turned into a resounding, No! No! No! But the man wasn't put off, you even got the feeling he was taunting the room by taking his time choosing a hat. And that he'd buy this one to spite the room, though he didn't like himself in it that much. He smiled at his own reflection in the mirror, he made different kinds of smiles, from having his lips barely parted to a big grin with a row of perfect white teeth like you only ever see in the movies. I mean, everyone knows what people's teeth are mostly like. Most people should never smile, never speak even. He pushed the hat back from his forehead, then pulled it forward, assuming a mysterious expression. He tipped the hat to the left, then to the right, like he wanted to look like someone he'd seen in a movie. Or he went right close up to the mirror, almost touching it with the brim of the hat, and looked at himself eye to eye, hat to hat. Or he suddenly stepped back and studied himself full length, from the hat all the way down to his feet. He put a hand in his pants pocket, one then the other in turn, or both at once, assuming a relaxed posture. Or he straightened his necktie, smoothed his jacket, and stood stiff as a ramrod. One time he seemed visibly disheartened when he looked at his reflection, another time like he'd be prepared to come to terms with this hat and with himself, but he lacked the willpower. At that point he would turn helplessly to Mary where she sat absorbed in her magazine:

"What do you think, Mary? Take a look. Do you like me in this one? It's not at all bad." But Mary, even if she raised her eyes, she would just lower them again without a word. And the man would regretfully shake his head. "No, not this one after all."

At these moments all of us in the rec room shared his sense of regret. You could tell from the creaking of the floorboards and benches, because everyone straightened themselves at the same time. No one whistled or swore or laughed. But it wasn't ordinary regret. He ought to strangle that bitch, you could hear someone whisper in a bitter voice. I'm sorry, those were everyday expressions at the school, other words couldn't have conveyed one feeling or another. Just as no words could comprehend why Mary was so uninterested in it all. Was it so hard to say yes, no, especially since it was only a hat?

At times Mary lifted her eyes from her magazine, other times not. And even when she did, it was with an increasing sense of boredom. And she made the room increasingly irate. We were all convinced it was her fault that he couldn't pick out a hat. Though if you thought about it, what had she done, she was was just sitting quietly reading a magazine. But it was enough for the man to turn to her and say, Take a look, Mary, what do you think, Mary, what about this one, Mary? It was like the room caught a fever. They were starting to express not just their rage, but rage mixed with helplessness, pain, despair even. Against Mary, that's right. But for what? You tell me. It was the man who was trying on hats and not liking himself in any of them, how was Mary to blame?

He could have realized that in all that trying on of hats he wouldn't like any of them. And he didn't. Maybe he wasn't trying on hats anymore so much as battling with them. But what can a person battle a hat about? About himself, you say? Still, the hat's always going to come out the winner. It made no difference whether he took it off his head right away or no, if he kept it on longer, even if he posed in it in front of the mirror. It came out the same. He could have tried on hats through the entire film, he could have tried on hats till kingdom come, it would have made no difference. Trying things on that way only ever ends along with the end of everything.

True, those hats just kept coming and coming. It wasn't just any old shop. Wherever you looked there were hats. The clerk even kept bringing more and more from the back, always with a new rush of hope that this one or that one would be to sir's liking. So there were plenty of hats to go before the clerk would lose hope too.

Though maybe the man would have lost hope first. The more so because there were already signs of discouragement on his face, in his gestures, as he gazed at himself in each new hat in the mirror. He would put the hat on and take it off as if casually. He stopped saying thank you or apologizing. He took each new hat from the clerk and gave him back the one he'd just taken off. He seemed to be doing nothing but moving the hats from the clerk's hands to his head then back from his head into the clerk's hands, barely even glancing in the mirror. He ought to have stopped trying them on, but he was evidently incapable even of that. Or maybe he'd started to feel sorry for the clerk, who had been fetching all those hats in vain. That's why he kept trying more and more on.

All at once, with one of the hats that wasn't particularly either good or bad, when we were already certain he'd take it off and say, not this one, he hesitated. His hands fell to his sides, he went up to the mirror and stood motionless facing his reflection. His face was still too but it conveyed distress, should I take it off, leave it on, take it off, leave it on, take it off, leave it on. The rec room froze. There was a silence so profound it was like everyone's hearts had stopped beating. As he stood there you could feel the fever rising and rising. Till at one moment it crossed the bounds of expectation and it made no difference whether he took it off or not, since he'd reached the point where it was no longer right either to take the hat off or leave it on. The only path open to him was to take out a gun and shoot himself through the hat. True, the clerk was already waiting with a new hat, inclining in a half-bow, the same smile on his face, which would suggest that he refused to envisage such a turn of events. But all of us in the rec room demanded exactly that, that he take out a pistol and shoot himself through the hat. Then his final words would be spoken as if to spite Mary:

"Mary, pay the man for the hat."

He may well have been about to put a gun to the hat when suddenly Mary twittered in an animated voice:

"Listen Johnny, it says here that this season brown felt hats are in for men. Try a brown felt one!"

"I already did."

"But it says here!"

You might have thought that a shot would ring out at this moment. I thought the same when I tried to imagine how the film might have ended. It would only have been right. You can't keep trying things on endlessly, even hats. Have you seen that film? Too bad. You could have told me whether he buys a hat or shoots a gun. I never got to see what happened, there was a power outage and the movie stopped. There often used to be outages. Especially in the evenings. And it rarely happened that the power got turned back on again soon. At the earliest after an hour or two. Most of the time, though, when the electricity went off in the evening it didn't come back till morning.

Oftentimes we'd return from work, barely able to walk, and on top of everything they'd have made us sing on the way, then when we got back there'd be no light. We'd have been breaking rocks for road-building, in the dust and swelter, everyone would be sweaty and thirsty, our hair sticking to our heads, and here there was no light. You couldn't wash, eat, undress. On top of which, by morning your uniform had to be cleaned, your boots polished, because the next day we had class, and in class you had to look like a student. We didn't have a change of uniform or boots. They'd only give us new ones when the old uniform or boots couldn't be darned or mended anymore. And evening was the only time you had to wash something, sew it, patch it. And here the lights were out.

One time the music teacher gave us a big funerary candle he'd bought for himself. Another time, before Christmas the boys stole a packet of Christmas tree candles from somewhere or other. But we used them all up even before Christmas, because the power went off almost every day. So our little Christmas tree had no candles. Yes, they let us have one. It stood in the rec room. They got it from the woods, it was decorated with something or other, we made our own ornaments and chains and streamers. But without candles it wasn't a proper Christmas tree.

You like having a Christmas tree? I used to too. But it had to have real candles burning. It didn't need to have much in the way of decorations, but it had to have lighted candles. It was always us kids that lit them, according to age, except backwards, first me as the youngest, then Leonka, then Jagoda. I couldn't reach the highest ones so father would lift me up. They were real, of course, they burned with a living flame. They had to be real so the tree would be real too. I was an electrician, but I don't like electric candles, that's the truth. These days everyone has electric ones, but in my book those aren't real candles. Their light has no life in it.

Wigilia – Christmas Eve dinner – always began with lighting the candles on the Christmas tree. Then mother would put a white tablecloth on the table and bring in the different dishes. There were always twelve of them. First we'd share the Christmas wafer, then we'd all sit at the table. Everyone had their own place at Wigilia. And everyone ate carefully so as for goodness' sake not to spill anything on the tablecloth. Even Granddad only took small spoonfuls so the soup wouldn't dribble. And he would eat like he never used to, without slurping or smacking his lips. Grandmother even complimented him, couldn't you eat like that every day?

It wasn't just an ordinary tablecloth. Mother only ever used it for Wigilia. She'd woven it and embroidered it herself, intending it all along to be only for

Wigilia. Everyone knew how much work had gone into that tablecloth. She'd even sown the flax for the linen herself, in the best soil. She sowed it sparsely so the sun would reach each stalk. Then she went out every day to see how it was doing. Whenever a weed would poke its head out of the ground, right away she'd pull it out. So when the flax grew, it was a handsome crop, let me tell you. She cut it herself with a sickle. Exactly, you didn't know what a sickle is. She used a sickle so as not to break the stalks. It dried for a long time in the sun, then later for a bit longer still in the barn. Then it was bound in sheaves, fastened with pegs down in the Rutka where the current ran fastest, and soaked there. Then it was dried again. Then she broke it up in the brake. I won't go into what a brake is. In other places they call it a flax mill. She threw out any fibers that were too thick or too short. You can't imagine how much sorting and combing there was. Till all that was left was a kind of gossamer. So every Wigilia, Grandmother would tell us the tablecloth was woven from gossamer.

Once the fabric had been woven, she washed it and dried it several times over. When the sun shone she'd spread it out on the grass to make it even whiter. Though it was hard to imagine it could get any whiter than it was. All summer long almost, day after day, if only the sun came out she'd spread the tablecloth in the sunlight. It wasn't till winter that she set about embroidering it. It was supposed to be ready for Wigilia that year, but she kept embroidering it more and more, and it wasn't till Wigilia of the following year that it was finished. As she worked on it she taught both Jagoda and Leonka to embroider. She embroidered a whole Garden of Eden. It was fancier than you see in some pictures. Grandfather, once he'd taken the edge off of his appetite, he liked to move his finger over mother's embroidery.

"That's where we'll be," he would say. "See, that's where we'll be."

What did we eat at Wigilia? First a little cheese with mint, to represent the shepherds. Then Żurek sour rye soup with wild mushrooms and buckwheat kasha. Pierogies with cabbage and mushrooms. Potatoes boiled in their skins, and salted. Whey soup to wash it down. Pierogies with dried plums, sprinkled with nuts and slathered with fried sour cream. Noodles with poppy seed. Boiled or fried fish. You have no idea how many fish there were in the Rutka back then. These days, in the lake you won't find half of what there used to be. I see it, people come here to fish and they sit for hours and hours by their poles. Sometimes I go watch, and it's rare that any of them gets a bite. Back in the day you could catch something just by dipping a basket in the river. You'd put it in near the bank, tap a stick against where it had holes, and every time something would end up inside it. Before Wigilia, when the Rutka froze over, you'd cut a hole in the ice, drop a net through it, and wait till a fish came along. Anyway, after that there'd be cabbage and peas, or cabbage on its own, fried in linseed oil. If it was cabbage on its own, then separately there'd be green beans in honey and vinegar. If it was cabbage with peas, there wouldn't be any green beans, just broad beans, that you had to take the skin off of. Then cranberry jelly. And finally compote from dried fruit.

We'd eat till we were fit to burst, even though it was always just a little of each dish. After that we'd go to midnight mass. Us children, we were usually sleepy by then, since the mass started so late. But we still had to go. It was only then that we'd put out the candles on the tree. To be honest, it wasn't the dishes, it was the candles that kind of proved it was Wigilia. When they were lit like that, I was prepared to believe anything. I believed in mother's tablecloth and in what grandfather said about how that was where we would be going, as he passed his finger across the embroidery. Sometimes I even had the feeling we were already there.

Maybe that's why for the whole of my life I've always liked to see candles burning. Whenever I was at some party abroad, if there were candles burning as well as ceiling lamps and wall lamps, I'd always remember that particular party. Whenever I invited anyone to my place, I'd always have to have candles. When the guests left, if the candles were still burning I'd not put them out. I'd sit there till they burned out by themselves. You might not believe me, but it hurts me to put out a candle. I have the feeling I'm shortening its life. As if something was suddenly ending, while nothing else was beginning. As if I were extinguishing something inside myself. I don't know how I can explain it to you.

Let me put it this way. In my view, there's something in a burning candle. Maybe everything. The same way that a drop of water contains all water, every body of water there is. Try putting out a candle one day.

I have two candlesticks. Silver. I bought them when I was living abroad. As if I knew you'd come visit me one day. If not right away, then at some time in the future. Shall I fetch them? They're through there in the living room. On the sideboard. I can put candles in them, we'll light them and watch them burn, and you'll see. I used to sometimes swing by an antique shop on the ground floor of the building I lived in. For no particular reason. I liked looking at all the old furniture, pictures, objects. All those cabinets, chests of drawers, writing bureaus, looking glasses, lamps, clocks, or even the inkstands, blotters, paper knives. When you think about it, all that furniture and those objects contain an infinite number of human touches, looks, how many heartbeats, sighs, sorrows, tears, fears, and of course smiles, excitements, outbursts of joy, though a lot fewer of those, those are always rarer. Or how many words, just think about it. Now all of that has gone. But has it really? For instance, a mortar for grinding pepper or cinnamon, when I touched it, you have to believe me, it would speak to me. It's just that it wasn't given to me to hear it.

I'm sorry for asking, but have you never had a similar longing to live both here and there? Never mind when. Never, not even for a moment? A moment is important.

So one day the antique shop owner, who always gave me a smile whenever I came in, although until then we'd never spoken – anyway, he came up to me and asked:

"Excuse me, I know you, I've often seen you come by, but so far nothing's caught your eye. Tell me, is there something in particular you're looking for? I can keep an eye open for you."

And though I'd had no intention of buying anything, I surprised myself by saying:

"I'm looking for a nice old candlestick."

"Oh, I have plenty of candlesticks. Take a look." He pointed to the cabinets lining the walls. "Brass, bronze, porcelain, majolica, lacquer, silver. Whatever you like." He began opening one cabinet after another, unnecessarily, because they had glass doors and you could see inside. He took a candlestick from one of the cabinets and placed it before me, singing its praises. "Maybe this one?" He took out another. "Or perhaps this is what you're looking for?"

"No, not that one," I said to each one he lifted out. "I've seen all these ones before. This isn't my first time here."

"Right," he acknowledged. "Could it be a pair?"

"Of course," I said. "It's actually a pair that I'm after."

"In that case I have something for you. I asked because they can't be separated. I couldn't sell just one of them."

And from a heavy cabinet with solid wood doors that he unlocked with a key he kept in his vest pocket he took out the two that I ended up buying. He stood them in front of me.

"Have a good look. Are these not the kind you're looking for? I knew it right away. They're baroque. Venetian. Superb craftsmanship, I'm sure you'll agree. I have to warn you though –"

"I can imagine," I said, interrupting him. "The price is immaterial. Please wrap them."

He probably wasn't expecting me to buy them, because as he was wrapping them up he continued trying to persuade me:

"It's a miracle they survived to the present day. And both of them together. You can only imagine what their story has been. You know, the stories of objects are as curious as human stories. And just as tragic. For example, imagine recreating the story of these candlesticks. Not their history, their story. At the same time we'd learn a great deal about the people who owned them. Things that might seem the most ephemeral, but which, who knows, might be the most important of all, though we'd never find out from any documents. Because sometimes a person can only count on objects to understand him. Sometimes he entrusts something to an object that he'd never entrust to anyone. Sometimes it's only objects that are truly capable of co-existing with us. I hope these candlesticks will be like that for you . . . Please come again."

Shall I bring them through, so you can take a look? I could light some candles. You say the light we have is enough for shelling beans. You misunderstand me. I didn't mean that we'd have more light. Oftentimes I don't feel like reading, I don't feel like listening to music. Especially when it's like this, in the fall or winter, the evenings are long, and I'm with the dogs, I sometimes bring the candlesticks in here to the kitchen, put in candles and watch them burn. And you know, as I watch I stop feeling that it's me watching. It's like there was someone here in my place. I don't know who. Besides, it makes no difference. The dogs will be lying just like they are now, over by the wall in the shadows, sleeping or pretending to sleep, while inside me it's as if everything is passing and I'm being overcome by an even greater calm. I become almost indifferent to myself, the whole world becomes indifferent to me, that it's this way and not otherwise. I even have the sense that I've refound myself in an order I never knew before. And like you see, you'd think they were just ordinary candles. They burn and say nothing. But maybe in that silence of theirs there's something more than silence, what do you think?

6

Now this was a true rebellion. We'd rebelled before, of course. How can you be young and not rebel? Especially in a school like ours. There were any number of reasons for defiance. It could be all sorts of things. The food, because the food was lousy. Or to protest the punishments. For instance, when one of us was missing a button on his uniform, the whole team would have to stand at attention half the day. One time they made us clear snow without gloves, also as a punishment. It was bitterly cold at the time.

They weren't big revolts. Once we came back from work in the late afternoon and the power was out. Not for the first time. So we decided we'd not go to class, or to shop, we wouldn't do anything connected with work. We all gathered in the rec room and sat there. They didn't give us lunch, they didn't give us supper, and in the morning, when we failed to appear for muster, they didn't give us breakfast either. They reckoned they'd defeat us with hunger. Except that each of us was thoroughly familiar with hunger. You might say there was nothing we'd had as much practice with as hunger. A good few of us had survived the war because hunger had bound us to life. Hunger showed you were still alive. Hunger woke you up, hunger put you to sleep. Hunger held you, consoled you, caressed you. Often hunger was your only refuge, because like I said, we were all from who knows where.

It lasted three days. The teachers came and tried to talk us out of it, they argued, threatened that it would end badly. The commandant himself came by. He was festooned with medals, he wore a Sam Browne belt, he only ever dressed like that on special occasions. He even started calmly, in a paternal way you might say, telling us we had to understand. He didn't blame us. He knew what it meant not to have electricity. They, that is, the teachers, also had to go without. Him too, even though he was the commandant. But we needed to realize that we were all still licking our wounds after the war. We of all people should know that. There was still very little power being produced, while the needs were colossal. Factories had to be set in motion, steelworks, mines, hospitals, schools. Our school for example. He gave us a long list. How much electricity was needed for cities, not just for the houses but for the streets as well. Soon the villages would need it as well, because they'd already begun the electrification that was finally going to end the age-old inequality between city and country. We ourselves were being trained with that in mind, after all. We'd be electricians by the time we left school. Had we not been given a challenge to be proud of? Future electricians, rise to your feet! No one stood up. That sort of cooled his enthusiasm. But he cleared his throat and went on. It was a thrilling task. One to suit our young hearts, our youthful zeal. He got so carried away the medals bounced on his chest. He was a fine speaker, that I'll give him. We had to understand and we had to understand, he said, the country still couldn't afford to give to each according to his needs. But in time, gradually, through hard work and vigor and patience, we'd get there. And through studying, studying was the key to strength. And it would depend above all on us young people as to who would finally win the peaceful war that was now being waged. Though he, the commandant of the school, he could already guarantee that we would be the winners.

We understood less and less of what he was saying. That there was some new war going on, even a peaceful one – that was beyond our ken. In any case no one had heard about it. After that he went back to saying, we had to understand, we had to understand. And we had to stop repaying the school with ingratitude. The school had taken us under its wing, looked after us, taken the place of home and family, made it possible for us to grow up . . .

All of a sudden he was interrupted by a whistle from someone or other, then all of us together, as if we'd planned it, we started shouting:

"We don't want to grow up! We don't want to! We don't want to! We want them to stop cutting off our electricity!"

He froze as if he was paralyzed. But not for long. Raising his voice to drown out our shouts, he began to yell:

"Who are the ringleaders? Who are the ringleaders? The rest of you will be let off! I want to know who the ringleaders are!"

This brought even louder whistles and shouts and stamping of feet. He gave as good as he got. He tossed his head and waved his arms. His face was red as a beetroot. It looked like blood was about to come bursting from his eyes and nose and mouth.

"All of you, on your feet! Ten-shun! On the parade ground, now! We'll sort you out. We know how to handle you! You're trash! Criminals! We know what you have on your conscience, every one of you! We have a file on everyone! Robbery! Arson! Rape! Murder! We know everything. And we'll use it! We'll send you where you should have been sent to begin with! Rebellion cannot be tolerated! People who do that don't deserve school, they need to be sentenced and put behind bars! Otherwise we'll never clean this country of tainted blood! Youth is no excuse! Enemies need to be destroyed whatever age they are! Destroyed, destroyed without mercy! The sooner the better!"

"Best of all in the cradle!" shouted one of the boys, his hands formed into a trumpet.

The rec room burst out laughing. He was struck dumb. His eyes seemed to fall still. And calmly, but with energy, like an order he barked:

"Who said that? On your feet this instant! Show you've got the guts! Well, I'm waiting!"

Everything went quiet, it was like the laughter had been cut off with a knife. He took out his watch and held it in his hand.

"Well? You've got ten seconds. If you don't come forward . . ."

We all stepped forward, the whole room as one. His eyes scanned us furiously.

"I see." Then he roared: "Just you wait!" He virtually ran from the room.

So we waited, expecting the worst. We didn't know what it might be, since it's always hard to conceive of the worst. We imagined various eventualities. In the end we came to the conclusion there was no point in waiting. We'd run away. The whole school would run away. The very next night. We agreed on which hut would go first and which would go last. The first was to leave before midnight. Then after that, the other huts at one-hour intervals. By the afternoon we'd end the revolt and go back to our huts, the teachers would relax and be sound asleep, and then we'd run away.

But that morning the music teacher paid an unexpected visit to the rec room. He was a little tipsy already. He pulled out his bottle, took a swig, and asked:

"Anyone want a drink?" Then he said: "They sent me to talk you out of it, boys. But I don't know how. I couldn't talk myself out of anything. I thought I might write a song for you. Every rebellion is remembered in song. But I'm not in the right frame of mind for it today. Forgive me. So what's to be done here? What's to be done? You can't just sit around like this. If I wrote something you could sing a little. How about that? Or maybe we could have an orchestra practice? I ought to have done it long ago. That was the pedagogical task I was given from the beginning. Come on, let's do it."

He pulled out his bottle and took another swig. Then he had us take up our instruments.

"Stand over there with them, boys." He pointed to the end of the room.

Each of us grabbed the first instrument that came to hand, because we thought it was some kind of game. We'd never had orchestra practice before. He would just tell us from time to time that that was why he'd been sent here.

Plus, with him drunk what kind of practice could it be. One of the boys asked him if we could take the broken instruments as well. He probably thought the teacher would say no, get mad. But he nodded yes. Everyone laughed, and some of the boys made a point of choosing a broken instrument.

I picked up the saxophone, but to my surprise he stopped me.

"Not the saxophone. There's no saxophone in this score. Back then the saxophone didn't exist, son. Take a violin."

There was only one violin left. It had no strings and the neck was cracked. There was no bow.

"This is the only one there is," I said.

"It doesn't matter," he said. "Stand at the back behind the other ones."

He started arranging us. Violins here, violas there, here the woodwind, there the brass, cellos on this side, behind them the double basses, and so on. We started to laugh again. By now we'd been occupying the rec room for three days, we thought he was trying to amuse us, to prevent us from getting bored. But he was far from laughter. He was serious as never before.

"Don't laugh, boys," he said. "Today is my day too."

It seemed he was done with arranging us, but he still wasn't content, he told one boy to move over there, another to come here, a third one to scoot to the side a bit, a fourth to step back a little. It was as if he still didn't quite trust himself not to have overlooked something. All of us were standing the way he'd organized us, but he still had one boy give his violin to someone else, pick up the other boy's horn and take his place. Another boy he had swap his bassoon for somebody else's trombone, a third one had to hand over his flute and join the cellos, while one of the cellists moved to the double basses. The whole time he was unsatisfied. As if it was us who didn't match our instruments. Or perhaps we spoiled his recollection of some other orchestra.

It was a big orchestra. We filled almost a third of the rec room. And like I said, the place took up an entire hut. The group of boys that hadn't found a place in the orchestra was much smaller, they were standing at the other end of the room.

He must have felt tired from arranging us all, because he sat down on a bench.

"Forgive me, boys, it's just for a moment. I need a breather." He drank from his bottle, wiped his forehead with his handkerchief, gave a couple of deep sighs, then stood in front of us again. "Don't laugh now. Be serious. Each of you, hold your instrument as if you were playing it. But don't try to actually play. Please don't actually try to play."

He evidently decided he wasn't drunk enough yet, because he pulled out his bottle and took another mouthful. Then he handed the bottle to the closest boy, who seemed like the first violinist.

"Put it over there. All right, pay attention now boys."

He spread his arms and froze. He stood for a moment in this position. Then he raised his hands over his head. At this point one of the boys in the orchestra laughed again.

"For the love of God, don't laugh. I'm asking you. It's the anniversary today. I'll explain later. All right, attention now, one more time."

No, he never told us what anniversary it was. But no one laughed anymore. In the meantime he spread his arms again and stood there for a long time, as if he could neither lower them nor raise them higher. He inclined his head slightly and narrowed his eyes. We were sure he'd fall over, because he'd been pretty well gone when he came in, and since then he'd tipped the bottle back a good few times. But for a drunk guy he was quite steady. He stood there. Again someone in the orchestra gave a quiet laugh. This time, though, he seemed not to notice. He stayed in the same pose, arms wide, leaning forward, his eyes half closed. At one moment he whispered in a voice that I may have been the only one to hear:

"It's like you weren't alive, boys. Forgive me. You don't have mouths or hands, just instruments."

His arms shot upwards. Then he flung them as far apart as he could, jerking his body and making him stumble. The hair on his head flopped back and forth. He was no longer restraining his arms. He was utterly engrossed in what we were supposedly playing for him, and he arranged it with his arms. Later on I saw various different orchestras, but I never saw a conductor like him. It's another matter that when you see something for the first time in your life, even the most ordinary things seem extraordinary. Even a tiny thing like a ladybug, so all the more so a conductor. Though maybe that sort of seeing is the only real kind? A music teacher, in a school like that, and a drunk to boot, yet here he was like a bird trying to fly into the air on his own arms. Back then we might not even have known the word conductor. In any case I didn't. In the village bands I'd seen up till then, one guy would tap his foot, another would give the key, then they'd just play without a leader.

Those arms of his stretched out so far that the whole orchestra craned their necks to see. Then they curved, made circles and zigzags, sliced from left to right, right to left, from top to bottom, diagonally. It was a theater of arms. I saw a performance like that one time in another country. Nothing but arms, yet they showed everything there is here below. You know, if someone were to watch our arms here as we're shelling beans, what might they imagine, do you think? There you go. It was the same with him. Because of course we couldn't hear any music. The only music was his arms. But the fact that we couldn't hear anything was neither here nor there. He heard for sure. He only needed us so he could hear what he wished to hear.

At times he would draw his arms in towards his chest, and at the same moment it was as if he liberated them from the bondage of his drunken body, tossing them far from himself. At other times I had the impression that his arms were circling over his head. Above him, in front of him, closer, further away, flying off, coming back, and all he was doing was following their movements with his ears. Perhaps that was how it actually was, who knows. Because as the orchestra, we were simply standing the way he'd arranged us. The violinists were holding their violins tucked under their chins, with the bows on the strings, the flautists had their flutes at their mouths, and we were all poised with those instruments of ours as if under a spell. As if he'd cast a spell on us with his arms.

No, no one laughed anymore. Even the boys who weren't in the orchestra, and who had retreated all the way to the far end of the room.

I forgot to mention that when he rose up on tiptoe, as if he was stretching himself along with his arms, it made him look tall, though he was only of average height. He stood on his toes like a taut string, his hands fluttering somewhere overhead. After which he would come down from his excitement onto his heels, bend his knees, and with his outstretched hands he'd seem to be lifting the music up from the floor. Or maybe he was begging it to lift him up. It's hard to say when you don't understand much and you can't hear a thing. Or he'd fling one arm above his head and keep it there stiff and straight, while the other one described a broad semicircle in front of him, his fingers wiggling as if he was searching for something in the music.

We were worried that his drunken body would pull him backward or that he'd crash forward onto us, because with someone tilting to and fro like that and rising up, even if they'd been sober they may well not have stayed on their feet.

At one moment, as he rose once again on his toes he suddenly staggered. He would have fallen, but luckily one of the boys standing close by jumped forward and caught him. He slipped to the floor in the boy's arms. We helped him up and laid him on a bench. He was white as a sheet, bathed in perspiration, you couldn't even tell if he was still breathing. Someone wanted to go get the commandant. Someone else said we should call an ambulance. All at once he gave a crooked smile under half-closed eyes.

"It's nothing, boys, it'll pass," he whispered. "I've had too much to drink for that kind of music. If only you'd heard what you were playing, boys. If only you'd heard. Sometimes, boys, it's worth being alive."

And you know what, you won't believe it but we stopped wanting to run away.

A few days later we were told to assemble on the parade ground. We see a truck parked there. Next to it is the commandant with the teachers. He's a changed man, self-satisfied, smiling, almost fatherly again.

"Come here, come here. See what they've brought us. Lamps. Kerosene lamps, it's true. But you can't look into the future the whole time. Once in a while it's good to look backwards also. You might find something that'll come in handy today. Come on now, carry them in." He turned to the driver: "Did you bring kerosene too? How many cans? Good."

There weren't even so many lamps that it was worth summoning the whole school. Each dormitory got one. There were four for the rec room. And one for each of the teachers. Nothing special, just regular lamps. In some of them the glass was loose. But at least we had something to give light when the power went out. You could wash and eat and go to bed like normal people. Make a repair even, sew something on or darn it. Even if it's second-rate light, people still need it. In any case, we never revolted again about the light.

But this time it was different. We weren't protesting about the light. It was about the film that had broken off. And at a crucial moment. You have to admit you couldn't make up anything so cruel. Did he buy a hat or not? Or did he shoot himself? Plus, there was that Mary. That it was all about a hat? What if it was about her cheating on him, what difference would it make? It can be about a hat. I've worn hats all my life, still do, I know what I'm talking about. I've several of them, I brought them from abroad. Some of them I wear on ordinary days, some are for Sundays and holidays. One of them I always wear when I go into the woods.

That one is the dogs' favorite. When I put it on they jump up and down and nuzzle up to me, their eyes laugh, they know right away we're going to the woods. Why are you so surprised that their eyes laugh? What don't you get? What is there to get here? If you had a dog there'd be a good few things you'd understand. You'd even be forced to admit that dogs are doing us a service by living with us in this world. And people should return the favor somehow. Not just by feeding them and giving them a roof over their head. In that case, tell me if you think people can get as attached to dogs as dogs are to people. I doubt it. I mean, it's just not the same kind of attachment. If you ask me, dogs have a lot of advantages over people. For instance, dogs don't wage war, and they don't break laws, because they don't have any need to write them down, they carry them inside themselves. You often hear about how people treat dogs. They throw them out of cars. They take them and dump them in some remote place, leave them when they go on vacation, or to the sanatorium. I used to see lost dogs like that when I spent time in a sanatorium. They'd stick to whoever came along in the hopes that in them they'd find their person. Or like my Rex, they tie them to a tree in the woods.

I'm telling you, that's why it's harder to understand a dog than a person. Where does all that attachment come from, regardless of whether their person is a decent human being or a swine. Have you ever heard of a dog that willingly abandoned a human? Just like that, up and left, never came back? Or for example if someone attacks us, did you ever hear of a dog that ran away? It could be David against Goliath, he'll at least grab the guy's pants leg or bite his ankle. And he'll rage and bark, never mind that there's nothing he can do. Or a dog leaving a sick person or abandoning someone that's dying, did you ever hear of that? You couldn't have. And it happens that dogs die of grief after their human dies.

Us, we can't even sense what's coming tomorrow. We can't sense other people. Dogs, they can sense death. At most they might not let on. Like these dogs of mine, they're lying there quietly, maybe they're asleep even. But we don't know what they've sensed coming. Well, yes, they have a sense of smell. But it's not just that. Dogs are more than just smell. What else? I don't know. If I did, I'd know a lot more in general.

But all you need to do is compare what happens when a human is hurting and when a dog is hurting. It's like it's two different kinds of hurt. The human at the very least is going to complain, sigh, he's going to groan; the dog just mopes, or at most he'll stop eating. With a person, the slightest pain can be seen plain as day; with dogs all you see is fortitude. Or take a look in a dog's eyes, what's reflected there? Is it the same thing that's in our human eyes? You can say he's looking at the same things we are, but does he see them the same? Have you ever thought about it? A human, depending on what he's looking at, his eyes get wider or narrower, they flicker or they smile. Dogs, their eyes stay still whatever they're looking at. Or, what do people look like in the eyes of dogs? How about that? Do we look like we do to ourselves when we look in the mirror, say, or when other people see us, or in our own satisfaction or dissatisfaction, in our own memory, our own hopes and fears and despair? What can dogs be thinking about people? What are those dogs of mine thinking about us right now, as they watch us shelling beans? It's the first time they've seen you here in my house, they must be thinking something. See, they've woken up. Well, Rex? Well, Paws? The gentleman and I are sitting here talking.

Or the heart, dogs have hearts after all. You often say about someone that they have a good heart. They say that a person has God in their heart. But when He looks down on it all, would God not rather just go and live in the hearts of dogs? We don't know, true. But we can guess. Besides, what *do* we know? We don't know the most ordinary things. A dog's hackles will rise and we often don't know why. He'll wag his tail and we don't know why. He'll whine for no reason, we don't know why either. See, he couldn't possibly sense all that he senses through smell alone. He can even sense who's come here for what purpose.

You might find what I'm going to say surprising, but sometimes I wouldn't mind being a dog, at least for a short while. Not permanently, just for a while. Maybe then I'd find out for instance if they dream about me. Everyone would like to know if they're dreamed about. Not you? I'm sure you would really. How do you know no one ever dreams about you? Maybe it's just that no one ever told you. All I want to know is what my dogs dream about me.

The revolt? Oh, I didn't finish the story. Well, the power went out and the film broke off. Maybe if it hadn't happened at exactly that moment. Maybe if it hadn't been that particular hat. And then there was Mary. You remember what set off the Trojan War. Exactly. First there was a huge groan of disappointment when everything went dark. Luckily, just when it seemed that the darkness was about to explode, one of the teachers who'd been watching the film with us called out:

"Settle down now! We'll go check, it's probably just a fuse!"

One after another they scuttled out of the room. They must have reckoned that if they all go check, it'll for sure turn out to be a fuse. So all the more we'd remain calm. And in fact, considering how packed the room was, you could say we did stay cool. Actually, they must have been furious as well at that moment. Or they wouldn't all have left. So we kept a lid on it till they came back. We quieted each other. We told each other off. Take it easy! Simmer down! And we waited hopefully for the expected moment when one of the teachers would appear in the doorway with a shout of triumph:

"It was a fuse, boys! Just like we said! It'll be mended in no time!"

But time went by and no one came. Perhaps if the projectionist hadn't suddenly spoken, the tension would have been dispelled just through waiting. We might have raised a bit of a ruckus, maybe started singing. But in the silence and darkness his voice sounded like a verdict:

"What are they talking about? How long does it take to fix a fuse? I'm going to rewind the film and put it away. There's never once been a time when I was showing a film and the power came back on after an outage."

At that moment, the silence exploded so abruptly you'd have thought the whole hut was about to fall apart. There were whistles, shouts, howls, stamping of feet. First the innocent projectionist was the target, as if his words had been the spark to set the silence on fire. The boys at the back of the room jumped on him, pushed him to the ground, pummeled and kicked him. They smashed the projector. They pulled the film from the cans and draped themselves in it like it was streamers. One of them took out a box of matches and was about to burn the film to make some light. Make some light! Thank goodness we put it out in time. You can imagine what would have happened. Then all the windows in the room got smashed. Whatever anyone had at hand, or rather whatever they grabbed in the darkness, they threw that. Stools, benches, musical instruments. I tried to save the instruments. I begged them, shouted, snatched them from their hands:

"Leave the instruments alone! Leave them alone! What did they ever do to you!"

Some of them came to their senses, but others only seemed to find release with the instruments. They broke them, smashed them up, tossed them out of the windows. They even wanted to throw the grand piano out, but fortunately it wouldn't fit through the window. One of them got so mad he climbed up and started stomping on the keyboard.

I was at the other end of the room when I heard the crash of feet on the keys. I pushed my way over and grabbed the kid by the legs. He put his hands around my neck and started to throttle me. I couldn't breathe, but I managed to get him off the piano and onto the floor. We didn't have anything to hit each other with, since he was holding onto me and I was holding him, so we set about biting each other. We bit till we bled. He was a budding pianist. The music teacher often said he had promise.

Most of the instruments that got thrown out of the window survived in better or worse shape. The ones that remained were generally not so lucky. It was just as well that some were overlooked in the darkness. Especially because rage can darken your sight even more. The next day, if you'd seen the ones that had suffered the most damage it would have broken your heart. But not one teacher showed his face. Though it was precisely because of them that the revolt had gotten so furious.

Have you ever taken part in a revolt? Not even at school? You've never rebelled? Against what? It's not like there's any shortage of things. Right from childhood. The fact that they force us to eat when we're not hungry. With the years, there's one revolt after another you could start. Against school, because who actually wants to go to school? I don't mean our school. That's a whole other story. And just in general, against life, because it's the way it is, not some other way. Against the world, for being like it is instead of the way it should be. Against God because he exists but he's not there. Not even against yourself ever?

Though a revolt doesn't have to have a reason. In fact, I'm not sure that any revolt actually begins for the reasons we say it does. Not to mention there are revolts where afterwards, we regret having revolted. Except you can't go back to the way things were before. What can you do, people will never keep still, they're always seething, in ferment, and even if they have no reason, they're always going to revolt. They're a perpetual reason in themselves. They're going to rebel till the end of time. If you ask me, the world has a good many revolts still to come.

So our teachers might have been doing the smart thing by leaving us to our own devices. Because eventually we would have had to calm down of our own accord, since it wasn't a fuse and there was no hope of the power being turned back on right away. It was just that, as often happens, chance intervened. The screen unexpectedly came away from the wall. You're probably thinking, so what? But at a moment like that, the smallest thing can take on great power. Perhaps it had been carelessly hung. Or it might have come loose from all of our shouting, yelling, smashing everything, because the whole hut was shaking from it all. Everyone rushed up and started trampling on the screen. Like it was its fault for the lights going out. Then one of the boys picked it up from the floor and shouted:

"Guys, let's make a noose! Let's hang someone!"

Everyone else chimed in:

"A noose! A noose! Let's have a hanging!"

The first boy explained later that his intentions had been good. He wanted to prevent any more instruments being damaged, because we wouldn't have anything to learn to play on. They would have destroyed all of them. And as for hanging, they'd never have actually hanged anyone, because aside from us there wasn't anyone left in the school. They started tearing the screen into strips and debating who they should pick. There were various candidates. From among the teachers, it goes without saying, because who else? In cases like that, teachers are always the best bet. Especially ours. But no one could agree on who it should be. They braided the rope as they argued. They were in the dark, so they weren't doing that great of a job. The rope was plaited like a braid of hair, it was all loose. Besides, the screen wasn't good material for a rope. It was made of cotton, like a bed sheet or a quilt cover. For rope, hemp is the only thing. Then you can be sure it won't break.

When they had to take Uncle Jan down, the rope was hemp and it couldn't be cut even with a kitchen knife, it was so tightly twined. They kept hacking away at it. In the end father had to take an ax and cut Uncle down along with the branch he was hanging from.

All of a sudden, one of the boys gave a triumphant shout:

"Let's hang the commandant!"

The whole room whooped:

"Hurrah! The commandant! The commandant!"

It was as if only the commandant matched the scale of this revolt. In any case, he seemed the best choice. Above all, it was as if in his person he made it possible for us to cross a further boundary. The revolt, which had seemed about to turn from a disagreement into a fist fight, flared up all over again.

"Let's get the commandant! Let's hang the bastard!"

Someone sang:

"The executioners have spilled our blood so long!"

It goes without saying that by now the rec room was too small for the revolt. We swarmed out the door and through the windows into the parade ground, whether we were for or against hanging the commandant, it was all the same. We marched up to the teachers' hut where the commandant's office was. We started chanting:

"Commandant! Commandant! Come out, commandant!"

No, the commandant didn't live at the school. He traveled to work each day. At that time he was nowhere to be found. We knew that, of course. But the revolt had blinded us so we forgot. Of course no one came out. The hut stood in darkness and silence. There wasn't so much as a glimmer of light in any of the windows. It was like all the teachers were gone too. Maybe they'd run away, every last one of them, when the film stopped. Or they were sitting inside without making a sound.

We hammered on all of the doors, all of the walls. In the end we smashed all the windows. Nothing. There wasn't a living soul. Someone brought up the idea of burning the hut down, since there had to be someone in there. There were always at least three teachers on duty at any given time. Someone else said we should burn all the huts, even the ones we lived in. Burn the whole school down. If there was going to be a fire, let there be a fire. We could go up on the hill and watch it all burn. At least that. Nero set Rome on fire the same way. I didn't know what Rome was, I didn't know who Nero was. But there were a few kids in the school who knew this and that. Then we'd run away. Good-bye, goddamn school!

One of them volunteered right away to do the Rome thing, he said he knew where they kept the cans of kerosene, he'd run and fetch them. Someone else said it was better to hang somebody. We had a rope made from the screen, and the film had been the cause of it all. Otherwise why had we bothered to braid it? We set off around the parade ground, attacking all the other huts, smashing windows everywhere in the hope that we'd draw someone out, bring them into the open, because it wasn't possible we'd been left alone with our revolt. Our rage had reached its peak. It was a huge letdown that nobody was there. Some people started shouting that we should go back to the rec room and get the projectionist, maybe he'd have come round by now.

Then we heard someone coming. They seemed to be walking heavily, slowly, one step at a time. The square was paved with gravel, and you could hear it crunching louder and louder. Even when the steps paused, the gravel still sounded under the person's feet, as if they were rocking on it. Can you guess who it was? That's right, it was him, the music teacher. Who else. Only a drunk could have been so unaware of the danger. We recognized him from far off. We stood there and waited. He was well gone. He took one last step as he loomed out of the darkness, then suddenly staggered. One of the boys darted forward and caught him, otherwise he would probably have fallen.

"Thank you, thank you," he mumbled. Though it seemed that it was only with his next step he could actually see us. "Why aren't you in bed yet, boys?" he asked, half surprised and half not. "Don't take me as your example. I hardly sleep at all anymore."

"This is a revolt!" someone exclaimed.

"A revolt?" He hiccuped so hard his whole body swayed. "Good for you. I was in a revolt one time myself. You can see where that got me. But maybe you'll do better out of it. All right, just let me through now. For some reason I feel like going to bed tonight."

"It's a real revolt!" another boy shouted virtually in his ear.

"We've smashed all the windows! Now we're going to burn the school to the ground! All the huts!" They were yelling over one another across his nodding head, forming an ever tighter circle around him.

"I believe you that it's real," he murmured. "I believe everything nowadays, boys. All right, let me through. I want to sleep, to sleep."

Then out of the middle of the crowd there came a shout, though afterwards no one fessed up to it:

"We should hang *him!* He's so drunk he won't even feel it!"

Someone else objected. But a third person screamed:

"A revolt's a revolt! It's all the same who we hang! There's no better or worse choices! Put the noose on him!"

He'd been so drunk he could barely stand, but he sobered up at once:

"For what, boys? For what?"

"We have to. It's a revolt." Whoever said it, their voice cracked as they slippd the noose around his neck.

What do you think about that? I mean, he was the only one of them we actually liked. Of all the teachers. Whether you wanted to learn to play an instrument or not. Actually most boys didn't, but still all of us really liked him. Maybe it was just that we didn't know the rules of revolts, and we were bursting with rage. He on the other hand, he must have known, because he treated it like a joke.

"Hang away, boys, if you must. Just let me have a drink first." He took out his bottle, from this pocket here. "Be a pity to leave even a little drop." Though I think the bottle was probably empty, it kind of rang hollow when he lifted it to his lips. "Well, at least I'll die like a true artist. At the hands of those dearest to me. That's something." At that point he checked the noose, which they'd already tied around his neck. "Are you sure this thing will hold, boys? It doesn't seem that strong. I'd prefer not to have to come back."

We started to lead him along by the rope, looking for a place to hang him. But it turned out there weren't any protruding beams, or any trees nearby. Everyone racked their brains about where to do it. The music teacher was getting antsy:

"Well then, boys? I'm ready."

At that moment someone ran out in front of the others and kicked his legs from under him. He dropped to the ground, his hat fell off, and the bottle he'd been holding in his hand slid off somewhere.

"My bottle! My bottle!" he gasped. "Don't let it get smashed!" Then more calmly, with a touch of resentment, as he struggled to get up: "Too soon, boys. I'm not hanging yet."

And what do you make of this, the same boys that tied the noose around his neck hurried forward to help him up. Others looked for the bottle in the darkness. Someone put his hat back on his head, someone brushed off his clothes. The one that had brought him down, the others beat him and kicked him. Then the whole mob together walked him back to the hut where he lived.

"Too bad, boys," he said in farewell. "I'd finally have been done with it all. Find me my bottle tomorrow. Right now I want to sleep."

And that was the end of the revolt. No, they didn't show the film again.

Besides, who would have wanted to watch it now? The power came on the next day, as usual. There were no musters, reports, speeches. All they did was make us clean up. They had us bring in the instruments that had been thrown out of the windows. Lessons and shop and work were all put on hold. We got breakfast and lunch and dinner as before, not reduced portions. Right away glaziers came in and started putting in new windows, starting with the rec room. Then the insurance people came to assess the damage. So it seemed like our revolt had been insured. Nor could you tell from the teachers that there'd been any kind of rebellion. They even got more lenient. In any case none of them raised his voice or frowned. The commandant responded to our bows, which came as a shock, because up till then he'd hardly ever nodded back when you bowed to him. Mostly he didn't notice you. Unless something he didn't like caught his eye, in which case he could even slap you in the face. In front of everyone else, to make it worse.

Our biggest surprise, though, was the music teacher. Not the fact that he was going around sober. It was that when he was sober he was a completely different person, quite unlike himself you might say. Lost in thought, older, and he rarely showed himself. No, we never did find his bottle, though we did what he asked and scoured the entire parade ground the following morning. That was the strangest thing of all, it was like the bottle had vanished into thin air. I'd understand if there'd been grass or bushes, but the whole square was covered with gravel. There was nothing on it but gravel and huts. We even wanted to buy him a new one, because it wasn't just an ordinary bottle, these days flat bottles like that are everywhere, but back then there were only round ones. Where he got it from I couldn't say. I think he went looking for it himself as well, because he'd sometimes come out in the morning and walk around the parade ground.

Otherwise, nothing happened. One time only, once the windows had been fixed in the rec room they had us all assemble there. There was the commandant, the teachers, and us. They told us to think about our revolt, about whether it had been worth it. Whether we'd have it easier without the school. No one said anything about the film. The whole affair was pretty short. The only other thing they said was that until order was restored, until the damage had been repaired, they were giving us some free days to think about everything. We were being punished by being made to think, as one of the boys put it.

So, whereas to begin with we'd reckoned that things wouldn't end there and it was only the calm before the storm, eventually we stopped suspecting anything, since they'd told us to reflect on it all. Some of the boys even began to regret we'd not at least burned down the teachers' hut.

Maybe a week passed, maybe less, in any case we still had free days, and here there was a muster at the crack of dawn. Not a normal one, but like something unusual had happened. We ran out onto the parade ground and there were three military jeeps. You know, cross-country vehicles. They had us fall into line two deep, and told us we'd be questioned after breakfast.

They sent us off to eat. They must have been eating also, because they waited a long time. The sun was already well up in the sky when they began calling us in to the rec room for questioning. Not in alphabetical order, not according to age, not team by team or room by room. At random. There had to be some principle at work, but we couldn't figure out what it was. It wasn't even who had shouted the most during the revolt, who had been the loudest or the most involved. Nor was it who had been the first to suggest we should make a noose and hang someone. Though everyone knew who that had been. They started with one of the boys who happened to have fallen sick after the revolt and had had a fever.

They were seated at a table, a handful of civilians, a few military, and our commandant at the end. The table stood by the far wall of the room. It was a long one, made of several tables pushed together and covered with a red cloth. There were two vases with flowers, and everyone had glasses of tea in front of them. It even looked nice, they smiled at us in a friendly way, not just the civilians but the army guys as well. They asked us their questions politely, no one raised his voice, it was like they'd just come by to chat with us.

What did they ask us? Most of all about the teachers, as if the main thing was whether they treated us well. For example, do we often ask the teachers questions, and how they answer. What do they say when the power goes out. Or what do they say when the food is worse than usual. Do we ask them about that. That question none of us could understand, since the food was always worse than usual. They must have known that. But they didn't ask anyone what we actually ate. If they had, they might have learned that a great deal depends on food. It's not always about a film. The film, it was the first time they'd shown it. Whereas we ate every day. Things depend on food, and on what you eat it from and with what, on the plates, spoons, knives, forks. Us, we always ate from beat-up old mess kits. We'd been told the army had donated them to the school. But no one believed it. There were rumors they'd been gathered from dead soldiers at the front. So you could imagine that you're sitting there eating from a mess plate, and next to you is the dead guy whose plate it was. Even if you had a nice pork chop on the plate, do you think you're going to enjoy it? Heck no, we never got pork chops. If there was any meat, at most it'd be a piece of liver or spleen, or very rarely heart or kidneys. All the time it was kasha, potatoes, potatoes, kasha. Pearl barley it was. To this day I can't stand it. The soup was usually watery. Often the boys would just dip their spoons in it, then flick it over each other, they were so mad. They'd start at one table, and pretty soon the whole cafeteria would be splashing soup over one another. Little thing like soup, but it could have led to a revolt. The spoons and forks were made of cheap aluminum, they'd get bent and you'd keep having to straighten them. Not to mention that most of the forks were missing a prong, sometimes two. And there weren't enough knives to go around, when there was something to cut up, of course. Luckily they weren't needed that often. And they really didn't know about all that?

With the teachers, it was like they were trying to analyze them in detail. But there wasn't much we could tell them, because in our eyes all the teachers were alike. Besides, what was the point of dwelling on the teachers when it was all about the film breaking off when the power went out? Some of the boys did their best to tell them about the man in the film, and about Mary. That he kept trying on hat after hat. But they interrupted as if that was of no interest to them. At one moment apparently one of the military guys even smiled, though it wasn't me being questioned at the time. In my opinion, first they should have watched the film, and only then questioned us. And it should have been stopped in the same place it was for us. Maybe then they would have understood how a revolt can break out. You don't think they'd get it? You reckon they'd think it had to be more than the film? Or that they wouldn't understand how it could all be about the hat? I have to disagree with you there.

In any case, they wouldn't listen to anything about the film. And as far as the revolt itself was concerned, they asked us for instance what we shouted, they told us to tell them if not the exact words, because we might not remember, then at least the gist of what was said. They also asked each of us what each boy did during the revolt. As if each person could be doing something different in the middle of a revolt. A revolt means everyone does everything together, and no one's aware of what they're doing individually. One person shouts, and everyone thinks they're the one who shouted. Or like one person's at the front of the crowd, but everyone will think they were at the front. It's like in a war, one man dies and all the others think they've died as well. If someone is alive it's only because there has to be someone who remembers that the others died. Running away is the only thing you do on your own.

Maybe they got something out of us after all. You know how things are in that kind of questioning. You don't want to say something, yet you don't even realize you've already said it. You have nothing to confess to, but between the lines you confess all the same. In general, in questioning what they ask is more important than what you answer. The questions contain the answers they're looking for. Your guilt is already in the questions, even if you don't feel guilty. Whether you say you don't remember, or whether you say nothing, you confess. Especially with silence, because that way all you're doing is confirming your guilt. Inside you is enough guilt for every possible question. Even those that no one has ever asked, and maybe no one ever will. Because what is a person if not a question about guilt? The only good thing is that at least he rarely demands an answer of himself. It's just as well, because he wouldn't be able to give it.

On top of everything we were afraid they'd arrest us all, so we could have accidentally given various things away. They asked us for example about the ringleaders, as one of the army guys called them. He explained right away that that meant the ones who had led us, who had been the most eager, who had shouted the loudest and the most, that we should give their names. Each of us gave a different name, so maybe it turned out we were all ringleaders, because they didn't arrest any of us.

But the matter couldn't end there. And it didn't. You know who they arrested? That's right, the music teacher, who'd done nothing wrong whatsoever. Maybe someone had let slip that we were going to hang him. That was enough for them. That was enough of a clue. Because no other clue led to anyone else. True, later on word went around that he'd been under an obligation to inform them about anything that happened in the school. And he'd failed in that obligation. But you know what it means to say "word went around," so none of us believed it. How could it have been him, the music teacher. A guy who was almost always drunk, aside from anything. What could he have seen or heard when he was drunk. His eyes were permanently misted over, his ears must have been filled with other sounds. The sounds might have been in his eyes too, because often he didn't know which way he was going. There were times he couldn't find his own room. He needed to be led there. You had to take the key from his pocket, open the door for him. Help him off with his hat and coat and shoes. Lie him down on the bed. Who knows, we might have been no more to him than sounds he kept trying to put together in a way that made sense, and when he couldn't it wasn't his fault but ours.

Would you have believed it? There you go. But that's what people said. And the worst of it was that no one knew anything, no one said anything, but the rumor went around as if the information had come into being of its own accord. Where does such a thing come from, can you tell me that? Maybe there's something like the spontaneous generation of words, what do you reckon?

When we heard they were taking him away we ran to the rec room, grabbed whatever instruments we could, whether or not they were working, and we stood on the parade ground the way he'd arranged us that time as an orchestra, in any case more or less like that, it didn't really matter. The ones who didn't have instruments also gathered around us, because the whole school turned out. When they led him out, we all took up our instruments as if we were about to start playing. But we didn't play, we just stood there.

He was walking with his head down, he didn't even look at us. They put him in the back seat of the car, one guy on one side of him, another guy on the other. They were just about to set off when he jerked forward and shouted:

"Long live music, boys!"

7

You didn't know him? That's too bad. Did you know the Priest maybe? I don't mean an actual priest. That was just what we called him, the Priest. He even let me call him that, though I was a lot younger than him. A welder, he was. We worked on a building site together. Because I was thinking that if we found some people we knew in common, maybe we'd find ourselves too, the two of us, at some time or other, some place or other. I sometimes think of somebody I used to know, and he leads me right away to some other person I knew, then that person leads to someone else, and so on. And I'll be honest, there are times I find it hard to believe I used to know one guy or another. But I must have, since they remember meeting me someplace, at such-and-such a time. One guy, it even turned out we'd played in the same band years ago, him on the trombone, me on the sax. Though he's dead now. But people we know can lead us all kinds of ways, even to places we'd never want to go.

One guy abroad told me about these two brothers he used to know who'd fought on opposite sides in a civil war. Brothers on opposite sides, you can imagine what ruthless enemies they must have made. But the war was ruthless too. People killed each other like they wanted to drown each other in blood. Civil wars are much worse than ordinary wars, as you know. Because there's no greater hatred than the kind that comes from closeness. So when the war ended they continued to be enemies. They lived in the same village, but they wouldn't allow their wives to talk to one another, or their children to play together. And it goes without saying that they themselves never spoke a word to each other. But they both used to go to the same bar. It was another matter that there was only one bar in the village. They'd sit at separate tables, drink their beer, read the paper. If there was only one newspaper, when one of them finished reading it he'd put it back where he got it, even if his brother's table was nearer. The other one did the same thing if he was the first one to read it.

But the one who finished reading first didn't leave. He went on drinking his beer, as if he was waiting for his brother to finish reading. Almost every day they'd show up at more or less the same time, as if they knew when they were supposed to come. They drank their beer, read the paper, the second one after the first one or the first one after the second one, then when their glasses were empty they'd leave. The second one after the first one or the first one after the second one, just the same. It never happened that one of them finished his beer sooner and left. They didn't have to sneak glances, you could easily see the beer in their glasses. Or maybe because they were brothers they had the same rhythm? In any case they drank at the same pace. And that seemed to show they hadn't stopped being brothers. Because as for words, the war had killed the words in both of them for good.

The years passed, and they got older. One of them went gray, the other one lost his hair, and they kept coming to the bar, one of them at one table, the other one at the other, they drank their beer and read the newspaper. And each time they'd put it back where they got it. They needed eyeglasses to read now, and they weren't that steady on their feet. But neither of them would give the paper to the other one when he was done with it. Then they'd finish their beer, one of them would leave and the other one would leave right after. All those years, neither of them said so much as:

"Here, here's your paper."

That one sentence might have been enough. Because who knows if with that single sentence they wouldn't have said everything they hadn't said to each other all those years. You can fit an awful lot into one sentence. Maybe everything. Maybe a whole lifetime. A sentence is the measure of the world, a philosopher once said. That's right, the same one. I sometimes wonder if the reason we have to say so many words throughout our life might be in order for that one sentence to emerge from among them. What sentence? Everyone has their own. One that you could utter in a fit of despair and not be lying. At least to yourself.

If only you'd known the Priest. You know, the welder. I couldn't tell you. I don't even know what his first name was. Everyone always just said, the Priest. His first name and last name got lost somewhere along the way. You know what, you even resemble him a bit, now that I look at you. Hand to God. There's something of him in your features, in your eyes. Of course, I mean when you were younger, as I imagine you. He was still young then too. A lot older than me, but I was no more than a kid back then. It was only my second building site, and I worked on the first one less than a year. When you lift your head a bit that way it's like I was looking at him. Stop shelling a moment. When your hands stop moving your face is clearer. Now I'm not so sure. Maybe a little.

Why Priest? He'd trained to be a priest, spent three years in seminary, but he gave it up. That he never told me. But he kept his surplice and stole, and his Bible, he had them in a separate little suitcase that he kept locked. Though on a building site like that, who wouldn't open another person's suitcase and take a look inside? Especially one that was locked. Before he went to sleep he'd always kneel by his bed and pray for a long time. He never missed Sunday Mass. So it was all the more of a temptation to open the suitcase. Work on the building site often continued on a Sunday, especially if it was running behind, but he always had to go to Mass.

Of course he got into trouble, he was written up, they docked his bonuses. At the worksite meetings they claimed it was because of people like him that the building was behind schedule. That there were too many believers on the site, and he was an example to them. Though he was no exception. All kinds of people worked on building sites in those days. Building sites were like hiding places. So if they'd wanted to get rid of all those of one kind or another, there wouldn't have been anyone left to do the job. Not to mention the fact that there'd have been no tradesmen whatsoever. And he was one of the best welders. Maybe even the best of all. All the other welders would go to him for advice. Plus, he was hard-working. If there was some urgent job that needed doing he wouldn't leave the site till it was done, even if he had to work through the night. He didn't drink, didn't smoke, didn't go to dances. He kept away from girls. In his spare time he read. In that respect he was an exception, because everyone else drank in their spare time. Even before he went to sleep, however exhausted he was, he'd always say he had to take up his book and read at least a couple of pages. One time when I'd climbed the scaffolding to where he was, he said to me that books are the only way for a human not to forget that he's a human. Him, in any case, he couldn't live without books. Books are a world too, a world that you choose for yourself, not the one you've come into.

He kept trying to persuade me, till in the end I started reading too. I thought to myself, it's no skin off my nose, I'll give it a try, especially because I liked him. He'd asked me one time if I wouldn't like to read a book. I was reluctant, said I had to do this and that, I didn't have time. In the end, just to please him I told him to bring me something. He had a few books, he kept them in another suitcase, that one he didn't keep locked so no one looked in it. And that was how things began. There was a second book, a third. Then he said there weren't any more books for me, because the ones he had would be too difficult. So he took me to the library. There was a little library on the site, a few shelves. He poked about and in the end he picked out something for me. When I'd finished it he went back with me and chose something else. Let me tell you, out of respect for him I eventually started to read of my own free will. And like him, before I went to sleep I had to read at least a few pages.

It's strange you didn't know him. Everyone on the site knew him, he was well liked. He was always impartial and fair. Well-disposed towards everyone. He'd stop and talk with each person. Even if he was in a hurry he'd at least ask you about this or that. And he always remembered when something had been bothering you the last time you spoke to him. He'd lend you a few zloties if you needed it. If a cat or a dog wandered onto the site, he'd feed them. And the best proof of what a good welder he was is that he worked on the highest places. When a building was going up he'd always be at the very top. He was never secured. Never held on to anything. He didn't even turn off his torch as he moved from one joint to another. He walked across the girders like an acrobat. And you have to know that the higher up the work, the better a welder you have to be.

Sometimes he'd look down from way up there and see me crossing the yard, and he'd call to me to come up to him for a moment because there was some- thing he wanted to tell me. I'd go up there if I didn't have anything urgent on. He liked me, I couldn't say why. I was just a kid compared to him. He said it was a good excuse for a break when I went to see him. No, it wasn't like we talked about anything special. He'd ask me if I'd finished the book he picked out for me last time at the library, if I'd liked it, what I thought about it. It wasn't that he was checking whether I'd read it, rather if I'd got it. He guided me in how to understand it. He'd relate it to different things, life, the world, people in general. And always in the course of things he'd say something that made me think for a long time afterwards.

We didn't only talk about books. He'd say that it was only here, up at a height, that we can feel human. That was a truth I only grasped much, much later. Espe- cially because down below people mostly didn't talk, there the work hurried you all day long, or you were driven crazy because they hadn't delivered some materials or other and the work was at a standstill. Unless it was over vodka, but then you had to watch who you drank with, because they'd sometimes snitch on you. Actually, they also snitched on you when you didn't talk. Even if all you did was let out a sigh.

He said that on all the building sites he'd been on, he always worked as high up as he could get. And since he'd worked on so many sites, the high places were sort of his territory, so it was no surprise that it was up there he most liked talking. Down below, when he came down after work, he read, fed the dogs and the cats, and he didn't keep company with anyone. Despite the fact that, like I said, everyone liked him. Naturally he earned a lot more working up there. But it wasn't about the money for him.

So can you imagine it, one day during lunch, word went around that the Priest had fallen to his death. Some people said he'd fallen, others that someone else must have had a hand in it, still others that he'd fallen deliberately. Otherwise he would have been holding his torch and had his goggles on. Whereas he'd set the torch aside and taken his goggles off. But we never learned the truth. The cause of it may have been concealed up above there. The construction had already reached the fifth floor. And the floors were high ones, the building was going to be a factory. When you get used to the high places like that, maybe you can't get over the fact that you live down below. With high places there's no messing around. Me too, whenever I climbed up to visit with him, I always felt something either pulling me downwards, or drawing me even higher.

If you ask me, though, the truth lay elsewhere. There was a girl. She worked in the cafeteria. No, nothing of that sort. I told you he kept away from girls. He liked her, the feeling was mutual. He was gentle, polite, not like the rest of us. The most he did was when she'd bring the soup or the main course, he'd admire her braided hair, say how beautiful it was, how you hardly ever saw hair like that anymore. It was true, her braid was as thick as my wrist here. And it reached all the way down past her waist at the back. Everyone would tug at it as she brought their food.

Not me. For some reason I was too shy. Besides, I'd only recently come to work on the site. When she put my soup or main course in front of me I didn't even look at her, I only ever saw her from a distance. The other guys had known her for a long time. She'd gotten used to having her braid pulled. I won't lie, I liked the look of her from the start. And she knew it right away. One time she leaned over to my ear and whispered, You should tug on my braid too, see what it feels like. I didn't. But I decided that even without that, she'd still be mine. When the right moment came I'd tell her. For the while I didn't let anything show. I never even said to her, You look nice today Miss Basia, or Basieńka – Barbara was her name. Though everyone said that to her every day. When she brought me my plate I'd say, Thank you. That was it. Other guys, they wouldn't have been able to eat if they hadn't pulled at her braid or at least said, You look nice today Miss Basia, or Basieńka.

Sometimes she'd spill the soup because someone tugged at her braid before she'd had time to put the bowl down. Plus, some of them had hands twice the size of yours or mine, rugged and strong. She'd even break a plate at times trying to free herself from a hand like that. A good few plates or bowls got broken because of that braid of hers. Same when she was clearing the empty plates away.

One day she was carrying plates with the main course on a tray, six plates if I remember correctly, when someone grabbed her braid, even though she wasn't going to his table, she was just passing by. The tray wobbled in her hands and all the plates crashed to the floor. They were going to fire her on the spot. Luckily the guy did the right thing and paid for all the plates and all the food. After that the men were more careful, they only tugged at her braid once she'd put the plates on the table, otherwise every last plate would have gotten broken, and not through any fault of hers. Unless you could blame the braid. If you ask me, girls or women who work in cafeterias, especially on building sites like that, they shouldn't be too good-looking. Nice, polite, of course, but not too good looking.

Sometimes she'd wear her braid up on her head in a bun. Maybe it was for self-protection, because how else can you protect yourself when you've got the kind of braid that just begs to be grabbed and held for at least a moment. Or perhaps she wanted to look nicer, who can tell. Though in my book she had no need to look nicer. Without the braid, though, she looked quite different, she became kind of unapproachable, haughty. When she put the bowl or the plate in front of you, she seemed to be doing you a favor. I didn't like the bun. I thought to myself, when she's my wife I'll tell her I prefer the braid. With the braid, when it swung back and forth behind her back she looked, I don't know how to put it, like she'd only just risen into the world.

You're smiling . . . my imagination's a bit old-fashioned, right? But that was how I felt back then. Though if you think about it, don't you reckon we continue to imagine things the way people have imagined them? However much the world changes. However different we are. Or maybe we just pretend to be different so we can keep up with the world. While in our innermost longings we're all still the same, we just hide it from ourselves and the rest of the world.

Besides, tell me yourself, can anyone imagine nicer hair on a girl than a braid? Naturally, for a braid like that you need a mass of hair, and not the thin kind. You need hair that's a gift, as they used to say in my childhood. Here, on the lake, in the season, when people come on a Saturday or Sunday or on vacation, you sometimes see nice hair. But it's best not to look too closely. It's all dyed, and often colors that you never see in real hair. Real hair has a different color on each person, have you ever noticed that? In addition to which, their hair looks like it's been all puffed up by hairdressers, with all those conditioners and shampoos and gels. Often their heads look like bunches of flowers. And the whole bunch could fit in your hand if you plucked it from their head.

In general, something wrong is going on with people's hair. Maybe it's a sign that something bad is starting to happen in the world? Despite what you might think, more often than not the beginning is hard to spot. It's rare for anything to start with big things or big events. It's usually from something little, often something insignificant, like people's hair for example. But have you noticed that more and more young men are bald? And they're getting younger and younger. When I was their age everyone had a shock of hair.

When you only look at people's hair, or for example only at their bare feet, for instance here at the lake, or only at their hands, their eyes, their mouths, their eyebrows, you see them altogether differently than when you look at them as a whole. It gives you all kinds of insights. It gives you lots to think about.

It was that braid of hers that was the start of what came next. Though no one suspected it could be the braid. A braid is just a braid. It was tempting to grab it and feel it, that was all. Though let me tell you, when it sometimes accidentally brushed against my face as she was clearing plates from the table, it gave me goose bumps, as if death had brushed against me. Though I couldn't have imagined her with any other hair.

Actually, there was something odd about her in general. When they took hold of her braid she'd always blush, when she should have been accustomed to it by then. She'd served so many meals, there'd been so many lunches since the building site was set up, she ought to have gotten used to it. But she blushed even when someone just looked her in the eye when she was bringing the plates. She'd blush whenever someone said, You look nice today, Miss Basia, or Basieńka. She always looked nice, but they'd say that to her. I mean, there just aren't that many words you can use when you want to say something nice to a girl, especially in a cafeteria, when she's giving you your soup or your main course or clearing the dishes away.

It's another matter that as far as words are concerned, something has happened between men and women, don't you think? Someone here said to me once that words are unnecessary, that they're dying out. It's obvious what a man is, what a woman is, what do you need words for. True or false ones, wise or unwise, elegant or clumsy, either way they all lead without exception to the same thing. So what are they for?

True, on the building sites things weren't that great either when it came to words. You used them as much as was needed on the construction. And you can imagine what kinds of words they were mostly. One job followed another, so you just dropped by the cafeteria to quickly eat your lunch and then hurry back to work. You were dirty and sweaty, you didn't even wash your hands sometimes. Plus, while you were eating there were other men waiting for your place the moment you were done. Where could you be expected to learn other words? You look nice today, Miss Basia, or Basieńka, that was all some of them could manage. And those were the ones we reckoned knew how to talk. It was much simpler to just grab hold of her braid.

Were any of them in love with her? I can't speak for the others. Probably all of them would gladly have gone to bed with her. But were any of them in love with her? As far as true love is concerned, not many people are capable of that, as you know. It's hard to find, especially on a building site.

The construction wasn't finished, it was three quarters done at most, when here the machinery started arriving from abroad, in accordance with the plan. Soon after that a crew came to install it, including a couple of men who worked for the foreign company that had sent the machinery. It looked like they wouldn't have a whole lot to do for the moment, but they suddenly got all busy. They told us to quickly finish off one of the shops, and began installing some of the machines. Luckily for us they had to redo the measurements, because something had come out wrong, they even had to redraw their plans, and that gave us time to catch up with our own schedule. They were constantly sitting around the table in management, adjusting, arguing, threatening, saying it was supposed to be this way and not that.

They were classy guys. Every second one was a qualified engineer. A whole separate barracks was prepared for them to stay in. They even started calling it a pavilion instead of a barracks. They plastered the outside, painted the interior, weather-stripped it, put in new doors and windows. Each of them had his own room. Those of us who'd been living in that barracks before, they moved us to private lodgings, cramming seven or eight guys into one room. They bought the newcomers shiny new furniture, big wide beds, plus sofas, armchairs, wardrobes, tables, stools, bookshelves, bedside tables, night lights, lace curtains in the windows, drapes. There weren't many private homes that were as nice as those rooms. Also, in each room there was a radio, a rug on the floor, a mirror on the wall.

When we lived in that barracks, we had iron bunk beds and one wardrobe between six of us. The most you could do was hang your suit in there if you had one. You kept the rest of your things in a suitcase under your bed, or in old cookie boxes or cigarette cartons. No one would have dreamed of putting drapes on our windows, let alone lace curtains. It was difficult enough to get your turn at the soap or the towel. We bought a piece of calico and hung it over the window on nails at night. Or a mirror. The only mirrors were in the shared bathroom, nearly all of them cracked. Most of the time you had to use a cracked mirror to shave, brush your hair, or for example to squeeze your zits, or tie your necktie on a Sunday. And if you just wanted to take a look at yourself, you looked like you were made of broken pieces like the mirror. In the cafeteria they gave the new guys a separate area by the windows – that was where they had their tables. However late they came, those tables were always free and waiting for them. No one else dared sit there. There were times when all the other tables were occupied, and however big of a hurry you were in, because you were in the middle of an urgent job, you still had to wait till someone finished eating, even though those other tables were free. And often it wasn't just one or two of us, there'd be a dozen or more guys hovering over the ones who were eating. We'd even tell them to get a move on, eat faster, as a result of which some of them would deliberately draw out their meal. It was infuriating, here your stomach was rumbling, here there was work to do, and right in front of you there were empty tables, almost taunting you. On top of that, often they only showed up when the last men were eating, any number of us could have eaten at their tables in the meantime. It sometimes happened that someone couldn't wait and went back to work without getting their lunch. At most they'd grab some herring or an egg from the snack bar, or a bit of sausage, though they didn't often have sausage, and they'd go back to work still half hungry.

And just imagine, she fell in love with one of the guys from those tables. In front of everyone, on the very first day. He came in, sat down, and she served him his soup. He looked at her, and she didn't blush, she just looked back at him. For a moment they looked at each other like that, and the whole cafeteria stopped eating for a second. Even if someone was lifting a spoonful of soup to their mouth, or a fork with potatoes or meat, they froze and watched. All the time they'd been grabbing her braid and saying, You look nice today Miss Basia, or Basieńka, and here some complete stranger had shown up and she wasn't even blushing.

He was holding his spoon also, but he hadn't yet put it in his soup, as if he couldn't tear his eyes away from her as she stood over him, or maybe he'd lost his appetite. She couldn't take her eyes off him either. Even though she'd put his soup down in front of him and she should have gone away, the way she'd go away from each of us after she put our soup down. She only snapped out of it when the cook leaned through the kitchen hatch and shouted:

"Basia, don't just stand there! These bowls need taking!"

She said to him:

"I hope you like it."

She'd never said that to any of us.

He said:

"Thank you. I'm sure I will."

And he watched her walk away, right till she reached the hatch. He ate his soup, but it was like he wasn't eating. It was *krupnik*, barley soup, I remember. Do you like krupnik? Me, I can't stand it. Ever since I was a kid I've hated it. Eating a bowl of krupnik was torture for me. Then she brought him the main course, and he didn't so much as glance at the plate. He took her braid in his hand, but not the way the others would grab hold of it. Rather, he lifted it up on his outspread palm as if he was weighing it to see if by any chance it was made of gold. She didn't snatch it back the way she did with the other men.

"Where on earth do braids like this grow?" he said.

Which of us would have known to say something like that, where do braids like that grow. But she didn't blush. She looked at him as if it was all the same to her what he did with her braid, as if she'd let him do anything he wanted with it.

He could have wrapped it around his neck, he could have cut himself a length of it, he could have unbraided it, she wouldn't have pulled it away. She only said:

"Please eat, sir. Your food'll get cold."

He said:

"I like cold food."

That was another way he was different from the rest of us, none of us would have said we liked cold food. With us, if something wasn't hot enough we'd make a fuss about it on the spot:

"Why is this soup cold? These potatoes look like leftovers! What kind of meat is this, it's bad enough it's offcuts! Miss Basia, tell them in the kitchen there! Take my plate back, have them heat it up!"

Whereas he'd said he liked cold food. He was on a building site, in the cafeteria, and he liked cold food. I don't know if anyone enjoyed their meal that day. I couldn't even tell you what the main course was. Probably meatballs, because we mostly got meatballs. They were more breadcrumbs than meat, but they were called meatballs.

You probably think she drove a dagger into my heart, as they say. Well, it did hurt. I didn't finish my main course. I went back to work. Though I didn't much feel like working either. In the end I made myself feel better by saying I'd wait him out. They'd install all the machinery in the cold storage plant and he'd leave, and I'd still be there. I just had to be patient. Besides, I found it hard to believe it could have happened just like that on the first day. She'd given him his soup and his main course, and that was that.

But from that day she changed beyond recognition. She looked and she didn't see. Even when you said to her, Good morning, Miss Basia, or Basieńka, sometimes she didn't answer. When she gave us our plates it seemed like it was all the same to her which of us was which. She knew the cafeteria like the back of her hand, she could have found her way among the tables blindfold, but she began to make mistakes. The next table had been waiting longer than us, but she served us first. She'd never gotten the order wrong before. She knew virtually to the second who had arrived first, who had sat where. The opposite happened too. We'd be calling, over here, Miss Basia, or Basieńka, we were here before them. She'd give us a distracted glance and serve the guys who'd come after us. Or she'd bring the main course to a table where they hadn't had their soup yet, while there were other men waiting for their main course at a table that was even closer to her.

It's possible to fall in love at first sight, but to that extent? It was enough to see what happened when he showed up in the cafeteria. If she was carrying bowls or plates to some table, the tray would shake in her hands, the plates would clink, then when she served them it was like she wanted to chuck them all down at once. And right away she'd run to the hatch for his soup. He'd still be eating the soup and already she'd be bringing him his main course. While us, when we finished our soup we always had to wait for the main course till she was done serving everyone their soup. Sometimes we'd even tap our forks against our bowls because we'd been waiting too long for the main course. Him, he never had to wait.

You should have seen her when he didn't show up at the usual time. You'd have thought it wasn't her that was serving the meals, her hands were doing the job all alone. As for her, she didn't even see what her hands were carrying. She was just one big tormented waiting mass. Here she'd be putting plates down on the tables, but her eyes would be fixed on the door. I'm telling you, when you ate you could virtually feel that torment of hers in the spoons and forks and knives.

Suddenly he'd appear. We'd be bent over our food, no one was looking at the door, but everyone would know from her reaction that he had come in. Right away she'd perk up, smile. Like she'd come back to life. Her braid would swing. Her eyes would sparkle. She'd almost be dancing among the tables. You had the impression she was all set to tear the braid off her head, put it in a vase and stand it on the table in front of him to make his meal more enjoyable.

And all that was only what you could see in the cafeteria. You'd often meet them walking along, their fingers interlocked. Or he'd have his arm around her, and she'd be pressing against him. When someone nodded to say hello, he'd nod back for both of them, because she wouldn't see. I have to admit he had good manners. He didn't put on airs. Whenever he needed my help as an electrician, or someone else's, he'd always wait till you finished what you were doing, then ask politely. He knew how to make people like him. And honestly, we even did like him.

Her, on the other hand, she seemed to be getting more and more impatient. She'd clear up in the cafeteria, but for example in the kitchen she wouldn't want to wash the dishes because she was in a hurry. Then later you'd see her waiting somewhere for him to get off work. Mostly she'd pace up and down on the other side of the street from the building site. Or even along the perimeter, right outside the chain-link fence. Though there was no path, just mounds of earth dumped there for the purposes of the site. She just walked back and forth on those mounds, sometimes holding on to the fence. When she saw him coming she'd run so fast her braid would bounce up and down. Sometimes she'd take off her shoes and run barefoot so she wouldn't miss him. If it was too far to go around by the gate, she'd squeeze through the nearest hole in the fence. There were all kinds of holes, people used them to thieve things from the site.

However long it took him to get off work, she'd wait. Everyone knows you can't always clock off at the time you're supposed to. All the more so on a building site like that, especially when you're behind schedule. Plus, they were on a foreign contract. We weren't, but even in our case you rarely got off when you were meant to. When things really fell behind, no one counted the hours.

She waited even when it was raining. She got herself a little umbrella, or perhaps he bought it for her. And even when it was pouring she'd wait under her umbrella. Or by a wall under the eaves, or in the watchman's hut by the gate when the rain was really heavy. You'd sometimes see her in the library too. I'd go there to get something to read, and here I'd see her at a table by the window with a book, and the window would just happen to look out onto the site. But she never glanced up to see who'd come in. Not many people visited the library.

So the librarian loved it when anyone appeared. But her, she didn't look up. She even seemed to sink deeper into her book, so as not to draw attention to herself.

So I would not notice her. Or God forbid I should ever ask what she was reading. That might have embarrassed her, turned her against me, hurt her even. And what for? I knew she was waiting for him. And who cares what she was reading. It was better she was in the library than standing or pacing to and fro in the rain. You know, I often felt more sorry for her than I did for myself.

It goes without saying that people told all kinds of stories about her. I don't even want to repeat them. For instance, there were rumors that she cleaned his room, did his laundry, washed his shirts, darned his socks. That she spent the night there. See how her eyes are all puffy, what do you think that's from? It never occurred to anyone it could be from crying. It was like that love of hers was the property of everyone. Like anybody had the right to walk all over her love the way you walked about the site, trampling it, even tossing down your cigarette butt. All because she served in the cafeteria.

No one said anymore, You look nice today Miss Basia, or Basieńka, she couldn't look nice with her eyes swollen. They said she'd lost her looks, she'd gone to the dogs, that her braid wasn't what it used to be, or her eyes. Maybe she was pregnant, she moved more slowly now, she wasn't so brisk when she brought you your meal. They said various things. Someone supposedly even overheard her say to him, You promised. To which he answered, We'll do it. You just have to understand. She says, What do I have to understand? I'm not as dumb as you think I am. Just because I work in a cafeteria? And she burst into tears.

The librarian, though, she was easy on her, she was an older woman and she'd probably been through a lot herself. Even after it was time to close up the library she'd keep it open if it was raining outside and the other woman was still sitting over her book. She'd tidy the books on the shelves, replace torn slip covers, catalogue new items.

Sometimes though, despite the rain she'd suddenly give back her book and leave as if something had agitated her, and at most the librarian would say to her:

"It's good you have an umbrella, Miss Basia."

She'd apologize to the librarian, explain that she'd just remembered she had something urgent to do.

"Never mind, never mind, Miss Basia. I understand, it happens. I'll just put a bookmark at your page. I'll leave the book over here, it'll be waiting for you."

"Oh, please do. Thank you." And she'd almost rush out, as if she really had remembered some pressing errand.

Then a moment later you'd see her somewhere by the fence, waiting for him. And the librarian would also see her from the window. Or she'd ask the watchmen to let her in to the site, and she'd wait there. She'd sometimes be wandering around till evening, till nighttime if he didn't show up. When someone came by she'd slip behind a crane or a backhoe, or behind a pile of bricks, some reels of cable, a heap of crates or barrels or used tires, there were mountains of stuff like that all over the main yard. Wherever she could hide.

Why would she hide when everyone knew anyway? Exactly. I wondered about that myself. Especially because I often used to run into her myself on the site in the evening. Though she hid from me too. Maybe that was the nature of her love, that it was somehow at odds with the world. Or maybe she wanted it to be that way.

In the end they got married. It was a strange wedding. It wasn't a civil one, but it also wasn't in a church. Apparently he'd so turned her head that she agreed to have the Priest marry them. That's right, the welder. She had wanted a church wedding. He wouldn't agree, because as he explained to her, he could lose his job over it. As she knew, he was on a foreign contract, and he needed the backing of important people. He couldn't even tell her who, it was an official secret. Besides, what difference did it make whether it was in a church or not. The main thing was that they should be married by a priest. A church was just where there was a priest. And she knew him after all. And the fact that he was a welder, what of it? He was a priest. People found themselves in various situations these days, even priests. He had a surplice and stole, and a Bible, he kept them in a suitcase, what could they be for other than to perform services? He'd be sure to agree. He knew what times were like. And he'd certainly keep their secret. Because for the moment it had to be a secret. At most he'd invite three or four of his closest friends. They wouldn't breath a word of it, he guaranteed. She shouldn't invite anyone from her side, not her father or mother, no one.

They agreed on a Saturday evening when the site would be deserted, so no one would see it. A lot of people working on the site would leave after work on Saturday to travel to their families. The watchmen at the gatehouse would get a bottle of vodka so they wouldn't see anything or hear anything. Just in case, he'd tell them it was his birthday. They'd cover the window, the table would serve as an altar, they'd cover it with a white cloth. He'd buy candles. It would be good to have a crucifix, he didn't know if the Priest had one. Maybe she had one at home, she should bring it. But she should make sure no one saw her. So she did. Do you think she was being gullible? I doubt it. Desire is stronger than suspicion.

She wanted a wedding dress, a white one, because she'd always dreamed of getting married in a white dress with a train. He gave it some thought. No problem, she'd have one, he'd buy it for her. He'd go into town and buy it. She didn't have to go with him. He'd get her the most beautiful one, the most expensive one. If she went with him someone might twig. She shouldn't worry, it would be the right size. It'd fit her like a glove. How tall was she exactly? That's what he thought. And her hips and waist, and here? That's what he thought. So why did she need to go? What if someone saw them together in the store, and her trying on a wedding dress, then there'd be problems. It wasn't their fault they were living in such times. He wished they'd met in a different age. But she herself could see it was best if he went alone. White shoes? He'd buy her white shoes. What size was she? That's what he thought. Just in case, she should draw the outline of her foot on a sheet of paper. That way he'd be more confident. Especially since with shoes it can happen that even though they're the right size, they turn out to be too tight or too loose. Would she also like white gloves? He could get her some white gloves while he was about it. What else would she like?

How do I know all this? You've never worked on a building site? Then you don't know much about life. On a building site everyone knows everything. You don't even need to eavesdrop. You don't need to see, you don't need to guess. You could say that what happens, what's said, what someone feels, what they think about, that first off everyone knows it. Then what comes next only confirms it.

Anyhow, she didn't want any white gloves, because why should he spend more money on gloves. No, she didn't want gloves. It was it was going to be an expensive enough business as it was. The dress alone, you say it'll be the most beautiful one, the most expensive one. Then how much will the shoes cost? Plus, she'd never seen anyone get married in gloves. She used to go to nearly every wedding at her church. Every wedding kind of changed her life for a moment. She'd gone since she was a girl. Even when it was total strangers getting married, she'd still go. When old people got married there was never much of a crowd, but she would be there. So what if they were old? It was still a wedding. And when they promised they'd never leave each other she would feel her heart pounding in her chest, tears welling in her eyes. But she'd never seen a bride in gloves. I mean, they had to put rings on their fingers, and what, was she supposed to take off a glove at that moment?

All of a sudden she realized he'd forgotten about the rings. He had to buy rings. He didn't have to because he already had them. He'd thought ahead. He took them out and unwrapped them, told her to try one on. How did he know it would be the right size for her finger? If it didn't fit this finger it would go on that one. Try it on. If it's too big, later on we'll give it to a jeweler and have it made smaller. If it's too small, she can put it on her pinkie finger for now. Later on we'll give it to a jeweler and have it enlarged. He'd bought them some time ago, before he was working on the foreign contract. An opportunity had come along when someone lost at cards and didn't have anything else to pay with.

No, he didn't play cards, not him. He'd bought them off the guy that lost. He'd figured they might come in handy. And they had. He'd forgotten about them, it was only when he saw her in the cafeteria that he remembered he had them. It was like those rings had chosen her to be his wife. Though they wouldn't be able to wear them for the moment. After the wedding they'd take them off and he'd keep them safe. Once his contract was over they could put them back on. Maybe they'd go away somewhere. Maybe abroad. He'd try and pull some strings in the foreign company whose machinery they were installing.

Who wouldn't have swallowed it all, you tell me. Common sense might have made her suspicious. But common sense always loses out to life. She was working in a cafeteria, and bam. Soup, main course, bam. Anyone who wanted could grab hold of her braid, but he lifted it on his outspread palm and weighed it to see if it was maybe made of gold. Common sense tells you to be wary of any love, because you never know where it might lead you. Common sense tells you you should be wary of yourself. But it isn't people that create common sense for themselves. And what is common sense anyway? You tell me that. And I'll tell you back that no one could survive in life by just following common sense. Common sense is all well and good . . . But all it really is, is what you say when you don't know what else to say.

It's too bad you didn't know him, you could've warned her. You didn't know him? Though she wouldn't have believed you anyway, of that I'm sure. No one can ever be drawn away from love. And if you ask me, they shouldn't be. When someone's drawn away you never know where they'll end up.

I thought the Priest might not agree. But they made him. Is it so hard to force a man to go against himself? We go against ourselves all the time just to avoid trouble. They forced him to do it by saying they'd put the word out. I told you he kept away from girls. No, that no one knew. There has to be something you don't know even when you know everything. He'd quit seminary, that much was known. He kept a surplice and stole and a Bible in a suitcase, that much was known. Before he started his lunch in the cafeteria he would cross himself, he prayed every evening before he went to bed, he never missed Sunday Mass, so everyone thought he still kept up his calling. Even I didn't know, and we'd often had long conversations together when I climbed to where he was working up aloft. How did the other man know? I couldn't say. I don't want to make accusations without any proof. In any case, if word had gotten around, his life on the site would have been miserable. It wouldn't have made any difference that he was one of the best welders, in fact the very best. And it would have followed him to other sites. He would never have gotten his life back.

They covered the window just like he said. What it looked like inside, we only knew from what one of the watchmen said. The other watchmen had sent him from the watch house to ask for another bottle, because they'd finished what they'd been given. But the moment he crossed the threshold they stuck the bottle in his hand and pushed him back out the door. So he didn't get to see if the table was covered with a white cloth, whether candles were lit, whether there was a crucifix. All he saw was that they were all drunk, especially her. He didn't see if the Priest was there. Maybe he left right after the wedding. Though it would have been strange if he hadn't gotten drunk too.

Besides, what could a watchman like that actually see when he was drunk himself, and every drunk thinks that it's other people who are drunk, not him. The watchmen had supposedly been given a crate of vodka, and they'd drunk the whole lot when they sent him out for another bottle. You can imagine how far gone he was. The watchmen were like that. They had uniforms and rifles, but things were always getting pinched from the site. One time someone even stole a tractor. And they didn't see a thing. So how could you believe him? But he said what he said, and other people repeated his words after him.

In any case, after the wedding bad things started happening between them. Him, he didn't even look up when she served him his soup or his main course in the cafeteria. And as for her, it no longer made a difference whether she was putting the food in front of him or someone else. Her eyes seemed to be losing their shine from one day to the next. You couldn't say, You look nice today, Miss Basia, or Basieńka, because she looked like she might burst into tears. She unbraided her hair and just tied it behind with a ribbon. It still looked nice, but it wasn't the same as when she'd worn the braid. But no one had the courage to ask her why she'd done it.

The Priest stopped coming to the cafeteria, and that made you wonder as well. Apparently he went to some tavern to eat. Then one day she happened to be bringing the main course to the table where I was sitting when someone ran in to say that the Priest had fallen from the scaffolding. Either he'd fallen or it was something else, in any case the guy shouted to the whole cafeteria that he'd fallen. She had one more plate to put on the table and, as chance would have it it was mine. The plate fell from her hands to the floor. She burst out crying, covered her face with her hands and ran into the kitchen. What went on in there I couldn't tell you. But people in the cafeteria could have thought it was because of the dropped plate.

We all rushed to the door, people came hurrying from the offices and from management, everyone was running, a crowd gathered and it was hard to push through to the place where he'd fallen. Someone checked his pulse and his heart, but he was dead. Soon an ambulance came, the police, they started questioning people and asking about witnesses. But it wasn't by accident that it had happened at lunchtime, if you ask me.

I didn't see her again that day. And him, he left that same evening. For the next few days she didn't work in the cafeteria. One of the cooks took her place. They said she'd taken some sick days, but she'd be back soon. And she did come back. Only, you wouldn't have recognized her. She took soup to the men from the foreign contract and right away she asked them when he was coming back. They didn't say anything. She brought them their main course and asked again when he would be coming back. When they still said nothing, she made such a scene that they got up and left. She was crying and shouting that they'd come to get their meal and they'd left him to do all the work. He'd get exhausted working so much. As it was he didn't look well. He was pale, he'd lost weight. The next day she was fired.

After that, from time to time she'd come to the cafeteria, stand by the hatch and say to the cooks that she just wanted to serve him his meal when he came. And the cooks, like you'd expect with cooks, they'd say to her, Come in to the kitchen, sit yourself down, we'll tell you when he comes and you can serve him, we can see the door from here, when he comes in we'll let you know.

You'd also meet her outside the gate waiting for him to get off work. Everyone had already left, but she'd sometimes wait till dusk, till night. It would be raining, pouring even, but she'd wait. She didn't have her umbrella anymore, who knew what had happened to it. Out of pity the watchmen would sometimes bring her in to the watch house so she wouldn't get so wet. Or they'd tell her to go away, that there was no point in waiting.

"My husband works here," she would reply.

"He used to, but he doesn't anymore. And what do you mean, your husband?"

"He's my husband, he took an oath. I wore a wedding gown, a priest married us."

"What do you mean, a priest. He was a welder. Besides, he's dead now."

Sometimes she'd beg them to let her onto the site.

"Let me in."

"Come to your senses, girl."

"I'll just tell him I'm waiting for him."

Occasionally they'd let her in. If not, she'd squeeze through a hole in the fence. She knew all the holes, after all. Even when they saw her wandering around the site they didn't drive her off. They turned a blind eye. If someone from management had seen her they had a good excuse, that they'd not let her in through the main gate. Besides, she was quiet, all she did was walk around the main yard. She never stopped anyone, never asked any questions. If someone came along she wouldn't hide anymore. No one asked her any questions either, everyone knew. Sometimes she'd sit down somewhere and lose herself in thought, like she didn't even know where she was.

From time to time I'd cross paths with her when I happened to work late on the site. One time it was almost evening, she was sitting on a crate.

"Oh, Miss Basia," I said.

"It's not 'miss' anymore," she said. "I'm married. Who are you?"

"An electrician, Miss Basia."

"Oh, right. I remember you from the cafeteria. I used to think you were cute. You were a shy one, I remember. You used to want me to be your wife. A lot of them did."

She surprised me, I'd never told her that. I wanted to say to her it wasn't that I used to want her to be my wife, I still did now. You might not believe it, but I suddenly felt like I wanted to be in her unhappiness with her. True love is a wound. You can only find it inside yourself when someone else's pain hurts you like your own.

But before I could explain this to her she said:

"Except that you guys working on building sites, wherever your site is, that's where your wife is. What do you know about love."

My courage failed me.

"Help me find my way out of here."

"The gate's over there," I said. "I'll walk you out."

"I don't want to use the gate." She looked at me as if with those old eyes from the cafeteria. "You know, I still think you're cute. But I already have a husband."

8

Let me tell you, he changed my life. You know, the warehouse guy. I told you about him. The warehouse worker that turned out to be a saxophonist. I don't know why you find it surprising. I mean, back then hardly anyone was who he was. A welder would turn out to be a priest. There were all kinds of guys working on building sites, hidden behind different occupations. But often it was only over vodka that you'd find out stuff like that. And not the first time you drank with them. Anyone who didn't drink, or only occasionally, they weren't trusted. It was because of that that I turned to drink. They'd ask a few questions but in only a general way. It wasn't till later they'd start to probe into your life. Or your conscience. Especially since our consciences had turned out to be something different than before. You think a conscience is something permanent? Too bad you never worked on a building site back then. It was probably the same in other places. But I worked on building sites and that's all I can speak about. You know, any change in the world is an assault on people's consciences. Especially when it's an attempt to make a new and better world.

In any case, you'd never have met such a mixture of people anywhere else. Bricklayers, concrete workers, plasterers, welders, electricians, crane operators, drivers, delivery men, all kinds, same in the offices, and it would turn out that one of them had been one thing, another had been something else, one was from here, another from there, they'd been in camps, prisons, one army or another, they'd fought in the uprising, in the woods, they had kidney problems from being beaten, they were missing teeth or fingernails, they were ageless, or still really young but already gray-haired. Every building site in those days was a true Tower of Babel, not of languages, but of what could happen to people. Though there were also folks, a good few of them, who had changed profession of their own accord so they could take part in building a better world, because they'd stopped believing in the old one.

I don't remember now which site it was, but on one of them there was this guy that worked in the planning department. People would say, the planning guy, and everyone knew who you meant. So one time, over vodka he let on he'd been a history teacher. He couldn't hold his liquor, he got drunk and started talking about how history had deceived him. Imagine that, history had deceived him. Like history could deceive anyone. It's us who keep deceiving history, depending on what we want from it.

Besides, if you ask me everyone lives his own life, and every life is a separate history. The fact that we try and pour it all into a single container, into one big immensity, doesn't lead to any truth about humanity. You can imagine a history of all the individual people that ever lived. You say that's impossible? I know it is. But you can imagine it. Yet nothing exists in the abstract, especially people. I don't know how you see the world. Me, like I said, I see it from one or another building site. They were always individual people, each one different from the next. They'd be called a team, the way you talk about history, but that was only at meetings.

For instance, on one site there was a philosophy student. Actually he'd completed his studies, he only had one exam to go when the war broke out. Then after the war he learned to lay parquet floors. He was even a foreman, I was friends with him a bit. He drank like the blazes. He had a strong head, and not just for philosophy. One time, when we were drinking he began talking about the studies he'd broken off, and someone asked him:

"Why didn't you finish? You could have done it after the war. What's one exam?"

His eyes became bloodshot, and we hadn't drunk so much at that point.

"What the hell for? What use is philosophy to me after all that? No mind could comprehend it. Plato, Socrates, Descartes, Spinoza, Kant – none of them could have. Screw the lot of them!" He slammed his glass down on the table.

We all exchanged glances, because none of us knew who all those people were that had gotten under his skin like that. No one dared ask either, because maybe we were supposed to know. Someone just said:

"You find the same sons of bitches wherever you go, sounds like. Not just on building sites." He poured the other guy a brimming glass. "Here you go."

Believe me, if I hadn't worked on building sites, and also, well, if I hadn't been a drinker . . . Anyway, it was on building sites that I learned how to live. And it was thanks to all the different people I met, that I wouldn't have run across anywhere else. I really owe them a lot. I might even say that each one of them might not have actually felt like living. They all had their reasons. But they *were* living. Above all I'm grateful to them because even though it often seemed a particular price was too much to pay, and there was nowhere to borrow from, still you had to keep on living. And most important of all, I realized that I myself wasn't an exception. Or if I was then the world was filled with exceptions. But those things only came out over vodka. So how could you not drink?

For instance, one person worked in the benefits department handing out bars of soap, towels, rubber boots, work gloves, they could have been just anyone, but over vodka they turned out to be one thing or another. Someone else operated a backhoe, it seemed like other than the backhoe all he knew how to do was drink vodka, but after a bottle or two he'd recite poems from memory. With another guy, it was Cicero in Latin. And thanks to the vodka you could even enjoy listening to it.

On another site there was someone who'd been a policeman before the war. I don't know if you'll agree with me, but I reckon any change in the world starts with the police. He'd had to hide his past, because during the war he'd also been a policeman, the organization had ordered him to be. It goes without saying he had no certificate after the war to prove it. Who could it have been from? With an official stamp to boot? The people who could have corroborated his story were apparently dead. And how many of them could there have been anyway? Two or three at the most. So after the war he moved from place to place to cover his tracks. He'd learned a couple of trades in the meantime. On our site he was a plasterer. But he drank too much, if you ask me. And when he did, he'd tear open his shirt and pound his own chest till it rang, shouting that the organization had ordered him to. Even over vodka there were always limits as to how open you could be. Me, I never said too much at such times, at most I'd talk about how things had been on other sites. Whereas him, once he'd gotten all emotional about how the organization had ordered him to do it, he'd always swear by Our Lady of Ostra Brama, which made it all the more suspicious, because Our Lady of Ostra Brama wasn't in Poland anymore. A policeman, yet he couldn't keep a cool head when he was drinking.

There were other guys that even when they were dead drunk, they could have been drowning in misery and their hearts bursting with revelations, but still they wouldn't say a word more than they wanted to. Someone who has a calling to drink, who doesn't just drink from one opportunity to the next, they know ways to say a lot while saying nothing, how to laugh when inside the last thing you feel like doing is laughing, how to believe in something when you don't believe in anything, even in a new and better world.

I don't know what happened to the policeman, because soon after that I moved to another site. Not for any particular reason. Maybe I thought that on a different site I'd drink less, or stop altogether. In general, whenever I'd worked on one site for too long I got the feeling it was winding itself around me, sucking me in. I couldn't stand it, and I'd move to another site. You probably think I was impatient, like any young person. It wasn't that. I just couldn't get attached to any one place. Actually, the thought of getting attached scared me.

No, I didn't have any problems with that. I was a good electrician. They always assigned me to the toughest jobs. When it came to hooking up new machinery or equipment, it was always me. There wasn't a problem I couldn't fix. I got complimented the whole time, they gave me all kinds of certificates. I never missed a bonus. Or even when something needed mending in the apartment of one of the directors, they'd always bring me in, at the request of the director or his wife. Anyone could have done it, it was only the iron or the hot plate, or just a light bulb that had burned out, but I was the one they asked for.

Did you change jobs often? Never? How is that possible? You liked it so much in one place? What job did you have, if you don't mind my asking? Did you not want to get ahead? That I don't understand. Everyone wants to move forward, if only to the next level. For most people that's the goal in life. So it was all the same to you? I don't get it. What kind of institution or firm was it? You're not at liberty to say? I understand. I'm sorry for having asked.

For me, it was never better somewhere else. Not in that sense, because the pay got better and better. Maybe I was driven a bit by the thought that where I was going things would at least be different. But everywhere it was the same. There was drinking just like at the previous site. In the end I turned to drink completely. It was only on the site where I played in the band, and I met that warehouse guy, that I worked till the construction was finished. Though it dragged on forever.

On one site, which one was it again? Actually, it makes no difference. Anyway, there was this one guy that worked there, well, you couldn't really call it work, he kept the overtime records. We didn't know the first thing about him. He didn't even make you curious about who he was. Because what kind of job is that, keeping overtime records. He rarely drank vodka, except when we invited him when it turned out he'd done a good job of recording our overtime.

Then one day two civilians and one military guy showed up in a car and asked him if he was him. He was. They twisted his arms behind his back and handcuffed him. Then they manhandled him into the car and sped off. He never came back. And we never found out who he was. He kept the overtime records, that was all.

True, we might have wondered, he always went around nicely dressed, coat and tie, pants with a crease in them, always freshly shaven and smelling of cologne. When he greeted women, whether it was the cleaning lady or the head accountant, he'd always kiss their hand. And he always referred to women as the fair sex. The fair sex, gentlemen. With the fair sex. He never got on first name terms with anyone. Maybe if he'd drunk more often with us. But we only invited him because we wanted to thank him for the overtime. Though he knew how to behave. He was our guest, but still he'd always bring a bottle at least.

Oh, I just remembered one other detail. He'd never take a piece of sausage or pickled cucumber from the tray with his fingers, like all of us would do. He'd always use a fork. He'd bring one whenever we invited him over, it would be wrapped in a napkin. If you don't mind, gentlemen, I'll use a fork, that's just my way. And he never ate the sausage with the skin on, he'd always peel it. I sometimes think to myself, maybe if it hadn't been for that fork. Maybe if he would've just used his fingers, like the rest of us, and not peeled the sausage. Sometimes there'll be a little thing, but it leaves marks like a trail in the snow.

And then there was the warehouse man. I think I mentioned that we were building a glassworks. In the middle of the countryside. The grain was almost ripe, but they weren't letting people mow it. We even volunteered to help with the mowing, it was a pity to see so much grain go to waste, how much bread would be lost, when there were often shortages of bread. But it was no, because the plan was behind schedule. Construction was supposed to have started the previous year, then it was supposed to have begun in the spring. They were always urging us to get a move on, faster and faster, high days and holidays, extra hours, overtime, working all hours of the night. The cities were waiting for windowpanes, the villages were waiting, factories, schools, hospitals, government offices, as if everything was to be built out of glass. While here they still hadn't delivered this thing or supplied that, something was wanting and the work kept getting held up.

So anyway, on that site there was a clerk in the warehouse. He didn't look like a warehouse keeper, let me tell you. If you'd seen him, you wouldn't believe that's what he did. He stooped, he had trouble turning his head on his neck. When he walked it was more like he was shuffling his feet than taking steps. People said it was from the war, from being interrogated. Though apparently he never gave anyone up, never admitted to anything. I don't know if that was true or not. I never asked him about it, and he didn't say anything either. In those times people didn't like to reveal things. Also, his left arm was partially paralyzed, in rainy weather he'd often rub it. He never explained that either, though that particular thing looked like rheumatism. When someone asked him, he'd say it was nothing. His right arm wasn't all that good either. When he wrote you a chit, he'd press his indelible pencil down with all the strength in his arm to stop it from shaking. The pencil itself was no more than a stub, you could barely see it between his fingers.

He'd always cut a new pencil into four, and use little short ones all the time. Not out of thriftiness. If you have a whole pencil sticking out of your hand, however hard you press down it's still going to give you away. You could see the shakiness on the chit, even if all he'd written was something like, Screw: one count.

Oh, and also he couldn't really see out of one eye. To cover it up he'd look at you with the eye that didn't see properly, and half-close his good eye. Or he'd take turns, first one eye then the other, which hid it even more. And he was a grumbler, he complained all the time. When you went to the warehouse for some item you'd get a virtual inquisition, why do you need it, what's it for, where's it for, before he'd scribble the chit and give you the thing. And all the time he'd be going on and on about how we damaged everything he gave us, you could have built a whole other glassworks with the materials we'd spoiled, plus we were probably pinching stuff. He knew, he knew full well. Maybe not you, kid. But they all steal. They reckon that what they're stealing isn't theirs.

On the other hand, there wasn't the slightest thing wrong with his hearing, let me tell you. Maybe it was because of his hearing that they made him a warehouse keeper. You'd be standing in front of him while he filled out the chit and he'd ask without looking up:

"Why are you creaking like that?"

"What do you mean, creaking? I'm just standing here."

"You're creaking, I can hear it."

Or:

"You have asthma or something?" The guy would be healthy as you like. "Keep drinking and smoking and you'll run out of breath before you die."

Or whenever he gave out a part, he'd always have to hold it to his ear. If it was something heavy, he'd bend over it. And he'd say, It's good, or, I'll give you another one.

You know, hearing means a lot in a warehouse, maybe even more than sight. The warehouse took up an entire hut, he'd have had to always be walking around and checking up. As it was, he just sat at his desk and he could hear the whole place from one end to the other. He would have heard a mouse, let alone someone trying to remove a window pane at the other end of the warehouse.

No one on the site knew that he'd been a saxophonist. He never let on. He hadn't actually played in a long while. But sometimes, when you went into the warehouse without warning, it seemed like he'd been wrapped up in listening to something. Because as he used to say, you can hear music even in a rock.

No one would have found out either. But they decided to form a band at the site. A directive had come down from above that if there was more than x number of people working at a given site, and the project was a long-term one, then there ought to be some musical ensemble or a dance troupe or choir, or at least a drama club, since working people needed entertainment. So they started asking around the site about who could play an instrument. I told them

I played the sax. True, I'd not played since school, it had been a few years. And I thought I'd never play again. Though I won't deny I felt the urge. Sometimes, when I couldn't sleep I'd imagine I was playing. I heard myself play. I could taste the mouthpiece between my lips. Oh yes, every mouthpiece has its own taste. Well, actually the reed. I even felt the fingering, I sensed the keys against my fingertips. I felt the instrument weighing from the strap around my neck, maybe even more than a real saxophone would have weighed. Sometimes I could even see a firehouse full of people, I could see them dancing as I played for them, because I'd never known any other venue than firehouses.

But that was mostly when I couldn't get to sleep. During the day there was never time to imagine anything. Or you were so exhausted by work that vodka, vodka alone, was the only thing that could give you back the will to live. They were pushing us so hard, often it would be nighttime by the time you got off work, because like I said, the job was behind schedule the whole time, and at those moments only vodka would do the trick.

I didn't think they'd accept me. But I thought, I'll give it a go. Because I'd tried everything. I'd tried reading, I'd tried drinking, I'd tried believing in a new and better world, I'd tried falling in love. Maybe that would have been the best option. But to fall in love, you can't work from morning to night, because after that all you want to do is sleep. You have to go to dances. But to go to dances you need to know how to dance. And me, I couldn't even dance. No, they never organized dances at our school, and we weren't allowed to go to dances any-where else. One time the older kids had gone to one on the sly, they'd gotten into a fight with some local boys, there was a whole investigation, then after that they started checking up on us even in the night, to make sure we were asleep.

Sometimes we'd have a pretend dance on a Sunday evening, in the rec room. In fall and winter the evenings were long, there were no classes, on Sundays we didn't go to work. We'd decorate the rec room and put up a poster saying there was a dance. A few kids were chosen to be in the band, the younger ones were made the girls, the older boys were the gentlemen. But what kind of dance could it be when we didn't know how to dance – how could we have? Maybe one or two of us knew this or that, but most of us just stepped on each other's toes. There was constant cursing and name-calling. You so-and-so, you trod on my big toe, you trod on this, on that. You stepped on me with your whole boot, goddammit! The hell with girls like you. The worst words were thrown about. Get off my toes and dance, you son of a b . . . , and so on. Pardon my language, I'm just repeating what was said.

Though how could you step on their toes when everyone was wearing hob-nailed boots? We wore them for dancing too – we didn't have anything else to change into. We wore them summer and winter. The most you could do was dance barefoot. We tried that, but you got splinters in the soles of your feet because the floorboards were rough and jagged, they were all torn up from the nails in our boots. When someone got an accidental kick on the ankle from one of the boots, it made them howl. They sometimes whopped you if it was the girl who'd kicked them, or if one of the younger ones had kicked an older boy.

And when the band played a faster number, it wasn't just your dance part-ner, the whole room stepped on everyone's feet, people bumped against each other deliberately it seemed, some of them knocked other ones down. At those moments the insults and curses erupted like volcanoes, there were scuffles, sometimes someone even pulled a knife. Plus, can it really be a dance when no one throws their arms around anyone, no one whispers tender words in anyone's ear? At most one of the gentlemen would say to the girl he was dancing with, hold me tighter, you little shit.

The dances were mostly about the older boys, which is to say the gentlemen, taking it out on us, which is to say the girls. They took it out on us every day anyway, but at the dances they went the whole hog. The teachers? They didn't do a thing. Once in a while one of them would show up, watch for a bit, then leave. At those times, we'd just happen to be dancing nicely. No one trod on anyone's toes, you never heard a single cuss word. But the moment the teacher left, you can imagine what happened. It was total pandemonium, sometimes they even turned off the lights. And what went on when the lights were out, well, it's best not to say.

Oh yes, of course there was a master of ceremonies. This kid that was one of the oldest ones. It was always him, at every dance. He'd pin a bundle of ribbons on his lapel. He could actually dance a bit. He was a smooth talker, though he also had a mouth on him. But he always took the side of the older boys. He might have been the worst of the lot. He was pleasant, never swore, never called people names, when you stepped on his toe he'd just make you apologize. But before the number was over he'd lead his girl outside, supposedly to go take a walk, and there he did what he liked with her. Often he beat her till she bled. Complain to who? It would have cost you dearly afterwards.

He called circles, baskets, pair by pair, swap partners, and white tango. For the white tango, us girls had to ask the older boys, that is, the gentlemen. As master of ceremonies he decided everything, he'd say, you go with him, you go with so-and-so. If anyone tried to object, he'd grab him by the scruff of the neck and drag him across the room, now ask him and bow to him, get on with it before I kick you in the pants. And you could feel his hand gripping the back of your neck.

Let me tell you, for a long time after that I was afraid to dance. I was put off by the idea of dancing, which sort of goes against the nature of the thing, because after all dancing is supposed to attract people. Maybe because all through school it was as if I was the girl, and that makes you look at everything entirely differently, experience it all differently, it's hard to even trust to the dance. It was only when I began playing in the worksite band that I finally started to like dancing. A band has to know how to dance, not just how to play music for dancing. Especially a saxophonist.

They chose seven of the guys who'd put their names forward. An instructor came, brought instruments, listened to us play. And he said, We'll practice, we'll learn to play together and we'll make a decent band. No, it wasn't till the next time that he brought a saxophone, he auditioned me separately. He even asked where I'd learned to play, seeing I was so young. Had I been in a band before? A school band, I told him. It must have been a really good school. You must have had excellent teachers. Yes, I said, one of them in particular was.

On each instrument they painted an identification number to show it was official property. Just like they had on all the desks, office machines, telephones, equipment, towels, everything that was company property. Each of us had to sign a list to say we'd been given such and such an instrument to use, and that we'd be responsible for it. They also bought us company outfits so we'd all look the same: gray suits, white nylon shirts, neck-ties all the same color and the same pattern. The outfits were kept in a closet in the social department, we had to sign them out whenever we had a show. The only things of our own we had were our shoes and socks.

After that, for several months the instructor came and we rehearsed with him two, sometimes three times a week. After work, it goes without saying, because they only let us off overtime. And so we wouldn't lose out, they added two extra hours each day for the rehearsal. To tell the truth, after a couple of rehearsals we didn't really need the instructor, each of us knew more than he did. There was a cement mason, a welder, a tile layer, a crane operator, an office worker, and another electrician, and aside from me they'd all played before in various bands. One had been in a military band, another one had played at a spa resort, one had been a street musician during the war, or before the war. One of them had studied for a time at a conservatory, one was an organist, and one of them had a father who played fiddle at the opera, and his father had taught him to play even better than him, he said.

They chose me because I was the only one who'd come forward as a saxophonist. You know, in those days the sax wasn't a regular instrument. You didn't often see one in a band. Elsewhere in the world sure, but not here, not in company bands, especially from a building site. Though it was precisely the saxophone that made us so successful. Those guys have a saxophone – it gave us an advantage over other bands. Pretty soon we started getting invited to play here and there, on other sites, factories, army units. And not just for dances, but other things too, we were asked to perform at celebrations, anniversaries, holiday events.

Let me tell you, our band often did more for the site than management. So you don't think I'm just saying that, one time we did a special event at a cement works. Maybe you know how things were with cement in those days. With everything else too, it's true. But on a building site, without cement you couldn't do a thing. You'd sometimes have to beg for every ton of it, organize parties for the cement works management or their workers' board, remember the name days of this or that person, which people were important and who made the decisions, bring gifts. Or send telegrams, call. And when nothing helped, who to call higher up, though that was always the least help of all. The site would grind to a halt and stay that way.

They asked me to perform solo on the saxophone especially for the wife of the director of the works, because it happened to be her name day or maybe birthday that day. And they announced that I'd play solo for her, the rest of the band was only going to do backup. I didn't want to do it, I told them I'd never appeared solo before. But then I thought to myself, when it comes down to it it's a challenge. She was sitting in the front row, next to the director, she was a decent-looking woman, a brunette I remember. I started playing, I saw she was beaming, so I went all the way. I finished my solo, and the place was dead, there wasn't even the faintest applause. It was only when she jumped to her feet in the front row and started clapping without looking around that the whole room burst into applause, some of them clapping even louder than her. After that there weren't any more problems with cement. At most the delivery would be a day or two late. And the whole band got bonuses.

That was later, after he and I had gone our separate ways. You know, the warehouse keeper. It happened because there was a performance at our site, it was some holiday or other, a few people got medals, a bunch of certificates were handed out. The next day I went by the warehouse for some item, and as he was writing out the chit he said in a kind of hurt voice:

"You were all over the map. You'll never be a real band. You don't play well together, you're not that good."

It got to me, because who was he to say things like that. Some warehouse keeper. The room had rung with applause, it was even louder than after the director's speech, everyone congratulated us, people kept shaking my hand, and here was this warehouse guy. I thought, I'll just get the part I need and I'll say something to him as I'm leaving. But all of a sudden he softened up.

"You, you have something. But with the saxophone, don't go getting any ideas. You'll be wasted in a band like that. They'll clap for you, sure they will, because who ever heard a saxophone out here in the countryside."

I did a double take. Where had *he* heard a saxophone? It was then he let on that he'd been a saxophonist, he'd played for many years before the war, and in lots of different bands. I was dumbfounded, because on the surface you wouldn't have given ten cents for the guy, as the saying goes. I forgot that I'd come for the part, and honestly, to this day I can't remember what it was. I just wondered, should I believe him or not?

Words didn't come easily to him, you could see he had to force them out. Two or three of them, then a break, with big gaps in between, as if he had trouble joining them together. Or maybe that was just my own impression, because I couldn't get over the idea that the chit was being signed not by some warehouse keeper but by a saxophonist. From what he said, he'd played every kind of sax, though most often an alto. Then when he started listing the places he'd performed, I have to say I thought I was dreaming. Vienna, Berlin, Prague, Budapest, and those were just the capitals, he'd worked in all kinds of other cities. He'd traveled in any number of countries. He started naming the venues he'd played, and I thought he must be making them up. The Paradise, the Eldorado, the Scheherezade, the Arcadia, the Eden, the Hades, the Imperial. I wanted to ask him what all the names meant, but I was too shy. Because he might think,

And you want to be a sax player? Oh yes, he also performed on a passenger ship sailing to America. I stopped wondering whether he was telling me the truth or not, because the very fact that the saxophone can take you all over the world like that was making me think differently about it.

Once again I got the idea of maybe beginning to put money aside from my wages on the first of the month, or at least a part of what I spent on vodka. I couldn't play a company saxophone for the rest of my life, after all. And what if I moved to another site and there was no band there? One day I was back in the warehouse to pick up something or other, and as he leaned over the chit he asked:

"Do you have your own sax?"

"No, just the company one. I saved for one once, but then the currency change happened. I was thinking about starting to save up again."

"Don't bother," he said. He finished writing the chit, and didn't utter another word.

I thought, probably he reckons there's no point, because there might be another change of currency. And a currency change is like death, you always end up not having enough time. He must know life.

A couple of weeks went by, then one day I was passing the warehouse when he shuffles out and calls me:

"Come over here!"

"I don't have time now. I'll swing by later." I really was in a hurry.

"No, now. Later's usually too late."

"Is it something urgent?" I could see there was a case lying on his desk.

"Look inside," he said.

I opened the case, my heart pounding, and I couldn't believe my eyes.

"A saxophone," I said, though it was like I still didn't quite believe it.

"A saxophone," he said. "I went home Sunday and brought it back. Why should it go to waste?"

"It's golden," I said. I felt I was trembling.

"Yes it is," he said. "An alto. It's seen a good deal of the world with me."

"How much would you want for it?" I finally got up the courage to ask, while in my mind I'd already begun to borrow from everyone I knew on the site, in the offices, in benefits and loans. Where else could I try, where else. My thoughts were racing like a hunting dog, because I was certain all the money I'd be able to borrow would not be enough. He also seemed to be wondering what he should ask:

"How much? How much? How do you know I want to sell it? Things like this aren't for sale. Sometimes all that's left of your whole life is what you didn't sell."

And he said to me that if I wanted, after work or on Sundays I could come by, to his warehouse, and we could play. Or rather I would play, he would listen. It'd be better for me than vodka or cards. Especially as I couldn't play that much yet, and a saxophone has as many secrets as a person. Some of them he'd show me, others I'd have to discover on my own – not that he was trying to keep anything from me, it's just that he himself hadn't managed to unearth them.

"How much would that cost a month?" I asked.

"It won't cost anything. You'll play and I'll listen. I can't play myself, as you can see. I'm barely up to this job. It's only thanks to good people, a few still exist. I'm not well, I don't have long."

And that was how it began. First he hammered it into me that the saxophone isn't just a tool for playing music. You won't get anything out of it by being angry or mad at it, or by sulking. It needs patience and hard work. Conscientious hard work. If you want the saxophone to join with you like a soul with a body, you yourself have to open up to it. If you don't hide anything from it, it won't hide anything from you. But at every deceit of yours it'll dig its heels in and not give an inch. It won't go any higher or lower, however much you blow your lungs out. Actually, your lungs won't be enough, you'll be playing but it will be lifeless. You have to play with your whole self, including your pain, your tears, your laughter, your hopes, your dreams, everything that's inside you, with your whole life. Because all that is music. The saxophone isn't the music, you are. But

I'd have to try, really try, he kept repeating to me, if I wanted to hear myself in the saxophone. Because only then would it be music.

I have to tell you, I was even afraid of that thing. What kind of saxophone was it, I wondered. I played the company instrument, that was a saxophone too, but I didn't feel any of what he was talking about. And to begin with I played much worse on his sax than on the company one. Actually, you couldn't really call it playing, we mostly just practiced scales. That is, he told me what to do, I practiced. On and on, nothing but scales, up and down the whole range of the saxophone. It made me mad, but what could I do. Then he brought some sheet music and we started doing exercises and short extracts. He never let me play any piece of music in its entirety, I only practiced separate parts over and over, and it wasn't till later that he let me put the parts together. Also, often he'd make me play one sound till I ran out of breath, then he'd have me repeat it time and time again till he'd say, Good enough.

I'd go to him after work, and not leave till night had fallen over the site. Afterwards I wouldn't be able to sleep, I'd be playing things over in my mind, then often I'd dream about them. One time he told me I was holding the mouthpiece wrong, and it was making me blow more than I needed to. My lips weren't in the right place, I was pressing them too hard to the mouthpiece and air was escaping out the sides of my mouth. We have to change that. Another time it was that I was fingering too heavily, my fingers were too stiff, they needed to be loose, I should only touch the keys with the very tips of my fingers. And my fingertips should be so sensitive that they'd feel a sunbeam if it touched them. Because when I played, I wasn't supposed to touch the keys, I was supposed to touch the music. Those hands of yours are like turtles, your joints are clumsy. Keep practicing. See here, at the end they need to bend at a right angle. Practice at work as well. Though it was from work that my fingers were that way, because electricians don't much need to move their hands.

Sometimes I used to doubt whether he really had been a saxophonist, or whether he just sat in that warehouse of his and out of boredom imagined that he'd played the sax, like he could have imagined that he was anything other than a warehouse keeper. Maybe he did play a bit at one time, hence the saxophone, but all the rest was wishful thinking. Someone like that can put themselves through hell, then try and drag other people into their hell with them.

He never once took the saxophone in his hands to show me how one thing or another should be played, since I was doing it wrong.

"I would show you, but how?" he would say. "With one hand? I can barely write chits. As you can see."

But in that case, how could he know something was wrong? Not like that, play it again. Oh, he knew, he did. It was only years later that I came to understand.

I went to him every day for maybe eight months, then I got sick of it. I started coming every other day or so, though he would stay back in the warehouse every evening, waiting for me. Why didn't you come yesterday, why didn't you come the day before yesterday. It's been four days. You haven't been since last week, and I keep waiting here for you.

I would explain that there'd been an emergency, that we were having big problems with a repair, it'd be another few days yet. Or that they'd kept us later than usual on the site because of something or other. That the previous week we'd been doing contract work, because we were behind schedule. I made up excuses, and he seemed to understand.

"Yeah, that's how things are on a building site. That's how things are." He would just ask a while later: "So, is the work back on schedule?"

"Not exactly," I'd mumble.

"Your work might be, but getting yourself back on schedule won't be so easy," he'd say, a note of reproach in his voice.

Then one time, though I'd only skipped a single day, he said:

"Evidently I was mistaken."

That stung, and I was on the verge of saying I wouldn't be coming anymore when he spoke again:

"There'll come a moment when you won't be able to play and work on a building site at the same time. Not just yet, but at some point you're going to have to make a choice. For now, just drop out of the band. At least let them stop ruining you."

"What do you mean, drop out?" He'd actually made me jump.

He leaped up and started clumping around the warehouse. I'd never seen him so worked up.

"In that case, play all you want with them. Some people can't see further than the tip of their nose. Play all you want. You all love the applause, that's the fact of it, whoever's doing the applauding and why. Plus you get overtime."

That really needled me. I told you they gave us two hours of overtime each day. But that wasn't why I was in the band. That wasn't why I'd put in more effort than almost any other kid when I was in school. That wasn't why I'd saved up for a saxophone, taking food out of my own mouth. He'd really touched a nerve. And I stopped going to him at all. I thought to myself, how long do I have to listen to him saying, Not like that, not like that. You're not doing it right, not doing it right. Play it again, play it again. If he'd at least have praised me just one time. And on top of everything else he wants me to drop out of the band.

I left without a word, but let me tell you, I was clenching my fists so hard my hands bled. For several days nothing went right at work. I burned a transformer – myself, an electrician. He wants me to drop out of the band, kept running through my head. Drop out of the band. When that band was my only hope. Not to mention that we were more and more successful. Not long before, we'd been shifted half time to the band, we only worked half time on the site. Plus, in a few weeks we were supposed to play at a masked ball for some bigwigs. They chose us over who knew how many other bands. We all thought it was something to be proud of. Not just for the band but the whole site, management, and all that.

In preparation for our appearance the management got us new suits, dark, with a pinstripe, new shirts and ties, they even thought about having us wear bow ties, opinions were divided. This time everyone got black shoes, black socks, and a handkerchief. We heard they'd wanted to buy us matching over-coats as well, since it was autumn, but they ran out of funds. You have no idea how much we were looking forward to that ball. We were counting down the days. The night before they were going to pick us up I barely slept at all.

It was a Saturday. They sent a truck covered with a tarpaulin, but with benches along the sides. When we got in they told us not to look out from under the tarpaulin. In fact there were holes in it, but since we'd been told not to look, no one even dared so much as to peep through the holes. Besides, there were two soldiers sitting at the back watching us the whole time. They'd lowered the tarpaulin the moment we set off, and it was like riding in a dark box.

They told us it would take about two hours. It couldn't have been all that far, but the road went up hill and down dale, we bounced in our seats, the benches kept sliding into the middle of the truck, and we had to keep a tight grip on our instruments. So when we got there it was already completely dark. I don't know what kind of building it was. It was a big sprawling place, and it was in the woods, maybe a park. You couldn't see any more. Besides, after we got out of the truck they didn't let us look around. They hurried us to a kind of corridor in the left-hand wing, then from the corridor into a small hall. Here one of the soldiers who'd brought us reported to another soldier with two stars on his epaulette that the band had arrived and was ready to play. The second soldier told us to take off our overcoats and hats and hang them on pegs. I had a beret instead of a hat. I'd intended to buy a hat, and in fact I did. With those first wages, like I said, on the first building site I'd worked on after the electrification of the villages. But now I was working on maybe my fourth site, and I wore a beret.

We took off our hats and coats like he asked. Right away two civilians came through from the next room, one of them carrying a list. The one with the list checked our ID cards and marked them off on the list. The other guy went over to our hats and coats and he started feeling them, looking inside every hat, squeezing my beret in his hands. Then they patted us down to check we didn't have anything. Exactly what I don't know, they didn't say. But the clarinetist had a pocket knife, a regular pocket knife. You know what a pocket knife looks like. It's not a real knife, you can fit the whole thing in the palm of your hand. Two folding blades, one longer, one shorter, a folding corkscrew, a can opener, maybe a nail file, though I don't recall whether pocket knives had nail files back then. They told him to leave the pocket knife, that he'd get it back after the ball.

Then my heart nearly stopped, because one of the civilians asked the other: "Was there supposed to be a saxophone?"

The other one immediately went through into the next room. He stayed there for a really long time, or so it seemed to me. True, when it's fear measuring time instead of a clock, even a moment can drag on forever. He came back and nodded, but I didn't feel the slightest relief, I was bathed in sweat. They examined all the instruments closely. They shook the violin to see if anything rattled inside it, tapped on the drums to make sure the sound was clean, looked into the bell of my saxophone. Then they asked if we'd brought a list of the tunes we were going to play. Of course we had, since beforehand they'd required us to bring a list. We gave it to them. Had we brought the music to go with the tunes? Did any of it have words? We hadn't been told that anyone would be singing, so we were taken aback. They explained that that wasn't what they meant. Of course we had the music with us, though we knew by heart all the pieces we played regularly. We always had the sheet music with us anyway, since it looks more serious when a band plays from sheet music.

They spent more time on the sheet music than on anything else. One of them went through it all, then handed it over to another guy. The other guy, it looked like he knew music because he studied each page in turn, and from his eyes you could tell he was reading everything from top to bottom. He even took out two or three pages and held them between his fingers, after which he went into the next room again and stayed there for a long while. This time it really was long. We thought there must be something they didn't like, though we'd only chosen tunes that we'd played before at all kinds of parties and functions.

Finally he came back. He handed the music over. He said, It's fine. It turned out he hadn't held on to any of the tunes. But when we checked to make sure he hadn't put things in the wrong order, we saw that at the top of every page there was a handwritten note saying, Approved, and an illegible signature.

The soldier with the stars said, Let's go. He led us down one corridor then another one, to the ballroom. At the doors he told us to wait, while he went in first. I don't know why. Perhaps he had to report to someone that the band was at the doors. They were reporting to each other at every step. You couldn't move unless one of them reported to another one that you were there.

When we'd been getting in the truck to go there, one of the soldiers that later sat in the back to watch over us had first made us line up, after which he reported to another soldier sitting in the cab next to the driver that the band was ready for departure. Only after that did he drop the tailgate and tell us to climb in.

The one that had gone into the ballroom came out again and arranged us in a line according to our instruments, violin, viola, clarinet, trumpet, trombone, percussion, and me, saxophone. I didn't know if it was because I was the youngest, or because of the saxophone.

We were supposed to play something as we entered, then only after that make our way to the place for the band. Imagine walking into a huge, brightly lit room, there are streamers, balloons, but you don't see any people, there's nothing but masks. Someone called out:

"Bravo, the band is here!"

There were a few more bravos, and someone added a double one:

"Bravo! Bravo!"

It came out that we were late. Though not through any fault of our own, of course. Let me tell you, I didn't know what to think of it all. Here the people who were supposed to be enjoying themselves were waiting for us, while the other guys were checking us over like they didn't give a hoot about the first lot. I thought to myself, could it be that the second ones are more important than the first ones? It was because of the second ones we were late, they'd kept us back for such a long time. Maybe that was why they weren't wearing masks, while the first lot had masks on.

The ball was nothing special. It wouldn't have been any different from a regular dance if it hadn't been for the masks. Some people were dancing, others were going through to an adjoining room where there must have been food and drink. We couldn't actually see, there was a civilian standing by the door and he closed it every time someone went through. But when they came back, virtually every one of them was unsteady on their legs. They alternately danced and went out. Whether they kept their masks on to eat and drink, that I couldn't tell you. They didn't even let us through there for supper. They took us to a different room where again they reported that we'd come for supper, seven count. And they brought seven portions.

It was the first time I'd seen a party with masks. I couldn't get over it. Plus, all the masks were the same, like they'd all been given one, the men and the women alike. They covered their faces from forehead to chin, with holes for eyes and nose and mouth, as if instead of faces they only had those holes.

Later on, abroad, I played at many a masked ball, but there everyone's mask was different. Even in a mask each person was trying to stand out. Not to mention that every mask glittered with various colors, silver and gold. And there were all kinds of shapes, stars, moons, hearts. Some were so narrow they only covered the eyes, others revealed the eyes and nose and mouth while the whole of the rest of the face was hidden. Also, everyone's costume was different. Here everyone was dressed the same, or in any case the differences were small. And all the masks were black.

I wondered how they could dance in those masks. You couldn't smile at the other person, or show surprise, or make a face, through the holes. Maybe they could talk, but when a voice came through a hole like that you couldn't even tell whose voice it might be. And when you're dancing, your faces are next to each other.

Maybe that was why they went out more and more often to the room where the food and drink was. And they were increasingly wobbly when they came back. Some of them were staggering even. At times there were barely two or three pairs on the dance floor, most of them were eating and drinking in the other room. More and more noise came from there, while we played for the two or three pairs. There were moments when no one at all was dancing, but we kept on playing.

During one of the last breaks, I think it was, I went to the bathroom. I heard someone in the next stall. It wouldn't have been at all unusual, except that I heard what sounded like someone talking to someone else. I listened closely, whoever it was was speaking indistinctly, mumbling, I figured they must be well oiled. I was only surprised that the other person wasn't saying anything. The partitions of the stalls didn't reach the ground, so I bent down and got an even bigger shock, because I only saw one pair of shoes. Not patent leather shoes, just regular lace-ups.

"So, are we going to build a new and better world, what do you think?"

Who on earth was he talking to? True, sometimes you might say to yourself, What do you think. You're right, people like to talk with themselves more than with anyone else. If you ask me, even when you're talking with someone else, when it comes down to it you're really talking with yourself.

In any case, I could barely breathe from curiosity. Especially because he was talking about a new and better world, something I believed in too. All at once he raised his voice, he almost shouted:

"It's nonsense! Not us, not them. It's all nonsense, pal."

I climbed up onto the toilet, grabbed hold of the top of the partition, pulled myself up carefully till my chin was over the top, and what did I see? Someone was standing at the toilet, but alone. His mask was pulled away from his face onto the top of his head, so from above all I could see was the mask. All the more so because he was stooping over and rocking, with one hand on his fly, looking downward, and muttering downward so it seemed:

"Socialism, capitalism, none of it's worth a damn thing. You're the power.

The world stands on you. Though what are you? Well, what are you? You sit there inside our pants. Nice cozy place. A refuge, you might say. Many a time people would hide there themselves if they could. And there's plenty to hide from, that's the truth. Relax now, otherwise I won't be able to piss."

Pardon me, but it's just us men talking. I'd never say that in front of a woman. I wanted to see his face but he never once looked up. Actually he seemed to lean over even further. True, I wouldn't have recognized his face either. I didn't even know where we were, where we were playing, who for, who all those people were, they were all wearing masks. On top of that, they'd brought us there under a tarpaulin and forbidden us to look out.

My hands started to hurt from holding on to the top of the partition, and my arms were getting tired. I let myself down, as carefully as before, first onto the toilet, then from there I stepped down quiet as anything to the floor. I wondered if I should flush the toilet, let him know someone was in the next stall. But my curiosity held me back. You know how hard it is to know even about yourself, what you'd do in a situation like that. I decided I'd just give a cough. So I coughed, but it didn't have any effect. He even kind of raised his voice a little:

"You sure have a nice life. Your only worry is which pants leg to be in. And even when you get old and decrepit, no one's going to throw you out. We should all be so lucky – I won't say who the luck should come from. Me, you know, I can't even be sure of tomorrow. I can't be sure of anyone's words. Everyone's wearing a mask, how can you tell whose words are whose. Which ones mean one thing or another. Which ones are good wishes and which ones are judging you. You have to beware of every mask. What, are you looking at something? The future maybe? You don't have eyes. You'd like to see me? It's not worth the trouble. I'm standing at the toilet and because of you I can't take a piss. Let me tell you, people have to do too much thinking. You don't know everything, if only you did. There are times a person doesn't feel like living. But what do you care about that. You only have one thing on your mind. Though supposedly it's actually my mind. But truth be told, what does it mean to say 'mine'? Eh? That it's in my head? That doesn't prove it's mine. I mean, I've got you in my pants, but are you mine? I've never felt that way. More like I'm yours. I'm attached to you so there's someone to carry you, move you here and there, take you out, hold you up, put you back and so on. Maybe it'd be better if we were separate. What do you think? If we were only occasionally together. Maybe if that were the case I'd want something more. Because being a man from morning till night isn't as enjoyable as you think. Maybe for you. But what do you know. You squirt your load and you're happy, whereas me, I have to do everything else, it all comes down to me. Not to mention that I have other responsibilities. Conferences, meetings, consultations, councils. Going from one to another, all day long, sometimes even into the night. To the point that I even forget you're there, that's what my life is like. A walking contradiction, you might say. Do you know what a walking contradiction is? The idea that you and I are one. That's a load of baloney. If the new and better world is supposed to be that way too, I'm out of there. Or maybe I'm already long gone from it, what do you think? So what if I'm pissing? That's no proof of existence. And as you see, without your say-so I can't even do that. Just relax. Oh, you . . . I know what you're after. I even understand you. But get real. With a mask? Do you know who might be behind the mask? You don't. And neither do I. Do without for now. We'll have to get through this ball somehow or other."

In the end I flushed and left the stall. He came out right after me, but his mask was already on.

9

Did you just arrive in this world? Because everything surprises you. Yes it does. I'm not pinning anything on you. I'm just listening to what you say. I can even see that your hands are surprised by the beans. You could never shave with a straight razor. A straight razor needs a cool hand, one that's indifferent to whatever's going on inside you. Or someone would say something you weren't expecting, and you'd cut yourself right away. You ever shaved with a straight razor? Never? You probably use an electric razor. You don't shave at all? How is that possible? See, now it's my turn to be surprised. But that's something a person can still be surprised at. You don't have any stubble, it's true. I can see your face is smooth. Unless these days there's some other way of dealing with beards. In that case you probably don't even know what a straight razor is. I have one here, in the drawer. Somewhere I have a brush as well, and shaving cream, and aftershave lotion. I could give you a shave. It doesn't matter that you don't grow a beard, you'd still see how nice it is to shave with a straight razor. You can only learn that when it's your own face. You're scared? Of what? I don't understand.

No, I don't shave with a straight razor anymore. I couldn't do it, not with these hands. But I did for many years, before I got the rheumatism. It's really not that hard. I taught myself. When I was little I always used to watch my father shaving, and my grandfather, and Uncle Jan. Uncle Jan was always the most careful. He'd always shave twice. He'd shave, then soap up again and shave a second time. He used to say he had an angular face, and so to make sure he got all the hollows and bumps properly, he'd shave two times. His hands shook by that time, but he always used a straight razor. He'd sometimes cut himself, the blood would run down his face, especially under his Adam's apple, but he'd always do it twice. And he shaved every morning. But when he decided to hang himself the next day, he shaved the previous evening. I remember like it was yesterday. No one thought twice about it, though he never shaved in the evening. That time too he cut himself and he had to stop the blood with alum.

It wasn't because the razor was blunt, he sharpened it before every shave. First on a whetstone, then on a strop. After he sharpened it he'd check the blade. If it wasn't good enough, he'd sharpen it some more. Do you know the best way to check if a razor's sharp enough? You pull a hair out of your head, hold it between two fingers like this, and split it with the razor blade.

Hang on, I'll get the razor and show you. It's a good one, Swedish steel. The best ones were always Swedish. I brought it back from abroad. I keep it as a reminder that I used to shave with a straight razor, that my hands were that good. From time to time I take it out and run it over the strop, so it's sharp. You need to choose the right razor for your face, that way you get the best shave. A hard beard likes soft steel, and vice versa. Plus, you need to know your own face. That way you don't cut yourself. And the best way to get to know your face is by shaving with a straight razor. You're never closer to your own face than when you shave that way. Believe me. With an electric razor you're shaving, but you're thinking about something else. You can't do that with a straight razor. Even if you cut yourself and bleed, you know it's your own face. You feel it more than when you just see it in the mirror.

Look here. I pull a hair from my head. Then I hold it up in the air, best of all against the light, and I draw the razor across it. Not quickly. Gently. If it's too quick even a blunt razor will tug the hair away. But it won't cut it. That was always how people checked. Now pull a hair out of your own head. We'll try it with one of yours, you'll see. What, you don't want to give up a hair? It's just one hair. Think how many come out when you brush your hair in the morning. How many fall out when you wash it. One hair won't even hurt. If you'll let me, I'll pull one out. You're even afraid of me pulling a single hair from your head? I don't get it at all. You don't trust me? Yet you came to get beans from me!

Me, I started shaving when I was still at school. Once in a while. My chin was only just starting to get covered with fluff. But since the older boys were already shaving, us younger kids wanted to be the same as them. We shaved each other with a razor we borrowed from the custodian. At a price, you understand. Every Saturday we had to sweep out his yard and the sidewalk in front of his house, and clear the snow in winter. I only bought my own razor when I went to work on a building site. When I was working on the electrification of the villages I still used to borrow one from the guys I roomed with. I was saving up for a saxophone, I didn't want to spend money on a razor.

As it happened, there was this blacksmith in the next village that made razors out of tank bearings. You can't imagine what those razors were like. The only thing that might have come close were the Swedish steel ones, and even that I'm not so sure of. In the fields there were still all these smashed-up tanks from the war, he'd remove the bearings and make razors out of them. They were a bit unwieldy, true, the handles were awkward to hold, they were thick, made of elm wood or acacia, but the blade took your beard off all by itself. I bought two, I used one of them and kept the other in reserve, then later I gave it as a gift to the warehouse keeper who taught me the saxophone. He wouldn't take any money for the lessons, like I said, so I thought I'd at least give him a razor. He tried to give it back when I stopped going to him.

No, from that time on, even when I needed some item from the warehouse I'd ask one of the other electricians to go get it for me. I don't remember how long that went on. Then one day I was passing the warehouse, he must have seen me through the window and he started knocking on the pane, but I pretended not to hear. I thought to myself, he probably wants to tell me again how bad the band is. A week before it had been Women's Day. There was a celebration, and we performed in the musical part of the evening. He came, I saw him there, he sat right in the back. There were speeches, flowers and chocolates and stockings for the women. Construction was still going on, the plans were way behind, but they always had various celebrations in the course of the year. Though Women's Day was the most enjoyable.

I'd already passed the warehouse, but he called after me. He was standing in the doorway shouting:

"Are you pretending not to hear? And you say you want to be a saxophone player! Come back here!"

I turned around and went up to him.

"What do you want?"

"I'll buy that saxophone back from you."

"What saxophone?" I didn't follow, I didn't have any saxophone. He hadn't told me to save up, so I didn't. The one I played on in the band belonged to the company. And his, the one he taught me on in the evenings, was with him.

"The one that used to be mine," he says.

"It's still yours," I say. "And you still have it."

"I have it, but it's yours," he says.

"What do you mean, mine?" I still didn't know what he was talking about.

"It's yours. I gave it to you. I meant to tell you a long time ago, but I never got around to it. Now I'd like to buy it back from you. Take this as a down payment." He stuck a wad of banknotes in my palm. I pulled my hand away but he caught hold of it, pushed the money into it and closed my fingers over it. "Here."

Let me tell you, it was like the will went out of my hand, the blood went out of it. I stood there not knowing what to do, what to say. One banknote fell out, he leaned down and picked it up.

"Don't lose this. Count it, make sure it's all there. There ought to be . . ."

I didn't even hear how much. I could only feel my heart pounding. There was a tightness in my throat.

"I'll pay the rest bit by bit. Every month on pay day. Don't worry, you'll get it all down to the last penny. The amount it's worth. I don't expect any concessions. I'm not trying to pull one over on you. I never cheated anyone in my life. The amount it's worth. And it's worth quite a bundle. Every month on pay day. If you don't believe me, make sure you're standing behind me every month in the line for the cashier. I'll give it to you right away, the moment I get my wages. Every month. I can't give a lot each time, I don't earn that much, as you know, I need to be able to live. But each month. They won't close the site down, a job like this'll take a long while yet, I'll have time to pay off the whole thing. Even if they finish earlier, the warehouse will still be here. They can't get by without a warehouse. They promised they'd let me keep my job till I retire. But even if I don't finish paying it by then, don't worry about that either. I've thought it all through. You can write me to say where you are and I'll send you the money, every month. I'll even pay for a money transfer, so you're not out. I thought about taking a loan from payroll, but I'd prefer monthly payments, if that's OK with you. I don't like paying off one debt by taking on another. Then you have two debts to fret about. And there's nothing worse than getting tied up in debts. Life's a debt as it is, even if you don't owe anything to anyone and you haven't borrowed anything from anybody."

It goes without saying that I didn't take his money. How could I have? He was going to buy his own saxophone back from me? He died about a year and a half after that. Construction was still going on. Someone went to get something from the warehouse, he wrote them a chit and all he needed to do was sign it, when his head tipped forward. And that was that. But he didn't drop the pencil, can you imagine. As if he'd meant to sign off on his own death, one death, check.

A signature is an important thing, let me tell you. Especially when you sign off on your own death. Why shouldn't a person sign for his own death? You sign for all kinds of trivial things all your life. Whether you need to or not. Most of the time it's not even needed. Imagine counting up all the times someone's signed their name in the course of their life. As if they kept having to vouch for the fact that it really is them, not someone else in their place. As if there even could be anyone taking your place, say, or mine. So why shouldn't he have signed off on his own death? It was his, after all. If you ask me, death shouldn't have stopped his hand. Death itself should have needed him to sign.

You say that people are born without signing to say they want to be born. That's understandable. There are very few people who'd want it, if it depended on their signature. Death is a different matter entirely. You should at least be free in the face of death. In any case, what difference would it have made to wait a short moment. What was a moment like that for death. You're talking as if I were only referring to appearances. Let me tell you that even if that were so, appearances shouldn't be scorned. When the truth turns against us, thank goodness there are still appearances. There are times when after a whole life, appearances are the only record of a person's life.

For that year and a half I took lessons from him. It was as if one day we were practicing together, then the next day he died. I tried much harder than before. Almost every day, if only they didn't keep us back at the site, right after work I'd quickly wash, change, eat something or not, and go to him. He'd always be waiting for me, sometimes dozing with his head resting on the desk. But the moment I walked in he'd start up.

"Oh, it's you. I was beginning to think you wouldn't come today, and every day counts."

He took a piece of chalk and drew a circle on the floor that I had to stand inside when I played. He made another one for himself, at a suitable distance, in which he sat on a chair.

"I measured it out, this is the best distance for sound quality. I'll be able to hear you best from here. This warehouse is no concert hall. Or club. I get consignments of piping, sheet metal, wiring, tires, all kinds of stuff. Every time the sound changes."

He brought more sheet music this time. And he made me a stand for the music. When I arrived the stand would already be waiting in my circle with the music lying open on it.

"Let's begin with what you have in front of you there," he would say, to stop me from changing the order of the sheets. Then he'd put his chair in his circle, and have me take my place in mine. "Stand up straight though. Not like in that band of yours, where you all slouch."

He always had to run down the band. I guessed it must be his new way of weaning me off them. He did it kind of casually, in a mild way, because he'd stopped telling me to quit the band.

Often my legs would be shaking under me, after all I'd been working on my feet all day long on the site, but he never let me sit down even for a minute. There was another chair in the warehouse, when he was writing out a chit he'd offer you a seat. But whenever I came for my lesson, the other chair would always be put aside at the far end of the warehouse.

"You need to be on your feet," he'd repeat. "When you're standing your diaphragm works better, you take more air into your lungs. Breathing is really important with the saxophone. You, your breathing is too shallow, and so you're not blowing the instrument properly. Plus, a saxophonist has to have strong legs, a strong back, the whole spine has to be strong, then it's easier to play. When you end up having to play all night because the party's still going on, you won't have to say your legs hurt."

And let me tell you, my legs never feel tired. Sometimes here I have to walk and walk. Especially now, in the off-season. Like I said, during the day I'm obliged to make three rounds of all the cabins on both sides of the lake. And at least one in the night. When I walk around I know I'm really keeping a good eye on the place.

Excuse me, I have to get a drink of water, my throat's dry. When you shell beans there's always dust, that's why. Would you like a drink too? It's good water, from my well. No, it was here already. I just had it deepened and cleaned out. I had a pump put in, and they piped it up to my place. See, all I need to do is turn on the tap. Perhaps you'll try some after all? Here, you're welcome. It's good, right? Spring water. They tapped into a spring. Let me tell you, nothing quenches your thirst like this stuff. Even when I'm drinking coffee or tea, I have to have a glass of water to go with it.

When they were going to sink the well, father brought in a dowser. I don't know where he found him, he brought him back in the wagon. The guy searched and searched, his rod kept getting pulled down toward the ground, but he wasn't satisfied. Finally he said that he'd felt the cold, they should sink the shaft here.

Lots of people from the cabins come and get water from me. They can't say enough about it, It's so good, it's so good. Whoever went around praising water back in the day, you tell me that. The most you might say is that it was hard or soft. Spring water's always hard. For washing hair or bathing we'd collect rainwater. The animals were watered in the Rutka. Laundry was done in the Rutka too. River water is soft. When they're leaving for home, they bring canisters here so they'll at least have water to make coffee or tea. A few canisters each. A line forms at the well and I have to go out and keep order so no one pushes in, and everyone gets an equal amount. Because some people even take it as a gift for their neighbors in the city. What are things coming to, giving water as a gift. Regular water. Would you ever have thought something like that would happen with water? Let me tell you, that's the clearest measure of what's wrong with the world. At times I have to limit them to two or three canisters each, the well isn't bottomless. If the pump starts sucking up dirt it has to be cleaned afterwards. Then it takes at least twenty-four hours for the spring to fill up again.

You have to admit it's good water. Another glass maybe? I'll join you. Here where I'm standing there were always buckets of water, and on the wall over them was an embroidered motto that read, "Good water means good health." More or less where you're sitting, that was where he sat in his circle, and where I'm standing, that's where I stood in mine. Let me tell you, I wasn't convinced by those circles, I thought it was just some nonsense of his, and one day I told him so.

"Maybe we could try without the circles. People are making fun of me on the site. What do circles have to do with playing music?"

"They matter. One day you'll figure out why," he said. "Just keep standing there. Get used to it. You think you'll have more space? Life isn't lived sideways, it's lived going down deeper. Likewise, you don't play sideways, you play deep."

He'd say that if I'd played the accordion I could have sat down, or the cello, a few other instruments. But not the saxophone. The sax was played from the legs, all the way up above the head. In that way the air flows into the instrument by itself, you don't have to blow so much. You don't have to puff your cheeks out and tense your jaw. You, you're still all tense. You need to make the shape of the sounds with your lips, pass your tongue over them. Then the saxophone will become as tender as pain. Between you and it there ought to be pain. Otherwise you'll remain strangers to one another. It's a saxophone. But who are you?

You know, he became a lot gentler. He didn't correct me so often, he listened more. At times I finished and he seemed to still be listening. It was only as I was leaving that he'd sometimes say I needed to improve this or that, work on one thing or another.

It's also true that I was trying like never before. I was filled with a kind of doggedness, a hunger for playing. He'd say, That's enough for today, and I'd ask him to listen to just one more thing or another, I'll play it differently, just listen. He'd close his one good eye, you might have thought he was sleeping. Then suddenly he opened it wide:

"Play that again, I missed something the first time."

Sometimes the watchmen would come in and tell us to wrap it up, because the warehouse couldn't be open so long. They had to put the seals on. As it was they were turning a blind eye. When I left it would be nighttime, the site was so quiet I could scarcely believe it was the same place as during the day.

Each Sunday he'd give me the saxophone so I could practice when I got back from Mass. No, he never asked if I'd been. He only asked, So, did you manage to practice? At the rooming house I never could. From morning they'd be playing cards and drinking vodka there. Even when someone went to church, they'd come home and immediately go back to their vodka and cards.

When the weather was good I'd go into the fields or on the meadow. On Sundays no one was out in the fields, and on the meadows at most there were cows. Empty fields aren't a good place to play. You play, but it's like your music melts away. The meadows were a bit better. In the meadows I'd go out among the cows. And let me tell you, the saxophone took on a sound that it never did afterwards in other places, not just the warehouse, but in any night club, not even in a concert hall. You won't believe it, but the cows would stop tearing up the grass, they'd lift their heads, stand still, and listen.

I tried playing in various locations to see how the sound changed depending on where I was. I don't know how it would be here on the lake, in the woods, or when the Rutka still came through this way, in the village when there was still a village here. I really learned a lot from that. Same saxophone, same mouthpiece, same reed, and of course I was the same, but each place was different from other places. For example when I stood by a river, it was different where the current ran fast than where it flowed slowly.

It was worse when it rained, or in wintertime. What was I to do then? I'd go to the building site and stand under the roof of an open shelter. The watchmen would let me in. I'd slip one or another of them something from time to time. Once the construction had a roof things were a little easier. I'd go into one of the shops. Though in winter, especially when there was a severe frost, you couldn't practice for long. I had these gloves where I'd cut off the fingertips, down to about here, so only the ends of my fingers would show. But I still had to breathe on them every so often, because they'd go numb.

I don't know where that determination of mine came from. I'm not going to claim that I knew he was going to die soon. Maybe the saxophone had moved something in me, the fact that it was mine. And without needing to scrimp and save, without having to go to huge lengths. One day he said to me:

"I often thought to myself, why am I keeping the saxophone? I don't play, it just sits there in its case. I've got a grandson, but he's in the slammer. When he comes out he's only going to sell it for a song when I die. He's your age. Go on, go stand in your circle."

I went and stood where he told me to. He sat in his circle. His eyes were closed, he was listening to me play. All of a sudden one eye opened, the blind one. I could have sworn he could see me with that eye. It even glinted, and I stopped playing.

"Come to Mass with me on Sunday, ask the priest. The church is empty most of the week, maybe he'll let you practice there. The truth is, this warehouse is useless. You really should have a proper space. What else is there around here? The firehouse? That's even worse."

He died, the construction was finished, I moved to another site then another one after that. We were building a cable factory, I remember. One day I went to the store to get a loaf of bread, and I heard someone talking about a ruined church in the neighborhood, it had been like that since the war. They held their services in a hut somewhere else. After the war they'd taken prefab panels from camps and barracks that were being torn down, and in the areas with a lot of war damage they used them to put up apartment buildings, barns, cattle sheds, government offices, community centers, schools. They'd built the church building out of those kinds of panels. It stood at one end of the village, while the ruined church was at the other end.

One day I went to have a look, and on the off chance I took my saxophone in its case. The place wasn't completely ruined, that is, not to its foundations. But the war had left its mark. The steeple was gone. Half the roof was missing. The other half was riddled with bullet holes. There were big gaps in the walls. Not a single window had survived, though once there must have been stained glass windows, you could still see the remains of colored glass at the edges. The main doors had been torn off. A bomb must have hit the organ loft. You went in over rubble, with bits of the smashed organ poking out from among the debris. I accidentally stepped on something and it let out a moan that gave me quite a scare. But there wasn't any way in except through the rubble. There wasn't a single pew, no sign of confessionals, and where the main altar and side altars had been there were just empty spaces. On the floor were the remains of campfires. Soldiers must have burned the pews and confessionals and altars to cook food or keep warm. The walls looked like they'd been shot up by machine gun fire, the figures of the saints were all smashed. Here there was part of a head, over there an elbow or a foot in a funny-looking sandal. I picked up a hand, it was missing the thumb right here. I started to look around, see if I couldn't find it someplace. I found another hand, it had all its fingers and it was clutching part of a rosary. But it turned out not to be a match for the first hand, even though one was a left hand and the other a right. I won't say any more about the other fragments, I'm sure you can imagine. You had to watch where you stepped. In a word, there was debris and wreckage everywhere. On top of that, the rain had been pouring in for all those years since the war, snow had blown in, there'd been hard frosts, and there was no indication that anyone had tried to protect the place from further ruin.

The only thing still in any kind of shape were the Stations of the Cross. Though they were shot up and blackened, some of them had lost almost all their paint, so you couldn't tell if Christ was carrying his cross or if the cross was moving along on its own. That and the pulpit. It was mighty strange that that survived, let me tell you. It was also peppered with bullet holes. But there wasn't even one step missing. Yes, it was made of wood. Maybe they made speeches from there to keep the soldiers' spirits up. Or maybe there'd been some anniversary. Holidays are celebrated just the same during wartime.

I went into the pulpit. I had no intention of playing, the ruins had really depressed me. I only wanted to look down on it all from up there. I'd never been in a pulpit before. When I was a child I always thought that from the pulpit the priest could see everything in people's heads. Even if someone had a lot of hair, or if the women had winter headscarves on, he could still see everything. So during the sermon I'd hide behind father or mother so he wouldn't tell me off in front of the whole congregation, saying, See, over there, in that little blond head evil is already lurking, and remember that evil grows as a person grows, brothers and sisters. Because every sermon was always about evil. He'd often call out the first and last names of some man or woman in that regard.

So now it was me standing in the pulpit, looking down from above on the devastation. And after a moment, it was as if some voice whispered to me to start playing. Maybe it was even the ruins themselves. I opened the case, took out my saxophone, put the mouthpiece between my lips. Though I still wasn't sure. Then all at once my saxophone seemed to start playing on its own. It played and played, and I only seemed to be listening to what my playing sounded like amid the destruction. At that point I see someone making his way across the rubble. Disheveled gray hair, a walking stick raised and being waved in my direction. He was shouting something and straining as if he was trying to rise into flight. But his right leg wouldn't let him, at every step he sank down on it so low it looked like he'd collapse before he reached me. I had the impression of someone rising up out of the debris. Gasping and sweating, he finally hobbled up to the pulpit and as if with his last breath he shouted:

"Get down from there! Stop making all that noise! Get down, do you hear?" He went under the pulpit and started hammering on it from below with his cane. "Get down! Get down!"

I kept on playing. He came out from underneath, stood still, tipped his head back to look at me, and seemed to start listening. He was evidently unable to keep his head in that position, because he put both hands on his cane and rested his chin on them. He stood motionless and listened. At a certain moment he looked up again.

"What's that tube you've got there?" he asked. "The thing you're playing?"

"It's a saxophone."

"Never heard of it. Do you think God would like it? He used to always listen to the organ. But the organ's lying under the rubble, like you see. If you gave me a hand we could fish it out. I can't manage on my own. I'm too old. And when I put my cane aside I can't keep on my feet. I was the organist here my whole life. That was one fine organ! Over there in the hut they don't need me. They don't even have a harmonium. So I stayed here. God stayed with me. He wouldn't go someplace where they don't have music."

He walked up to the debris and tapped on it with his cane.

"See, you hear that? Come down and clear away this piece of wall for me, it'll be easier to hear."

"What will be easier to hear?"

"You don't get it. I sometimes come here, I sit in the ruins and listen. There, you hear that? If you'd only move this piece of wall. Come down. You're young, you'll be able to do it."

I went there almost every Sunday and helped him dig out the organ. That's to say, he sat by me and I did the digging. Every now and then he'd stand and try to pick some piece up, but the moment he leaned over he'd lose his balance. In the end I told him to stay put, I'd do the clearing myself. He hardly said a word, didn't ask any questions, maybe he was listening. Because when I moved some bigger piece of rubble he would always repeat:

"Now you can hear more clearly. Dig over there now."

One day I'd been digging and digging till I'd uncovered the keyboard. I sat down, tired, and he said:

"We're close now. Listen."

I swear I couldn't hear a thing. I asked:

"Close to what?"

"God," he said, "Close to God. God is music, only after that is He the Almighty."

One Sunday I came as usual, looked around, I couldn't see him. He would always be there before me, sitting in the ruins and waiting. The next Sunday I didn't see him either. Or the next. I cleared away the whole organ. As you can imagine, it was nothing but wreckage. I gathered up the tiniest parts. But he never came back. Maybe he'd had the good fortune to die before I dug out the organ. Because if he'd seen it . . .

10

What happened after that? After that it snowed. That much you know. How do you know I hid in the potato cellar? I didn't hide, mother sent me in the morning with a basket to fetch potatoes. The zurek soup was already on the go, she'd put the potatoes in and for sure what was in the pot would have been enough. But she suddenly decided it wouldn't do. Get the basket and bring a few more, son, I'll peel them and pop them in. She always liked to make big amounts of everything, because you never knew who might show up hungry. And if not, it would still get eaten.

It took a while for me to fill the basket, then clamber up to the little door of the cellar, the place was deep and I wasn't that strong, I had to go one step at a time, first lift the basket onto the next step up and only then climb after it. I'd almost reached the door, I had one more step to go, when out of the blue I heard shots. I put my eye to a crack in the door and I saw soldiers running and shouting, pouring something from canisters all around the house and the barn and cattle sheds. I let go of the basket, it crashed back into the cellar. Instead of rushing out and running back to the house, I hunched over till my head touched my knees. I shut my eyes, covered my ears with my hands, and sat there not hearing and not seeing.

Let me tell you, to this day I can't understand my own behavior. I can't forgive myself. No, it wasn't what you think, it wasn't fear. Fear would have driven me out of the cellar. Fear would have made me hear my heart, but in my case my heart stopped. I couldn't hear the least murmur through the hands over my ears. I was all numb.

I don't know how long I sat like that, like I'd frozen for good in that position, hugging my knees, hands pressed to my ears. I don't even know when I fell asleep. Can you imagine that, I fell asleep. Is that normal? True, I'd never liked getting up early in the morning, I always had a hard time waking up. Even when I could hear mother leaning over me and saying, Come on son, get up, it's time, even then I could never wake up. So more often than not it would be father who came to wake me up. He'd pull the covers off of me and say loudly, Come on, on your feet or I'll pour cold water over you! After that I'd walk around still sleepy for the longest time. I'd wash and get dressed in a daze. We'd have breakfast and I'd still be in a daze. They'd have to keep reminding me to eat instead of falling back asleep. I'd still feel sleepy when I went to school. Often, the schoolteacher would finally wake me during the first lesson. Or in vacation time, when I led the cows down to the pasture it was more like they were leading me, and I was following behind, still asleep.

Anyway, when I woke up everything was covered with snow. I'd never seen snow like that before. You have no idea. The trees were a third buried in snow. Nearby in the orchard there was an old beehive that the bees had left. Father had been planning to set up a new bee yard, he kept promising himself. The hive was completely covered in snow. It was coming down in big flakes, it was so dense you could barely see anything at all. And it kept falling. You had to peer through it like you do with fog. We'd not had snow all winter. There'd been frosts, but not a hint of snow. When it had started I couldn't tell you. But it was only when it stopped that you could see how thick it lay. It came up to more than half the height of the cellar door. Luckily the crack I could see out of was right at the top of the door. The snow shone so brightly it was hard to see through the crack.

Snow like that changes the world. For instance, when you walk through the woods among the trees all heaped with snow, you really feel like just lying down under one of the trees. Especially when it falls in big flakes, even if it were going to cover you up, you'd still lie down. Why not? Is it so difficult to imagine you're lying there in bed, in the sheets, under a fluffy quilt, plus no one's waking you up, while here over your head there's, let say, a happy fir tree. That's right, trees can be happy or unhappy too, it can happen. Like people, they're not so different from us. I can see you don't believe me. Let me tell you, when I was little I could tell at a glance which trees were happy and which ones weren't. When I went berry-picking or mushrooming with mother, she'd be looking for berries or mushrooms, whereas me, I'd be looking at the trees and seeing which ones were happy and which were unhappy. Often I'd call her over to come take a look, she really had to see. She'd come away from her berries or mushrooms, thinking something must be wrong. But she never told me I was talking nonsense, that I'd taken her away from her berries or mushrooms for no reason. Try and imagine this: two oak trees next to each other, both of them just oaks, but one of them is happy, while the other one is kind of stock still in its distress. On the first tree the leaves are all atremble with the joy of life, on the other one they look like all they want to do is fall off.

These days I can't tell which is which. I often walk a good ways through the woods, but I can't figure it out. They all look the same to me, and whether a tree's happy or unhappy, I can't say. Often I'll take the dogs out and watch to see if they know. But neither of them so much as sniffs at a tree. How can I get them to? What are they even supposed to sniff for – to see which trees are happy and which ones aren't? You'd have to explain to them what that meant. The thing is, no one knows. Besides, the woods themselves may mean something different to dogs. In any case, for me they're no longer the same woods.

When I got cold looking through the crack, I went back down to the bottom of the cellar. It was much warmer down there. I slept there, ate there. Oh, there was plenty to eat. Not just potatoes. Carrots, beets, cabbage, turnip. When I was thirsty, I drank snow. I managed to push the door open a tiny bit, just enough to reach out my hand and get a handful of snow.

I didn't count on anyone finding me there. To be honest, I didn't want anyone to find me. Besides, who could it have been? The whole place was deserted, silent, nothing but the snow. You'll find this hard to believe, but I was actually beginning to feel comfortable there. I felt the way I did when I was lying in the bottom of the boat in the reeds, and they'd be calling me, father, mother, my sisters, and I'd pretend not to hear. I'd imagine them scolding me later, Where on earth were you? You're nothing but trouble. We were calling and calling.

No animal came by, no bird flew over or perched on a tree. It was only some time later that I saw a hare, though even then I just caught a glimpse of it on top of the snow. Some time after that, I don't know how long it could have been since I saw the hare, I wasn't counting the days – I guess I could have put one potato aside each day, say, but what for? When you count, it means you're counting on something. Whereas me, I wasn't counting on anything, like I told you. Anyway, after a while a deer appeared. I didn't think it was real. I stared and I couldn't believe my eyes. I thought I must be dreaming, because it was standing more or less where the kitchen had been. Plus it was calm, tame, you rarely see deer that calm and trusting. It stood there like nothing could scare it away. It must have been hungry, it started grubbing in the snow with its muzzle. I thought about tossing it some potatoes, it might come even closer. But I couldn't open the door any wider. Then suddenly, though nothing had startled it, it just vanished. You know, when you look at nothing but snow, and through a crack in a door at that, everything happens in a different way. And different things happen than when there's no snow.

I'd glue my eye to that crack in the door, and it was like looking through a stereoscope at Christmas postcards. For instance, one time a Christmas tree decorated with candles appeared where our living room had been. The candles burned so brightly that everywhere else all around became dark as night, even though it was daytime. Or suddenly, beyond the woods a star began to fall from the sky, big and glowing, with a shining tail. I had to take my eye away from the crack, because I couldn't stare at it for long. Then one day I looked out and the three kings were passing by. How did I know they were kings? They wore crowns. They looked lost, because they walked a ways, turned around and went off in a different direction.

One time father took me to market and we went into a store to buy notebooks. Under the glass counter top they had postcards like that, among other things the three kings walking across snow, and someone was pointing the way to them, not this way, that way. I couldn't tear my eyes away. It was the first time I'd seen postcards. I even got up the courage to ask the clerk what you did with them.

"You send them," he said.

I started badgering father:

"Daddy, let's buy one and send it."

"Who to?" He tugged me away impatiently. "We don't have anyone to send it to. Everyone's here."

One time there was the sound of sleigh bells. I stuck my eye to the crack. It got louder and louder, it was clearly coming in my direction. Then, suddenly it started to move further away, till it faded completely. I never saw the sleigh, or who was driving it. Another time, carol singers appeared. They were walking in single file, one after another, they could barely lift their feet clear of the snow. In the lead was the Star, after him King Herod, the Marshal, the Jew, the Watchman, while the Devil brought up the rear. I was surprised Death wasn't there. I thought to myself, who's going to cut Herod's head off? But maybe Death was there after all, it was just that Death is white, and against the snow you couldn't tell if he was there. The way you sometimes can't tell dreams from waking life.

Mr. Robert, ever since we first met, every Christmas he'd send me one of those cards, and I'd send one to him. We'd choose the kind I'm talking about, with Christmas trees, carolers, the three kings and so on. He'd often select one that he made fun of in what he wrote on the back. I'm sending you what's left of our naivety, check out the other side.

One Christmas I was picking out a card for him when I saw one that was just like what I'd seen through the crack in the door. Exactly the same. A star was falling beyond some woods, and the world lay under a blanket of snow. I bought it, bought a stamp right away, addressed it almost without thinking and sent it. Not to Mr. Robert. To this place. With no message. I mean, what message could I have sent? Ever since then, every Christmas I would send a card like that. Without a message. One time only, I wondered about signing it: Yours. But what does that mean? Whose? They never came back. How could they, I never gave a return address. Pointless, you reckon? I thought so too. But Christmas would come around again and I'd send another one. You might not agree with me, but to my mind it's only on postcards that the world is still the way we'd like it to be. That's why we send them to one another.

No, I didn't think about what would happen when the snow melted. I ate, I slept, I looked through the crack in the door, and when it came down to it I wasn't sure whether I was alive. Maybe I was simply waiting, thinking I would melt along with the snow. Why wouldn't I? When a person isn't sure that they're alive, maybe they could melt with the snow.

Then out of nowhere, one day a group of partisans appeared. That morning the sun was shining brightly, the woods had become transparent, it was like the trees had parted, and I could see them coming from a long way off. You might not believe me, but I wanted them to walk on by. Shout that I was there? No way. I'll say more, it was only then that I started to be afraid. I went back down to the bottom of the cellar, I even climbed up on a pile of potatoes by the wall. To one side there were potatoes, on the other there were the carrots, beets, cabbage, turnip. In the middle was a clear space where you could stand, put your basket down and fill it.

It wasn't that it was because of them it had all happened. Whoever it might have been, I didn't want to be found. They often came to the village. In summer, in winter, at any time of the day or night. In wintertime they'd stay the longest. There wasn't a house where they didn't make themselves at home. At times there were more of them than the people who lived there. They'd sleep in attics, barns, in the regular rooms too if someone had more than one room. The officers always stayed in the houses. They had to be fed, and they'd tend to their wounds. Often a doctor had to be fetched, though I don't remember anyone in the village ever bringing a doctor for themselves. People would make their own treatments, they had herbs and ointments, they drank infusions, gave rub-downs, did cuppings. And when that didn't help, they died. There were all kinds of ways of treating sicknesses. For example, do you know what hare's-tongue is? No, it's actually fat. It's the best thing for an infected wound. For burns, aloes. For rheumatism, you'd sting the affected place with nettles. Me too, I sometimes go and put my hands in nettles. Or you'd put bees on them. Even the worst broken bones, there were people who knew how to set them. Without plaster, they used firewood sticks. Or do you know what it means to say a child is dry? It's when a baby's born with a dislocated hip. Grandmother always mended hips like that. They'd bring her the child, say it wouldn't stop crying. First she'd place the baby's legs next to each other to see if the folds lined up. If they didn't, it meant it was a dry child. At those times you had to leave the house, the baby would scream so much in her hands. But in our village no one limped. Not every illness could be treated. But treatment isn't always about having a solution. It's enough for someone to know there's no solution and that's why they have to die.

You know, fetching a doctor was easier said than done. It was a long way, plus not every doctor was willing to take the risk. One time they made father go, and we all prayed until he came back. Then he had to take the doctor back again, and again we prayed for his safe return. So sometimes people were sick of the partisans. Especially because on top of everything they drank, and you had to have moonshine to give them. They even organized little dances. Some of them played the harmonica, they'd gather all the unmarried girls, and the girls were raring to go. Afterwards one or another of them found herself pregnant.

Each time they came to the village, a few of them had died in the meantime. That didn't stop them drinking and partying. When they drank they'd some-times fire their guns in the air. The village was in the middle of the woods, far from highways and the railroad, they thought no one would hear. Honestly though, it was kind of fun when they were there. It was like a different place. Not right away. When they first arrived, their faces were always hollow-cheeked and dark. Their eyes were sleepy, bloodshot, every glance they gave seemed like suspicion. When one of them smiled it didn't look like a human smile. They all had long beards, as if they hadn't shaved since their last visit. A few of them would have bandages around their heads, in some cases blood was still seeping through. One had an arm in a sling. Another would be limping. Some only had one boot on, the other foot was wrapped in bloody rags. A few of them were being carried. Those were the ones they usually called the doctor for. And let me tell you, they stank to high heaven.

The first thing they did was delouse themselves. Maybe because lice itch even more than dirt. When they bite, they're more trouble than wounds. We never had lice in our home, mother saw to that. If even one showed up, she'd launder everything at once. Then she'd iron it all with an iron so hot it hissed. Especially along the seams. That was where the lice most liked to hide. We all had to take a bath, wash our hair, comb it with the finest comb. There were special combs for when you had lice. The teeth were so close together there was barely any space between them. On top of that she'd slather us with sabadilla. You don't know what that is? In those days it was the most effective thing for head lice. There were guys who came selling stuff around the villages, they had buttons, safety pins, snap fasteners, needles, pins, threads. They also sold hair clasps, tape for lining, ribbons to make bows for little girls. What else? All kinds of things. Shoelaces, shoe polish, bunion cream, rooster powders – that was what they called pain medication, but only for headaches. Rooster powders. They had pretty much anything that might come in handy around the house. The housewives would look forward to them coming. People rarely rode into town to market, only when they had more than usual to sell. But sabadilla was always needed. It was almost like holy water.

So the lice would appear the moment the partisans showed up. They hadn't learned to delouse themselves. Not all of them, some of them must have been shown how to do it by their mothers or grandmothers. Because they'd find them and just throw them away. You've never had lice? Let me tell you, if you've not had lice you've not truly been in this world. One war after another and you've never had lice, that's pretty strange. I'm just saying in general, not about you in particular. In this world you have to have had lice at least once, and you have to know how to get rid of them. Grandfather even wondered how they knew how to fight if they didn't know how to delouse themselves. He said that the first duty of a soldier is to know how to deal with lice, then with hunger, then with the home he's left behind. Only then is he fit to kill other soldiers or civilians. Though that didn't stop grandfather sitting and watching them delouse themselves. He'd even point and say, look, there's one, there's another. It was hardly surprising that later he brought the lice home with him.

Then they'd bathe, shave, get a haircut, wash their hair, launder their clothes, dress their wounds, till they became completely unlike the men who had arrived. The ones who'd arrived were old, and these were young men. Some were still children. In many cases it was hard to believe it was the same person. They arrived barely dragging their feet, then afterwards they'd want to dance.

All of a sudden the snow crunched outside the cellar, the door creaked, and a shaft of light fell across the floor. I couldn't be seen in it, because as I said I was sitting outside on a mound of potatoes. But I heard a girl's shrill voice:

"Hello? Is anybody there?"

In the first moment I wondered if it could be Jagoda or Leonka. They had girlish voices.

"Hello? Is anybody there?"

It was only then that I knew it wasn't either of them. They'd probably seen where I'd scooped out snow to drink from beside the door, and figured out there must be someone down in the cellar. She came maybe one step down, her voice got louder, though it was still girlish, it even sounded a little afraid:

"Is anybody there? Say something!"

I didn't step out, I swear. All at once something happened that couldn't have been predicted. The pile of potatoes I was sitting on collapsed with a crash, and I came tumbling down with them. No, it wasn't fate. We'd been taking potatoes again and again from the pile, it was bound to tumble sooner or later. All it would need would be one more potato being taken, and the pile wouldn't hold together anymore. The only question is, why at that particular moment, not some other time. The bough of a tree breaks off right at the second someone's passing by. Is that fate? I heard her shout up above me:

"Oh my lord!" She scrambled out and started shouting:

"There's someone alive in here! There's someone alive!"

There was nothing I could do, I had to show myself alive. When you hear an almost angelic voice above you, at a moment when it seems the world doesn't exist, and you don't exist in it – it's as if the voice was summoning you and the world to life. What was I supposed to do, shout out that I wasn't there? I started to clamber towards her, the light flooded my eyes, so the first thing I saw was an armband with a red cross on her sleeve, before I saw the rest of her. She said in a shocked voice:

"Lord, you're nothing but a child!"

I must say she cut me to the quick with that comment about being a child. I thought, damn girl. And it turned out I was right. She was really young, with such fair hair, though in her army greatcoat and forage cap she might have seemed a lot older than she was. Especially because the coat was much too big for her, the sleeves were rolled right up to here, and the cap would have also been too big if it hadn't been for her hair. Her voice was the only indication of how old she might be. As you know, appearances can deceive but the voice, never. All the more so in uniform. In uniform the youngest soldier always looks much older than he actually is. Even children – when they're in uniform it looks like it'd be no problem for them to kill, slaughter, burn. Besides, even aside from the uniform, when you were as young as I was then, even someone who's just a few years more than you looks virtually old. Later it changes, the years draw closer together, and the closer you are to death the more everything evens out. In particular since death doesn't choose among us according to age. I wouldn't say it's random. Death has its own wisdom.

She was a medic, you could tell from the armband with the red cross. When I came out from the cellar I saw that over her shoulder she was carrying a bag that also had a red cross. The bag was too heavy for her, her shoulder drooped. There was a whole drugstore in there. Actually, it wasn't just the bag that was too heavy for her. She was the only medic for the whole unit, can you imagine. I never heard her complain, but it was clear that the whole thing was beyond her strength. Constantly she was washing bandages, dressing wounds, handing out pills for aches and pains and fevers, she'd wipe the men's foreheads, clean away the blood and the dirt – often from head to foot – when one of them was too weak to stand on his own two feet and kept calling her to come here and go there, day and night.

Even today, when I think of her I find it hard to imagine that someone could be so young and work without any relief – anyone her age deserves a break. I couldn't tell you exactly how old she was, she never mentioned her age, maybe she was embarrassed, but she put up with it all like someone much, much older.

Actually, in the depths of my soul I wanted her to be a whole lot older. Not for the reason you think. It's only up to a certain age that you want something like that, then your desire starts to turn back. You think that from that moment we become worse people? I don't think I agree. We're already worse when we play in the sandbox.

Did you ever play in a sandbox when you were a child? Me neither. Why would anyone have made a sandbox for children in the village? There was sand everywhere, in abundance. Wherever the river turned, one bank would be sandy. You could roll in the sand, bury yourself, build things in sand, whatever you felt like. And not just by the Rutka. Though village kids aren't drawn to sand the way children in the city are. You've got fields, meadows, woods, everything is wide open in every direction, above you, in the distance, who would want to play in sand? You could play anywhere. Like living, people lived wherever. Big houses weren't necessary, no one needed to be apart. People lived in the yards, in the barns, in the cattle sheds, the orchards, the fields, on the meadows, under the sky, by the Rutka. The whole world was our home, while our actual home was only there so we could all come together at the end of the day. So everyone wanted to be as close as possible to the next person. In some houses there wasn't even a separate living room, just one big room, then you were closest of all. It was only when you were tightly crammed in that you could truly feel you were together. Who would have made a sandbox for the children, when the children also wanted to feel they were part of everyone else. If it had occurred to anyone to build a sandbox like you see in the cities, do you think any child would have wanted to play in it? You could have tied them there on a chain, they would have broken free. And the sandbox would have become a home for chickens and geese and ducks, they like to play in sand, they would have made a big old mess in there and that would have been the end of the sandbox.

When I was abroad I spent a lot of time watching sandboxes. Wherever I lived, in among the apartment buildings there were always sandboxes. As I mentioned, I like children, and so whenever I had a little time I'd sit on a bench by one of the sandboxes, among the nannies and mothers and grandmothers. And let me tell you, when I watched the children playing in the sandbox, I'd sometimes be moved, but also fearful.

Believe me, a sandbox is a whole world. A couple of square yards, but it's an entire world, humanity, future wars. Nice rosy little faces, you'd think they were all quite innocent, but you could already tell who would bury who in the sand, and who would hide from who in the sand. Which of them would one day find the sandbox too small, and which of them would soon get lost in it. Was the sandbox really to blame? Some people reckon so. But when I think about it I sometimes have the feeling that we're all exiles from the sandbox, whatever our age. Me too, though I never played in a sandbox.

You know, when I was abroad I even saw sandboxes with colored sand.

Green, blue, pink. I think it was dyed. Where could they have found sand in those colors. But can colored sand make us different? It's true that we're affected by colors. But not everyone is influenced to the same extent by the same colors. And we've no idea who is more affected by what color. Or which color fades in which person or which one grows brighter. And are the colors we see the same when they're within us? Besides, tell me this: Can anyone come up with a wiser color for sand than the color of the sun? A wiser color for leaves than green? Or blue for the sky? White for snow? Of course colors are wise. Didn't you know that? If it hadn't been for the white snow back at that time, then . . .

What's my favorite color? What are you, a journalist? No, that much I know for sure. You don't even look like a journalist. What color? Oh, I don't know. I wasn't expecting that question. I don't have a favorite color. Anyway, would it mean anything if I said, for instance, green? Because which green would it be? Each tree in the woods, each bush, each leaf, even moss, is a different kind of green. And in you, all of that turns into a different kind of green again. So can you say that something is green? Green is an infinity. Each color is an infinity.

As I stared through that crack in the cellar door, I was amazed to see one kind of whiteness turned into another, then a moment later into a different kind again, without ever going back to the previous one. It was like waves of whiteness rolling over the white snow. So what do you think the color white is? You're messing with me. You'd like to see me spend my whole life in the sandbox. I'd want that too. Except that no color is forever. Color is change, like everything else.

When I was abroad I'd sometimes visit art galleries and museums. You too? Then you must have noticed that for each artist, the hardest color is the flesh of a woman. Even with the same artist, from one picture to the next. I don't mean that the color changes, just that there's a kind of helplessness in the face of that color. So can you say that a woman's body is such and such a color? Since the color might depend, say, on the painter's self-doubt? Or on his fear, his anguish, his despair? Yes, sometimes his desire as well. As I looked at the paintings I'd often have the impression that all those colors were unequal to some challenge, as it were. No, not what you think – not unequal to the model. Then what challenge? You'd have to provide the answer yourself, if you've been with women.

The sister wasn't at all shy in front of me, she would bathe naked. Sister, that was what everyone called her, me too. Actually, that was the first word I spoke. Sister. Because for the longest time I didn't talk at all. I just didn't. It was like I didn't know how. Like I didn't know any words. I was simply mute. In fact, she was the one who taught me that first word. Call me sister, she said. That's what everyone calls me. Go on, say it: sister. Say, sister. Sis-ter.

She'd always have me stand guard when she bathed.

"You can see me," she'd say. "But make sure none of the others are watching."

Wherever there was a little stream or creek or spring, she'd always bathe. Actually we only ever stopped at places where there was water. After all, you had to have something to drink, to clean yourself in, and there was always a lot of stuff that needed washing. Bandages for a start. I helped her with it all. Whatever needed washing I'd carry down to the water, then later hang it out on branches to dry. I didn't speak, but I understood what was said to me, by her and by the others. Whenever she was dressing a wound I'd hold things for her, take things out of her bag, use the scissors, help her tie the bandage. When she had to wash someone because they were lying there like they were dead, I'd hold his head up, or his side if he needed to be turned on his side. I'd take his boots off, because she'd always wash his feet as well, even though his feet weren't injured, she'd say it'd be easier for him with clean feet. You can't imagine what state their feet were in, covered in blisters, sores, scabs, often rubbed to the point of bleeding, infected.

One time we came to a biggish lake in the woods. We stopped there for longer than usual. They said the place was untouched by humans, no one would find us there. It was true, you could even tell from the trees, they were falling over from old age. You could pick your fill of mushrooms, blackberries, wild strawberries, blueberries. And there were birds everywhere you turned, let me tell you. Birds to your heart's content. Right from daybreak the woods echoed with birdsong. On the lake there were moorhens, ducks, swans. It was the perfect place to rest up after all that walking, catch up on some sleep, lick your wounds, and even forget about the war for a short while. The truth was that I didn't know if it was still going on or if maybe it was over. No one said anything. We kept trekking about in the woods, avoiding the villages. I remember one time we crossed some railroad tracks, another time we went over a bridge, and one night we spent in a windmill. All I saw was them carrying out full sacks of something and putting them in a wagon. They told me to sit on the sacks. Then they walked alongside, and I rode on the wagon. In the end I fell asleep, and when someone eventually took me down from the sacks we were already back in the woods. Another time we were at some country estate, though only in the grounds. They brought out some food for us, we ate then moved on.

The sister always led me by the hand. Every so often she'd ask if I was tired. Sometimes one of the men would give me a piggyback ride for a bit. In the winter they made dugouts and we lived in them, so the war could have been over by then. At home they always used to talk about how it'd be over by Christmas, or by Easter. Here no one said anything. Not around me, in any case. Whenever they were talking about something and I came by, they'd fall silent. One time they didn't notice me, it was evening, a bunch of them were sitting by the campfire. The only thing I caught was, Till the final victory. I might have heard more, but I trod on a dry branch and they stopped talking.

Truth be told, I didn't particularly want it to end. I liked being with them. The sister was like a real sister to me, I grew attached to her, and I couldn't imagine that we could ever be parted. I could have figured out one thing or another, but I preferred not to. For example, it sometimes happened that a small group of them, or a dozen or more, would all of a sudden grab their guns and head out. They'd come back in the early morning, or the following night, when I was asleep. Where they'd been, I had no idea. How could I ask when I didn't talk?

We always ate better after one of those trips. There'd be bread and lard, sometimes a bit of meat in the soup. The soup itself would be different, instead of being made from a little of everything as it seemed, we'd have for instance pea soup. When it was pea soup everyone rubbed their hands in anticipation. We also ate better when they caught something in a trap or a snare. They weren't allowed to hunt with guns. Otherwise, we mostly just ate millet porridge. You know what millet is? No? Well, I'm not going to explain it to you, because ever since then I've hated millet porridge. Where they got it from I couldn't say. Just like I couldn't say where they went with their guns.

One time, from one of those expeditions they brought me back a tin of acid drops, another time a ball, then once it was a game of checkers, and one of them taught me how to play. Then I would always play with him. Another time a book, *Andersen's Fairy Tales.* Do you know it? They said that if I started to read, maybe I'd begin to speak as well. Though when they took their guns it wasn't so they could bring me acid drops or a ball or checkers or a book of fairy tales. I tried to read in my head, because I couldn't do it with my mouth. I barely got to the end of the page, it was such hard work I'd rather have been shelling beans. Though like I said, I couldn't stand shelling beans.

I basically couldn't read, though in school I'd been the best reader. I read pretty well. I liked reading. At home, in the evenings I used to sometimes read aloud to everyone. Jagoda and Leonka were both older than me, Jagoda was two classes ahead of me and Leonka three, but they weren't as good at reading as I was. The sister noticed one time that I was having trouble.

"Here, I'll read to you," she said.

From that time, not every day because she didn't always have time during the day, and in the evenings we didn't use lights, but when she could she'd read to me. At least a page or two. Though often her eyes would be closing from exhaustion. Sometimes one or another of the men would listen in, sometimes a few of them. Grown men listening to fairy tales, you can imagine? And partisans into the bargain.

She'd always mark her place in the book with a dry leaf. Later she'd keep the leaf, because she'd say she couldn't bring herself to throw away such a beautiful leaf. And she'd mark the new place with another leaf. I would find the leaves for her, I'd hunt around for the nicest ones. I often went all over the woods. Then, of the best ones that I'd gathered, we'd choose the nicest one of all.

"Shall we use this one?"

I'd always want to use the one she picked.

"Where do you find such lovely leaves?" she'd ask admiringly each time.

Let me tell you, to hear that admiration of hers I would have climbed up into the trees, not just looked around on the ground underneath them. There were oaks, beeches, maples, elms, sycamores, all kinds of trees. She virtually filled the book with leaves. We only had a few tales left to read, but she didn't manage to finish the book. Later I'll show you the book. I have it in the living room. Don't worry, I'm not going to read to you. The ones that are unread, let them stay that way. No, the copy with the leaves got lost. This one I bought myself.

I went to get some sheet music one time, and the store also carried books. I'd already bought the music, and I was just browsing idly among the books. All at once I see *Andersen's Fairy Tales*. My heart pounded. I paid, brought it home and put it on my bedside table. I was living alone, my wife had left me not long before. I'd always read at bedtime. Whether or not I was tired, I always had to read a page or two at least. Even after just one page I'd feel myself calming down and everything resuming its place, then after five or ten more pages my eyes would start to let me know they were about to close. I didn't need sleeping pills. But the remaining tales, the ones she didn't manage to read, somehow I could never bring myself to read them either.

These days I supposedly have much more time, now that the season's over. I don't need to sleep because I don't have to be fresh in the morning. But still I've never turned to those fairy tales. I do read, just not so much anymore. Nowadays not even books can make me fall asleep. Besides, I have the sense that books can no longer help me understand the things I'd like to understand here at the end.

When I was working on the electrification of the villages, in one house where we were installing the wiring I saw *Andersen's Fairy Tales* lying on a windowsill. I asked the owner if I could borrow it. He said:

"You can have it. We don't need it. It belonged to our boy. He got killed. Stepped on a mine."

I took it back to our lodgings, four of us were rooming together, and I meant to read a bit in bed that evening. One of the other guys whose bed was next to mine noticed the book and started to laugh.

"What, are you reading fairy tales?"

Another guy piped up from another bed:

"What you need is a girl. One that's the right shape here and here, got some flesh on her."

I was embarrassed, I pulled my suitcase out from under my bed and stuffed the book beneath my shirt and socks and other things, right at the bottom. Then I started work at the building site, but I never reached for my suitcase to take the book out and read it. In the end I gave it to one of the guys to give to his son. He was going home one Sunday and he was worried that he didn't have a present for his kid. I asked:

"How old is he?" I took out the *Fairy Tales*. "Give him this. It's just right for his age. I was the same age."

But why was the sister not shy in front of me? I don't know. Maybe because I didn't speak? Or for some other reason?

One time I was on guard to make sure no one was watching her, I was standing with my back to the lake and she was undressing on the shore. Suddenly she called out:

"Turn around! Do I make you feel uncomfortable? Come over here! When was the last time you bathed?" I didn't know how to tell her it hadn't been that long. "I bet it's been ages," she said. "All of you here like being dirty. Take your clothes off. You can wash with me." I stood there rooted to the spot. "What are you staring at me for? Haven't you had your fill of looking yet?" I averted my eyes. "Don't just stand there, get undressed. Come on, I'll help you." Left to myself I don't think I could have so much as unfastened a single button on my shirt. "Lift your head up. Give me your arm. Raise your foot. Have a good look, look all you like. At your age what do you know? You haven't even got any hairs down there. So it can already get stiff? Still, you've got time. Though the rest of us might not be alive by then. Not me in any case, that's for sure. Come on, hop in the water with me."

She leaped in. Like a colorful blur, that's how I remember her. All the colors were in her. I've never found her since in any painting. I don't remember her face anymore, but I can still see the blur of her body.

"Come on, jump in!" she repeated, emerging from the water. "Let's swim to the other side! Don't be afraid, I'll be right by you!"

I wasn't afraid, I was a pretty good swimmer. I'd swum many times in the Rutka, downstream, or against the current. She swam by me, and when we got near the other side she asked:

"Are you tired? Let's climb out and sit awhile."

We got there, sat on the shore and gazed out.

"The lake's even more beautiful from this side," she said. "It would be beautiful to die in it." She lost herself in thought, then a moment later she said: "Look at me. Don't turn your eyes away. I want you to remember me. Will you remember me? Tell me you will. You'll survive for certain. Because us–" She broke off. I looked at her. I thought I was seeing things, but no, tears were streaming down her cheeks. "I'm not crying," she said, though I hadn't said anything. "My face is wet from the water, that's all. Yours is too. I could just as well say you're crying."

But I actually was crying. Not on the outside. I felt somehow as if the tears were flowing inside of me, on the other side of my eyes. Have you ever known tears like that? For me, it was only that once. And for the first time since she'd found me in the cellar, I felt words in my mouth.

"Sister . . . ," I said. I got stuck. Then: "I'll . . ." Then: "always . . ."

She didn't let me finish. She burst out in joy:

"You're talking! You're talking!" She wiped the tears from her cheeks. "Let's swim back! We'll tell everyone you're talking!"

What was I trying to say then? I don't recall. Perhaps it wasn't anything important. But for me those had been the most important words of my whole life that I'd wanted to say but hadn't said. If you sat down and thought about it, how many unspoken words like that must have disappeared forever? And they may have been more important than all the ones that were spoken. Don't you think?

There was only one thing I couldn't understand: why she hadn't wanted to admit she was crying. And she was, I could have sworn she was.

At that age, there are a lot of things you maybe don't understand, but you feel things deeper than if you'd understood them. Plus, you see everything, you see it through and through. Life can't be concealed from anyone, least of all a child. There's no curtain you can use to hide it. A child will even see through a curtain. Sometimes I wonder if children aren't our conscience. Later you see less and less. The world's no longer willing to be reflected in people's eyes. Although a child doesn't even have to look. The world pushes under his eyelids of its own accord. The world is still transparent at that age. Unfortunately, you grow out of it. Today I find it hard to believe I was once a child. I used to graze the cattle, but what proof is that of anything. Before that I minded the geese. Then grandfather took over the geese, and I took the cows from him. And I imagined that we'd just keep swapping like that the whole time. Grandfather would take over the cows from me, and I'd take the geese again. Then he'd mind the geese once more, and I'd mind the cows. And it would always be like that, cows to geese, geese to cows. I was convinced that since grandfather had always been grandfather from the beginning, I'd also always be a child.

Though if you ask me, geese are harder to mind. Yours get mixed up with other people's, they're all white, and afterwards there's no way of telling which are yours and which aren't. Not to mention that they often fight till they bleed, they latch onto each other so hard you can't pull them apart, especially the ganders.

We kept a lot of geese, to have down to stuff quilts, and pillows for Jagoda and

Leonka for when they got married. Mother wanted them to have down bedding, and for that you need lots and lots of geese. And you'll be plucking away for years. It takes a huge amount of down to make a feather quilt, and there's not that many feathers on a goose.

So I always preferred minding the cows. To make a long story short, I'll tell you one thing. Mother would sometimes despair over me:

"You were such a good child when you minded the geese."

The pasture was the road that led directly to adulthood. Whoever graduated from the pasture was no longer a child, even if they were called one. And the sister always treated me like a child. From the first moment of surprise when I emerged from the cellar. Lord, you're nothing but a child! And so on till the very end. Maybe that's why it was OK for me to look while she was bathing, whereas she was afraid of letting all the others see? I don't know, that's exactly what I don't get, especially after what happened one night. So I stood there and kept guard to make sure they didn't peep.

Oh yes, almost all of them. When one of them saw she was going down to the lake, he'd sneak off immediately and follow her at a distance, hide behind a bush or a tree, or even climb a tree if there was one nearby on the shore. Sometimes even the wounded would drag themselves down to the lake. Some of them would back off when they saw me standing guard. But not everyone. A good few of them, it made no difference whether I was standing there or not. Many of them would give me an earful. Or tell me to keep my trap shut and sit tight. One guy, he had binoculars, he'd lie down right next to me, by a bush or under a tree, and it was like I wasn't even there. When I moved he'd say, Stay still or I'll shoot you. He was a huge guy, with a nasty look in his eye, as if he didn't even like himself that much. For a guy like that, shooting someone was like eating a slice of bread. I was terrified of him. So I'd stand there stock still whenever he came to watch.

One time he told me to stand and not say a word, while she had undressed on the shore and it looked like she had no intention of going into the water, she was just enjoying the sun. He lay down, put the binoculars to his eyes and watched and watched. My heart was beating harder than ever before. All of a sudden he smashed his fist against the ground, rested his head on the earth and groaned:

"Dear Christ, dear Christ." He turned his face upwards. "What I'd give to be between her legs. A guy would know what he was fighting for." He wiped his eyes from the binoculars. "They're going to kill us all anyway, what difference would it make to her." He held the binoculars out towards me. "Wanna look?" I shrugged. "Right, maybe it's best you don't."

As it happened, a few days later there was a muster in the middle of the night, the men formed two lines, it was, count off, they all shouldered arms and marched off. The sister went with them. I stayed back with the wounded and some sentries. The others only came back three days later, around daybreak. They looked like a hounded pack of wolves. Several of them were wounded, two were being carried on stretchers made from branches. And the one I was so afraid of had the sister in his arms. She was dead. He himself had a head wound, his hair was caked with blood, blood was running down inside his collar. He'd refused to let anyone else carry her the whole way. They'd wanted to make another stretcher and carry her on it, but he wouldn't allow them. Four others had died too, but they'd been left behind. He'd risked heavy rifle fire to retrieve her body. That was when he'd been injured. She'd died dressing the wounds of one of the men who had fallen. It had been pointless. The man had only been able to open his eyes and say, There's no point, sister. Then he was dead. Who heard it? You ask like you didn't know there's always someone who hears. There's no situation in which there isn't someone who hears.

You know, she sensed that she was going to die. Or maybe she just didn't want to live? One time I helped her take the laundry down to the lake. There was a lot of it. As she washed and rinsed the things, I took them and hung them out to dry on the branches. It was one of those days that don't come along very often. The sky was blue as can be, without the tiniest cloud. The lindens were in bloom, you could smell honey in the air, bees were buzzing, the heat was intensifying, it was the perfect weather for washing and drying. All at once she dropped the clothes, sat down on the shore, pulled her knees up under her chin, put her arms around them, and stared and stared at the lake.

"I really don't feel like doing the laundry today," she said. "What I'd most like to do is go lie down on the lake, you know? Just lie there. What do you think, would I sink?"

She jumped to her feet and started to undress.

"I'm going to go bathe. You keep guard. Go stand over there."

And she leaped into the water. I watched her swimming, and I began to choke with fear that in a moment she'd lie down on the water and stop moving. Luckily she swam for a bit and came back. She got dressed again.

"Now get on with the laundry, sister," she said, telling herself off. In between giving me items of clothing to hang out, she said: "You know what, you should move in and live with me, would you like to? Goodness, it's hard to even call it living in these dugouts, these pits." When I took the next piece of clothing from her to hang it out: "None of them have tried anything with you?" I didn't know what she meant. "What are you staring at me for? That's why you're going to live with me. Too bad I didn't think of it sooner. Maybe I'll be able to sleep better too." I didn't understand either why she couldn't sleep.

She brought a litter and made a place for me next to her. She had to squeeze over a bit so there'd be room for me. After picking out all the pine cones and acorns and twigs from the litter, she covered the litter with dry grass. So it'll be nice and soft for you, she said. Then she laid some old rags on top. Sometimes, on a cooler night she'd ask if I was warm enough and put her coat over the blanket I slept under. But I didn't sleep that well with her. Even though neither of us snored, or smoked cigarettes, or swore, or shouted in our sleep. She slept as quiet as anything, often I couldn't hear a thing. It was just that the silence was hard for me to bear. It was the silence itself that woke me up several times a night.

I'd jerk awake, listening fearfully to see if she was asleep. If I couldn't hear her breathing, I'd get up from the bedding and place my ear close to her. And though I'd be reassured that she was sleeping, I often couldn't get back to sleep myself.

One night, I don't know why, I woke terrified, I sat up and gently touched her forehead to see if it was warm. She jolted upright, equally scared:

"Oh, it's you. I had such a fright. Don't touch me ever when I'm sleeping. Remember, don't touch me."

"I just wanted –"

"I know," she said. "Lie down and go back to sleep."

There were also times when she would sit up from her bedding and, holding her breath, she would listen to see if I was asleep. When she was sure I was, though in fact I was pretending, she'd take her coat if she hadn't put it over me and she'd go off somewhere. All kinds of thoughts rattled around in my brain at those times, and I'd wait till she came back. When she did, sometimes I'd pretend to have just woken up.

"Did I wake you? I'm sorry. I went to bathe. In the nighttime at least no one watches you," she explained. "The water's so warm. It's a full moon. The lake is even lovelier than during the day."

That was how it was every time. So I decided I wouldn't wake up anymore when she came back. But one time when she returned, and I was pretending to be asleep, she lay down and all of a sudden I heard her crying.

"I know you're not asleep," she said. "I can't take it anymore. It's so hard for them. But I can't take it any longer."

11

Lost yourself in thought there, did you? What were you thinking about, if I may ask? True, there's a lot to think about. And there doesn't have to be any particular reason. There's just lots of things to think about in general. In one country I once saw a sculpture. This man lost in thought. You've seen it too? There you go. I stood in front of it and began to wonder. I really wanted to ask what he was thinking about. But how can you ask a sculpture? If a person really decided to think about themselves so hard, they'd probably become a sculpture too. But in that case, tell me, is it only sculptures and paintings and books and music that can think about themselves, while we can't?

I don't mean anything in particular. I was just asking you, as if I were asking that sculpture. Of course I know I won't get an answer either from you or from the sculpture. Sometimes people ask a question without expecting an answer. You have to agree there are questions that are sufficient in themselves. Especially as no answer would satisfy them anyway. And if you ask me, it has nothing to do with what we're asking about. It's a matter of who is asking who. Even when we're asking ourselves, there's always one who's asking and one who's being asked. It only seems like the person doing the asking is the same one giving the answer. If you think about it though, it's always a different person asking and a different person answering. Or not answering, because maybe for instance they're lost in thought. Every question selects an appropriate someone inside us. Even the most trivial question chooses a different person. Not just the person who's supposed to answer it, but also the one who's supposed to ask it. And with each question both the one and the other will be different people. After all, inside us there's a child, and an old man, and a young man, and someone who's going to die, and someone who doubts, and someone who has hope, and someone who no longer has any. And so on, and so forth.

If things were otherwise, no one would ever have to ask themselves anything, or have to answer anything. Yet no one can say of themselves that that's me, that's the way I was and the way I'm going to be in the future. No person can draw the boundaries of their self or establish themselves as themselves. That's why we keep having to ask ourselves questions, first from one self, then from that one, then from another one still, and ask first one person, then another, then a third person, even though none of the questions is going to be answered anyway.

See – we're sitting here shelling beans, you could say you're here, I'm here, and between our hands we feel every pod, and every bean that we shell from it. Yet what's more important still is how you and I imagine one another, how I imagine myself in relation to you, and how you imagine yourself in relation to me. The fact that we can see each other shelling beans doesn't prove anything. If all we were doing was shelling beans, that wouldn't be enough to experience the shelling. It's only our imaginings of one another that fill out the fact that we're shelling beans. Just like they fill out everything. Honestly, I even think it's only what's imagined that's actually real.

Why does that surprise you? Then I don't understand why it was me you came to for beans. I mean, you couldn't have known I grow them. A few, just enough for myself, like I said. So all the more you couldn't have expected me to have any to sell. And at this time of year who would come and visit me here? At the most someone from the dead. So I couldn't have expected you either. Besides, I was going to go to bed soon. I would just have done my rounds of the cabins. I usually go to bed about this time. It's early, because nightfall's getting earlier these days. Though I read in bed a bit, listen to music, before I fall asleep, or don't fall asleep, it varies. If I do get to sleep I'll wake up after an hour or two, read some more, listen to music again, till I drop back off. Then when I wake again I'll get up and do the rounds. Sometimes, though, there'll be a night that's like daytime, I go to bed but I know I won't fall asleep. On nights like those I get up and repaint some nameplates. It takes me a long time, as you saw, but I hope to get them all done. If I had the hands I used to have, when I played . . .

Here there was a knock at the door, and I wondered, who could it be? It was you, and you were asking about beans. I'd understand if you'd been asking for directions, how to get out of here, which way to go. Or which cabin is Mr. Robert's, because you want to stay there, then I would have shown you, it's that one over there, and told you where the key is. But you must admit, the fact that you wanted to buy beans from me could have made me suspicious. What if I hadn't had any? Besides, you were convinced I wouldn't. You didn't think you'd be at my place long. Don't deny it. I even wondered, do I have any or not, because maybe this much life would have been enough. It was just that I'd noticed how you remind me of someone. Especially in that overcoat and hat, we must have met before, even if only by chance. Do I have any or not, yes or no, I started scouring my memory. But memory is like a well, the deeper you go, the darker it gets.

Forgive me for asking, but how would you define chance? Why do I ask? Because one time, when I was living abroad I was on my way to rehearsal one afternoon, and I see someone coming toward me who actually looked a little like you, now that I've gotten a good look at you. We hadn't yet crossed, there were still a few yards between us. I might not have noticed him at all, but all of a sudden he tipped his hat and nodded to me. Or maybe I was the first one to nod, because I'd seen him smile at me and raise his hand to his hat to tip it, and I wanted to beat him to it. Besides, it makes no difference whether it was him or me. And like that, him raising his hat over his head, me raising mine, and smiling at one another in the conviction that we knew each other, we passed.

But the moment we crossed, I turned around to look at him and I saw he was staring at me also. Where we'd met and when, I couldn't recall. Nor could he, because why would he have looked back at me if he'd remembered when and where. I walked on a few steps and turned again. Believe it or not, he had also turned back again. I decided to go up and ask where we knew each other from. At that exact moment he also started towards me, with the same intention as it transpired. We walked up to one another, raised our hats again, but I see he's a little embarrassed, and I'm disappointed, because we can both see we don't know one another.

"I'm terribly sorry," I said. "I don't believe we know each other."

"I'm afraid I don't remember you," he replied.

"Oh well, just an unfortunate chance. It happens. Once again I'm very sorry." I raised my hat again and was about to walk away. But he held me back.

"It isn't chance, my dear sir," he said. "There's no such thing as chance. After all, what is chance? No more than a justification for what we're unable to understand. So we shouldn't part like this. Let's at least go get coffee. On me. See, we're even standing outside a cafe. They have good coffee here. I stop by sometimes."

The coffee was indeed good. But the conversation never took off. Especially at the beginning. I barely said anything, I mean, what was I supposed to talk about with a person I'd mistaken for someone else. So I gazed around the cafe, though there wasn't much to look at. It was just a regular cafe. Not that big, a dozen or so tables, rather dimly lit. I don't like dark cafes. The lower half of the walls had dark wood paneling, the top half was wallpapered in dark gold. The tables seemed too bulky for a cafe. The backs of the chairs were almost as high as your head, and the chairs themselves weren't especially comfortable. The only thing I liked were the wall lamps and the chandelier that hung from the ceiling. Each wall lamp was in the form of two female figures holding candlesticks in their outstretched hands, and there was a candle in each one, as if there were no electricity. Each lamp had women from a different historical period. The chandelier also was not electrified, it was filled with real candles and decorated richly with cut glass in different shapes.

He noticed me looking around the cafe, and began to tell me about it. Hardly anything had changed here since the cafe first opened, he said. He mentioned the year, I don't remember exactly when it was, but the place was almost two hundred years old. The tables, chairs, lamps, chandelier, paneling, even the wallpaper was the same color and pattern as two centuries ago. And the candles were lit at dusk just the same. This wasn't only known from descriptions, he said, there were photographs, and a number of paintings of the interior. One artist had gathered all the famous personages who had come here over those two hundred years, as if they'd all come by and taken a table on a single day and at the same time. He mentioned some of them by name, though without telling me what they were famous for. He probably assumed I would know. But at that time none of the names meant anything to me.

At some of the names he lit up as if he used to meet with them here himself, though they'd lived fifty or a hundred years before, or even earlier. He knew a lot about them. In many cases he knew who used to sit at which table. And if they'd been alone or with someone. Whether they drank coffee or tea, or if they preferred wine, and what kind. Which cakes they most liked, or if they didn't like cakes.

There'd also been someone who used to sit at the table we were at. It was the first time I'd heard the name. You knew him? So you know what work he did. That was the only name that stuck in my memory, of all the ones he mentioned. Maybe because, like you just said, he worked on dreams.

Later I bought a book about those dreams of his. We could find ourselves in there too. You, me. Anyone. Supposedly they were just his dreams, but really they were dreams about people. Apparently he would come to the cafe every day. And always at the same time. No more than a minute earlier or later. You could have set your watch by him. Actually, he'd always take out his pocket watch and check whether he'd arrived punctually. And everyone else in the cafe would take out their watches and check they were running right. Some days he'd drink coffee after coffee, especially when he was making notes on a paper napkin. Other times he'd only ask for a glass of water as he sat there lost in thought.

"Was he waiting for someone maybe?" I asked, trying to show I was listening.

Because you have to agree that when you don't arrange to meet someone but you want to see them, then every day at the same time you'll go to the place where you usually meet with them. As if the place itself were capable of making them appear. It's a mistaken belief, that places are more constant than time and death.

"That I don't know," he said. "Waiting is a permanent condition within us. You know, often we don't realize that from birth to death we live in a state of expectation. He'd probably grown attached to the cafe, this table. Those kinds of attachment are often stronger than to other people."

I didn't say anything. I simply didn't understand that anyone could get attached to a cafe, let alone a table.

So when he came into the cafe and saw that his table was occupied, he'd leave right away, even if other tables were free. The proprietor would have to send him an apology and assure him it would never happen again. He was even capable of scolding whoever had taken the table. Once he struck the table with his cane. Two young people were sitting at it, it may have been the first time they'd been in the cafe and they had no idea it was his table. Besides, like all young people, the world still belonged to them, including some table in some cafe or other. So they refused to move to another table, why should they. Everyone knows that cafes are for everyone and that anyone can sit at any table they like. Whoever sits there first, it's their table. And here someone was claiming they'd occupied his table. If I were them, I'd not have moved. Maybe if he'd asked politely, said that he couldn't sit at any other table, because the coffee or tea would taste different. That I'd understand. But he evicted them from the table like he was throwing them out of his own apartment.

One time he slapped someone in the face with his glove because they'd had the temerity to sit at his table. It would surely have ended in a duel, because the other man responded by throwing down his own glove, which meant he was demanding satisfaction. Fortunately the proprietor of the cafe picked the glove up and somehow managed to smooth things over.

After that incident a card was stuck in the napkin holder saying the table was reserved. But he never came back.

Then suddenly the other man said something that made me think:

"The proprietor of the cafe died. His son took over the place. Then his son after him. But on that table, in the napkin holder, the whole time there was a card to say the table was reserved. Perhaps if he'd known it was reserved, that it was waiting for him . . . Then war broke out, and before it ended the cafe was taken over by soldiers. They didn't care whose table was whose, if one of them was reserved or not, because all the tables were theirs. They sat wherever they flopped down, they'd even put their feet up on the tables."

All at once he asked me if I'd like some cake.

"Gladly," I said, though I avoided cakes, just like I wasn't supposed to drink coffee. At that time I had a duodenal ulcer. He beckoned the waitress. She brought over a tray with various cakes, she smiled at him, she evidently knew him, because it wasn't the usual smile you get from a waitress. He looked the tray over and said:

"You should take one of those. They don't have them anywhere else."

I nodded to say that was fine. He chose the same thing for himself. When the waitress took the tongs and was about to put the cake on his plate first, he directed her to my plate and only then let her serve him.

"Delicious, isn't it?"

"Absolutely," I agreed, though I didn't really like it, it had too much cream.

But what else can be said about a cake . . . So we both fell silent. It was my turn to say something. He'd told me all about the cafe, and I hadn't spoken a word. But I didn't know what to talk about. I wasn't particularly disposed toward conversation. Maybe I was overwhelmed by the fact that after greeting each other by mistake on the street, now we were sitting together like old friends, but in fact we didn't know one another. Besides, I was starting to feel a slight pain in my right side, below the ribs, which was a clear consequence of the coffee I'd had, and perhaps also of the cake. I was afraid that the pain would flare up for real, because if that happened I'd be in no state to come up with anything at all to say. Normally when the pain would get worse and worse, all I could ever do was remain silent. Though at moments like that even silence cost me dearly. True, I had my tablets with me, but I wasn't going to start swallowing tablets in front of a stranger. He might ask what was wrong with me. And the conversation would move to duodenal ulcers. Then if he had some illness too, we'd spend the whole of the rest of the time talking about illnesses. Illnesses help out any conversation, as you know. But had we really greeted one another on the street by mistake just so we could talk about illnesses? He'd even claimed it wasn't chance. I preferred not to say anything at all. I put in a word from time to time, but it was more to agree with what he was saying, like with the cake, when he said it was delicious and I said absolutely.

"You know," he said, finally breaking the silence, "they make the cakes here according to recipes that are as old as the cafe itself. Don't you think the coffee tastes differently here than in other cafes?"

"Absolutely," I agreed.

"Yes, the way coffee used to taste," he said, yielding to some kind of nostalgia.

I didn't know what he meant by "the way coffee used to taste," because from my own childhood I only ever remembered ersatz coffee with milk. And then the coffee at school after the war, without milk or sugar, it had the taste of bitter water.

"That's why I come here from time to time," he said. "I wonder how they make it? I asked the owner once, he only said he was glad I liked it. Funny that even cafes have their secrets. The way coffee used to taste . . ." He grew pensive. Then he suddenly snapped out of it: "Have you ever thought about how powerfully we're bound to the past? Not necessarily our own. Besides, what's our past? Where are its boundaries? It's something like an undefined longing, but for what? Is it not for something that never was, but nevertheless has passed? The past is just our imagination, and the imagination needs longing, it actually feeds on longing. The past, my dear sir, has nothing to do with time, despite what people think. Besides, what is time anyway? Does something like time even exist outside of calendars and clocks? We use ourselves up, that's all it boils down to. Like everything else around us. Life is energy, not survival, and energy gets consumed. As for the past, it never goes away, since we're constantly making it anew. It's created by our imagination, that's what determines our memory, gives it its characteristics, dictates its choices, not the other way around. Imagination is the ground of our existence. Memory is no more than a function of our imagination. Imagination is the one place we feel connected to, where we can be certain that that's where we actually live. Then when we come to die, we also die in it. Along with all those who have ever died before, and who help us die in turn."

He abruptly reached into the inside pocket of his coat and took out his wallet.

"Will you let me take care of this?" I said, thinking that he meant to settle the bill, and that by the same token he was indicating that our meeting was over.

"Out of the question," he said. "It was me who invited you. You're my guest, remember? But actually I was going to show you something."

He began rummaging through the compartments of his wallet, taking out various photos, business cards, documents, folded pieces of paper, tickets. He tossed it all on the table and something fell on the floor, but before I could reach down he swooped like a hawk and got there before me.

"Could it be that it's not there? How could that have happened? I always have it on me," he said with worried self-reproach. "I don't have it. I actually don't have it. I don't understand. I'm terribly sorry." He replaced the wallet here, in his breast pocket. "Would you like a glass of liqueur?" he asked suddenly, as if forgetting what he had meant to show me. "They have an excellent almond liqueur. Then wine, perhaps? Too bad. No, I won't take any on my own. If I were alone it would be a different matter. Though I don't know whether in that case I'd feel like drinking anything. You have to have some purpose to also have the desire. That applies just as much to the desire for life. Where are you from?" he asked out of the blue.

I was taken aback. We'd been sitting there quite a while, our cups were empty, there were nothing but crumbs on the plates. In such situations I was usually asked at the very beginning where I was from. That was understandable, you could tell from the way I talked. The moment I opened my mouth it became natural to ask where I was from.

"I thought so," he said. "Actually, I was certain of it. Right back then, on the street, when you apologized. But I was the one who greeted you first. Who knows if I wasn't sure of it the moment I saw you reaching for your hat. My face couldn't have looked familiar to you, but yours could to me. It appeared to me in a brief flash. I immediately started asking myself where and when. Then all of a sudden it came to me – of course!"

"You've been there?" I asked, though it may have been rude on my part to interrupt. Yet I had the impression it was expected, he might even have been intending for me to do so.

"No, never," he responded brusquely, almost as if he were brushing my question away. "Pity they don't allow smoking in here," he said. "I don't smoke, but there are moments when I feel like a cigarette. Do you smoke?"

"No," I said. "I used to. Gave it up."

"Good for you. Really. It's not good for your health." He suddenly stared at something with a fixed gaze.

I wondered if maybe he'd seen one of those people who'd come there over the previous two hundred years. Maybe he'd even seen the man who used to sit at our table, standing in the doorway. I expected him to jump up in a moment and say, excuse us, we're just leaving. Then, in a quiet, blank voice he said:

"My father was there."

"Oh, then maybe you went with your father one time," I put in encouragingly, pleased at the chance to contribute more to the conversation.

"During the war," he said, breaking in.

His words had a strange effect on me. Perhaps because I was already immersed in what I'd been planning to say, since I had the opportunity, and as if speaking over his words I said:

"It's always nicer to go with someone who's been there before. Especially your own father."

"My father is dead," he said, cutting short my enthusiasm.

"I'm sorry. I had no idea. Please accept my condolences."

"But you didn't know my father," he said, almost bridling. "Still, thank you."

I felt uncomfortable. I sensed a slight pressure beneath my ribs on the right side, the pain in my duodenum was showing signs of flaring up again. That was how it usually began, initially just a faint pressure under the ribs on the right. Sometimes it went away, like a moment ago after the coffee and cake. But now it seemed more substantial, it was starting to spread around my side to my lower back. I began to worry that if it kept increasing, in a short while it would be unbearable. I'd turn pale, start sweating, and it would be hard for him not to notice.

"Are you not feeling well?" he'd ask. And what on earth could I say to him then? That it was because of the coffee and cake? The coffee was excellent, the cake was delicious, I'd said so myself. No, no, please continue, it wouldn't have been right to say that either, because it wouldn't have been right in general to admit I was ill. Especially at such a moment, he starts telling me about his father, and I respond that I have a duodenal ulcer? You have to admit it would be awkward to say the least. One pain should never be pitted against another. Each pain is unique to itself.

I was wondering how I could slip my hand under my jacket without him noticing, so I could put some pressure on the rising pain, because that sometimes helped. I often saved myself in company in such a way. Or in the night, for instance. The worst pain would usually come in the night. When I couldn't take it any longer, I'd get out of bed, squat down, and kind of push the pain into myself with my hand, pressing on it with my whole being, my chin doubled over to my knees. Sometimes I spent all night like that, it was the only thing that brought relief. And that was how I lived with it. Since when? It started on one of the building sites. At first it was only in spring and fall. Once in a while I thought about going to a doctor. But in summer or in winter it would pass and I'd forget. I got skinny as a rake. Everyone kept asking me, what's up, you look awful. Are you sick? No, I'm not sick, this is just how I look.

I couldn't stand anyone's sympathy. If I happened not to be in pain, and someone expressed sympathy, it would start to hurt right away. I did take flax-seed oil, you bet. I did just like you said. I'd dissolve a tablespoon of it in luke-warm water in the evening, then drink it on an empty stomach in the morning. It helped a little. I hardly ever drank vodka anymore. And I tried to eat only boiled food, nothing greasy. Later I went on a very restricted diet. On the advice of a buddy, the pianist in the band. He'd had the same thing. Though he'd gone to the doctor.

You'll find this hard to believe, but when I played it never hurt. We'd play till late at night, often into morning, and it never hurt. Can you imagine, for a guy of my height I weighed forty-five pounds less than I should have. My jawbone jutted out from my face like it had no flesh on it, my cheeks were hollow, my nose grew longer. Later, much later, when I got over it and put on some weight, my wife confessed to me one time that as she looked at me she thought there'd come a time when my jaw and my cheekbones would grow level with each other.

When I had a tuxedo made for my wedding, the tailor took all my measure-ments and after a pause said:

"Pardon the comment, but you're awfully slim. Oh well, I'll leave some room in the seams if you should ever want to alter it. When you make a tuxedo it's not just for a single occasion."

I guessed that he'd been going to say "skinny," but used the word "slim" out of professional courtesy. Besides, how could I not be skinny given how little I ate. Whenever I ate anything at all, right away it hurt. I'd already stopped drinking wine and beer. At a party for instance, everyone else would be eating and drinking and I'd ask for a glass of milk. Milk was the only thing I could still drink. No one could understand. He's healthy, there's nothing wrong with him, and here he's drinking milk. They'd try to persuade me, give me advice, they made jokes at my expense, raised a toast to me, and I'd raise my glass of milk in return. All I wanted was for them to leave me alone, forget I was there.

It was through the milk that I met my future wife. The double bass player in the band was having a birthday party, and I asked for my usual glass of milk. The milk attracted her attention. I hadn't noticed her till that point. Besides, when you're in pain you don't even see beautiful women. It was another matter that there was a big crowd at the party. I was standing to one side, and she emerged out of the mass of people and came up to me.

"You like milk? Me too."

"I can ask for another glass," I said.

"No," she said. "I'll have a sip from yours. Can I?" After that we danced together.

Subsequently I went to various doctors, I spent six months in the hospital, they examined me and in the end they declared that an operation was the only thing. I refused. So they gave me injections and tablets. I still remember one of the medications was called "Robuden." For a year I felt better. But then I had a relapse, it was worse than before. I thought it was all over for me. My wife cried, in secret, though from her eyes I knew right away she'd been crying. With some eyes, you can't tell they've been crying. You just need to wipe them. But with others, the tears linger long after the crying. Hers were like that.

I pretended not to have seen anything. But one day I came home late from the club and she was still awake. She looked at me, and I had a suspicion.

"You've been crying," I said.

"No I haven't. Why do you say that? I have no reason to."

"With me you'll always have a reason," I said. "You made a bad choice. That glass of milk let you down."

"Don't make jokes." She burst into tears.

A short while later she took me to an herbalist. He was a doctor, but he treated people with herbs. In those days doctors didn't believe in herbs. I don't know how she found him. She made an appointment and went with me. He was an old man, when I told him my symptoms and how long I'd had them he mumbled to himself. Then he gave me a big sack of herbs. My wife prepared infusions and made sure I drank them regularly, three times a day at the same times, morning and midday twenty minutes before eating, in the evening twenty minutes after eating supper. Though the evening one she'd put into a thermos for me to take to the club.

And would you believe it, within a month I'd already begun to feel better, it hurt a lot less, I started to put on weight. In four months I was already back to my regular weight. I could eat anything, I even had a glass of alcohol from time to time, with no ill effects. I drank the herbs for a whole year, then after that only in spring and fall. And since then I've been fine.

Would you like to write them down? I'd just need to find you a slip of paper and something to write with. Well, maybe later. I remember what they were, I've not forgotten. If only I could remember everything like that. Though could anyone live in such a way? Actually, I don't think that sort of memory would be any more real.

No, my wife and I broke up for a different reason. I didn't want to have children, as I mentioned, and she very much did. I liked children, I still do, as I said. But I didn't want any of my own. Why not? I'll leave it to you to figure out. Me, I might not tell you the truth. Do I regret it now? Maybe yes, maybe no. We broke up when I was already well again, I'd almost forgotten about being sick. Wives don't leave you when you're sick. Especially her, she'd never have left for a reason like that. True, for a long time I hadn't let on I was ill. When she found out, she even said to me one time:

"I'll leave you if you don't get treatment."

I didn't want to worry her with my illness. I'd never presume to worry anyone with my own ill health, especially my wife. It hurt and that was all there was to it. You can get used to any pain if it hurts constantly. Like back then in the cafe, it hurt, but I kept listening to the man. And maybe it was under the influence of the worsening pain in my right side, under the ribs, that I asked:

"Was he unwell?"

You should never ask questions based on your own pain, as I realized immediately.

"No," he said. "He committed suicide." He spoke calmly, you might say, but at the same time he lifted his cup to his lips even though it was empty. And he added: "It was years and years ago, but I still find it painful. More and more painful. So thank you for letting me buy you coffee."

That I did not understand, let me tell you. We'd nodded to each other by mistake, and here he was thanking me. Out of the blue he asked:

"What year were you born in? That's what I thought. I was more or less your age when my father came back from the war. Luckily, or unluckily, he wasn't taken prisoner. He was in hiding for some time, so he didn't come back right away. We didn't think we'd see him again. Then one day, unexpectedly, he showed up, dressed in civilian clothing, unshaven, gaunt. You'd think all the more that there couldn't be anything more joyful. That's what people usually think when someone comes back from the war. . . And rightly so. Any return from the war has joy written into its very nature. Unless it's someone coming back to an empty house, to ruins. Think about what a return from the war always meant. Someone came back, someone else didn't, that alone is a measure of our experience. Someone comes back, someone else doesn't – that pretty much sums up our own predicament. As if human fate were forever vacillating between joy and pain. If you look at war from such an angle, it might seem to be exclusively for homecomings of that kind that wars are fought. As if there were no greater measure of a person's happiness. Or greater pain when someone doesn't come back. Coming back from the war might be the clearest proof that life can triumph over death. Yet it's a triumph for which we need constant evidence. Because it's like a return from another world. So even when someone comes back a cripple, armless, legless, eyeless, the very nature of the situation means we should greet them with joy. They bring joy across the threshold of the house along with their saved life.

"Too bad we didn't even have time to express our joy at father's return. As he walked in he glanced at us with cold eyes. Then, when mother burst into tears and tried to throw herself into his arms, he held her back. The same went for me and my little brother, when we hugged him he moved us away from him. He at least ought to have picked my brother up and said, My, how you've grown, son.

"I mean, that's one of the basic principles of homecoming. Especially since when he went to war, my brother had just been learning to walk. He asked mother for a glass of water. As he drank it we both looked at him almost greedily, as if it was us who were thirsty. His Adam's apple bobbed up and down in this funny way. To give vent to the joy he'd dampened in us, we laughed at his Adam's apple. Mother made the best of our laughter, she evidently had a premonition, and she said:

"'See how happy the boys are.'

"He didn't say a thing. He just looked at us with those cold eyes, and the laughter died inside us. He handed the glass back to mother and walked into the living room without a word. He dropped heavily into an armchair. Mother started to ask him if he wasn't tired, maybe he should lie down, or perhaps he'd like to take a bath and change his clothes. She had everything ready. All his shirts and pajamas were washed and ironed, his suits were cleaned. She'd borrowed a razor and had the neighbor hone it, he could shave. She'd even managed to get hold of some shaving cream. Or maybe he'd rather have something to eat first. There were a few eggs, she'd gotten hold of them by some miracle. Would he like them fried, or would he prefer soft-boiled?

"But nothing she said had any effect on those cold eyes. He sat there without a word, lost somewhere deep inside himself. Perhaps he didn't believe he was home, that he'd come back. Mother was helpless, she didn't know what to do or say anymore. She smiled and cried. She kept hurrying out to get something as if she'd just remembered about it, then she came back empty-handed. I felt sorry for her. I thought to myself, I'll go and play something for him on the piano, maybe that'll convince him that he's home, that he's back.

"Whenever he used to hear me playing, however busy he was he'd always come into the living room, sit down and listen. He never asked me to play any particular piece, he just listened. I knew he wanted me to carry out his own unfulfilled ambition. He'd wanted to be a pianist, apparently he had ability, but it all came to nothing after his father, my grandfather, died in the previous war. Every generation has to have its war, as you see."

I didn't know if he expected me to agree, or to offer a different opinion, because he broke off and became pensive, he was gazing off somewhere. Though I hadn't caused his outpouring in any way, I somehow felt as if I'd intruded into his life. And it was making me more and more uncomfortable. I decided it was time to look at my watch and say, I'm really sorry but I ought to be at my rehearsal by now, which as it happened was true. Till next time maybe if you feel like it. The next coffee's on me. We can even meet here, in this cafe, tomorrow, the day after? At the same time? Here's my card.

He spoke before I'd had a chance to say anything:

"What's your instrument?"

I was shocked, because I hadn't yet told him I was supposed to be at rehearsal.

"The saxophone," I said. I was about to seize the opportunity to say I had to be getting to my practice, since I was running late as it was, I was very sorry.

With what seemed to me a hint of scorn he repeated:

"The saxophone." And again: "The saxophone." He drifted into thought once again. "It makes no difference what a person plays. What's unfulfilled remains unfulfilled. So I had good reason to think that if I played for him . . . and for our sake too. Because we also found it hard to believe he was with us, he was back. Mother had cried her eyes out all through the war. All through the war we'd prayed for him. Hope faded as the war dragged on. His letters came less and less frequently, then in the end they stopped altogether. Mother wrote him, he didn't reply. So she started getting us used to the idea that we'd have to live without a father. The war ended and he still hadn't come home, so our hopes were almost extinguished. And now, out of the blue here he was, he'd returned. You must admit that in such instances it's easier to come to terms with the fact that someone will never come back than to believe that he's here, he's returned. Tears may be more in place at those moments than joy. Tears seem more appropriate in a situation where you don't know what to do with yourself. But we kept our tears in check, and we couldn't imagine tears appearing in those cold eyes of his. If there weren't to be any tears, music was the only thing. When hearts are bursting, music is the only thing.

"My fingers were already over the keys when he raised himself from the armchair and said:

"'I'm going to go get some sleep.'

"Mother tried to hold him back, have him wait a moment, she'd make the bed, in the meantime he could have something to eat, take a bath. It was like he didn't hear her. With a heavy step, almost as if he were hauling his own body, he dragged himself to his study, not to the bedroom. Mother took out a blanket and pillow and hurried after him. For a long time she didn't reappear. My brother and I waited for her just outside the door of the study. As she came out she led us away from there, then she told us God forbid never to go in to where father was. Not even to go near, to stay away from the door. And in general to keep quiet. Me, I shouldn't try to play the piano under any circumstances.

"From that moment on he slept in the study on the sofa. He only left to go to the bathroom. Even then he'd first crack open the door, and if he saw me or my brother nearby, he'd close it again at once. Besides, mother kept an eye on us and made sure we didn't hang around the hallway needlessly. One time I asked mother why father didn't want to see us.

"'Not for the moment, son,' she replied. 'He needs to rest. You understand how exhausted he must be.'

"He didn't eat with us either. Mother took his food to him in the study. Three times a day. Always on a silver tray. The same one the maid had once brought our meals on. Because of the war we'd learned to eat without niceties, and we'd completely forgotten about the silver tray. We'd not had a maid for a long time either. Plus, what we ate didn't merit a silver tray or a maid. Often there was nothing to eat at all. Mother sold various valuables to buy food. She'd even thought about selling the silver tray, because if father didn't come back it wouldn't have been any use to us. Once she took the tray from the dresser intending to finally sell it, but then suddenly, as if she had a presentiment she said:

"'What if he comes back, what will I serve him his meals on?'

"And instead of the tray, she sold their wedding rings.

"When she was taking him his food, even though she carried the tray in both hands she wouldn't let my brother or me open the door for her. The tray would be loaded, there was a tureen of soup, a dish with the main course, a plate, a bowl, the teapot, cup and saucer, sugar bowl, silverware. She would place the tray on the floor, check that neither of us were about, and only then knock at his door. She was taking food to her own husband, but still she'd knock. It's hard to imagine a more bizarre situation. Not that he ever opened the door for her. She would always open it herself. She'd pick the tray up from the ground and only then go in.

"She usually sat with him till he was done eating. Sometimes, though, she was there much longer. I was often tempted to sneak up to the door and listen in to see what they were talking about, and in general if they were talking at all or if they were just silent all that time. Of course, we'd been taught that eavesdropping was wrong. But the war made us unlearn a lot of things we'd been taught. It wasn't that that held me back, but rather the fear of what I might hear. Especially because when he didn't feel like eating, which sometimes happened, my mother's eyes would be brimming with tears as she came out of his study. And that was how hatred toward my father began to grow in me. I hated him so much sometimes for those tears of my mother's. Nowadays, yes, nowadays I can guess what went on between them.

"With every meal my mother took to him it became more and more important whether she'd leave there tearful again, or whether her expression would be calm. Even when I was in the furthest room I'd be listening for her coming out of his study, and I'd run to meet her to see if there were tears in her eyes or whether there was even the least hint of a smile on her face. I even tried to guess if it would happen when she took him breakfast or lunch or dinner. It was then that I first became aware of how much I loved my mother. While my father, every time she left his study crying I hated him more, never mind that he'd come back. I actually felt that it was my job to protect my mother from him. I had the feeling that every time my mother brought him a meal, he was taking her away from me. In fact, my love for my mother also protected me from him. It still protects me today, even though my mother is no longer alive either. If it hadn't been for that, he may well have pulled me along after him. Because I inherited his bad conscience. I often feel as tormented as he must have been. You seem surprised that a bad conscience can be inherited. Everything can, everything can, my dear sir. We have to inherit it all, otherwise what happened will keep repeating itself. We can't simply select from our inheritance only the things that won't weigh us down. That way we'd be utterly entangled in hypocrisy. As it is we wallow in falsehood. Have you not noticed that lies have taken on the appearance of truth? They've become our daily bread. A way of life. Almost a faith. We absolve ourselves of our sins with lies, convince ourselves with lies, justify accepted truths with lies. Just take a good look at the world. In any case, I've inherited that from him. And I want it that way. Otherwise I might not have become as aware of the undying love I felt toward my mother.

"One day, as mother came out of the study carrying yet another uneaten meal, her eyes filled with tears, she looked in my direction and said abruptly:

"'Your father wants to see you.'

"I felt no joy, believe me. Not even relief. I knocked at the door, my heart pounding. He was sitting on the sofa, in his pajamas, in rumpled bedding, wearing house slippers. He was hunched over, as if the simple act of sitting were agony for him.

"'Come here,' he said.

"His voice seemed alien to me. I wouldn't have recognized it."

"'Closer,' he said. At that moment I noticed that his face was even thinner and more sallow than when he'd first appeared. His cold eyes seemed almost lifeless. They were turned in my direction, but I couldn't tell if he actually saw me. My heart was thumping ever more loudly in my chest, though all I was doing was standing in front of my own father. He was a good father, please believe me. He was exceptionally mild-tempered, he never got angry. He never so much as laid a finger on me, unlike my mother. I'd get up to mischief sometimes, and he'd always go easy on me. Now, for the first time I was afraid in his presence.

"'I want to make my confession to you, son,' he said. 'To you, not to God.' A shiver ran down my spine, though I didn't really understand these opening words. 'God forgives too easily.' It was as if he was wrenching the words out of himself. I had the impression he was speaking not with his mouth but with his entire body that had been exhausted by the war, that was so skinny his bones poked through his pajamas. I felt like I could hear them rubbing against each other at every word. 'Fathers should confess to their sons if memory is to survive. I don't need you to forgive me. I need you to remember. Your memory will be my penance.' He had tired himself, he lowered his head and for a long time we remained like that, me standing stiffly in front of him as if I were at attention, him on the sofa like he might come crashing head first to the floor. With a great effort he raised his eyes to me. They were no longer cold and lifeless. It was more as if they didn't believe it was me standing there. He looked at me for a long time. He looked and looked, and still he didn't seem to believe it was me. 'I was ordered to check whether anyone else was still hiding there. In the orchard between the farmhouse and the barn there was a potato clamp. In those parts they dig pits, a bit like a cellar. I ran up to it, yanked open the door, and I saw you. Now that you're standing here in front of me I'm even more sure it was you. I saw the terror in your eyes. Come closer.' He stared into my eyes for a long, long time, from so close up I could almost feel our eyes touching. 'Yes, these are the same eyes. They didn't believe that the soldier with the smoking gun barrel, who could pull the trigger again at any moment, was your father. I hesitated for a second. That second made me realize that I have no right to live. Me, your father, I felt disappointed that it was you. I slammed the door, furious, and shouted back that there was no one there.' He'd grown tired, he was clearly short of breath, but a moment later he took my head in both his hands and laid it on his shoulder. His body was shaking. 'It would have been better for all of us if I'd not survived,' I heard him whisper by my ear. 'But I so wanted to see you all before I died. So very much. I love you, son. But that's not enough to live. Go now.' He pushed me away from himself."

We sat there, both silently immersed in those last words of his father, because what can you say after all that, I'm sure you understand. The cafe was slowly filling up, it was getting more and more crowded and noisy. At some point he nodded to someone, or returned a nod. I didn't look, thinking that at such a moment it would have been wrong even to show curiosity. Then, greeting someone again, he said:

"But no one could have predicted what would happen soon after. And while he was shaving, with a razor."

After these words it was as if the life went out of him. Or perhaps he'd come to the conclusion that after what he had said, our meeting could return to being pure chance. And he no longer felt like talking. As for me, nothing came to mind to keep up the conversation. I only noticed to my own amazement that the pain in my right side under the ribs had gone away. I hadn't even noticed when. It had ceased, just like that. So I'd have gladly had another slice of cake and another coffee. I was about to ask him if he felt like having more, but at that moment he glanced at his watch and said:

"I didn't realize it was so late. I'm deeply grateful to you. Unfortunately I have to be going."

He brought out his wallet, counted out the money and stuck it under the sugar bowl. As he was putting the wallet back in his pocket he suddenly hesitated and took it out again.

"Just a minute, maybe it's in here somewhere."

He began rummaging through the compartments as before. I thought that maybe this time he wanted to give me his business card. I put my hand inside my coat to get my own wallet and give him mine.

"No, don't bother looking, you won't find it in your wallet. It ought to be somewhere in here. I'm certain I have it." He was rifling ever more anxiously through the wallet. "I wanted to show you a really interesting photograph. Extremely interesting. The person who took the picture captured the exact moment when my father was standing in front of me. Where on earth is it? I refuse to believe it's not here. The most extraordinary thing about it is that we're looking into each other's eyes. My terrified eyes looking at my father, and father's face fixed in a grimace, his eyes staring at me. Both our faces can be seen together *en face*. It's hard to credit, but you must believe me, both faces are opposite one another and both are *en face*. The place the picture was taken from seems physically impossible, to have two faces opposite one another and both at the same time looking at the camera. I've tried to figure out where that point must have been – so far without success. Because it was somewhere, the picture itself is the best proof of that. If I manage to find it it'll be quite a discovery. Who can say if it won't be a new dimension of space that for the moment is inaccessible to our senses, our imaginations, our consciences."

His hands were trembling, again he began tipping out the contents of the various sections of his wallet, emptying them to the last slip of paper.

"Take a look." He handed me a photograph. I thought it would be the one he was looking for. "My mother."

"A beautiful woman," I said. She really was beautiful. But he didn't take after her. Except perhaps for something in the eyes, the mouth.

"That was how she looked before father came back from the war," he said absentmindedly, busy looking for the other picture. Now he was searching for it among all the things he'd tossed out onto the tabletop. "Perhaps it isn't possible to find that point in our everyday space. Especially as we're overly used to it, we've become one of its dimensions. But after all it's space that determines who we truly are. Just as it determines everything else. Not only in the physical meaning of the word. To judge from the photograph it may not be a physical space. That's what I'm trying to figure out. Sometimes, indications of that space can be seen in the old masters, in their most perfect paintings. The usual laws of physics would never have allowed such a place. But that's the thing with great art. I mean art as a world, unfortunately one that includes humans. Oh, if only I could find that point. Too bad, I don't seem to have the photograph," he said resignedly, as if he'd let himself down. "I'm sorry." He began gathering up all the things he'd scattered from the wallet and putting them back unthinkingly, without worrying what had been in which compartment. "I'm really sorry," he repeated. "I was certain."

"Don't worry about it," I said. "You can show me the next time."

"You'd like to meet again?" he said, surprised.

"Of course. It could even be here, in this cafe. And if this particular table happened to be free . . . ," I added hurriedly, to assure him I wasn't just being polite.

"The thing is, though," he said as he put his wallet back in his pocket, "I'm not sure that would be possible. In fact, I don't think it would be," he repeated emphatically. "We'd have to not know each other again, and again say hello to one another by mistake on the street, convinced that we'd already met someplace, some time before. But where, when? Otherwise you'd be right in saying it was just an unfortunate chance."

12

You know, I wonder whether he just didn't mention it, or whether his father hadn't told him, that when he ran up to the door there was a pig standing in front of it. It had clambered out of the pig shed when the sheds began to burn. The sheds were a little off to one side, I could partly see them through the crack in the door. It walked slowly, it was old. Usually you don't hold on to pigs as old as that, but this was an uncommon pig. It so was fat it could barely support itself on its short little legs. You could barely see its feet under its flabby sides. You had the impression it was moving along on its sides alone. It headed straight for the potato cellar where I was and started grunting, rubbing its snout against the door. Probably it could smell me. Plus, I was the one it was most attached to. Wheezing and snorting, it plopped down right by the door. He kicked it, and it struggled to its feet. Then, after he slammed the door shut and shouted to someone that there was no one there, out of rage he let loose with a burst of shots at it. He kept firing, though it was dead already. Till his last bullet. Flesh spattered everywhere. How do I know it was his last shot? He had to switch out the magazine.

You can't imagine what that pig was like. Right from when she was little we called her Zuzia. And from when she was little she wasn't like a pig. I don't know if you know it, but pigs are the most intelligent creatures. Even when she was still suckling she stood out from all the other piglets. Whenever you came into the shed she'd just up and stand in front of you with her snout in the air, wanting to be picked up. She was most comfortable around people. We'd often bring her into the house so she could be with us. She knew each of us: father, grandfather, grandmother, Uncle Jan, he was still alive when she was little, Jagoda, Leonka, and me. Me, she'd always nudge on the leg with her little snout. She never confused me with anyone else. It was easy to see she liked me best of all. She went everywhere with me. Many times I didn't know how to get rid of her. I'd go graze the cows on the pasture, and here she'd be following behind. I'd be going to school, I'd look behind me and there she was. I'd have to turn back and lock her up in the pig shed. I'd often be late for school because of her. The teacher would ask why I was tardy, but I couldn't say it was because of a pig. So I'd get a D for behavior that day. I got so many Ds because of Zuzia that by the end of the year I was bottom of the class in behavior.

My mother would send me to the store for something. I'd go into the store, try and close the door behind me, and Zuzia would be blocking the doorway. The store lady would shout at me, what did I think I was doing bringing a pig into the store. Get out! How do you like that! That boy! People would be laughing, and I'd get all embarrassed. Often I'd not buy what I was sent for. And no threats or pleas did any good. Go home Zuzia, go on, go now. Go home, because this or that or the other. While Zuzia, she'd just raise that little snout of hers and look at you kind of reproachfully. Or when I went mushroom picking, there was no way to explain to her that she couldn't pick mushrooms herself. She didn't know mushrooms, and besides, what would happen if, God forbid, she should get lost in the woods? You had to pick her up and carry her back to the pig shed.

Though that at least was doable till she got too heavy. After she'd grown some there was no way she could be carried. You're not going to pick up a pig that weighs, say, over a hundred pounds, and she was getting heavier by the week. When you locked her in the shed she always found a way of getting out. When you took food in to her she'd slip past your legs and be out in the farmyard. Plus, from spring to fall the sheds were left open during the day so the animals could have some fresh air, especially when the weather was hot. She spent entire days roaming around the yard.

You'd close a gate behind you when you were going somewhere, but still she'd appear. She didn't need to go through the gate, there was always a hole in the fence somewhere or other. She made the holes herself. Father would fill them in, and she'd just make another one right away. Though of course, did you ever see a fence without holes? That's just how it is with fences.

One time mother was certain that father had plugged all the holes. She was on her way to May devotions at church. She closed the gate behind her and latched it. May devotions were usually held at a roadside shrine that had been made in a hollow oak tree near the woods. People said it was the oldest oak around, that it remembered everyone who had ever lived in those parts. It didn't die because it contained the shrine, any other oak tree of that age would have fallen down long ago. There was a host of women gathered around the tree, it was mostly women that took part in May devotions. They sang and sang. All at once my mother feels something wriggling about by her skirt, she looks down. It's Zuzia. She had to pick her up, and the rest of the service she sang with Zuzia in her arms. Zuzia was still little then.

There was a guy from town that was courting the neighbors' daughter. Actually, I repainted her nameplate just recently. He'd always come on Sundays and they'd go for a walk together in the afternoon. He had a camera, and when they went walking he'd always have the camera around his neck. Of course, back then cameras weren't as common as they are today. A young man with a camera, well, no young man that only had land could measure up to him.

One Sunday Zuzia had been following me and I was carrying her back to put her in the shed, when the two of them happened to be walking by. The neighbors' daughter burst out laughing, and the guy asked me to stop a moment. Everyone came out of our house, because the neighbors' daughter was in such fits of laughter. So he lined everybody up in front of the house, he had mother hold Zuzia in her arms and he took a picture of the whole family like that. One Sunday soon afterwards he brought us the photograph. We were all there, father, grandfather, grandmother, Jagoda, Leonka, me, Uncle Jan, and in front was mother with Zuzia in her arms like a baby.

Perhaps he'd wanted to make a humorous picture. But it was the only photograph with all of us in it. No, I don't have it anymore, but I remember it well. Though I have to say that whenever I think of it, I don't find it remotely funny that there's a pig in it. I'm even kind of grateful to Zuzia. Because it was thanks to her that we had our only family photo. So what if it's only in my memory? While everyone thinks a pig like that is just for fattening up and slaughtering. Really, how are we so different from her? Are we smarter? Better? Not to mention that animals have just as much right to the world, since they're in it. The world belongs to them too. Noah didn't take just humans into his ark. And have you noticed that in their old age animals start to resemble old people? While they're young and humans are young the similarities might not be so easy to see. But in old age they become just as decrepit as people. They get sick just the same, and from the same illnesses. And maybe the reason they don't speak and don't complain is that words wouldn't bring them any relief anyway, just as words don't bring relief to humans even though they can speak and complain. And if you ask me, they're afraid of death just like humans are. How do I know?

Pardon me for asking, but how old are you? It's hard to tell from looking at you. I couldn't say, really I couldn't. When you came in I thought you must be about my age. Perhaps because you were wearing an overcoat and hat. Whereas now you seem a lot younger. Or maybe older? I really don't know. Sometimes a person looks like they're no age at all. Perhaps you're one of those that time hasn't touched. Am I right? In other words, I was not mistaken. Well, too bad, it's coming to all of us sooner or later. Besides, I might have suspected it. The moment you said you'd come to buy beans, I might have suspected it.

Though let me tell you, years don't matter much either. Do you know how long a pig like that can live? Eight, ten years maximum, provided of course people let her live out the full time. But they don't. So it must have cost her a huge effort to get herself from the shed to the potato cellar. It wasn't far, but at her age . . . She barely ever got up, didn't eat much at all. I'd take her boiled milk with bran, because from me she'd still accept a little food. Though even I had to plead with her, coax her. Come on, Zuzia, eat, you need to eat, if you don't eat you'll die. Only then would she deign to stick her snout in the trough and have a little.

It was hard to see her in her old age. You couldn't believe that at one time you'd carried her back home. Everyone would be saying her name. Zuzia. Zuzia, Zuzunia. The day virtually began with Zuzia. How's Zuzia, Zuzia this, Zuzia that. And Zuzia herself would cling to everyone, not to mention following everyone around. At times she was a nuisance, we hoped she'd change when she got a little older. But she grew up and she didn't change. She just made bigger and bigger holes in the fence. And still, when one of us was going somewhere Zuzia would follow behind. And not just our family, she got so comfortable with people that whenever anyone was walking past our house she'd make her way out onto the road and follow them. At times someone would get all upset and come running to say, Take that wretched Zuzia, that's how they'd talk about her when they were mad, because they'd be walking along and Zuzia would be right behind. Whoever saw such a spoiled pig. You should slaughter her, it's high time, actually she's probably already over-fattened.

But at home, no one said a word about slaughtering Zuzia. Though you couldn't help but see she'd already grown to her destiny. After that, she even outgrew destiny. And everyone knows what a pig's destiny is. One time father said something, Christmas was approaching, he said maybe we could slaughter her. At that everyone lowered their eyes, father felt uncomfortable and added:

"Just an idea."

Grandfather put in:

"There could be a war, it's best to leave her be."

And so Zuzia kept growing bigger, and following everyone around. She got heavier and heavier. She wasn't allowed in the house anymore, so she'd lie down outside the door and just stay there. When someone went out to shoo her away, she'd have a hard time clambering to her feet. One time father got mad and said:

"If we can't slaughter her, we should at least sell her."

He went into town and came back with a broker. Brokering was mostly done by the Jews. If you had a pig or a cow, or geese, or just goose down, you'd give it to a broker and he'd find a buyer. He came into the farmyard, and Zuzia happened to be lying outside the house. She picked herself up, went up to him, lifted her snout, and for a moment they just looked at each other. Then she lay down at his feet. And get this, the broker, who surely had no interest in pigs aside from their meat and their back fat, scratched his head and said:

"You brought me here to see a pig, but I can't say if she's a pig or not. What she is, I can't tell. She might look like a pig, but I really couldn't say. Oy, I don't know."

He wouldn't even feel her to check how her back fat and hams were. And you should know that that's what any broker would start from. Before they gave a price they'd always feel the animal for a long time, and they'd always grumble:

"It's got no more back fat than the width of my finger here. And as for the hams, you can see yourselves that my finger goes in like I won't say in what. It's not at all firm. What have you been feeding it? Starving it, more like. What kind of price is a butcher going to give for a starved pig? Not a penny more. And if he won't give any more, there won't be anything in it for me either. I'm not interested in making big money, I just want my cut."

But this broker wouldn't even feel her.

"She's not meant to be turned into back fat or ham. She's lying here at my feet, for goodness' sake. Maybe she thinks badly of me, what then?"

It seemed like this was just his way of starting negotiations at the lowest price. Father kept asking him, swearing she was no different from any other pig, she ate the same things, and how long was she going to go following people about, she was too big for that. In the end the man had no choice but to start checking her over. The main thing is to feel for the thickness of the back fat. See, like here on my thigh. You have to spread your hand and feel with each finger separately, then make a final check with your thumb. A good broker can tell you precisely whether the pig has two, two and a half, three fingers. And in the same way, how firm the hams are.

"She has back fat, hams. Everything's fine there," he said. "But she wants to live. And you all should pray she keeps wanting to for as long as possible. It may be some kind of sign, but to know that you'd need a rebbe. I'm just a broker."

Let me tell you, to this day I can't understand it. What had Zuzia ever done to him? He emptied his whole magazine into her. You don't think the father told his son about that? Why wouldn't he? I don't know either, though I can guess. But I had no intention of asking him the next time we met. In fact, we didn't meet a second time. Or ever again. I often used to go by the cafe, even at the same time we'd run into each other that day. I'd at least look in on my way to a morning rehearsal. Sometimes I'd sit down, order a coffee, have some cake. I'd ask the waitress when it was the same one who'd served us that time. She knew him, you recall she'd smiled at him a different way than a waitress usually smiles. She remembered us meeting, she vaguely remembered me, but him she remembered well. She'd never mistake him for anyone else, she told me, but he hadn't come back once since then.

I couldn't stop thinking about that photograph he'd mentioned, and I would have asked him about it. I kept wondering where the point could have been that the picture was taken from. It still bothers me today sometimes. True, I've never seen the picture. But you can think about it even without the picture. Let's say someone took a picture of us as we're shelling beans. We're sitting here opposite each other like we are now, but in the picture we're both shown full face. Your face seems to be looking at the photographer, and mine also, but at the same time we're facing one another. The distance between him and me was no more than between me and you right now. I could see the muzzle of his gun like I can see your eyes now. So where could that point have been? Where do you think it could have been – here? Where could the photographer have been standing? There was very little space, no more than in this room. And here there's no war, the dogs are asleep, and we're sitting here talking and shelling beans. It ought to be a lot easier, don't you think?

Shall we go outside maybe? It's nighttime, but I could turn on the light in front of the cabin. I'd show you where it was. The cellar's caved in, it's overgrown with nettles and scrub. The door's gone, it rotted away, but the door frame is still there, it's made of oak and oak lasts. I might be able to squeeze through it, but if not we can still make believe. I could kneel down and you could stand in front of me. You'd just need to take some kind of stick. Well, you have to be taking aim at me with something. The way children play at guns. You say it's not something we should be imagining, even if we were children. Then who *should* imagine it? I mean, no one's going to take our place. No one can live for someone else, and no one's capable of imagining things on behalf of another person. No method should be rejected if it might lead us to ourselves. Maybe if we were in the place where it happened it'd be easier to find the point where we'd be closest. You wouldn't have to look for me all over the world. You wouldn't have to come to me for beans. We wouldn't have to wonder where and when. All the more so because as you see, we're gradually getting to the end of the beans. Though there's still a pod down by your foot. There's another one over there, and one there. And another one right here, you see it? If you root around you're bound to find more.

Maybe you'd like more beans? I've set some aside for myself, but I could bring two or three more bundles. You came by car, a little more won't make any difference. Surely you won't be leaving just yet. Why go driving at night? If I were you I'd wait till morning. We can have some tea or coffee later. Are you in a rush? The next time you come I might not be here any longer. If you hadn't come by for beans I don't know if you'd even have found me this time. Why not? Can a person ever be certain where and when he is in the world? You say, he's always here and now. Except that that doesn't mean anything. You might say that these days there are no boundaries, that what it's like here is what it's like everywhere. If you ask me, every world is past, every person is past, because there's only past time. Now, here, those are only words, each of them immaterial, like all the words we were speaking about. Now I couldn't even tell you what world this is. Or whether it exists at all. Perhaps we only imagine it exists. For you that probably makes no difference, because since you came to me for beans . . .

Perhaps you could buy a cabin here? What for? Oh, I don't know. I just thought you might be looking for a place. You wouldn't have to come every weekend. I'd even advise against it. Or spend all of your vacations here. One or two visits a year would be quite enough. And best of all at these kinds of time, in the off-season. I'd mind your place like I do all the others. You wouldn't have to worry about a thing.

A few of the cabins are up for sale. Twenty-two, thirty-one, and I think forty-six or forty-seven, I don't recall. There may well be others, I'd have to check. Oh yes, a lot of people have sold their cabins since I've been here. Recently there's not been much interest in buying. Once in a while someone comes through, takes a good long look around, and doesn't know if he wants to buy or if he's just looking. To begin with people would often drop by, they'd leave their address and phone number with me in case anyone happened to be selling a cabin. No one's building any new ones anymore either. Though it's a decent place, as you can see – there's the lake, the woods, the air's good.

The animals around here have gotten so tame that the deer sometimes come right up to the cabins. Not for food. Food they have in the woods, everything they need. The squirrels hop about on the decks and peek into the cabins. It's another matter that the people here spoil them rotten. They bring them bagfuls of nuts. More than the squirrels could ever eat, or bury in the ground. You walk along and at every step there are nuts crunching under your feet. I was even thinking of adding to the signs, saying, Do not feed the squirrels. Because so what if they eat from people's hands during the season? The season doesn't last forever. Sometimes a wild boar comes through here. Sometimes you see a hare scooting between the cabins. You can see weasels, martens. Often you're more likely to see them here than in the woods.

One time a moose appeared. And it didn't just stop for a moment on the bank. It walked right between the cabins, stopped here, stopped there. People started shouting, there was a bit of a panic. Some people took shelter in their cabins, others jumped into boats and canoes or hopped into the water, someone nearly drowned because they didn't know how to swim. Someone fainted – luckily some of the cabin owners are doctors. The moose went down to the lake, had a drink, bellowed, and calmly went its way. Even a moose sometimes has a yen to be among people.

Or if you were to get up before sunrise, when the birds wake up. If you got to breathe that fresh early morning air, you'd feel your lungs opening up, and what good air really is. In other places people are quite unaware they're breathing, or of what they're breathing. If you thought too much about it, you could lose the will to breathe altogether. I already told you about the mushrooms, the blueberries, wild strawberries, cranberries. But best of all is just to go into the woods and not pick anything, not think anything. When it's just you and the woods.

I don't even like to take the dogs. They get distracted by every rustle and off they rush. Then try calling them back, Rex! Paws! One time they chased a deer. I kept calling them, looking for them. In the woods the trees deaden your voice. In the end I got ticked off and came back alone, without them. They didn't come back home till the evening. Their muzzles were covered in blood. So now I had a deer on my conscience. Have you ever seen a deer's eyes when it's dying? Like in a snare or a trap, for instance. You'll never see such terror in any other eyes.

Let me tell you, when crowds of people start arriving here in high season, I sometimes have the feeling that I live in a different world from them. I won't deny it, their world is pleasant, cheerful, maybe even happy, I can't say, but I don't think I'd be capable of living in it. You're convinced that I actually do live in it? But how can *I* be sure of that? I mean, even with the sun, everyone has to have their own, their own sunrises and sunsets. I lived abroad for all those years, but wherever I was living, whenever I wanted to have a sunrise or sunset I always had to have it according to the sunrises and sunsets here. That was always the measure of any sunrise or sunset. The only measure, wherever I was.

It's another matter that especially in the big cities you can live your whole life and not see a sunrise or a sunset. How does the day begin? It just gets light. Then when night falls, a million lights are lit. It's not really night at all. They just call it that. True, here too I no longer know where the sun used to come up or where it went down. It doesn't rise in the same place, or set in the same place it used to. I get up with it, but I'm never sure, it didn't used to rise in that place. That's why I don't know how you found me, since I can never seem to find myself. Admittedly, finding yourself is no easy task. Who knows if it isn't the hardest of all the tasks people face in the world.

No, Mr. Robert's cabin isn't for sale, I already mentioned that. At least not until Mr. Robert tells me so. If I were you, I'd go for number thirty-one. There aren't many cabins as nice as thirty-one. It has a fireplace, electric heating, double-glazed windows, insulated walls, you can even live there in the winter. Two bathrooms, one upstairs and one down, both tiled, with boilers. And it's all in oak. Carpeted floors. There used to be antlers, but fortunately the guy took them with him.

I'd advise against antlers. You couldn't live with them. The walls were covered in antlers. Wherever you turned there were antlers. In the main rooms, the kitchen, the bathrooms. Over the front door there was the head of a wild boar with tusks this big. Not one single wall was empty. Whenever I went over there to check everything was in order I had to be careful not to get jabbed by an antler, because some of the bigger ones stuck out all the way into the middle of the room. I'm telling you, every now and then I'd sit down in an armchair, because sometimes I like to sit awhile in one or other of the cabins, he had these nice big leather armchairs, but something made me want to leave right away. He built the cabin as a place to keep the antlers. Apparently his wife had made him remove them from their apartment because there was no more room to put anything else up. No, she never came here. Whereas him, he'd be here every Saturday and Sunday. He didn't go sunbathing or swimming, he rarely even went on a walk, he'd just sit for days on end in his cabin. He often came in the winter too. And the strangest thing of all, imagine this, was that he didn't hunt. Those weren't hunting trophies. He did have a shotgun. Though what he needed it for I couldn't say. How can you enter someone's soul through antlers?

Then all at once, I couldn't tell you what had happened, one day he arrived in a truck with two hired guys, took the antlers away, and put the cabin up for sale. Some people said he'd found a good buyer for the antlers, others that he'd thrown them on the trash heap. The truth may have been something else again, though I can't imagine what.

You should think about it. He's not asking much. A cabin like that is worth twice the price. What would you do here? Well, what do I do? Especially if you were to come here once or twice a year, in the off-season. I could even plant more beans. If we didn't feel like shelling beans we could go for a walk in the woods. We could listen to music, I brought a lot of records. No, I don't play chess. You like to play? I somehow never learned. I had no patience for it. When I lived abroad I sometimes used to play bridge, but for bridge you need four people. When I worked on building sites, when we weren't drinking vodka, once in a blue moon we'd play cards. We'd play one thousand, *durak*, sixty-six, also blackjack or poker.

Before that, at school we'd play the matchbox game. Do you know it? You've never even heard of it? It's very simple. You take a matchbox, it has to be full, and you put it on the edge of the table, lying flat, so it sticks out over the edge, though not too far or it'll fall off. Then you flip it up with your index finger. You get points depending on how it lands on the table. The most number of points is when it lands upright, in other words on the smallest side, where you take out the matches. We'd always say that was worth ten points, though you can agree on a different score. Five points for the scratchboard, on either side. You know what the scratchboard is? Where you strike the match. And no points if it landed on its big side.

Oh, the game wasn't as innocent as you imagine. There are no innocent games. Everything depends not on what you're playing, but what you're playing for. We played innocently when our homeroom teacher would come by. At those times we didn't even write down the points. He collected matchboxes and almost every evening he came to see if we'd used up all the matches from yesterday's box. Later I'll tell you why he collected them. Sometimes he'd just sit there endlessly. There were times when we'd have to pretend we were getting ready for bed, otherwise he'd have stayed forever. One of us would start unbuttoning his shirt, another untied his shoes, someone else turned his bed down. Then when he finally went, probably thinking we were all about to get into our beds, we'd check the hallway one more time to make sure he'd left the building, and only then would we start to play for real.

Not for money. We didn't have any money. Sometimes those who knew how to remove a wallet from a pocket had a bit. Not for cigarettes. We smoked cherry leaves, clover, other disgusting things. The game was about not coming last. You're surprised the stakes were so low. Then let me say this: what was remarkable was that the stakes were so high. There was only one loser, however many of us were playing, and it was the one who got the lowest score. He then became the victim of all the other players. We could do whatever we liked with him, and he had to do what he was told to do. In other words, the game wasn't about winning, like all other games, where that's the whole point. The point of this game, as I said, was not to come in last. What it meant to be last, well, the best indication was that some of them would burst into tears. Some people would try to run away, but there was no way you could get away when there were so many winners. Other losers would try and buy off the rest with all sorts of promises. But no one could be bought. Some of them even reached for their knives. But that didn't help much either. When there are too many winners, tears and knives are useless. Just one time, one kid managed to escape. But he also never came back to the school ever. He'd had a feeling he was going to come out last and before the game was over he jumped through the window, which was closed, he smashed the pane with his head as if he was leaping into a pool of water.

But I have to say that we always played fair. None of the players kept track of the score. One boy was chosen as scorekeeper, and he got a pencil and a sheet of paper and no one was allowed to look at it. You can imagine the excitement once the game finished. Not who had won, but who was last.

There was one kid once who came last, he took it calmly but he said that first he had to go to the latrine. If we didn't trust him, we could go with him. We went. The latrine was in a corner of the parade ground, a little ways behind the barracks. I don't know if you know what a latrine like that looks like. It's a pit about as deep as the height of a person, maybe a bit more. I don't remember them ever emptying it, so it could have been deeper. It was about as wide as from you to the wall, and long enough for a dozen or more people to sit at the same time. There were two horizontal poles, you sat on the lower one and leaned your back against the other one. They were thick things, and they were propped up by struts so they wouldn't break. Around the latrine there was a solid high enclosure made of planking. I could stand on tiptoe and reach up my hand and still not be able to touch the top. Of course, I was a lot smaller then. There was a roof raised a foot and a half or so above the walls, to allow for ventilation. Though when it rained, it was hard to find a place on the pole where the rain didn't come in. And when it was really pouring, you could do your business on the fly, as they say, but you still got soaked.

The latrine was the only place you could go to talk, complain, curse, confide in each other, tell your woes, or every often even cry. Everywhere else, whenever a few people gathered together, however quietly they talked or even, God forbid, whispered, immediately someone would squeal. Whispers were the most suspicious of all. And they'd get hauled in right away.

"So what are these secrets of yours? We don't have any secrets here. Secrets are a selfish relic of old ways. And school isn't just about teaching you a trade, but how to behave as well. Out with it."

And you'd have to make something up on the spot. It goes without saying there were informers among us. But how could we tell who it was? I mean, they didn't exactly have "snitch" stamped on their foreheads. Even if you suspected one or another kid, he could still have been innocent. Whereas in your wildest dreams you'd never imagine it could be the guy who slept in the bunk above you or below you. He even hid under the blanket when he crossed himself.

Of course, you had to be careful in the latrine as well. Everyone would drop their pants whether they needed to go or not, and we'd all sit on the pole, while one guy would keep guard outside, his fly undone like he'd just finished. You should remember that back then flies were button-up, and fastening three or four buttons took longer than the zippers you have today. If someone we didn't trust came along, the kid outside would tip us off by whistling or coughing, then he'd start to button himself up. So when the person came into the latrine he wouldn't see anything wrong, because we'd all just be sitting there on the pole grunting away, often more than we needed to.

So anyway, the loser of the game said he had to use the latrine. We went with him. He unbuttoned his pants, sat down on the pole, there was no way anyone could have known it was just a trick. All of a sudden he slid off the pole and began to drop down into the pit. He didn't shout out for us to save him, because he had no intention of drowning. He just wanted to dunk himself in so he'd stink. He was quite right in thinking no one would want to come near anyone who stank like that, and none of the winners would order him to do anything. Even after he washed. After something like that getting rid of the smell is easier said than done, even if you take a bath every day. Plus he was fully dressed, wearing his boots. It would take the longest time for the smell to go away.

But he hadn't realized how deep the pit was. He was in up to his chest already, and his feet still hadn't touched the bottom. At that moment he began asking us, begging us, to save him, afterwards he'd do anything we wanted. What would we have him do? Whatever anyone of that age and at that school could come up with. I won't even tell you what. Another boy and I broke one of the support struts with the idea of handing it to him. The older ones wouldn't let us. Hold on a minute! Stop! Let it come up to his neck first! Then his chin. Let him eat the stuff, the little bastard. They were even making fun of him. You thought you could save yourself in shit. In the end he sank down to his forehead and we had to drag him out by the hair. That was what the game was like.

Supposedly it was just flipping a matchbox to see if it would land upright, scratchboard, or flat. And whoever came last, well, you might say it was a part of themselves that they lost. There wasn't anyone who didn't experience being last. That may have been why the limits of losing became blurred. When one of the older boys lost, us younger ones were no better. We'd make him do things that I don't even want to think about.

Then why did we play? Well, who starts playing a game with the idea that he's going to lose? Plus, in our game only one person lost, the one who came last. In any other game one person wins and everyone else loses. In this one, everyone wins except a single person. Tell me yourself, can you think of a more easy-going game? Or simpler? Exactly. Upright, scratchboard, flat.

Maybe we could take a little break from shelling, I could show you? I should have matches here somewhere. Here we are, the box is full even. You know, I actually sometimes play by myself. I take a box of matches, it has to be full, forty-eight matches, at least that's how many there used to be in a box back then, I sit down right here at the table, and I flip the box. Upright, scratchboard, flat. I don't keep score, what for? I'm not playing for anything. What could I play for, especially against myself? Unless you'd like to play for something. Then please say. At our age we can hardly play for the things we played for at school. Oh, I don't know. You're the guest here, you choose. I'm fine with anything.

Yes, the box is full. I don't use matches. I buy them sometimes just so I can play. I have lighters. Besides, it's all electric here. I am an electrician, after all.

The stove is electric too. Come sit at the table. Maybe you sit over there, I'll be here. Or would you prefer the other way around? See, this is how you place the box, it shouldn't be sticking out from the tabletop any more or it'll fall off. And you flip it up like this, with this finger, though you have to bend it a little.

Please, you go first. Look at that, your first time and you get it upright. That would have been ten points according to the way we played in school. My turn now. See, mine landed on the flat side. I'm not as nimble with my fingers as I used to be. Once the rheumatism gets hold of you it won't let go. Though it's much better now than it used to be, like I told you. It doesn't hurt much at all when I'm shelling beans. The finger that I'm flipping the matchbox up with, you see how crooked it is? No, it'll never go back to the way it was. I'd need an operation. At this point it's not worth it. Your turn. Upright again. How about that! I see it's sucked you in. And you were wondering why we kept playing. Every game pulls a person in, otherwise no one would play it. There, I got the flat side again. Maybe you'll want to keep score after all. Even when you don't play for anything, it can turn out that in fact you were playing for something, you just didn't know what it was. Especially after you've won. You'll remember? OK. I didn't want you to be mad at me later that you won and yet we weren't playing for anything. Upright again! You must have played before. I don't believe you. I can tell, if only from the way you flip the box up. It makes a half turn in the air, but it always lands upright. You just won't fess up.

There was this one kid in school, I remember that almost every time he got it upright. No one would play with him. You knew right from the start that he'd never come last. You must admit there's no way you can play with someone like that. You have to have equal amounts of hope and fear even in something like the matchbox game.

You wouldn't want to have been in a school like that? I understand. It's just that it didn't depend on whether you wanted to be there or not. Your turn. Upright again. Now me. And again, there you go. At school I was far from being the worst. Quite the opposite. It was another matter that I'd practice almost every evening I stayed behind in the rec room. I'd often take a break from practicing the sax or some other instrument and flip the matchbox at least a bit. Yes, I spent time in the rec room almost every evening. Mostly late when no one else was there. Though sometimes the music teacher would come by. I never minded that he was drunk. He'd sit down and I knew he was listening to me play. Again you got it upright. You should drop everything and just play the matchbox game. If you played for money you could make a fortune.

How did I end up in that school? You remember how the sister died, I told you about that. Soon afterwards I fell ill. I had a high fever, they gave me some pills, I sweated, but the moment the fever dropped it would come back again. I got all pale and skinny. I could pull myself out of bed, but I didn't have the strength to walk. The unit, though, had to move from the lake because they were beginning to be encircled. They took turns at carrying me, handing me from one to another for a time. We walked all night and all day, with short breaks. That is, I was carried. By evening they were out of the woods, they were planning to go into another woods, then all of a sudden they noticed a forester's cottage. They waited till it got completely dark. A light came on in one window. Two of them went to check. It turned out that the only person in the place was the forester's wife. They took me to her and left me in her care. She wrung her hands over me and said:

"Mother of God, if I'd only known you were so sick. Your forehead is burning up, you're all on fire. But don't die on me, I only just buried my man."

Feverish as I was, she bathed me in a tub, lamenting all the while:

"You're so skinny! Mother of God, skin and bone. Well, I'll just have to fatten you up, but get out of the tub now."

After that she cupped me. Then she rubbed me from head to foot with something that stung.

"Goodness, those cups left such dark marks. So dark," she kept repeating as she worked the stuff into my skin. "I've never seen such dark marks. I'd leech you, but I don't have any leeches." She gave me something to drink. I remember it was awfully bitter. "Drink up, it'll do you good." Then she wrapped me in an eiderdown.

Apparently I slept three nights and two days. She roused me now and then just to give me more of the bitter drink. I finally woke up completely devoid of strength, I couldn't even bring my hand out from under the eiderdown. But the fever was gone.

"I killed a chicken for you," she said, as if she was welcoming me into the world, "so you can have some broth. After a sickness like that, broth is the best thing." But she wouldn't allow me out of bed. "You just lie there, you need to stay put awhile. I'm not going to let you get up just yet." She fed me in bed, putting one spoonful after another into my mouth. A little broth, some noodles, a tiny piece of meat. "Come on, have some more, just a bit. One more spoonful at least. You have to put on some weight, otherwise you won't get your strength back. You're so skinny, mother of God but you're skinny."

She pulled the eiderdown back and looked at me. I was too weak even to be embarrassed. She was still young, as I remember her today. I just thought she was on the plump side. She might have been good-looking, I don't remember. Her face was rather bland, her eyes were sad but kind. She had black hair, she used to let it down when she brushed it and it would cover her up completely. Her breasts were so full they'd sometimes spill over the top of her nightgown when she was getting out of bed.

She had no children, and the forester had died not long before. The Germans had been hunting partisans, it was sunrise, and he had run out of the cottage to chase off some wild boars that were rooting around in the potato patch. They thought someone was trying to escape from the place and there were shots. She ran out after him and found him lying dead right outside the cottage, at the edge of the field. She often wept for him. She'd be peeling potatoes or making dough for noodles and suddenly she'd burst into tears. I'd comfort her as best I could:

"Don't cry, ma'am. Maybe he's in heaven now and he can see you crying."

"How did you get so wise?" And she'd stop. "Will you have something to eat?

I'll go see if the chickens have laid, I could make you some scrambled eggs. You need to eat. And dinner won't be for a long while." She'd keep telling me I was putting on weight before her eyes. "You know, you look better already. Much better, thank the Lord. Do you want something to eat?" That was the constant refrain: "At least have a slice of bread and butter. Maybe with some cheese? The butter's homemade, the cheese too."

She had two cows. I'd already gotten my strength back and I'd graze the cows on the pasture by the woods. Often it wouldn't yet be sundown and she'd come bring me either a slice of bread and butter with cheese, or two or three hard-boiled eggs.

"It's still aways to dinner. You must be hungry. Have this . . ." Sometimes she'd sit with me awhile. She'd watch me eating and keep saying: "Eat, eat. You've filled out even since yesterday."

One time we were already in our beds, her in hers and me in mine, when I heard her crying. Very quietly, but ever since I was little my hearing has been good, I thought she was maybe having a bad dream. I raised my head and listened intently. I could hear she was weeping.

"Are you crying, ma'am?" I asked. "Why?"

"It's nothing. There's no point telling you. It'd be different if you were older. Go back to sleep."

Winter came. She was still plying me with food, and as for me, I was helping with everything, whether she asked me to or not. She'd often say God had sent me to her, because how could she have managed on her own after he was gone. Meaning the forester. His hat lay on the dresser in the main room. It was sort of green, with a narrow brim, there was a cord twisted around it and tied in a figure-of-eight at the side. I might not have paid any attention to it, but one time she took it from the dresser, cleaned it with a brush, and hung it on a nail over their wedding photograph.

"It should go here," she said. "Don't ever touch it. It's a sacred thing."

As you know, though, sacred things are more tempting even than sin. One day she left to go to the store in the village. I took down the hat and studied the wedding photo. She wasn't much older than in the picture. The forester just looked like a forester. I thought to myself, he's dead, she's at the store, who's going to see if I try on the hat? So I did.

There was also one room that she kept locked up. She put the key behind a picture of Our Lady with the Infant Christ. But since she locked the room, that meant she didn't want me to go in there. And I didn't. But once she left the key in the door and didn't turn it. I felt an itch, and I peeked in. All I could see was a bulging bed covered with a patterned bedspread. Next to the bed was a cradle and a large wall mirror. I knew about the mirror. Whenever she washed her hair she'd tell me to do this or that, keep an eye on something, while she was brushing her hair in front of the mirror. And she'd go into that room, lock herself in and brush her hair for the longest time.

I looked into the mirror and let me tell you, in that first moment I had a fright when I realized it was me. It was like I was seeing myself for the first time. Like it was only now I was able to see that I existed. At home I never looked in the mirror, who looks at themselves at that age? When I was leaving for school in the morning, mother would always check me over, come here and I'll comb your hair, because otherwise I wouldn't even touch it. I couldn't tear myself away from that mirror, I couldn't believe it was me. Maybe because I was wearing the forester's hat, which fell down over my ears. Or maybe because I'd always imagined I was a lot older than the unexpected reflection in the mirror. A ruddy, chubby, well-fed face. I ran my hand over my cheek and I couldn't even feel a slight fuzz, but the boy in the mirror also ran his hand over his cheek, and I had the impression that he could already feel a fuzz. I stood and stood there, still unsure whether I should believe it was me. Especially because I didn't like the way I looked. The only thing I liked was the forester's hat. It even occurred to me to wonder, what if I were a forester?

I didn't notice that in the meantime the forester's wife had come back and was fuming. She burst into the room asking how I'd found the key. Snatching the hat off my head, she started saying that she was feeding me, looking after me, and here I was so ungrateful, so ungrateful, so this, that, and the other, going on till she made herself breathless. I'd never seen her like that before, gasping, her breasts heaving. Finally she sat down, exhausted, and cooled off a little.

"See what you've gone and done. I was thinking now that the war's over . . . But now . . ."

I didn't understand what she meant, but at least I learned that the war was already over.

Sometimes, especially when rain was in the air, you could hear a train rumbling and whistling a long long way off. Or if you put your ear to the ground, the rumbling sound would pass through it like electricity. Once I asked her:

"Where's that train?"

"Over there." She pointed.

"But where's the station?"

"It's that way. But it's a long way away."

Winter passed, spring, summer came along. One day I told her I was going to the woods to look for wild strawberries, and set off to find the station. I just went, with no particular intention in mind, just to see if maybe a train would come along. As I remember it today, I must have walked a good few miles. It was only a small station, but there were quite a lot of people waiting. I asked a railwayman when the train was due.

"Which direction?" he asked.

"It makes no difference."

"What do you mean, it makes no difference? Don't know you which direction you're headed in? Well anyway, if you don't know, one will be along any minute now."

And in fact a train arrived soon after. It was bursting with passengers, there were even people sitting on the roofs of the cars. The ones who were waiting, it didn't look like there'd be room for them. Especially because they all had suitcases, trunks, baskets, all kinds of bags and bundles. The ones already in the train pulled them in, while others pushed from the platform. I forgot to mention that the moment the train came to a halt, from the front and back two boys about my age jumped out. They were carrying baskets and as they ran along the platform one of them called:

"Pears! Apples! Plums!" While the other one shouted: "Tomatoes! Cucumbers! Kohlrabi!"

Hands reached out to them from the train windows, people bought from them. The train started to move off, but they ran down the platform and kept selling. At the last minute they hopped onto the step, just barely grabbing hold of the handrail. The train gathered speed and disappeared, and I felt kind of strange that I'd been left behind. I felt as if I'd been abandoned by the train and all the people in it. The railwayman I'd spoken to seemed surprised:

"Why didn't you get on, if it makes no difference to you which direction you take?" He laughed.

He went into the station building, while I took my time going back. I walked slowly, bothered by various thoughts, and when I got close to the forester's cottage I decided I'd run away from the forester's wife. She started scolding me for having been gone so long, and see, you didn't even pick any wild strawberries. And that in general I used to be more willing to do things, though I'd been much skinnier then and didn't have the strength I had now.

I took a basket of hers and a pint-sized tin mug to have something to measure with when I was selling wild strawberries, blueberries, blackberries, or other such things. And in the morning, before she woke up I crept out of bed and ran away.

I began riding the train like the boys I'd seen. I sold whatever I could pick in the woods or steal from people's orchards and fields. To begin with at any rate, because later, once I'd set some money aside, I bought things from the farmers. Sometimes they'd take pity on me and sell me produce for next to nothing, sometimes they'd even give me things for free. Then I'd sell the stuff either by the piece or by the mugful. If it was by the mugful, the person would need to have a small bag or at least a sheet of newspaper. I slept at the stations. Most of the time, though, I was riding. I'd hop from one train to another at the passing places, then just keep going, and do that the whole time. I got to know other boys who rode the trains like me, selling this or that. They taught me a lot, what was most profitable, what not so much, what was most popular and at what times. What sold best in different trains, morning trains and evening trains, there really was a big difference. In slow trains and expresses. Takings were lousiest in express trains. The express only ran once a day. Or for instance what people tended to buy in crowded trains versus less crowded ones, in second class versus third class. Back then second class was like first class today, and third class was like our second class. When you can charge more, when people won't pay as much. Sales were best when the train was packed. Except that making your way through a crowded train presented quite a challenge. Often the conductors couldn't even be bothered to check anyone's tickets. But at that age I was half the size I am now, and nimble. When I got better at it, I sold lemonade too. That was when I did the best business. Plus of course it never went bad.

One time I was going through a second-class car, second class usually wasn't as full, I called out:

"Lemonade! Lemonade! Pears! Pears! Apples! Apples!"

An old man beckoned me:

"I'll take one pear. But I want a good ripe one. How much do you charge for a pear?"

He paid me three times the price. He wouldn't take any change. He asked me to sit by him a moment. He started asking questions about where I was from, where I lived, whether my parents were still alive. I didn't say anything, because what was I supposed to tell him? Plus I was afraid he'd slap me with a fine, as naturally I didn't have a ticket.

"Would you like to go to school?" he asked.

I didn't say anything to that either, because I didn't know if I wanted to or not.

"You could learn a trade," he said. "You can't spend the rest of your life riding the train. What are you going to sell in winter, for instance? There are no fruits. Lemonade? Most trains aren't heated, who's going to want to drink lemonade?"

Let me tell you, he scared me with that winter. I didn't know people weren't thirsty in trains in the winter. He surprised me even more by saying that these days, after the war there were a lot of children like me. The train stopped at some station and without asking me anymore if I wanted to or not, he said:

"We're getting out."

I got out with him. There were *dorozhkas* outside the station. We went up to one of them. The driver evidently knew him, because he was pleased to see him:

"Oh, it's you, counselor. Greetings, greetings. Haven't seen you in a long time." Then he asked: "The usual place?"

We rode for quite a long time, till we pulled up in front of a building with bars on the first floor windows. There he handed me over to someone. They took me, and the first thing they did was shave my head down to the skin. Then they gave me soap and a towel and took me to a shower, and told me to give myself a thorough scrubbing. They gave me clothes and boots. I remember the boots were way too big for me. I'd left my own boots at the forester's cottage, I hadn't wanted to wake the forester's wife as I was leaving. I'd been going around barefoot, though summer was almost over. They took my picture from the front, from one side then the other. Then they brought me to a cafeteria. A few boys were already eating there. There was bread and jam and black ersatz coffee, I remember I didn't like the food despite being hungry. Then a uniformed guard led us all to a cell. The window was barred, there was a bucket in the corner and a few iron bunk beds. He said:

"You'll be more comfortable here than at your own mother's. Go to sleep." And he bolted the door from the outside.

No one slept though. The moment we turned off the light we began to get bitten by bedbugs. Ever been bitten by a bedbug? I wouldn't wish it on you. They bit all night long. There were hordes of them. We crushed them, but new ones kept popping up. It was my first time dealing with bedbugs. Believe me, fleas are nothing next to bedbugs. Our bodies were covered in welts, and they itched so bad you wanted to tear your skin off. We scratched ourselves till we bled. And the more we scratched, the worse it itched. It was like that night after night. We complained to the guard who locked us in at night, and all he said was:

"You need to sleep better."

It was only after several days that a van came for us. Not the usual kind of truck. This one had a metal hatch with barred windows, and another guy in uniform bolted the door after we got in. He sat next to the driver and he kept glancing through the barred window from the cab to see what we were up to. What could we be up to? We were being jolted up and down, that was it. The road was all potholes, so we spent more time driving in zigzags than going straight, and we kept getting thrown against the sides. The whole way I was wondering to myself what I'd actually done to deserve this. Was it because I'd run away from the forester's wife? Or that I was selling things in trains? That I didn't have a ticket? Anyway, this was how I found myself at the school.

Oh – we didn't decide how many turns we'd take. Whatever you like. At school we'd always agree to take a certain number of turns. It depended on how many of us were playing. Also on whether it was early or late we got started playing. And that would depend on when the teacher went away. But I was going to tell you why he collected matchboxes. You'll never guess. Look at the box we're playing with. What do you see? Right, here are the scratchboards, this is where you take the matches out from one side or the other, and here's the label. This one happens to say: Feed the Hungry Children. Some charity. Back then there were different ones. They'd change from time to time. When you'd used up all the matches, you'd go buy more or take some from someone else's pocket, and there'd be a new label. The previous one had said: Brush Your Teeth, while the new one said: Long Live May 1, or: Power to the Youth of the World, or: The Whole Nation is Rebuilding our Capital. If you didn't know what times you were living in, you could have figured it out from those labels. These days I don't know what they change from or to. Like I said, I hardly ever use matches, it's all electric here. I don't smoke either. But if you ask me, you could figure out any time on the basis of those labels. And it's been possible ever since there have been matches.

That's exactly what our teacher thought too. He had them make him a plywood display board in the shop. How big? Well, not to exaggerate, a little smaller than a classroom chalkboard. On it he would pin matchboxes in little rows. There was still a lot of free space, and so every evening he'd come and remind us to give him our matchboxes when they were empty. For each civics lesson we'd bring the display board to class. There'd be two or three of us carrying it, it was pretty heavy, and he'd follow behind and shout:

"Careful! Careful!"

The boxes mustn't have been attached very firmly, because every now and then one of them would fall off on the way. When that happened he'd get so mad, he'd call the boys who were carrying the board all sorts of names, say they were oafs, morons, good-for-nothings. And he'd educate us using the board, matchbox by matchbox. He probably thought that since we were constantly playing that game, we'd find it easier to learn in such a way.

He'd call you to the board, point with his stick at one box or another and ask you what you could see on it. But what you saw wasn't all, because after that it would be, Say more. Saying more was much harder. Even when one of us managed to say more, he'd still keep at him. All right, go a little deeper, think about how that should be properly understood. If anyone happened to understand something improperly, he'd fly into a rage, he'd shout about how we spent all our evenings playing matchboxes, even after he left us, we thought he didn't know but he knew everything. He knew what kind of game it was. And what we played for.

You know, it really wasn't such a stupid idea at all, if you think about it. Tell me yourself, how can you educate someone so they're in no doubt about what times they're living in? All a person cares about is the fact that they live from birth to death. But who needs someone who only lives from birth to death.

Often it seems to them that even that's too much. Plus, if they could pick what time they could live in, probably not that many people would choose their own. Living in your own times is the hardest thing of all, you have to admit. It'd be a lot easier in some earlier or later time, anything but your own. So educating someone is no simple matter. And you never know what might turn out to be the best method. Then why would matchboxes be any worse?

All right, it's your turn.

13

Did I not tell you? I thought I told you already. I went and bought it. Not to the nearest town. The nearest towns were backwaters, they might not have had anything like that there. I wanted a brown felt one. I walked all over before I found a hat shop. I might have passed it by, the display window was no bigger than my window here, and it contained nothing but caps and berets and a single drab-colored hat. Luckily, a bit further back, behind the caps and berets, kind of hidden, I spotted a brown felt hat. I perked up and went in. The store was dark, it long and thin like a hallway, the only light was what came from the display, and right at the far end, behind the counter, was the clerk. He looked to have been dozing, because when I came in he raised his head, yawned, and said quickly:

"Can I help you?"

"I'm looking for a hat," I said in an apologetic tone, as if for having woken him up.

"What kind?"

"A brown felt one."

"We don't have anything in brown felt. There aren't any in brown. Generally speaking, what you see is all we have, young man." He gestured toward the shelves behind him. There were peaked caps, other caps, berets, and no more than a handful of hats, most of them the same dull color as the one on display, plus two or three greenish ones, as far as I could make out in the gloom that reigned at that end of the store. "I bet you thought you'd walked into a shop, didn't you, young man?" He grew so animated he sat up on his seat. He was a short man, but all of a sudden he seemed a lot bigger to me. "But this is no shop. And certainly not a hat shop. Before the war I had a hat shop. Now if you'd come to me before the war . . ."

I broke in:

"What about the one on display?"

"I can't take anything down from the display."

"Why not?"

"I'm only allowed to take things from the display when the display is changed."

"When will that be?"

"Who can know. Who can know, young man. There has to be a new shipment so there'll be something to change." He seemed unwilling to forgive me for having interrupted his nap. "Besides, the one in the display is too big for you. You need the next size down, I can tell. Or even two sizes, if you got a haircut. Where did this taste for big shocks of hair come from? Everything evidently has to be changed. Everything's all wrong."

I figured my hair must have set him against me, since he himself was bald. At the time I had a full head of hair, and it made me embarrassed next to his shiny head.

"At least let me prove it to you," he said unexpectedly in a milder tone. He took a tape measure, came out from behind the counter, had me stoop down, and measured my head. "Like I said, too big. I've been in this line so long I don't even need to take measurements. One look at a client and I know right away, they'll need such and such a size. And what style will suit them. What's the right color for them. Before the client tries anything on I know all there is to know. If you want to give good advice you have to sense everything. Sometimes a different style or color might be better, but I take one look and I know which one the client is going to like himself in best, so I advise them accordingly. And which one they'll like themselves in, that requires a lot more knowing than size and style and color. You might say that every client is a mountain, and on the summit of the mountain you need to be able to see the right hat. Though why am I even telling you this? As far as the hats are concerned there is what there is here, and there aren't any more clients either. All of us, we're just the 'working people of city and country.' As for brown felt ones, I don't remember when I last had anything."

"Do you expect to be getting any in?"

"Who can tell. Who can tell anything these days? You can tell that the sun will rise tomorrow, that much we still know. I put in an order. Way back. Including brown felt ones. Personally I like brown felt hats the best. I have one from before the war, it still does the job. These days, putting in an order means sending the thing off then just waiting and waiting. And even if it finally comes, it's not the styles you asked for, or the colors, or the sizes. You're lucky if the number of items matches up. Numbers still count some. Numbers fulfill the plan, so to speak, not styles or colors or sizes. It's another matter that no one buys hats any-more nowadays. These aren't good times for hats. It's as if people are afraid to be too tall. Because hats make you taller. That extra two or four inches, depending on the style, it adds to your height. There was a time, everybody wanted to be taller. There were even special styles for shorter clients. I've worked in hats all my life, and in my old age I don't understand any of it. You'd have thought that someone like me, who had a shop before the war - and not just any old shop, I even imported hats from abroad - that I ought to be able to read hats like you'd read the book of wisdom. But evidently that book doesn't include present times. Before the war, if you'd come to me I'd have had just the right hat for you. What kind was it you wanted again?"

"Brown felt."

"I'd have had a brown felt one, yes indeed. Would you prefer darker or lighter brown? Wide or narrow brim? By all means. Higher, lower? You're quite tall, I'd suggest something a little lower. By all means. The client was actually a client. And the hats – you could tell a person from their hat. These days, though, big industry comes first, producing hats is a sideline. What about this one? It's your size." He took one of the dull-colored hats from the shelf behind him. "Try it on, go take a look in the mirror."

"No thank you," I said.

"Then perhaps this sort of greenish one? For a young face it's even better. And it's also the right size. I'd not suggest brown. Brown ages a person. Especially felt. There's no reason to hurry toward old age, even in these times. It'll come of its own accord. Oh yes, it'll fly here on wings. You expect it, but still you're taken by surprise. People aren't able to come to terms with old age. You, you're young, you don't need to understand how painful old age is. Though at times youth is painful too. That's how life is, there's something painful at every age. The worst pain comes from inside a person. There was this one client before the war, I'd order the very best quality hats for him . . . I'll never have clients like that anymore." All of a sudden he seemed to remember something. "Wait a moment, I have just the thing for you. It'll be perfect." He started rummaging about among all the caps and berets and hats on the shelf, and from somewhere deep down he produced a cream-colored hat. He straightened it and said with pride in his voice: "This is from my old shop. Try it on." When I said thank you but no, that wasn't what I was looking for, he actually begged me: "What do you have to lose. Please, try it on. Maybe it was just sitting here waiting for you. That's how it is sometimes, that a hat is waiting for a particular client. When the client finally shows up its destiny is fulfilled, so to speak. And not just the hat's. Unfortunately, the client I mentioned probably won't be coming back. Now there was a client. Simply brimming with life. He changed hats like he changed women, so to speak. I always knew he had a new woman when he came in for a new hat. The last time, he happened to be looking for something youthful, in cream. The color of desert sand in the glare of the sun, he said. In a whisper he added, there's going to be war. You have to enjoy life before then, right up to the final minute, because this may be the last time. I told him I'd have something in a month, please come by. But he never did. And this is the hat. The color of desert sand in the glare of the sun. Please, do try it on. That way I'd no longer have to . . . Especially as I hide it under the other hats. This is a state-owned store, and here I am selling my own merchandise. From before the war. What if they found it during an inspection? Luckily there's nothing to inspect here. They usually just have me sign a form that there was an inspection, the inventory was such and such, no discrepancies noted. Sometimes they try and reprimand me, saying the orders I put in are evidently too small and don't include every kind of headwear, because the plan includes all different kinds and so I ought to have more in the way of merchandise. Sometimes they ask if I have any particular requests. But what kind of requests can you have in a state-owned shop, in a state job, when requests have also been placed under state control, so to speak. I mentioned that it would be good to have more hats. Of course they wrote it down. Had me say what different styles, colors, sizes, they wrote all that down too. Now I'm waiting for those requests of mine to be granted. One request I had was that they fix the lamp in here. For the last month, when it gets dark I've had to light a candle, because I mean I can't shut up shop early. It says on the door that I'm open from such and such till such and such a time, and that has to be. When a client comes in I have to go up to them with a candle, how can I help you, because I never know if they can even see me here behind the counter."

"What happened to the light?" I asked, all set to leave, especially since he'd given me no indication that he might take that hat from the display and at least let me try it on to see if it really was too big.

"The usual – it went out and it doesn't work anymore. I checked the bulb and the fuses. They're fine. There's nothing more I know how to do."

"Is it just in your shop?"

"As if out of spite, they have power in all the neighboring stores. Upstairs too, on all the floors. Throughout the whole building. The only problem is in here."

"Do you have any tools? A screwdriver and pliers at least? I could take a look. Maybe something can be done."

"You?" he said in surprise.

"I'm an electrician."

"An electrician?" He was even more amazed. "Who'd have thought? Who'd have thought? I reckoned I could tell every client's line of work. Your line of work is your character, and everyone's character is written on their face. In their movements, their walk, their posture, their way of being. I was convinced . . . See what happens to a man when he works in a state-owned shop. These days it's getting harder and harder to know people."

"Do you have pliers at least?" I reminded him. "If need be, ordinary pincers might do."

"Sorry, no." He shrugged helplessly, as if he were confessing to some misdemeanor. "Wait a minute though, there's a tool shop a couple of doors down."

He scurried out. And before I'd had time to take a good look around – though truth to tell there wasn't a whole lot to look at, except maybe for the mirror, which reached from the floor to over halfway up the wall – he was back with an armful of various tools. Screwdrivers, flat-blade and crosshead, pincers small and large, pliers; wire-cutters, a small hammer, a wrench, a roll of insulating tape, even rubber gauntlets.

"Why did you bring all this?" I said with a laugh. "It won't be needed. First I have to take a look."

"Just in case," he said, visibly excited. "In the store they said that electricity is serious business."

"Luckily I know that already," I said.

He put it all on the counter, removing the hats he'd been offering me, and he rubbed his hands with satisfaction.

"Who'd have thought. How can anyone not believe in serendipity. And serendipity is precisely destiny. Even in a state-owned shop. I mean, if I'd had a brown felt hat in your size, I'd still be without light."

"That remains to be seen," I said, trying to calm him down a little. But he ignored me.

"You'd have tried the hat on and bought it, and I'd still be sitting here by candlelight."

"This switch is working," I said, screwing in the clips that attached it to the wall. "But it would be good to replace it. It's from before the war. The box has perished. I'll check the lamp now. I just need to push the counter into the middle of the room, I won't be able to reach it from a chair."

"Of course, of course. Do whatever you need."

I climbed onto the counter, took off the lampshade and unscrewed the bulb. The bulb was still good, but the socket was on its last legs, plus it was dangling by a single wire, the other one had broken off deep inside the line. I wrapped the socket in insulating tape to prevent it from falling apart completely, and cut away part of the line. I also had to cut a piece of it by the ceiling rose, because the insulation round the wiring came away in my hand. It was a fiddly job, it took me a long time. Meanwhile, the other guy seemed unable to settle down. He dropped onto a chair, but he couldn't sit still for longer than a moment, he stood up again right away. He tipped his head back and watched what I was doing. He was suddenly overcome by doubt:

"Maybe I was getting ahead of myself?"

"No, we'll figure something out," I said, "so long as the wiring in the walls is still good. But it all needs to be replaced. And I wouldn't put it off."

He sat down again, jumped back up, went into the storeroom and came back. The he started rearranging all the caps and berets and hats on the shelves.

"I'm looking for someplace to hide this hat, since you're not interested in it. Though I could already picture you in it, so to speak. On the street, in the park, walking along with the lady of your heart. You saying hello to people, smiling. Everyone looking back at you, wondering where you got a hat like that. The color of desert sand in the glare of the sun. And you got it from my shop from before the war. Could anyone ever describe the color of a hat in a deeper way?

Desert sand. And a perfect fit. It's like it was custom made for you. It'd stay on, I guarantee it. Because a hat ought to stick to your head like a soul to its body. It shouldn't be too tight, because then it leaves a mark on your forehead when you take it off. And it shouldn't be too loose, because that's even worse, the hat goes one way and the head another. The hat ought to be obedient to the head, when you turn it left or right the hat should turn left or right with it. You tip your head up toward the sun, it shouldn't slide forward; you lean down, it shouldn't fall off. And in general you shouldn't even feel you have something on your head. That's what it means to have a hat that fits. Hats I know like the back of my hand, so to speak. My whole life has been spent with hats. Trust an old hatter. Who are you going to trust, what you see is all that's left of hats, and before long it may all be gone. Then no one will ever be able to tell you anymore what hats once were. And that's a big thing to know. In other kinds of headgear a person shrinks, disappears, loses their uniqueness. Of a Sunday, when I'd go into town, so to speak, wherever I looked there were hats from my shop. It goes without saying I carried all the accessories that go with hats: scarves, neckties, bow ties, gloves, even umbrellas. And the clients would always follow my advice. Naturally I gave it subtly, tactfully, so he'd be convinced it was his own taste guiding him. It's common knowledge that not every person has the best taste. And taste is an important thing. Taste, so to speak, is more than just taste. Your taste determines how you think, feel, imagine, act."

I decided I had to find something for him to do after all, because my hands were starting to shake. Even standing on the countertop I could barely reach the ceiling rose – it was a pre-war building with a high ceiling, and with my hands stretched up the whole time the job wasn't going as well as I'd have liked. Plus there was his endless chatter down below. He'd evidently gotten carried away with the hope of having light, and perhaps out of gratitude to me he hardly even paused for breath.

"After all, isn't life a question of taste, so to speak?"

I thought he was talking to me and I said:

"Pass me that flat-blade screwdriver, please."

He handed it to me mechanically, and went right on.

"Some people like it, they're glad to be alive, others live because they have to. I'd never have come to know people if I hadn't had them as clients. Truth is, every one of us has the soul of a client. In that respect all souls are alike. It makes no difference who buys something and who doesn't. Or whether you carry what he's looking for or not. Excess or want, they both equally reveal the client in a person. Unfortunately, they don't do much else."

I asked him to go wash the lampshade, it looked like no one had cleaned it since before the war, it was blocking the light. He took it, but he didn't leave right away. He spun the lampshade in his hands like a hat. I had to remind him that it wasn't a hat, that he'd break it. It was only then he went into the back room. When he came back, I complimented him on doing a good job:

"It looks good as new." I started talking about lampshades, saying that these days you never got shades like the one in his shop, and telling him what kinds people put up now. But he took advantage of a moment when I had to hold a screw in my mouth, and he picked up where he'd left off:

"Generally speaking hats are headgear, as they say. But it's a different matter when it's on the head of a particular client. Then, when that client stands at the mirror, it's another matter again. Because who really sees themselves in the mirror at a moment like that? No one, let me tell you, no one. Who *do* they see? Exactly, who do they see? Maybe they themselves don't know who they see, even though they're standing in front of themselves. And that, so to speak, is the fascinating secret that makes it worth devoting your whole life to selling hats."

"Pass me the file," I said. "I can't reach down, I have to hold this up."

He started rooting around among the tools on the counter.

"It's in your hand," I said.

He gave it to me automatically.

"Now hand me those pliers." I reckoned if I kept him busy passing me this or that, he might stop talking. "Take the screwdriver from me. Now give it back again." Pass me that, take this from me. Pass that, take this. Instead of making the repair, it was like I'd succumbed to him, and I kept repeating: Pass that, take this, take this, pass that.

In the end I had him climb up on the countertop, stand next to me, and hand me tools or take them from me, because it was hard for me to reach his outstretched hand when he was standing on the floor, and I couldn't always bend down. He pulled up a chair, climbed onto it, stood next to me, but not even that prevented him from talking.

"There were times that from the first glance you could tell the hat wasn't right for the face, but the client said he thought this one looked best on him. You'd wonder who he was seeing that he'd chosen that particular one. Unfortunately you couldn't say, That one doesn't suit you, because it might sound like you were questioning not the hat but his face. What am I saying, face, it was as if you were questioning the image of himself that he carried. And after all, that's something everyone has a perfect right to, everyone bears that image within themselves . . ."

"I dropped a screw. Could you climb down and find it?" Once again I was trying to interrupt him.

He popped down almost like a spring, he was agile for his age. And wouldn't you believe it, he found the screw at once. You or I would have hunted all over for it. All he did was step down from the chair, lean over and pick it up. He climbed back just as quickly.

"Maybe it was like you were questioning his own unsatisfied need for himself, his thirst for himself, his longing for himself, because each of us allows ourselves something like that, it helps us to live. And you have to respect that in a client. Profit isn't the most important thing when you've been dealing with hats as long as I have. Besides, you outgrow the desire for profit, especially when you're nearer rather than further from the boundless place where profit counts for nothing at all. When you start to measure out your life with all the hats you've sold. When you're visited more and more often by doubt about whether everyone was satisfied with the hats they bought. If I'd been certain of that I would have said, All praise to the hat. Unfortunately, I'm not. Despite the fact that even before the previous war, when I was more or less your age, I worked as a clerk in a hat shop. I began life with hats, so to speak, and I'm ending it with them. That includes two world wars. You might think that when it comes to hats I know everything. It turns out though that I don't. And please believe me, young man, I learned this wise lesson only when my shop was taken over by the government. Though it is what it is, as you can see. In this way I was punished for daring to believe that I knew anything. Whereas in reality, what on earth do I know, as it turns out. The more so if you take as the highest measure of knowledge that you don't even know that you don't know, however much you know."

This time I told him an untruth, saying I'd dropped another screw. And imagine this, he got down, found it, climbed back up and handed it to me. After that I stopped trying.

"Pass me the bulb and the lampshade, then you can step down."

I replaced the shade and screwed in the light bulb.

"There's nothing more can be done here," I said. "Now it all depends on what the wiring's like. Turn the switch."

He turned it, the light came on. No, he didn't explode with joy. He simply said:

"Oh, the light's working." He turned the switch again, the light went off. He turned it on again, off again, on, off. All at once he was gripped by a kind of anxiety:

"When you leave, will it still come on?"

"Sure it will," I reassured him. "But all this is a stop-gap measure. You need to replace the fittings, the wiring, everything. And don't delay."

"How much do I owe you?" he asked, holding me back, because I was getting ready to leave.

"Nothing."

"But I have to give you something for your troubles. Wait a minute," he said, pausing to think. He suddenly went up to the display and took down the brown felt hat. "I can't sell you a hat from the display. But at least try it on. You'll see yourself that it's too big for you. I wouldn't like you to go away unconvinced."

I put it on and looked in the mirror, while he put one of the dull-colored hats in the display.

"See? It's too big, like I told you. And brown felt makes it look even bigger next to your young face."

The hat fell down over my ears. Plus, when I saw my reflection in the mirror I started wondering if that was me with the hat on my head. Have you ever had those kinds of doubts about whether you are you? I've had them all my life. I always felt as if I was divided within myself into one person who knew it was him and another person who felt no closeness with himself. Into one person, shall we say, who knows he's going to die, and one person who rejects the idea that it's him and thinks someone else is going to die in his stead. I've never been able to be together long enough even just to sympathize with myself. Let me tell you, a person shouldn't think too much about himself, or even more go probing himself. He is the way he is, and that ought to be enough. And whether he's himself or not, let that be resolved in due course.

Standing in front of the mirror, with the outsized hat on my head, staring at my own reflection, I became painfully aware of that division inside myself.

"Are you shaving already?" he suddenly asked. I was taken unawares, and over there, in the mirror, I went red as a beetroot.

"Of course," I said, though I don't think it came out very confidently.

"How often a week?" He wouldn't let up, as though he had some purpose in mind.

"It depends."

"Don't take offense, young man. I'd guess at the most once a week, on Sundays. I'm asking because brown felt isn't a good match for a face that's only shaved once a week. Actually, it's the worst match. Aside from the fact that this one is too big."

He caught me off balance with that remark, and I pulled the hat further down over my eyes, hoping it might not look quite so big.

"Not like that. Why hide your face?" He came up and tipped the hat back. "While your face is young it should be exposed, let the youth in it shine. It won't be able to shine when it's furrowed with wrinkles. Before the war it was mostly government workers that bought brown felt hats. In that respect nothing's changed. Whenever they come to do inventory, there's always one or another of them will ask if by any chance I have a brown felt hat. I don't, how could I? Never mind that, they pick out another hat or a cap, usually forgetting to pay. And that's the difference. Obviously I'm not going to say anything. I have to pay for it out of my own pocket. Though how can I do that when a month's salary doesn't cover a month's living expenses. Those guys ignore the fact that it's all state-owned, whereas me, I have nothing on my conscience. I mean, what could I have on my conscience in a place like this, you can see for yourself. This is all there is. Except that, unfortunately, it depends on them whether you have something on your conscience. Your conscience is state-owned too. There's no longer any need for God to remind us about our conscience. Hang on, maybe a bit further back, so your hair shows a little in the front."

He moved the hat so the brim pointed way up. And though I didn't think I could wear it that way, he said:

"There, like that. That's better. A lot better. Take a closer look in the mirror." He pulled it down again slightly. "No, it's too big after all. Too big. There's no way of arranging it so you can't tell." Then, stepping back from me, as if he was disappointed: "Anyway, why are you in such a hurry to get a hat? You'll have plenty of time to wear hats. You're young, maybe you'll live to see all sorts of different sizes, styles, colors. Someone has to have hope that someone else will live to see it. And who should have hope if not you young people. I'm too old now for hope, too old for this new world. That's what the government people told me, that this is a new world and that I don't understand it because I'm too old. I'd gone there to ask why the state was taking over my shop, they should just buy it from me. I wouldn't be crazy about selling it, but I'd do it. It was then that one of them told me I don't understand a thing. This is a revolution, citizen. I asked him, What does that mean? Revolution is revolution, the point is you have to believe in it. Don't ask any more questions, citizen. Just sign here. No need to read it. Of course I signed. I even thanked him for being so kind as to tell me I don't understand anything. Perhaps you'd like a peaked cap?" He went behind the counter and started taking peaked caps down from the shelves, one two, three. "Here, maybe this one. It's even your size. Or this one. Or perhaps this one. This one'd suit you better. Of all kinds of headwear, peaked caps bring out youth the most. Though maybe you don't want to look young? If that's the case, when are you going to be young? Now is your only chance to look young. There isn't all that much youth in a person's life. Especially if their life goes on and on. And it can't be put off till later. It's another matter that the present times are not too favorable for youth. These days even the young don't know they're young."

"Come on, things are not so bad," I said, daring to disagree, because as I stood in front of the mirror there was no doubt in my mind that at least on the outside I was young.

"Appearances, appearances, young man. It's dangerous to trust yourself so readily, especially as you can only see yourself in the mirror. You should think carefully about the brown felt hat, all the more since it's too big. The moment you came in, there was something in your face that troubled me. I mean, I know faces. My whole life I've been finding hats to match faces. And for that you need both experience and distrust. With every face, you have to ignore its vulnerability and first expose separately the eyes, the forehead, eyebrows, nose, mouth, cheeks, the whole thing, in minute detail so to speak. Then piece it back together again in all its fuzziness or excessive clarity, reduce it all the way to indistinctness, so nothing prevents you from seeing its special mark that's hidden, hidden deep as can be, but that exists in every face. Yes indeed, the face reaches deep inside a person. And each one needs a different kind of hat. Then it's much easier to pick the right hat. Though at the same time you have to remember that in the process of choosing we also have to deal with the other side of the equation, since hats can be fussy too, crabby even. At times they can mislead you so badly you forget what you're trying to match to what, the hat to the face or the face to the hat. Let me tell you, it hurt when a hat rejected a face but the client liked the way he looked in it. I felt sorry for every rejected face, though I ought to have been on the side of the hat. Not just because hats have been my whole life, that everything has revolved around them. Each new day would rise from behind my hats and go down again behind them at the end, so to speak. Hats swirled in my thoughts, my desires, my longings, my ideas. To the point that whenever I tried to imagine humanity to myself, it was always as an infinity of hats. There were times I started to wonder whether I wasn't a hat myself. Though on whose head? On whose head? So I admit that when the state took over my shop I felt a sense of relief, young man. It was as if someone had released me from some duty. More, that I'd been set free. I won't deny there was also regret, maybe even despair, but above all it was relief. Take the hat off a moment."

I removed it, he took it from me and went behind the counter. He bent down and vanished from view, as if he were looking for something stowed away somewhere deep. I could only hear his voice from under the counter:

"There should be a newspaper down here someplace. A client left it one time. I don't read the newspapers. Ah, here it is." He reappeared. "Step up closer, please. And watch carefully. Fold the newspaper more or less to the width of this inner lining. Not too thick, or it'll end up being too small for you." He slipped the newspaper under the lining of the hat and pressed it flat, working his way around the whole circumference. "Here, now try it on. At least it won't wobble about on your head. Or fall down over your eyes. If you take it off, just make sure you never set it upside down. The same when you hang it up, make sure the inside of the hat never shows. And most important of all, when you raise your hat to greet someone, never do it from too far off. The newspaper could fall out before you pass the person you're greeting. And for goodness' sake never ever lift the hat too high. You only need to raise it just above your head, or even just lift it up a little. It can be a big gesture, but the hat itself should only just be tipped upward. Let's give it a try. I'll give you a different hat and put yours on, I'll show you."

He gave me one of the dull-colored ones and had me step back by the display. He put the brown felt hat on and retreated to the counter.

"Oh yes, we should put the light on, since we have light now. It'll be easier to see. All right, so we're walking towards one another. Really slowly, like in a slow-motion film. There's no reason to hurry. You're approaching me, I'm approaching you. I'm the one who's supposed to say hello first, and you'll return the greeting. What I mean is, you're not you, I'm you, as I've got the hat with the newspaper in the lining. Pay careful attention. We're walking. I don't greet you yet, we're still too far apart. Only now, when we're almost passing each other. And you don't greet me, I greet you. You have to return my greeting. Don't snatch the hat off your head like that, the newspaper could fall out. Never mind that I'm wearing the brown felt hat, you're the one who's practicing. You raise your hand over your hat, like this. Slowly. Or like this, in a big broad gesture, depending on who you're saying hello to. It looks as if you're going to lift your hat almost to the height of your outstretched arm, but in fact as you pass one another you don't remove your hat at all, or you only raise it up very slightly. Sometimes a gesture alone can serve as a greeting. But don't forget to look back after you pass, just in case. Because if it turns out the other person has looked back as well, you can make an additional motion with your hand as if you were just replacing the hat on your head after the greeting. Let's try it one more time. This time you have the hat with the newspaper, and I'll take yours, and we'll switch roles. We'll see how you manage. Come over here, to my place, I'll go over by the display."

We practiced several times, and each time he corrected something in my greeting. Then in the middle of one of the practice runs, before we'd had time to greet each other, it was like he suddenly woke up, he came to a halt, winced winced a little as if from shame and said:

"Hand me the hat, please." He took the newspaper out. "Honestly, what am I teaching you here!" He put the hat back in the display, taking out the dull-colored one he'd put there in its place. "I'm going to the dogs. I'm not myself. What I've been showing you is an embarrassment. A hat lined with newspaper. At one time that would have been unthinkable. A greeting was a greeting, a ritual so to speak. You'd think I was trying to deprive you of all the pleasure of wearing a hat. I find it hard to even imagine you greeting a lady with a hat lined with newspaper. It's another matter that there are no ladies anymore either. They've all died off or flown away. Times aren't good for ladies either, so to speak. And if you walk down the street, you can see what's happened on the street also. You get elbowed, trodden on almost, and no one even apologizes. I rarely go out these days. Just to and from the shop. Not to mention what people wear on their heads. I try not to look. Have you noticed how ugly the world has gotten? So what that it exists? I've always been drawn to the beauty of the world, not just its existence. It's too big for you, it's too big. Not to mention that it's rejecting your face."

He opened a drawer under the counter, took out a thick notebook and almost tossed it over to me at the end of the counter.

"Please, write that you'd like a brown felt hat, in your size."

"What's this?"

"It's the requests and complaints book. Though I'd not use my own name if I were you. Just sign it: A client. I tell everyone the same." He picked the notebook up and turned the pages fretfully. "It's almost full. What people haven't written in here. See, there's a poem. And a picture, though it's dirty, very dirty, don't look at that page. OK, here's an empty page. Please. Please. You really must."

"What am I supposed to write?"

"Whatever you like. If you don't want a hat, you can write whatever you'd like to have. Clients write all sorts of things. Not just about hats. I never tell anyone what they should write. Either way I'll never show it to the inspectors. For them I have another book. This one, see." He took another notebook out of a different drawer. He flipped the pages and put it in front of me. "This one's empty, as you see. Nothing but stamps and signatures to say it's been checked. Whereas in that one, anyone can write anything they want. Because who are the clients supposed to write to? God? What if God doesn't know our language? Because if He did, if He did . . ." He took a handkerchief from his pocket and wiped his eyes, his nose, his forehead. "I'm so sorry. In the midst of all this I forgot that it's thanks to you I have light." He stuffed one notebook into one drawer, the other into the other. "I'm thinking about it . . . But no, no. It's too big, it really is too big. I knew the moment you walked in that it wasn't your size. I was even worried, because not only was it on display, but that would be the one you wanted, a brown felt hat, I could tell right away. At first glance, so to speak. The first glance usually tells us the most about someone. When that first glance of ours strikes against their face, and for a split second it becomes sort of dazzled, fully open, so to speak. So the moment you came in, my first glance told me everything about you. What could it possibly have said? Well, it told me your coming here was the kind of coincidence that sometimes turns malicious and changes into destiny. That's right, that's right, young man, destiny is no more than a particularly malicious coincidence there's no longer any getting away from. You came in here despite the fact that I don't have any brown felt hats in your size. You may not have known I didn't have any, true. But you're not aware of why you're so set on brown felt. It's not that you want something that isn't there. Though young people have the right to want what isn't there, even things that are impossible. Nor is it important that a brown felt hat wouldn't be right for your young face. That's not the point. The point is that you're passing yourself by, so to speak. You're walking past yourself and you don't recognize that it's you. I'd hoped you might go for the cream-colored one. But you scorned it. Against your own best interests. In discord with yourself. Then who are you? An electrician, you say. You work on a building site. You fixed the light in here, so that would confirm your story. Let it be so. I can see you have a young face, not fully hatched, so to speak. Let it be so. True, young faces are usually the hardest, in that a young face virtually by its nature is still unfinished. It's in constant flux, it brightens and darkens in turn. You think you've managed to grasp something permanent in it, then all at once it evades you, vanishes, the face you see before you keeps changing. But I'm absolutely certain that in your face I was able to grasp something. Namely, that in you nothing quite fits, so to speak. That you're the wrong size for yourself, in yourself even. And you're the wrong size for the one brown felt hat in the shop – not the other way around. Being the wrong size is your calling, so to speak, the hallmark of your existence, as revealed in the oh-so-malicious coincidence that there's only the one brown felt hat, and it happens to be on display, and I can't take it down from the display. Plus, it's too big for you. Everything in you is the wrong size that can possibly be the wrong size in a person. Which is to say, it's too big. To put it simply, you feel strange within yourself, you bump up against yourself inside, so to speak, you don't match up with yourself. The thing is, though, that you can't line yourself with newspaper, young man. Although who knows, who knows, these days the impossible sometimes becomes possible. In a word, in yourself you feel like that hat on your head, but in reverse. As if something were carrying you along and giving you an ever-changing shape, sometimes even blowing you away in the wind. I don't know why I'm saying all this to you. I've always been touched by younger clients. Especially since the state took over the shop and I've had a lot more time to think about things. Believe me, I can stare at a young face the way you stare at a painting. And even when no one young comes in for weeks on end, I can imagine such a face. The barely marked features that won't firm up enough to reveal the still distant shadow of death. Because death is the most exact measure of youth, old age doesn't need any measure. Youth is a state of weightlessness so to speak, the only one in your whole life. How can it be measured then, if not with death. There is no other measure, since a young person needn't even be aware of the fact that they're young. True, awareness always comes too late, regardless of age. That's the nature of our fate as humans, that it's always too late. Always when everything's already over. Because it's awareness that is our fate, not life. Whether our life was worth the living or whether it really might not have been – that's only decided by fate. Life is what goes on disconnectedly, without purpose, day after day, most often at the whim of chance, that since we're here we have to be here. Whereas people have made fate out to be a kind of validation of life. And it's only the short time of youth that allows us to see what a happy eternity could look like. So many years, so many years among these hats, and youth still awes me – me, an old hat seller. Especially when a young person is buying a hat for the first time in their life. This is your first hat, right? I thought so. I knew it the moment you walked in. Pardon me for asking, but how long have you been an electrician?"

"Since right after I left school. I first started work during the electrification of the countryside." I was getting ready to leave, my fingers were already on the door handle, but I was held back by his question.

"I see," he said.

I didn't have the courage to ask what he could see, because it seemed to me there wasn't anything to see.

"Why did you leave that job?" he asked.

"The pay was bad," I said. But there was something else in his question. It was like he knew I'd left because of the saxophone. To mislead him, I went on: "Rain or no, frost or no, you had to sit perched up on those poles –"

He didn't let me finish.

"How long have you been at your present site?"

"I just got my first wages."

"OK, now I understand everything." There was a clear note of dejection in his voice. "At such a young age, at such a young age a brown felt hat . . ." He went up to the display, took down the hat and said as he handed it to me: "Try it on again." Then he went behind the counter, sat down, rested his head on his hands and didn't say another word.

The hat was much too big. It seemed to fall even further over my ears than before. When I shook my head it wobbled. When I went up to the mirror, it looked too big. When I stepped back, it was still too big. All the same, I stood in front of the mirror waiting for him to confirm it: "See, it's too big. Too big. You must have finally realized it yourself."

But since I heard no word from him, I took the hat off and put it right by him on the counter. At that moment he asked unexpectedly:

"Will you wear it, or shall I wrap it for you?"

No, I wasn't pleased, as you might think. I'd realized I had no choice. And I said:

"Wrap it, please."

14

Let me tell you, it was the longest journey of my life. The one to buy the hat, I mean. Counting both going there and coming back. I sometimes have the feeling it's still going on. Since then I've traveled by plane, ship, express train, I even flew in a helicopter once, but it seems to me I never traveled that long. True, it was just a regular slow train. I don't know if you know what it meant to travel in those kinds of trains back then. Not only did it pull in at every station, every little halt, even places where there wasn't so much as a shelter to mark the fact that it was a stop. On top of that it would often be held up by the signals, or come to a standstill for no apparent reason at some random spot. Often it hadn't even had time to get up to full speed and already it was stopping again.

How many miles was it? Probably not all that many. Besides, it all depends how you measure it. I measured it by the hat I'd gone to buy. I left at dawn, and the previous evening we'd been drinking till late, because I had to buy myself into the good graces of the guys at the new job, the people I was working with, and especially the master craftsmen and the overseers. I was tired and I was hoping I'd get some sleep in the train. But I kept thinking about the hat, wondering if I'd find the kind I wanted, and I didn't sleep a wink. So I was counting on getting some shut-eye on the return journey.

The man in the shop advised me to go to the smaller station where the train originated, that way I'd be sure to have a seat. I managed to find a compartment all to myself. I curled up in the corner by the window, putting the hat on the shelf over my head. I began to feel drowsy right away. I don't know if I actually fell asleep. I was overwhelmed by everything I'd heard from the man in the shop. I was puzzled most of all as to why, when he handed me the screw that I hadn't even dropped, like I told you, he asked out of the blue:

"Do you play an instrument?"

"No," I said.

"Then you won't understand this. Me, when I was young I learned the cello a bit. Later I opened my own shop and my hats took up all my time. It was only after my wife passed away that I went back to playing. Today I couldn't make it through the day if I didn't have the hope of picking up my cello when I come home in the evening. It's not exactly playing, I just mess around a bit. Ah, the cello," he sighed. "It can resonate with the tenderest strings inside you. It's as if what's deepest, most mysterious, is concealed in the sounds. Every evening, so long as nothing gets in the way, of course. Though there's nothing left to get in my way anymore, so to speak. It's like I live only for those evenings. I come here, sit, supposedly selling hats, but every so often I take out my watch and count how many hours I still have to go till evening." He actually took a big "turnip" pocket watch on a chain from the pocket of his vest. Remember, they used to call pocket watches turnip watches. "Still a long, long time to go," he said in a disappointed voice. "At home, wintertime is worst of all. With every breath you puff out a cloud of steam. Because the coal rations they give you are pathetic. But I'm not complaining. I put on woolen gloves with the tips cut off, I wrap my legs in a blanket, put a woolen balaclava on, though you're not supposed to wear anything on your head indoors. Over the balaclava I put a hat, and I play. I try not to miss a single evening. I couldn't forgive myself. When words are no use, thoughts are no use, and the imagination won't imagine anything anymore, all that's left is music. All that's left is music in this world, in this life."

So I half-slept, in between my lack of sleep from the night of drinking and his question about whether I played an instrument. It was no kind of sleep, as you can imagine. The moment your eyes close, you wake up again.

After ten or fifteen minutes of this semi-sleep the train pulled into the main station where it officially started its journey. A crowd of people rushed to climb on board, and as I'm sure you know, in those days each compartment had doors on both sides of the car. At that point sleep was out of the question. Not just sleep. You couldn't even think anymore. And now I had to watch out for my hat as well. Plus, you know how it is with a person's thoughts in a train. They break off at the clatter of the wheels. And when the train goes over a switch, any thought you have is torn to shreds. The same happens at the stations, because either you look out the window, or someone asks what station it is. Not to mention people almost always talk in the train.

In the meantime more and more people joined the train, while very few got out. At each station it was like people were only getting on, not off. Getting on, that's how you can say it today. Back then they jostled and elbowed their way on, all of them at the same time. Plus, they were lugging bundles, bags, suitcases, baskets, packages, sacks, the compartment almost burst its seams. The conductors had to use the door to push people in so the compartment would close. And it was like that at every station. You'd have thought the train wasn't powerful enough to be carrying all those people and that was why it was barely inching along, stopping all the time, often in the middle of nowhere. And at the stations it stopped forever, so it was getting more and more delayed. At times it had to wait till a train coming from the other direction passed through and freed up the line. I'm telling you, I actually sort of felt sorry for the train for having to carry a burden that seemed beyond its strength.

When I was going in the other direction, on my way to buy the hat, and I was tormented by doubt as to whether I'd get the kind I wanted, a brown felt one – at that time I got mad even when the train stopped at regular stations. Now the hat lay above me on the shelf, and it made no difference to me whether we moved quicker or slower. I felt a little as if I wasn't going anywhere and I had nowhere to get to. At moments I even forgot I was in a train. I stared out the window at everything passing by, the fields, woods, rivers, hills, valleys, buildings, wagons, horses, cows, people – it all merged into a monotonous grayness, and it was only the telegraph wires rising and falling running alongside the tracks that lent the grayness a rhythm, showing that this was a living world. I felt completely outside of myself. You say it isn't possible to be outside yourself. But can't a person slip out of themselves just for a short while? What for? Where would they be at such a time? I can't say. But maybe you're right. Especially because you can't slip out of yourself when your hat is on the shelf over your head.

At one of the stations I shifted the hat to the opposite shelf so I could keep an eye on it. It was a good move. Soon after, the compartment filled up so much that people were standing squashed side by side between the seats. There was hardly any fresh air where I sat in the corner. A big fat woman stood right by me, or rather over me, pressing against me so I had to squeeze myself into my seat. There was no way I could have raised my head to check whether my hat was still there. Whereas I could somehow see through a narrow gap between the passengers to the other side to check it was still in its place.

The train was so packed you'd have thought there was no more room for anyone else. But here at the next station there were more bundles and bags and suitcases and baskets, and so on. And the people that came with them. You might find it hard to understand if you've never ridden a train like that. Did the trains stretch and get bigger, or did the people get smaller? Yes, people can become anything, a tiny dot if necessary. I had to use my arms to fend off the newcomers. I couldn't squeeze any further into the bench. I curled my feet under me as far as they would go, but still folks kept stepping on my toes, often so hard it made me wince. On top of that, all the curses that burst into the train along with the people seemed aimed at me, because I was sitting by one of the doors. And as if out of spite the train mostly stopped so my side of the compartment was next to the platform.

"The hell with all this!" the first person to come in would mutter, looking at me.

Everyone that followed, man or woman, without exception would be saying in my direction:

"Dear God, how can they do this to people! First the war, now this!"

"I thought this train would never arrive! We were waiting and waiting . . ."

"You have to wait for everything these days, why would trains be any different?"

"Why on earth is it running so late?"

"Did one ever come on time? I take the train almost every day, and I've never seen it come in on time yet. I mean, for fuck's sake!"

"Mind your language. God hears everything. Though it's like he's abandoned us too . . ."

"What's God got to do with any of this? God isn't the stationmaster or the dispatcher. It's those bastards in the red caps with the little paddles."

And I'd take it all as if it were directed at me, because I didn't have any problem with the train. My hat was on the shelf, I was in no hurry, what problem could I have? Actually it wasn't only the ones who'd just joined the train who were cursing, they also stirred up the people who'd gotten on earlier and who seemed to have come to terms with it all.

At one station a small man with a small suitcase who I helped to get on, because he'd been pushing and pushing into the already crammed compartment, suddenly asked me:

"Do you know if there's a problem?" I shrugged. "Does anyone else know?" No one answered him, so he turned to me again. "You're the youngest one here, right?"

"Give it a rest," the huge woman standing over me scolded him. "And keep your head out of my way."

"Oh, sorry, I do apologize, I was just asking if they're maybe repairing the tracks near here," he started to explain. "Or a bridge perhaps."

"They're not repairing anything, the train's moving the whole time."

"It's moving but it's still running late?" He found it hard to believe. "Even during the war the trains –"

"You should ask whoever's been on it since it first set out," someone interrupted him. He took this up:

"Has anyone been on the train since the start?"

People began looking around at each other as if they were searching for a guilty party. I said nothing. So they reminded themselves of who had gotten on at which station and who was already in the compartment. That gentleman? That lady? I could have sworn it was her. Or him. It wasn't you, ma'am? I remember you being here already. You were sitting right where you're sitting now. No, this gentleman was standing here even earlier. He was here when I got on. That lady over there was here too. Me? The nerve. You were the one who was here then. I was even wondering if you'd offer me your seat. But who gives up their own seat these days, even to a woman. Good lord, what's happened to people since the war? What's happened to them?

It was building up to be a scene.

Luckily the train stopped at the next station. Only one new passenger forced his way into the compartment, but he was groaning under the weight of enough luggage for several people. He started by throwing in his bags directly onto the people there, and only then got on himself. He basically pushed all the standing people toward the other side of the compartment, because otherwise there wouldn't have been room for him. He didn't swear or curse, he just gave everyone an angry look as if he thought it was their fault the train was running late. The shelves were already piled to the ceiling with people's luggage, but he started putting his things on top of theirs, flattening the other luggage and moving it around, putting one case on top of another. He was pretty much rearranging the whole compartment. But no one said anything, they didn't even tell him he shouldn't put this on top of that. Everyone quieted down, and, it goes without saying, they stopped accusing one another of having been first in the compartment. No one so much as whispered anything to anyone else. Maybe they knew him from the same route. I couldn't say. I don't know how he figured out that the package wrapped in paper and tied with string was a hat.

"Whose hat is this?" he asked in a menacing voice.

"Mine," I let on after a moment.

"Why is it here? You should have it on your side. Your belongings are supposed to be where your seat is."

He moved the hat to my side of the compartment, putting it up by the ceiling on top of someone's suitcase. He finally stowed all his things and then told people on the seat to move up, as he had no intention of standing the whole way. It was hard to do, but people squeezed closer without a word. When he finally sat down, he moved from side to side to give himself more room. He squashed the lady to his right and the gentleman to his left, they squashed their neighbors, and still no one said anything. At that moment the train moved off.

"We're on our way," he said. "And if we're on our way, we'll get where we're going." At that he settled more firmly into the bench and spoke again as if to himself:

"I used to have a hat before the war. A brown felt one. Cost a pretty penny. I joined the resistance and it got blown away by machine gun fire. We fired at them, they fired back, and that was the end of the hat." He cast a somewhat milder look around the compartment, as if he was absolving us of blame for the delayed train.

He rested his head against the back of the seat, closed his eyes, and a moment later his breathing became a little deeper. The train jolted and rattled, clattering over the joints between the rails as if it were going over potholes; it rumbled across switches. So you still couldn't hear his breathing. His lips were together, and it was only that they seemed to crack open with each outbreath pushing from inside. But I knew what was coming. Every great snoring has exactly that sort of innocent beginning. I was virtually cowering.

As I told you, I've loathed snoring ever since I was a child. True, everyone loathes it. But there's loathing and loathing. You can loathe it because you can't get to sleep when someone's snoring. Or let's say you're already asleep, then in the middle of the night you're woken by someone snoring and you can't get back to sleep till morning. Those are the usual aches and pains of sleeping in the same room as someone else. Husbands and wives put up with it their whole lives, assuming they stay together that is. Though as far as that's concerned, a change of husband or wife is no solution. You never know who you'll end up with next. But for me it wasn't just that I couldn't get to sleep when someone was snoring. Or that if I woke up, I couldn't fall back asleep. When someone was snoring, I'd feel like the pain from his whole life was rising into his throat, but he was unable to shout out and say what was hurting him. You might not agree, but if you ask me there are kinds of pain that only reveal themselves in snoring. There are endless kinds of pain in people. In any case, I would feel the other person's weakness as my own. And with them I'd seem to be choking on that weakness, on my own inability to shout out the pain. As if I couldn't break out of his sleep, yet at the same time I was fending off my own waking state. You don't hear your own snoring, of course, so there's no issue with it. There were times I'd be stifled by someone else's snoring, to the point where I'd have to get up and go outside for some fresh air.

Even at school some of the other boys snored, though only softly, and it wasn't many of them. Life was already painful for some of them, but the pain melted away through their whole sleep instead of pushing its way into their throat. Plus, back then we slept much deeper and our sleep could still hold back any kind of pain. Though I'd still sometimes wake up, even if someone was only snoring ever so slightly.

Later on, after I started working and I was mostly living with much older men, snoring became a nightly torment. Honestly, I was afraid of every coming night. We'd be getting ready for bed, but me, instead of starting to feel sleepy I'd be gripped by fear. Of course, I could wake one guy or another if his snoring got really unbearable. But he'd just turn over from his back to his side, or from one side to the other, and a short while later he'd be snoring again. I tried thinking about something, hoping it might stop me from hearing so intently, but I didn't have a thought in my head. I'd lie there like I was in a torture chamber. Hell could well be like that – not any of the stuff the priests frighten you with, but rather you're just lying there being tortured by someone else's snoring. It fills your ears, your lungs, your throat, your powerlessness, so you're unable to call out a single word. On top of that, it's as if you yourself were snoring, though it's not you who's doing the snoring. That's how it is – there are times when other people's pain is worse than your own.

In fact, at times I lived with guys you might call powerhouses of snoring. In waking life a guy like that was tiny, like a little dried-up pear. Anything that weighed a bit, you'd have to pick it up and carry it for him. If a screw got stuck you'd have to unscrew it for him because he didn't have the strength. But when it came to snoring he was a powerhouse. It felt like the ceiling was about to lift off and the walls were collapsing, that any minute now the whole place would come crashing down around us as we slept. In other men it was like gelatin boiling, and I'd be boiling along with it. Actually, there were lots of different ways they snored. Some moaned, some squeaked, some gurgled, some rumbled, and once in a while there'd be one who would keep exploding like a shell. You'd jerk awake thinking another war was starting.

In the lodgings the men were always older than me, like I said. Sometimes a lot older. They hadn't slept properly all through the war, they were still filled to bursting with war, so it was hardly surprising. Sometimes, over vodka one of them would tell a story that in itself stopped you from sleeping, and as if that weren't bad enough, the other guys would be snoring away. I tried plugging my ears with cotton wool or plasticine, or I'd put my head under my pillow instead of on top of it. None of it did much good. The snoring seemed not to be coming in through my ears, it felt as if it was flowing from someone else's sleep directly into mine. It was like somebody else's sleep took over the rhythm of my own. What, you didn't know that sleep has its rhythm? Everyone's is different.

But everybody sleeps to a rhythm, the same way we live to a rhythm. You can't separate sleep from life. Things'd be a whole lot easier if you could, if life was here and sleep was over there. Life here, sleep there.

Pardon me for asking, but do you snore? You don't know. You've never shared a bed with anyone who could tell you. I'm sorry to bring up such a question, but it's a normal human thing. A woman would tell you most honestly. Women sleep differently. Not to mention that they can hear in their sleep.

One time I was living with four older guys in the house of this widow; they put me in there as a fifth. The oldest of them could have been more than three times my age, or so I thought at the time. He was gray as a pigeon. True, much younger men went gray during the war. Often, at a meeting of the workforce I'd look around at everyone's heads and it was like a field of cabbage that had been blighted by frost. Why is it that most often it's a person's hair that shows what they've lived through? As I look at you, I don't see a single gray hair. I wonder how you've gone through life. You can see what happened with my hair. These days men go bald instead. And that too, there's no telling why. Even really young guys. Here in the cabins, you wouldn't believe how many young men are already bald, or balding. And there hasn't been a war in a long time, hardly anyone remembers the last one.

At the widow's place all the men had hair, but they were all going gray, and the oldest one was totally gray. And all four of them snored like the blazes, and when the four of them started up at the same time the widow would pound on the wall from her room. Especially when they'd been drinking.

One time I was so set on edge by it that I thought the only thing to do was smother them. But I got up and went outside instead. I sat on the stoop and lit a cigarette. It was summertime, the air was warm, dawn was beginning to break. I was intending to just sit there till it was time to get ready for work. The widow joined me outside. She hadn't been able to sleep either, even though there was a thick wall with plastering on both sides between her room and ours, not just a thin partition.

"They're snoring, huh?" she asked. "Yeah, they woke me up too. In the war I'd even sleep through the bombings. But I'm sensitive to snoring. Do you snore?"

"I don't know," I said. "No one ever told me."

"You're so young, at the most you might make a little bit of noise when you're dreaming. Give me a cigarette. I don't smoke, but I feel like one right now."

"I left them inside."

"Too bad. On a close night like this I feel like smoking." She fanned herself with her nightshirt, she'd come out in the nightshirt with a kind of shawl thrown over it.

"You can finish mine if you like, ma'am," I said. "There's enough for a few drags. If you don't mind."

"Why should I mind?" she retorted. "Women kiss men and they don't mind that." She drew on the cigarette and coughed so violently her breasts almost fell out of her nightshirt. "Ugh, these cigarettes are disgusting. How can you smoke them? Don't they make you sick? You're not even a full-grown man yet. And you work too much. I see when you go to work and when you come back. Plus, you never get a decent night's sleep from all their snoring. At your age you need more sleep. Later on you won't need as much. Today I can see you're going to go to work tired. And you work with electricity. Just be careful you don't get a shock. I admit it is pretty convenient with the electricity, but when I turn it on I'm always afraid."

"There's no reason to be afraid," I said.

"I'm sure you're right," she said.

I crushed my cigarette butt under my shoe and I was about to get up when she leaned down from where she was standing over me and stroked my hair.

"Come on, you can get some sleep in my bed. There's no point going back to their room. I don't snore. As it is you'll have to get up soon to go to work, but even an hour or two will do you good. My bed's nice and wide. There was plenty of room with my husbands, when we didn't feel like it we didn't even bump into each other. You shouldn't have to hang around out here till morning. Don't worry, you won't be late. I'll wake you up."

She took me by the hand and helped me up. Perhaps all those sleepless nights had suddenly overpowered me; in any case, I put up no resistance. While I was smoking I was somehow able to stay awake, but once I'd finished, my eyes started to close of their own accord. Maybe if I'd had another cigarette . . .

"You can barely keep your eyes open, I see," she said. "You really are short on sleep. Even an hour or two will help."

She was quite a lot older than me, though today I'd say she was still young. You know how it is. As you grow older, everyone around you gets younger. All the more so in memory. You often catch yourself thinking that back then someone seemed old, while at the time they were a lot younger than you are now. Or perhaps she seemed much older then because she'd already had two husbands. One of them she kicked out for drinking not long after they got married, the other one died from drink. And she was just thinking about whether to get married a third time. He drank too, but he was a widower like her, he had two small children, and that way she'd at least have children, she said. Because she'd have hated to get pregnant with a drunk, God forbid. Never with a drunk, she told herself. It would have been too much for her to see them born into unhappiness. She'd seen those kinds of kids. With this new husband she'd have a purpose in life, because it's hard to live with the thought that life comes to an end with you. And whether it's your own kids or someone else's, either way you never know what's going to come of them. Someone else's child could even be more caring later because you gave him your heart when the heart of his own mother failed. He might turn out to be a good husband, who knew? He only turned to drink when his wife left him with the two children. He didn't know what to do. A man's always drawn to vodka. But when he got drunk he'd sometimes come to her and weep at having gotten drunk. And he would beg her, help me, help me. So sometimes she'd weep with him.

He was completely different in his drinking from the other two. The first one, when he drank he slept like a log. And he drank almost every day, so every day she had a log in bed – or rather, every night. The second one, when he came home drunk he'd start by beating her. It was only once he'd beaten her that he'd make a move on her. He liked to make love with a woman like that, with her beaten and crying. Now this third one . . . Should she marry him or not?

"What do you think?" she asked, when we were already in bed. "Though never mind, you go to sleep. I'm not going to go back to sleep. I don't want you being late for work because of me. I don't know what to do, I go over it night after night in my thoughts. I might end up being too old for a fourth husband, if I take this third one. The older a woman is, the worse the guys that come along. The fourth one, I might have to make him take the cure. Or I'd kill him. And make no mistake, at times there's nothing you can do. True, even among older men you occasionally meet a decent guy that doesn't drink. But he could take to drink after he's married, or he'd feel closer and closer to dying, and I'd feel it too. And try dying with a drunk. Suffering for his drinking afterwards. By then it's too late to be thinking about a new husband. So you see how it is – you marry one person, but afterwards you have to live with a different one." She sighed so deeply a wave of warmth hit me. "But you should go to sleep. You have to get up soon."

I was so tired I was half asleep. Still, I was listening to her, especially because she seemed to be waiting to hear what I'd say about her troubles. But what could I say, I was appalled by her lust for life. By all those husbands of hers, she had two of them under her belt and she was already imagining not just a fourth, if the third one turned out to be a drunk after they got married, but more and more all the way till she died, and maybe even after death. How could I have any idea what it was like to be a third husband, or what it could be like for a woman to be with a third one.

"I don't know what to tell you, ma'am," I said.

"What are you calling me ma'am for?" she said, bridling, and I felt another wave of heat. "You're lying in bed with me and saying ma'am. Just call me ma'am when we're around the other men. I wasn't asking for your opinion. I have to figure it out on my own. What can you know." She slipped her hand under my head and held me to her. "Is this the first time you've been with a woman? I thought so, you're lying there all shy, all tensed up. But you should sleep. Today nothing's going to happen anyway. You need at least a bit of sleep before you go to work. See, the dawn's starting to come up. It'll be morning before you know it. Get to sleep. Lord, going without sleep night after night like that. Were you always sensitive to snoring? Me too. Good lord. If you like I can put a straw mattress down for you in the kitchen, and you can leave their room for the night, tell them you can't sleep because of their snoring. And sometimes you can come into my bed. I've never had anyone as young as you. You're a sweet boy." She shook me, as I was already falling asleep. She raised her head and leaned over me, suddenly bothered. "Are you telling the truth that it's your first time?" Relieved, she fell back on the pillow. "What a bit of luck. God must be making up for those drunkards of mine." She abruptly pressed my head to her breast. "I don't even know what to do with someone when it's their first time. When it was me it was quite an experience, I remember. I didn't like it. You probably have no idea what to do. But don't worry, I'll teach you everything. Whatever you do though, for God's sake don't let them persuade you to drink. You can have one or two drinks. That won't do you any harm. But not any more. It's not good for the man to have too much. Or for the woman either. Though for the woman it's not such a big thing. I've had drunken men, I know. I'm wondering where I could put that mattress down for you. I think I'll move the table against the wall. You'll finally be able to get some sleep. You don't have to come to me every night. Only when you're not too tired. I don't have the urge every night either. But go to sleep now. Today it's like you're with family. Brother and sister. I could be your older sister. Why not? There are bigger age differences. Though you sometimes hear about brothers and sisters doing it together. Nothing's sacred anymore." She stroked me, kissed me on the forehead, pressed me to her so hard that my nose was squashed against her downy chest. "Oh, you sweet thing."

Let me tell you, I started to be afraid of her. Maybe because what did I know back then about women. If I hadn't been so sleepy I might have gotten out of bed, said I felt like smoking again, I was going to fetch my cigarettes. But I was too timid to even get up.

"Go to sleep." She held me to her again. "This isn't the only night we'll have. There'll be plenty more! I asked your boss, he said the job's going to take a long while yet. We'll have lots of time to tell each other secrets. I'll leave the door from the kitchen to my room ajar so you don't have to move the handle. And I'll have the hinges oiled tomorrow. Go to sleep now. I won't turn around, I'll listen to you sleeping. When someone's asleep you can often tell a lot about them. One person sleeps like a child, while with someone else, God help him. It comes out of them in their sleep. Whether they keep turning from one side to the other, or they sleep on the same side all night long, or sleep facing you all night, you can know a lot. Or if they're curled up in a ball like they were clinging to their mommy. The worst ones are the ones that lie on their backs, like those drunkards of mine. The one and the other both slept on their backs. I always had to roll them over onto their sides to stop them from snoring so loud. Whenever I think of them I stop feeling sleepy, however tired I was before. When you want to go to sleep you ought to think of something nice. But how can you have enough nice things to last for every time you have to fall asleep. It's mostly unpleasant things that crowd into your mind, there's never any shortage of those. It looks like dawn's beginning. The curtain's getting lighter. And you can see the Lord Jesus better. He's always the first thing you see when the sun comes up. But you can still sleep a little at least. I'll wake you so you get up just before the other men. When you go in to get dressed it'll be like you were just coming back from the bathroom. Go to sleep. It won't be for long, but you won't be as exhausted as if you'd not slept at all. Especially working with electricity. Lord in heaven, what if you were to get a shock. Lord in heaven. I got a shock from the iron one time. I was only touching it to see if it was hot. It made me tingle all the way up my arm. Gave me such a scare. I burned a pillowcase. People say you get all kinds of illnesses from the electricity. Is that true?"

I don't know if I told her it wasn't, or if I only dreamed that I told her so.

"I won't deny it, a thing like an iron is really handy. All that work you used to have to do heating the charcoal, blowing on it. One time I burned my eyebrows, I've had to dye them since then. The flat-irons with the heated slug inside weren't any better. They were so heavy, and the slug would keep losing its heat. You'd have to be always putting it in the fire and taking it out. You'd use the kitchen stove. One time, a heated slug fell on my foot. Lucky I was wearing shoes. Now all you have to do is plug it in. It's convenient. Though if people start getting sick . . . Lord forbid. But there's no point worrying about illnesses ahead of time. If they come we'll deal with them, better or worse, either that or we'll die right away. Dying right away would be good. Even without electricity there comes a time of sickness. That's how life is. For now I'd rather just think about what it's going to be like with you. Your first time. Mother of God. I'm actually scared. My bed for sure never saw this coming. Though I have to change the sheets. I'll put the embroidered ones on. Quilt and pillowcases. I embroidered them myself. I'd be waiting in the evenings for those drunken husbands of mine, what was I supposed to do? I did embroidery. Though not for them. No sir. No way would I have let them sleep in embroidered sheets. And I'll buy us a new bottom sheet. Just make sure you wash. Your boss told me you have a shower over on the site. It's not you, I just know how guys wash themselves. Someone has to make sure you do it right. I'll have a good wash too. I'll soak myself in the bathtub. I'll fill it with foam, maybe even put in some fragrance. Will you make an outlet for me by my bed? I'd like to get a bedside lamp. We could turn it on sometimes. Instead of always only doing it in the dark. For once I'd like it to be light. I read somewhere it's a lot nicer that way. And I like to read from time to time. After you're gone, I'll be able to read in bed. Or think awhile with the light on. You probably have more pleasant thoughts that way. But you, don't think, go to sleep. I know what you're thinking about, but there's not much time. There wouldn't be enough. Best not to start. When you got up you'd be in worse shape than if you'd just not slept. Often your legs will barely carry you, and your head is whirling. The daylight's here, but it's like the night refuses to go out of you. You cook, you do the laundry, but it's still nighttime. As if you were doing everything in the dark. And you'd be mad at me. I don't want you to be mad. When a man's mad, someone has to be to blame. And the way it is, it's always the woman. Or you'd be late for work, and that'd be my fault too. But don't worry, I'll teach you, you'll see. There's always a first time. When you don't know what you're doing it can be all over before you know it, and I don't want that. I've had enough of that. I was raped by soldiers, I know all about that kind. There were five of them, with all these medals swinging to and fro over my head. I didn't even feel like crying. Though why am I even telling you these things. You don't need to know what the world was like only yesterday. Maybe you've come into a better world. You should want it to be better. If men want to fight, let them, but women and children shouldn't have to pay for their wars. Though those drunkards of mine weren't soldiers, and they weren't any better. They'd come home drunk, and it'd be the same thing, over before you knew it, without any feeling, then they'd be asleep a moment later. And when they did it that way it was like they were paying you back for something. Whether it was a soldier or a husband. For what? That the world's arranged in such a way that it takes two people? Surely the world is made for loving. Without loving there'd be no reason to live. Nothing but sleeping and eating, what for? Working, what for? Who'd feel like working in a world like that? I read a book once where some guy died while he was making love to a woman. His heart gave out. His heart, can you believe it. Everything collects in the heart. When too much gathers there it can't take it. Are you still awake?"

I'd been sleeping already, she'd woken me up. Evidently I'd not been deep asleep – sleeping with one eye open, as the expression goes. Because I'd not been at all sure she'd wake me. When it came time for me to go to work she might have fallen asleep. So I was kind of asleep, but alert.

"Here, let me see how your heart is." She put her hand on my heart. Who wouldn't have woken up then. "It's a bit impatient, like it's in a hurry. Now you put your hand on mine." She took my hand and placed it on her breast. A rock would have woken up at that. "Can you feel how much is gathered there? But do you know if a woman can die that way too? Though how could you know. The world isn't fair to women. Take your hand away." She removed my hand herself. "Like I said, not today. It's too late and you need to get some sleep. It's best to begin when the night begins, and not even think about the fact that you have to get up the next day. As if the night was going to go on and on, and day would never come. Also, bodies have to lie beside each other for a longer time before . . . They have to get used to each other, get comfortable with each other. Because they're full of fear. You don't think mine is? Let me tell you, it's got more fear in it than yours. After those soldiers, after those drunken husbands I'm afraid every time. I thought I'd never be a woman again. I didn't even want to be. I thought I'd just embroider, read, sing, cry a little from time to time. I want to buy a wireless, did I tell you? I put my name down for one at the store. They're going to let me know when they get some in. I'll be able to sit and listen. But you're only human. I was still in the mourning period for my second. I was still in black, and here I started to feel things gathering in my heart again. I went to church, I could see the men looking at me, not just the older ones, men that are younger than me as well. There I was praying, and I could feel them undressing me with their eyes. I was all embarrassed, it was a church after all, God was watching. But still it felt good. There was this baker, I get my bread from him every day, somehow I'd never noticed him in the bakery before, but here I see he's singing and he keeps sending me these looks that give me goose bumps. I feel my heart pounding. Forgive me, Lord, but you're the one who gave me my body. Actually, I looked good in black. Everyone said I should always only wear mourning clothes. I even had a mass said for that drunkard of mine. Let him have it. He left me this house, among other things. He didn't drink all of it away. Perhaps I shouldn't read books, what do you think? I sometimes read and read, and I start thinking to myself, if only my life . . . Because even when somebody else's life is sadder than yours, you sometimes would like to swap with them. Goodness, it's beating so hard. It's like it was about to give out too. Are you still awake? You could check to see if I'm only imagining it. It's like it wanted to jump directly to the next night, or come to you right now. But not today, no. The night's almost over. You need to get a little sleep. If we did it in a hurry, you might even be put off me. I often thought you must be awake with all that snoring. But I somehow never dared ask if you might want to sleep in the kitchen. I was suffering along with you, because they woke me up too. For some reason you can't hear them now – listen. The moment you moved in here I knew you'd never been with a woman. You kissed my hand, remember? It touched my heart to think that someone so innocent still existed in the world. So the first time mustn't be rushed. When it's the first time, everything afterwards is like that first time. Except for death. After death there are no memories. But while life goes on, you might remember me badly. Then you'd remember all the other women badly too. Because it would be bad with all the other ones. You might start to drink, and things would go on being bad for you. They'd be bad within yourself. Your whole life things would be bad for you. You'd lose your desire, and it would be bad for you. And it would be my fault. So for the sake of your whole life it's worth holding out for one night. You won't regret it. I'll make it up to you. Look, it's getting brighter. Go to sleep."

I think in the end I must have really fallen asleep, because I suddenly felt her shaking me:

"You need to get up. You'll be late for work. Get up. What a sleepyhead."

I was most surprised of all when she said:

"You snore just the same. But it's nice to listen to you. Things have gathered in you as well, I can see. When can that have happened? Mother of God, when can that have happened?"

Anyway, I never finished the story about the train. So the train was on its way, I was on it, and the hat was on the opposite shelf so I could keep an eye on it. It wasn't there anymore? Oh that's right, he'd moved it to the shelf on my side. At some station the train stopped again, no one got on, someone peeked into the compartment, saw it was filled to bursting, and slammed the door so hard the snorer opened his eyes. He lifted his head from the headrest, looked around at everyone to see whether it was the same people, checked that his bags were there, then nodded toward the window and said:

"Oh, we're at this station already."

So it looked like he might not be sleepy anymore. But the moment the train set off again his eyes began to droop, though he seemed in two minds about whether or not to go back to sleep. It was only when the train sped up and began rocking that his head fell back against the headrest as if of its own accord, his mouth opened, and the noise that came out was exactly like the sound of a distant wagon with ironclad wheels rumbling over frozen ground.

At a certain moment his head slipped down from the headrest to the shoulder of his left-hand neighbor. The neighbor allowed the head to remain on his shoulder without protest, but still, as the train crossed a switch and the whole compartment shook, he moved from that neighbor's shoulder to the shoulder of the woman sitting to his right, without interrupting his sleep. The woman accepted his head on her shoulder just the same. Yet the train, which was rocking like a cradle, must have sent him into such a deep sleep that his head slid from her shoulder to her chest. Her breasts were each almost the size of his head. It wasn't only that they were large, they seemed to be separate, independent of the rest of her body. There are women that seem to have been created exclusively for the purpose of carrying their own breasts. You might even have had the impression it was her breasts that were rocking the train, especially when it crossed a switch. What harm could it have done, then, for him to sleep his fill there? The woman, though, took as big of a breath as she could, breathed out, took another deep breath, breathed out. She was probably thinking that from the rising and falling of her chest his head would wake up. But he was evidently sound asleep, and so she suddenly exclaimed as if she'd been startled:

"Excuse me, what do you think you're doing?"

He must have heard. He didn't actually open his eyes and his mouth remained open, but with the force of his sleep alone he moved his head from her breasts to the headrest. And that was when it started. Not right away. To begin with it was like he was short of breath. His eyes were still closed, but his mouth opened even wider, though not the slightest sound came from it. You'd genuinely have thought he was dead. People in the compartment started looking at him and at each other, but no one dared say anything. In the end somebody finally got up the courage to half-whisper, as if they were trying to ward off their own unease:

"Someone sleeps like that, they must be making up for many a sleepless night."

Then someone else dared to say:

"He was in the resistance, you heard. You don't join the resistance to get a decent sleep."

A third person was even more emboldened by the previous speaker's words:

"His hat got shot up by machine gun fire. He must have been a brave one."

To her own misfortune the woman whose chest he'd tried to sleep on also spoke up:

"My man, when he gets drunk he sleeps like that."

Someone retorted indignantly:

"This man's sober, you can see that. He's just tired, tired from so many nights without sleep, years maybe."

The compartment fell silent. It was like everyone's mouth was stopped up. For the longest time all you could hear was the train, and the man's ever louder snoring. We passed one station, another, and finally someone spoke, obviously trying to kick over the traces of the previous conversation:

"If he's so exhausted it's no surprise that wherever he closes his eyes he sleeps like the dead."

"Who isn't exhausted these days?" The speaker was bristling. "Who is not exhausted? No one wants their life to be in vain. Those three sacks up there are mine, and I'm not as strong as I used to be."

Someone else swore:

"Exhausted, for fuck's sake!"

They started arguing about who was more exhausted than who.

"Take me, for instance –" someone was settling in to tell a longer story, when all at once a gurgling noise came from the sleeping man's throat. Luckily the train hit a switch that shook it, and the gurgling sound broke off. But not for long. When the car resumed its rocking rhythm, a great sigh came from his mouth as if from the depths of his soul. After which, still sleeping, he settled his head more firmly against the headrest and began to make a sound that was half-whistle, half-wheeze. The sound contained a distant murmur that grew with almost every breath he took, and became ever faster, closer, louder. It felt like the train, that up till now had been crawling, gathered speed each time he breathed. After a dozen or so breaths, it seemed to be hurtling along, that it had even stopped clattering over the rails and was virtually leaping across the switches, as if we were headed directly for some waterfall from which any minute now we'd plunge into the abyss.

I was gripped by panic, I felt actual pain in my chest. Please believe me when I say I never heard snoring like that before or after in my life.

The roaring waterfall we were approaching was making my head explode, it was pressing down on my chest, my legs began to twitch and I couldn't control them. I felt that along with his snoring, something deep inside my own existence was also being released. Maybe everyone in the compartment felt it, because no one had the guts to nudge him or to say, You're snoring.

I pressed against the window, hoping that help might come from that direction. And thank goodness, after a short period of torment the train pulled in to my station. Without waiting for it to come to a complete stop, I pushed open the door and jumped out.

The dispatcher was standing close by on the platform, and he tore me off a strip. "You there! What's the rush? If you break an arm or a leg the railroad'll be liable! Do you even have a ticket? Come here, let me see your ticket!"

I walked over, still shaken up by the snoring. I reached into my pocket, but I couldn't find my ticket.

"What did I tell you!" the dispatcher exclaimed almost triumphantly. "No ticket, and he jumps out of the train before it reaches the station."

I rummaged around in my other pockets. In the meantime the dispatcher gave the signal for the train to depart, and when I finally found my ticket it was already gathering speed. "I've got it," I said. "Here."

"Let's see if it's valid." He waved to someone in the departing train.

Without thinking I followed the direction of his waving hand; someone was waving back at him from a window of the train. All at once my heart leaped into my throat. My hat was on the train! Dear God! The last car was just passing. I rushed after it as fast as my legs could carry me. I managed to catch hold of the handrail on the very last door, but the train accelerated and I lost my grip. I still kept running, carried not so much by my legs as by despair that my hat was leaving with the train. Again I caught up with the last car and again I stretched out my hand, trying to grab the handrail, and again I seemed to have gotten ahold of it, all I needed to do was jump from the platform onto the step. But the train jolted forward again and I was thrown back onto the platform. Still I ran, till the last car was a long way off and getting farther and farther.

I was breathless, my legs shook under me, but I ran back toward the dispatcher. He was still on the platform. He may have been kept there by curiosity as to whether I'd make it back on the train. But he'd probably guessed what would happen, because he greeted me scoldingly:

"I bet you had a ticket to here and you were planning to continue on for free, eh?"

"No, I left my hat on the train," I gasped.

"What kind of hat?"

"A brown felt one. Please stop the train."

"Stop the train? You must be mad!" He turned around and set off toward the station building.

I blocked his path.

"Please stop it."

"Out of my way!" He tugged his cap tighter over his head and tried to push me aside.

I grabbed him by the lapels and shook him till he went as red as his service cap.

"Stop the train! Stop the train!" I shouted in his face.

"Let go of me!" he bellowed, trying to twist free from my grip. "Let go, goddammit! This is assault! You over there!" he shouted in the direction of a railroad worker with a long hammer who was tapping the rails. "Call the men! This lunatic won't let go of me!"

But before the other man could clamber up onto the platform, several railroad workers came running out of the station building.

"Don't let him go! Keep hold of him!" they were shouting.

"He's the one holding me!" the dispatcher yelled back furiously. "Son of a bitch won't let go!" he exclaimed to the men running up, as if out of hurt pride. "Just won't let go!"

One of the men grabbed my hands and tried to release my grip on the dispatcher's jacket. It did no good, it was like I was holding him with claws.

"Damn but he's strong. Little squirt like that."

The guy with the long hammer put in:

"One whack with this and he'll let go. Shall I?" He started to swing the hammer.

"Hang on," growled the dispatcher, still furious. "He'll let go himself. He'll calm down and let go. He left his hat."

"Where?" asked one of the men.

"In the compartment," replied the dispatcher. "He wanted me to stop the train."

They all exploded in laughter, while my hands dropped from his uniform by themselves.

"Stopping a train is like stopping the earth turning," one of them said as his laughter died away.

"He couldn't have stopped it anyway," added the worker with the hammer, peering after the disappearing train. "It had already passed the flagman's hut."

They all burst out laughing again. The laughter carried across the platform, it felt like it was drifting far above me.

"Where's his head?"

"Maybe he left his head there as well."

They laughed as if nothing as entertaining as this had ever happened on the railroad, except for crashes.

One of them must have felt sorry for me and said:

"Maybe we should call ahead? They could tell the conductor to go look through the cars."

The dispatcher retorted as he straightened his uniform:

"How's he supposed to make his way through the crowd? They're not even checking tickets on that train."

15

Did it start from the dream or from the laughter? No, it's no big deal, I just wonder about it sometimes. I see that surprises you. I'm not surprised you're surprised, because I'm surprised myself – what was it for? Especially as I don't even know what it was that supposedly started. I'm not looking for a beginning. Besides, does anything like a beginning ever actually exist? Even the fact that a person is born doesn't mean that that's their beginning. If anything had a beginning, it might continue in the right order. But nothing seems willing to go in the right order. One day won't march after another in an orderly fashion, one keeps pushing in front of the other. Same with the weeks, the months, the years – they don't follow each other one by one in single file, they charge at you in extended file as they say in the army.

No, I'm not a military man. When I was of an age to do my military service, my workplace got me out of it. The fact that I was an electrician wasn't enough of a reason. In those days I played in the company band, like I told you. I was the only saxophonist who'd come forward. They would have brought someone else in from another building site, but they'd never come across anyone that played the sax on those sites either.

The thing is, though, that when I sometimes try and make sense of my life, and who doesn't do that . . . Obviously I don't mean my whole life, but this or that part, it goes without saying that no one is capable of grasping their entire life, even the most meager one. Not to mention that it's always debatable whether any life is a whole. Each one is more or less broken into pieces, and often the pieces are scattered. A life like that can't be gathered back together, and even if it could, what whole would you make out of it? It isn't a teacup, or even some larger container. Perhaps it can be imagined as a whole after you die. But then, who's going to be around to do that? Each person is the only one that can imagine himself to himself. Not in all things, you're right. But as much as you can. There is no other truth.

Besides, am I really wondering about this life of mine? Why would I do that? It won't serve any purpose, nothing will be reversed or changed. If anything, it's life that wonders about me, I don't feel any such need. Why wouldn't life wonder about a person living it? It doesn't even need our consent. Just like with dreams. You dream things even if you'd prefer not to. Sometimes you have dreams you simply don't want to have, though they're your own dreams. Also, you have no influence over whether someone else dreams about you. How is life different from that?

What was the dream? How can I tell you briefly . . . I really don't know. It's not important. And even though I dreamed it much, much later, it sort of opened up the memory of that laughter, it singled it out from a series of many different events, and sent other, often more important ones toward oblivion. That much would be understandable. It's just that at the same time it was as if the laughter led to the dream I had decades later. To other things too, but for sure to that dream. Why don't you think a mutual influence like that is possible? I mean, I did say it isn't me wondering about my life, so it isn't me who's establishing a two-way symbiosis between one thing and another. It may simply establish itself. The more so because that often happens at the least appropriate moment, for instance when I'm walking through the woods looking for wild strawberries underfoot, or taking the dogs' bowl out with their dinner. Or sitting by the window staring at the lake. There's a swarm of people on this side, on the far shore, boats, kayaks, floating mattresses, heads in the water, like the water lilies and lotuses that used to grow in the bends of the river . . . That's right, I told you about that already. Shouts, squeals, laughter. So all my attention is concentrated on the wild strawberries, or on the dogs, or making sure no one's in trouble out in the water, no one's calling for help. You have to admit those are not the best moments for someone to be wondering about something else. And yet . . .

But I'm sorry – I interrupted you. Please, do go on. You think so? No, you can never go back to the same place. The truth is, that place doesn't exist anymore, going back there isn't even possible. Why not? Because if you ask me, places die once they've been left.

It only seems that they long for us. You shouldn't believe that. When I was living abroad, when I'd go for a walk in the woods it would be a foreign woods, with foreign trees, foreign bushes, trails, foreign birds, but I'd always feel like I was walking through these woods, along these trails, passing these trees, hearing these birds. So I stopped going for walks in the woods there. When a person's gone, it's no longer the same place. A person's only place is inside themselves. Regardless of whether they're here, there, wherever. Now or at any time. Everything that's on the outside is only illusion, circumstance, chance, misunderstanding. A person is their own place, especially the last place.

Did I mistake your meaning? We must be talking about two different things. We're talking about the same thing? In that case why did you appear only now? Why not back then? There were other opportunities too. I wouldn't have had to pretend all this time. It's true that our whole life we have to pretend in order to live. There isn't a moment when we're not pretending. We even pretend to ourselves. In the end, though, there comes a moment when we don't feel like pretending anymore. We grow tired of ourselves. Not of the world, not of other people, but of ourselves. It's just I didn't think the moment had yet come.

I'm taking you for someone else? I don't think so. To begin with maybe I did.

You came asking for beans, so one or another of them could have come asking for beans too, who knows who could've come. So I was justified in suspecting that we'd met before. Why wouldn't you be wearing an overcoat and hat? It's fall, the weather's chilly already. There'll be frosts before you know it. And at this time of year, in the off-season, who else could come, all the more so just like that, as if they were paying a formal visit? Once every so often the forest ranger stops by. Or someone from the dam comes on an inspection, they may or may not drop in. Or the mailman brings me a letter with money from Mr. Robert on the first of the month, he steps in but then a moment later he's gone. The last time he was here he said he probably wouldn't be coming anymore because his bike's broken, I'll have to go to the post office myself. Other than that, I don't think there's anyone.

People from the cabins? Yes, they do come. But not everyone will pop in and say hello. Besides, they don't appear that often, they know everything's fine here. I'm not talking about the ones who bring someone here. Those ones, of course they don't come and visit me. Quite the opposite. They try and make sure I don't see anything or hear anything when one or another of them is here. They usually arrive in the late evening. They think I'm already asleep because my lights are off. But me, I see and hear everything, it's just that, as I told you, I don't stick my nose into that kind of business. But I hear the car. When it's quiet like it is now, the slightest murmur carries all the way across the lake. When an owl hoots, and there's no wind, it's like a shot going off in the woods. When the wild boars come out of the woods you can hear the earth move under their feet. Plus, the dogs rush to the door right away, and I have to go out to see who's here. I don't get too close, just near enough to check who it is and which cabin, but so they don't see me. It goes without saying I don't take the dogs. When they go into their cabin I come back home. Everyone has to walk from the parking lot to their cabin, and that's enough for me to see what I need to. I stopped allowing them to drive up to their cabins. You can imagine what that would look like. Tracks everywhere. Plus, as you saw, most of the cabins are on a slope. What if the cars started to slide down into the lake? Who would be responsible? Me, because I'm the one that takes care of everything here.

There's only one angler who comes for a week or two at this time of year. For some reason he hasn't been yet, but he may still show. Let's just hope winter doesn't set in too early, because he wouldn't be able to get his fishing in. Though he avoids me too. I don't know why. He bought a cabin from another guy, way down at the end there, right by the shore. He doesn't leave his keys with me, so I don't go in. During the season you won't see him here, his cabin's locked up, he only comes here to fish round about now. But I couldn't say if he catches anything. He gets in his boat in the early morning and rows out onto the lake, sometimes to one end, sometimes the other. At the far end you can barely get to the shore, it's overgrown with reeds, alders, blackthorn. He disappears into the reed beds and spends all day there from dawn till dusk, in his boat. In the evening he doesn't turn on his light, I don't know if he goes to bed right away. I never even know if he's back from his fishing. And I mean I'm not going to go over there and ask him if he's caught anything. If he hasn't it's all the worse to ask. All I can say is, I've never seen any catch.

Maybe he doesn't fish? But in that case, why would he spend all day in his boat? He even stays in it when it's raining. He wraps himself up in his raincoat, pulls the hood up over his head and sits like that in his boat, in the rain. He has a fishing pole. Sometimes he fishes out in the middle of the lake, so I've seen it. It sticks up out of the boat like a regular pole. From time to time he pulls it out of the water, adjusts something on the hook, then casts it back. It must be a fishing pole. But I've never ever seen a fish thrashing about on it when he takes it out of the water. Of course there are fish in the lake. There were fish in the Rutka, why wouldn't there be fish in the lake? Different ones, but they're there.

If he fished from the shore I'd go up and at least ask, Are they biting today? Or look to see if his float ever moves. It's true, anglers don't like it when you check their floats. It's like looking at a card player's hand. But he always fishes from his boat. Sometimes, when he's opposite my windows I at least go out and sit on the shore. You can't talk from there. Not even to ask if the fish are biting, you'd have to shout, and I wouldn't want to scare the fish away.

I don't know. All I know is that he's an angler. I don't even know if he sees me when I'm sitting on the shore and he's out in the middle of the lake in his boat. Though I see him. What can I say, it doesn't have to work both ways, that since you see others they see you. That's how it is with everything. It's another matter that an angler has to keep an eye on their float the whole time, because if a fish starts to bite . . .

There are times the lake covers over with mist, especially around now, in the fall, and he disappears into the mist, so sometimes I call out to him:

"Hello, are you there?" I even walk along the shore calling: "Are you there? Are you there?"

He's never answered me. One time, just so as to hear his voice I went over there even before dawn, before he'd headed out, and I kind of told him off for not pulling his boat up onto the shore, there'd been a wind the night before and the chain of his boat was rattling so loud I hadn't gotten a wink all night. He'd probably been asleep and hadn't heard it. He said:

"I'm sorry."

That was it.

You know what, as I listen to you, your voice is sort of like his. I still have a good ear. At least that much is left from playing music. I won't argue about it. But I must have heard your voice once before. Say something more. Anything. It's strange, we're sitting here shelling beans, I'm listening and listening to you, but it's only now that I've noticed.

I always thought I'd recognize anyone from their voice. Not their face, faces change. Most often the face ends up looking nothing like itself. You're never sure if it's the same person when you look at their face. But when you hear their voice, even if it's someone from a forgotten memory you remember them. Also the face can be dressed up in all kinds of expressions, masks, grimaces. You can't do that with the voice. It's as though the voice were independent of the person.

I can even tell over the telephone, it's like I hear all the levels of the voice, from the highest level down to the breathing, to silence. Of course – silence is a voice. And it's words. Though words that have lost faith in themselves, you might say. Over the phone a person speaks with his whole self. Maybe if I'd heard your voice over the phone it would have been easier for me to remember.

Yes, I have a telephone, through in the living room there, except it's not working. I never reported the problem because I don't really need it. Who would I speak to? I've no one to call. If someone has something they need to talk to me about they can come visit me here. You say I ought to have a cell phone. What for? Oh, I see what cell phones are good for, here in the season. Everyone's got their cell phone stuck to their ear. Hardly anyone talks to anyone else the way we're doing now, they're all on their phones. Does that bring people closer together, do you think? People are more and more out of touch with one another. If it wasn't for those few months in fall and winter when peace and quiet come back, I don't know if I could bear it.

I sometimes wonder even whether next season I should add a sentence to the posted regulations: Cell phones are to be turned off or left in the cabins. Like in church, or the theater or the symphony. It's no different here than in those places. Peace and quiet can be a church, a theater, a symphony hall just the same. Only peace and quiet, because I don't know anything else that could be. You have no idea of its power. To just listen intently – in the off-season of course – to the sky, the lake, the early morning, the sunset, the night when there's a full moon, to go into the woods and listen to all the trees and bushes and plants, to lie down in the moss. Or if you listen to the ants. Lean down to the anthill, carefully of course so they don't get all over you, it's like you'd found yourself in outer space and you were listening to the universe. Why do people feel they have to fly to other places?

Sometimes I think to myself that if someone were ever able to record silence, that that would be real music. Me? Come off it. On the saxophone? Music like that isn't the same thing as a saxophone. Sometimes I regret not having chosen a different instrument. The violin, for instance, like that teacher at school was pushing. But I picked the sax. That was how it began, and that was how it remained. Plus, I played in dance bands, as you know. Not to mention that it's all moot now, because I don't play anymore.

Though let me tell you, I do wonder if I'd have played at all if I hadn't found myself in that works band. Maybe I wouldn't have gone any further than what I did at school. I don't know if things would have been better or worse for me, but at least I wouldn't have experienced what it's like when you can't play any longer.

What can I say, I was young. When you're young, how can you know what's going to be better or worse for you? And not right away, but in some distant future. No one gives it a second thought, there's nothing to think about. Not to mention that back then, young people were all the rage. They always are, you say. Perhaps, but not exactly in the same way. Back then, nothing could happen without young people. At every meeting, congress, celebration there had to be some youngster on the committee. Same with any deputation, it always had to include at least one young person. And one woman. About young people they'd say that they have their future ahead of them, that they would be the ones to build a new and better world, that everything was in their hands. True, everyone always talks like that, then the young folks grow old and leave the same world they inherited to the next lot of people. Yes indeed, the world isn't as easy to change as we think.

I sometimes even ask myself whether it wasn't for the same reason they decided it would be good to have someone young in the band. Because truth be told, I wasn't that good in those days. Also, I didn't think of myself as being young. I believed in a new and better world, because the old one, as you'll be the first to admit, it was nothing but shambles from the war. And it was only after the war that we found out what the war had actually meant, what a huge defeat it had been not just for human beings but for God. It seemed humans would never pick themselves up again, that they'd gone too far, while God had failed to prove his existence. I didn't need to understand anything. I myself was an example of it all.

I can tell that you disagree with me about something. Then why aren't you speaking up? Say what you want to say. Please, I'm listening. No, no. I wasn't the only one who thought the time for God had passed. Perhaps I didn't quite think like that, but I wasn't able to pray any more. The only thing that happened was that sometimes, when no one could see me, I'd burst into tears for no reason. So I was ready to believe in anything, so long as I could believe in something. And what's better to believe in than a new and better world? Especially because later, when I started working on building sites, each site was like a little part of that belief. Things got built, after all, you won't deny that. There were delays, it took a long time, often the work was done shoddily, there were shortages of materials, of this and that, stuff got stolen. But things got built.

Anyway, I'm not going to argue with you. You're my guest, let it be that you're right. It doesn't make much difference to me anymore. Wait a minute though, have I maybe seen a photograph of you before? And actually from those times, when we were young. You don't come out on photographs? How is that possible? Not even as a shadow? Or at the very least as a trace of light wherever you were standing or sitting? Not even that? There's nothing at all? Then I really don't get it. In that case the dogs . . . Whereas they're sleeping like babies. As you can see. Oh, they've woken up now. What is it, Rex? What is it, Paws? Were you having a dream? The gentleman and I have been shelling beans. Go back to sleep, go on. I'll wake you up when it's time.

I do have one picture. But I don't remember if you're in it. I'll show you later. What is it of? I mentioned that dream. I did, I really did. You were surprised I have nothing better to think about. It was when I was still living abroad. I rarely dreamed. Still don't, as it happens. When I was playing, I'd often get home in the middle of the night, I'd be so exhausted I wouldn't have the strength to dream. And even if I did dream something, when I woke up in the morning

I'd never remember it. Then one night I had a dream, and it was like my dream was being projected on a screen. I don't really remember, but I think it may still have been going on when I suddenly jerked upright and sat on the edge of the bed. I admit I wasn't sleeping alone, and she woke up too. She was concerned, she asked me what was wrong.

"I had a dream," I said.

"Tell me about it," she said.

But what was I supposed to tell her when I wasn't even sure whether I was dreaming I was sitting on the edge of the bed, and the dream was my waking life, or vice versa.

"You weren't in it, in any case," I said to reassure her. "Go back to sleep, it's the middle of the night."

"Were there other women?"

"Yes."

"You men always dream of other women." She fell asleep again right away.

I stayed on the edge of the bed, wrestling with my thoughts, trying to figure out if it had been my dream. And wondering if I could believe it was someone else's.

It was autumn, like now, I was walking through meadows, wearing a hat. You won't believe it, but it was the brown felt hat I'd left on the train. So many years had gone by since then, I could have sworn I'd forgotten all about it. No, quite the opposite, after that I always wore hats. My whole life I've worn hats. I couldn't imagine wearing anything else on my head. I even had a kind of respect for hats. Someone wearing a hat usually aroused my curiosity, in any case more so than with any other kind of headwear. Not to mention women. The women I best remember are the ones who wore hats. Myself, I always felt best in a hat. It was like I was someone else, someone beyond myself, someone for whom everything else fell into the background. Not that I was proud that way. Not at all. I was afraid to live. I felt like I'd only just emerged from a shell, and I still found everything painful. For a long time I was afraid to live. You'll find this hard to believe, but wearing a hat actually helped a lot. I began looking people in the eye, and not accepting things at face value. When I wore a hat, memory would somehow torment me less.

And another thing, I liked to greet people with my hat. That was a true pleasure for me. The fact is, there's no fuller way of greeting a person than by tipping your hat. And you can't imagine how I enjoyed it when a gust of wind would try and lift the hat off my head. I'd experience almost a sense of oneness with it as I held it by the brim. More, it felt like *I* was staying in place by holding on to the hat, often with both hands. Even if it was a howling gale, I knew I couldn't let it snatch my hat away.

Yes, I've had lots of hats through the course of my life, in all sorts of different colors, styles, various kinds and makes. I never scrimped on buying hats. Or regretted the time it took. I could spend hours in shops and department stores, trying things on till I finally found the right one. But I never wore any of them very long. I didn't just change them when the fashion changed. And I never threw any away. Life had taught me that everything comes full circle, the way the Earth does. Fashion's no different. What was unfashionable would later become the in thing.

That's true. But I never cared whether the fashion was for hats or for other kinds of headwear. Besides, it's never been the case that hats are completely out of fashion. Even these days you see women and men in hats. Hats may be the only thing left that testifies to stability in the world. Wouldn't you say so? Think how many things have disappeared and how many new ones have come along, but hats have stuck around.

My whole apartment was littered with hats. There was no more room for them in the closet. They lay on the bookshelves, on the books themselves, on the chest of drawers, on the windowsills, everywhere. I had this antique cast iron coat stand in the hallway which had spreading hooks like antlers at the top, ending in brass knobs. It was festooned with hats.

Yes, I made good money. Not right away, of course. Generally speaking dance bands pay well. Depending on the establishment, naturally. As you know, not that many people like classical music, but everyone dances. And I'll tell you something else, dancing isn't just dancing like you might expect. It's only in the dance that you can truly see who's who. Not in conversation, in dance. Not at a dinner table. Not on the street. Not even at war. In dance. If I hadn't played dance music I wouldn't have gotten to understand people so well.

I often wore a hat when I played in one band or another. For a saxophonist it's the right thing. There's even a certain style to it. The rest of the band would be bare-headed, I was the only one in a hat. Though sometimes the entire band wore hats. I forget which band it was, but we had a poster with all of us wearing hats. So it was at that time I had the dream about the brown felt hat that I'd only had on my head in the store when I tried it on. How can you explain that? No, it was definitely the brown felt one, it slipped down over my ears the same way.

From far off you could tell it was too big. Because as I was walking along it was like at the same time I was watching myself walking, from some undefined point. That happens in dreams. Though not only there. It was visibly rocking on my head with every step I took across the uneven meadows. When you're watching yourself like that, and you're also aware of it, you see it even more vividly than you feel it on your head. I was wearing an overcoat like yours. Underneath I had on a suit, and I think a necktie, though I don't remember the color or pattern. Besides, it was hidden under a scarf that also looked like yours. Whereas my shoes were tied together by the shoelaces and slung over my shoulder, and I was barefoot. Why barefoot? That's what I can't explain. I was doing well for myself, after all. My pant legs were rolled up past my ankles, but that didn't seem to be enough, when I looked down I saw my pants were wet from the dew all the way up to the knees. The grass was tall, it hadn't been mown in a long while. Also, there was a mist so dense that I would see myself then vanish again, I even lost the sense of whether it was me crossing the meadows, passing through the mist. It was only the hat that showed me it couldn't be anyone else. Especially since I could feel a biting cold on my bare feet, as if the grass was just thawing after a night frost.

I was walking rather briskly, though I wasn't in a hurry to get anywhere. The mist kept blurring the image, the painful awareness that it was me was still beyond me. If such a feeling is even possible. I seemed more like a hint of myself, as I watched from that unidentified point and saw myself moving through the mist, across the meadow. It was only the hat that was visible to me, perhaps because it was the brown felt one and it was too big. I had the moist cold taste of the mist in my mouth, I felt I was permeated with it.

At a certain moment I paused, wiped the mist off my forehead with my handkerchief, then I leaned down to roll my pant legs further up, and that exact second the hat fell off my head. I started looking for it in the grass and at that point I might have woken up, because without my hat I felt like I had one foot in the waking world. That would have been best for me, I wouldn't have had to keep on walking through the mist, across the meadows, I wouldn't have had to remember the dream after I woke up. It was just a dream, just meadows, just mist, they weren't worth bringing into my waking life.

All of a sudden the sun peeked out, because up till then it had been hidden behind the mist. The mist covered a wide area, but it also extended high into the air. There are mists like that. It was then I saw my hat, a few feet away in the grass. And next to the hat was the muzzle of a cow, as if it was sniffing at the hat. I reached down, carefully took the hat from under the cow's muzzle, then the whole cow emerged from the mist. At the same instant other cows began to appear on all sides, as if from the wall of mist. The sun was thinning out the mist almost as I watched, the meadows stretched into the distance and more and more cows had come, like someone had driven them out of the mist toward me. Some of them were raising their heads and staring, evidently startled by my presence. Some came closer till I could see their large mute eyes.

I was overcome by fear of them. I hurried away, and kept glancing back to see if they were following me. Though cows are the gentlest creatures under the sun. Of all creatures that exist, including humans. I used to graze them, I know. They weren't moving, they were standing there watching, as if they couldn't understand why I was running away from them. I tripped over a molehill and almost fell. I thought that maybe my grandfather was waiting for the mole with a spade. But no. It was because I'd looked around yet again to see if the cows were following me.

Glancing back constantly, I came upon a small group of women standing around a pile of dried potato stalks. You know what potato stalks are, right? The plants that are left after you dig up the potatoes. You make a bonfire of the dried stalks, you bake potatoes in it, there's always smoke everywhere. When you're driving in the fall, but earlier than now, you can see plumes of smoke from the fires rising here and there in the fields.

More and more piles of stalks appeared as the mist cleared. At each pile there was an identical group of women, all dressed in black. I was about to tip my hat and apologize for the interruption when one of the women turned to me with her finger on her lips, indicating that I should be quiet. It only lasted a split second, but I noticed a boundless sorrow in her expression. She was wearing a black hat with a huge brim; her eyes were big and dark, and her sorrow pierced me.

The women made room and another of them, who also wore a black hat though with a somewhat narrower brim, beckoned me to stand amongst them. I thought that they must want to light the bonfire, but they didn't have matches. Potato stalks, fall, meadows, cows, mist – everything pointed to this. Perhaps they were even planning to bake potatoes? I reached into my pocket for matches, but the woman standing closest to me stopped my arm and gave me a reproachful look.

I couldn't say how many of them were standing around the pile. I wasn't counting. Besides, you know how it is in dreams. Dreams don't like numbers. Most of the women were elegantly dressed in black overcoats, black furs, black hats and shawls and gloves. And the black of each woman's outfit was different from that of any of the others.

One of them had a black veil wound around her hat. Another wore a huge hat decorated with black roses – I think she was the one who had turned to me with her finger to her lips to stop me from speaking. I just hadn't noticed the roses at the time. Another had a tiny little hat, but with a black pearl the size of a poppy head pinned to the front. I know there are no pearls like that, but in dreams there are, evidently. One had no hat, only a black veil over her head, dark glasses in gilt frames, and a black fur that glistened with droplets of mist. Yet another wore a hat with a veil so thick that nothing of her face could be seen. That woman's sorrow seemed the most painful of all to me.

Among them were some country women. Muffled in shawls, in sleeveless jackets, wearing thin worn overcoats and crooked shoes, they hunched over, whether from sadness or from the drudgery of life. It must have been colder than it seemed to me, because they were blowing on their stiff blue hands. It occurred to me that perhaps the women in the elegant outfits were their daughters, daughters-in-law, cousins, who had come back from where they lived out in the world for the baking of potatoes. What could fine ladies like that be wanting for, if not the taste of potatoes baked in a bonfire.

"Have the potatoes been put into the bonfires yet?" I asked in a half-whisper.

"What potatoes?" asked the woman with the pearl the size of a poppy head, indignant at my question.

"Then what is it?"

"They're dying," said one of the country women in a voice filled with grief, as she blew on her hands.

"Who? Where?" I didn't understand.

"The old farmers here, in these piles, they're dying," the women in the hat with the black roses said softly in my ear.

"Lord in heaven," sighed one of the country women. Tears prevented her from saying any more.

"What do you mean, they're dying?" It was still a mystery to me.

The one in the dark glasses chided me:

"Please stop talking. Show some respect."

All the same I leaned over the pile of stalks, thinking I might recognize someone from our village. But there was only the narrowest of gaps, no bigger than a final sigh, and I couldn't see a thing. I was about to widen the crack a little, but I heard someone murmur above me:

"Please don't do that."

I looked to see who had spoken, and I realized I didn't know a single one of the women, either the fine ladies or the country women. Well, the one in the veil I might have noticed in passing at some point. But how could I see through her veil to check. The veil was dark as night, plus it was densely patterned with knots, they looked like little flies. I thought to myself that if I kept my eyes on her, at some moment she might need to wipe her tears, then she'd have to lift the veil. All at once a voice reached me from under the veil:

"Please don't look at me like that. Especially because this isn't me, despite what you think."

"Ah, the priest's here at last," said one of the country women.

I did in fact see a priest. He had risen from his knees at a nearby pile and was headed toward us. He wore a surplice, had a stole around his neck, and carried a Bible. I was about to shout:

"Hey, Priest! Remember me?"

I knew him right away. But when he came close, it turned out that it wasn't the welder from the building site, but a photographer. Without even asking, right away he took our picture. I'm standing with the group of women around a pile of dry potato stalks, in the brown felt hat. Can you imagine, I had so many hats in my life, but in the picture I'm wearing the brown felt one.

He clicked the shutter and took the picture out of the camera on the spot. It was in color, of course. My hat is brown, the meadow is green, the pile of stalks we're standing around is grayish, and the black of each woman's outfit is different. I believe he said which magazine he was from, but I don't remember. He said he'd just learned that here, on the meadows, in the piles of stalks old farmers were dying, and he'd come.

"The issue's going to sell like hotcakes," he said, crowing with anticipation. All he had to do was get into the middle of the pile.

He fixed a long lens on his camera. He knelt down by the pile and inserted the lens into the gap the size of a final sigh. He clicked and clicked, all excited, exclaiming: Excellent, fantastic, even better. Except that when he was done, it was like someone began to pull him into the pile. He struggled and struggled, calling out, Help me, someone, till in the end he had to let go of his camera. And that's how he lost possession of it.

You know, often when I look at that photograph, I'm tempted to take a peek inside the pile and see who's dying in there. One day I will. I'll have to. The only thing holding me back are the women standing nearby, even though I don't know any of them. Especially the one in the hat with the black roses. I don't suppose you know what black roses mean? Maybe the meaning of the whole dream could be made clear? I didn't mention that when she stopped my hand as I was about to take the matches from my pocket, and she looked at me with reproach, one of the roses came loose from her hat and fell at my feet. I was about to bend down and pick it up, but my hat warned me that if I leaned over it would fall off too.

Black roses must mean something, you don't find roses like that in gardens. One time when I was abroad I went to a rose show. Let me tell you, I was dazzled by all the shapes and colors. There must have been every kind of rose in the world, but there weren't any black ones.

Do you believe in dreams? I didn't until I had that one. I never thought twice about them. Whereas now, when I sometimes look at the photograph, I have the impression that I've simply dreamed myself from that dream into this world, and I'm here, I have to live here. I wonder if you'll recognize me. I'm a little younger, but not much. Maybe you'll recognize some of the women too. You may turn out to know one or another of them well.

What do you say, shall we have some tea? Or maybe you prefer coffee. Do you like green tea or regular? Me, I only drink green tea. Do you take sugar? Hang on, the sugar bowl should be around here somewhere. I don't use sugar myself. I only drink unsweetened green tea. I rarely have sugar at all. Ah, here it is. I'll put this stool between us if you've no objection, we can put our drinks on it. Yes, the sugar bowl is silver. I bought it in the same shop where I got the candlesticks. That was the time I was best off, it was my golden period. I was playing in a five-star hotel. We wore white tuxedos with green lapels, I remember it clearly. Well, not every evening. We had different outfits. And we'd play different instruments according to the evening and the clientele. Sometimes we'd change outfits in the same evening, depending on what we were playing. But the sax was always there, at most I'd change from an alto to a tenor or a soprano.

Here's the tea. We can drink it in these teacups. You like them? I'm glad. They were a birthday present from the band. Only two are left from the set. It's like they knew that one day you'd come and we'd drink tea in them. I never use them when I'm alone. Whether I'm having tea or coffee, I use a mug, like I do for milk. And before now I somehow never had the opportunity to serve tea to anyone. I've got two others like these, but smaller, for coffee. If you'd asked for coffee, instead of sugar I'd have given you honey. You could have tried it with honey. Have you ever had coffee with honey? I'll make some later and you can see what it's like. I only ever have honey with my coffee. Coffee with honey is totally different than coffee with sugar. You don't lose the taste of the coffee, but it's even smoother than with cream. Unfortunately I don't have any cream even if you'd wanted it. It's too late now, otherwise I could have gotten some at the store. The store's a couple of miles away, but in the car it's a hop and a skip. Like walking from here to the other side of the lake, no longer.

If I'd known you were coming I'd have made sure to have cream. I'd have been prepared. Too bad you didn't let me know in advance. You called? And what, there was no dial tone? Don't be offended, but I'll tell you honestly that it's a good job you didn't get through, because over the phone I'd have told you I don't have any beans. I'd have thought someone was pulling my leg. Or that they were mending my phone and checking to see if it works. Even if you'd introduced yourself, over the phone I wouldn't have believed you. I'd have thought you were pretending to be someone else. This way, at least when I see you I can be sure of one thing – that we must have met once before. Though where and when? We couldn't have just gone through life like that and never have met.

16

Maybe we should light candles after all? I could bring in the candlesticks. We've been shelling beans so long, we could have gotten to know each other well. The more so because I'm almost certain that once before . . . And when two people meet after they've not seen each other in a long time, it ought to be a special occasion, don't you think?

I'm sure you'll agree with me when I say that up to more or less halfway through life we know more and more people, so many that it's sometimes hard to remember them all, then in the second half there start to be fewer, till at the end you're the only person you know. It's not only that we outlive everyone else. Rather, it's life's way of indicating how much is already behind us, and how much still lies ahead. Almost all of it is behind, there's just a little bit still to go. So when someone like you comes by, if only to buy beans, and in addition they seem to have been an old acquaintance, it only seems right to at least light a candle. At those moments any person you've known stands for all the people you've known.

If I still played, I'd play something to mark the occasion. But what can you do. It goes without saying that I'm tempted. I often am. Sometimes I even take the sax out of its case, hang it around my neck, put the mouthpiece in my mouth, place my hands around the body. But I don't have the courage to run my fingers over the keys. For shelling beans my hands will more or less do, as you see. And for other jobs. But repainting those nameplates is torment. The saxophone is out of the question. My fingers start to feel stiff right away. I'm even afraid to blow into the mouthpiece. But I hear myself. You might not believe me – I don't play, but I hear myself playing. And those dogs of mine hear me too. I see them lying there all ears. Their skin is calm, neither of them so much as twitches, their muzzles are stretched out, but their ears are sticking up like they don't want to miss a note. I don't just imagine it, I play. They hear it, I hear it. I play with my mouth, my breath, with these hands that I'm afraid to place on the keys, with my whole being. Would I not recognize my own playing? I've listened to myself so often, my soul has listened, how could I not recognize that it's me?

And imagine this, it's only now, after I haven't played in years, that I've come to understand what kind of instrument the saxophone is. With that kind of playing, when only you can hear yourself, you hear more than the music alone. It's as if you cross some boundary within yourself. Perhaps it's the same with every instrument, but I played the saxophone and that's all I can speak about. You supposedly know what it's capable of, what it's good for and what it isn't, you know all of its parts, like you know your own hands, eyes, mouth, nose, you know which part is connected to which. But it turns out you knew almost nothing. It's only after you stop playing . . .

When I was picking out a new mouthpiece I'd try endless ones, the clerk would keep bringing them to me, before I found one that satisfied me. So you might think you know everything. Once in one of the stores I even heard someone say, We get people from all kinds of bands, but I've never known anybody to be so picky. Though two identical mouthpieces, made from ebonite let's say, they'll each sound different. Not because they're ebonite. They could be brass, silver, gilt. Identical mouthpieces, but the sound is different. And there's no knowing what causes it. It's the same with reeds, they have to be made of the right bamboo. But how can you say what the right bamboo is? What does it even mean to say it's the right kind? Well, it can mean anything. What soil it grew in, what kind of year it was where it grew, whether it had too little sun, too much rain, or vice versa. Whether it was harvested properly, dried evenly on both sides. And above all whether it's soft or hard. All of that comes out later in the sound. Even the hands of the people that made the reed are probably reflected in its sound. So every reed, I'd rub it down myself afterwards till I felt the sound was the fullest it could possibly be. Because let me tell you, the reed and the mouthpiece are the most important parts of a saxophone. Of course, every part is important, the neck, the keys, especially whether the pads are tight-fitting, the bell, each of them has its role, the cork around the mouthpiece is crucial, also what's called the tenon that holds the reed so it vibrates along its whole length.

But the mouthpiece and the reed are the most critical of all. Not just because they turn your breath into music. It's like they open up all the life that's inside you, all the memory, even the parts that aren't remembered, every single hope that's in you, your grudges against people, against the world, even against God.

So you think I'd have had a chance? It's just that saxophones are rare in the kinds of bands you're talking about. If I'd not been restricted to only playing dance music . . . Or if I'd studied somewhere, gotten a piece of paper that said I could play. You know how it is. You even have to have a piece of paper to say you were born. Without it even that would be impossible. You have to have one that says you died, or you wouldn't be able to die. That's how the world is, I don't need to explain it to you. We both live in it. You don't doubt that part, do you? I mean look, we're sitting here shelling beans, so we exist. Someone already said something along those lines, true. But that isn't enough. Everyone's existence has to be confirmed by something. Or someone. But while we're shelling beans we don't need any confirmation.

That wasn't what I meant to say. I meant to say that existence itself is no proof of anything. Existence brings us nothing but doubts. Please don't misunder-stand me. I'm speaking in general, not about you or me. I don't know you, after all. I may guess at this or that, but I don't know you. We're just shelling beans, no more. But at some point we'll finish, you'll drive away, and what then? I won't remember you, and all the more you won't remember me. What can I say, I never was the kind of person worth remembering. An electrician who played dance music. Even if you'd come to one of the clubs where I used to play, you'd likely not have thought twice about some guy in the band on the sax.

Forgive me, I don't mean to oblige you to say anything. For politeness' sake you might feel you have to pretend, yes, it goes without saying, how on earth would you forget, you have no doubt whatsoever, whether it was here or there, of course, here, there, absolutely, that's right, at such-and-such a time. Here or there, at this or that time. For what?

True, sometimes when you meet someone years later and no trace remains of who they were, you have to pretend that they're the same person as before. Or even if there is a faint vestige, what of it, when you rack your brains and you still can't remember any such person even existing. And moments like that, sure, you have to make as if you remember them. I sometimes wonder if anyone would have existed if we didn't pretend. If it would even be possible to have existed. Besides, what is memory if not the pretense that you remember. Though it's our only witness to having existed. We depend on memory the way a forest depends on trees, a river on its banks. More – if you ask me, we're created by memory. Not just us, the whole world.

So we should live as long as memory permits us. No longer. People live too long, let me tell you, though everyone thinks it's too short. You think so? If that's the case, what would my dogs have to say about it, or other creatures? Too long. When I think they could die before me, then it's too long by at least that much. A person's memory is suited to a shorter life. No one's memory can take in such a long existence. Just as well, you say? Why's that? You say no one could bear a memory like that? That the world would fall to pieces from it? That could be. Though whatever memory doesn't include, it's still lying in wait for us. And that's why we live too long in my view. Like I said, we should live as long as our

355 ·

memory allows, within the boundaries it lays down for us. Do you know of any other measure for life?

Forgive me for asking, but have you never had the feeling that your life is going on too long? That means you're fond of living, like most people. I can understand that, especially if someone thinks they're living in accordance with destiny. Oh yes, living in accordance with destiny is a lot easier. It's just that I don't believe in destiny. It's chance, chance, all chance. That's how the world looks, how life looks, if you were to check how things function here. So then, was it worth coming? All the more that I put you to work right away shelling beans. But you wanted to buy beans, remember? While all I had were unshelled. And as you see, I've been talking too long. I talked as long as memory allowed. Unless a person believes in dreams. Dreams are memory too, you know.

I might never have remembered that hat if I hadn't dreamt about it. I should have figured out what the hat meant right when I was standing with the women around the pile of potato stalks. Except that like I told you, up till then I didn't believe in dreams. It was only when I got rheumatism not long after. Rheumatism itself wouldn't have been so terrible, everyone knows sicknesses are for people and you just have to put up with them. But in addition it turned out I wouldn't be able to play anymore. And for me, playing was everything. You might say I wasn't interested in myself, only in playing. Beyond playing it was like I didn't exist. Who knows, maybe I actually didn't, and it was only playing music that kind of summoned me out of non-existence and forced me to be.

In fact, it was because of playing that I left the country. Back in those days that wasn't easy, as you know. But the firm I worked for got a foreign contract to build a cement works. And I never went back. I had no other reason. I could have continued to play in one company band or other. But I remembered what the warehouse keeper had said to me, that the saxophone had taken him around the world. Not to mention that I was trying to get away from my memories, which I always felt were pulling me back. I thought that the memories would stay here, while I'd be playing over there.

Then out of the blue there was this rheumatism. Everything came back with what seemed like redoubled strength. My whole life was suddenly reminding me it was there. I didn't even know I'd been carrying it inside me. If it hadn't been for the playing I wouldn't have cared much whether or not I was alive, or since when. Because when it came down to it, why should I be alive? Because of some lucky chance? Except, was it so lucky? Maybe it was just mocking me? Or testing me? In what way? I couldn't say.

Either way, my hands are better now. You saw when you came in how I was repainting those nameplates. And that's no easy task. If your hand shakes, the brush shakes with it. Plus, the paints these days are much better quality, they're harder to erase. Then you have to paint over the same letters, and often they've rubbed off, gotten rusty, you can't see them clearly. You might get people mixed up. I can shell beans as well, like you see. It's just that I can't play the sax anymore. For the sax you need fingers like butterflies. They need to feel not just that they're touching such and such a sound, but how deeply. This finger, see, it's a little swollen, and on my left hand I can't bend these two. They ache in the wet weather. But it's a lot better than it used to be. I can do almost anything. Make repairs, chop wood, drive the car when I have errands or it needs the mechanic.

There was a time, though, when I couldn't so much as lift a cup of coffee or tea, can you imagine it? Almost all my fingers were too stiff. And when you can't bend your fingers, how are you supposed to play the saxophone? Here you're blowing into the mouthpiece, and down there your fingers are afraid of the keys. No more playing. It's out of the question. There you were, playing away, and now there's just despair. Your whole life, and nothing left but despair. You beg your fingers, press them down, try to force them to bend, but it's like they're dead. You don't mind if they hurt all they want, they can hurt so much it's unbearable, they can throb and sting and burn, but let them bend. You can't imagine what it's like. All the hopes, desires, the suffering, all without meaning anymore. How can anyone come to terms with that?

Wait a moment, I'd never have expected you to say what you just said. I must have you confused with someone else. But I still have to figure out when and where we met. Something's not quite right here. I'd never have thought. If it were someone else . . . No, not at all, I understood you perfectly. I even think that who knows, you could be right. After all, that is one way out. Though now it no longer holds any meaning. Because the worst thing is when there's none at all. Yes, it's a way out. Though it's no longer of any importance. Maybe if it had happened back then.

The thing is, though, when something happens gradually, to begin with you don't notice it. Then you make light of it, then after that you reassure yourself that maybe things aren't so bad. Especially because other people also cheer you up by saying that some other person was in the same boat, or even worse, and in the end they were fine.

I came back one winter from a ski trip in the mountains and my hands started to feel strangely tired. And this finger here began to ache. Not the other fingers, the other ones just became kind of sluggish. I thought it was because of the ski-ing. That my hands had been overstrained by all the ski poles and ski lifts, the climbing, the falls. I was a pretty good skier. But I'd go for two or three weeks only, and not every year, and I was out of practice. It was hardly surprising it should make itself felt afterwards. But some time later my other fingers started hurting too, and getting stiff. When I was playing it would happen that I didn't press the key down on time, or I pressed it in the wrong way. That's not good, I thought to myself. I went to the doctor. He examined one hand, examined the other, bent my fingers this way and that, pinched them in different places and asked if it hurt.

"It does."

"I'm sorry to say, but it's rheumatism," he said. "And advanced. You'll need to get tests done. We'll take a look, and at that point we can think about treatment. But you'll have to spend some time at a sanatorium. Twice a year would be best."

"But will I be able to play, doctor?" I asked.

"What do you play?"

"The saxophone."

He gave me a sympathetic look.

"For the moment just think about your hands. Especially as it could spread further. You never know with rheumatism. Rheumatism's one of those illnesses …"

But I was no longer listening to him describing what kind of illness it was, I was wondering how I could exist without playing. At the end of the visit he tried to cheer me up by saying that it was hard to make any predictions without tests, so perhaps I'd still be able to play. If I followed his instructions, of course.

The results of the tests weren't particularly good, so I did what he told me to do, especially as he'd left me some room for hope. Aside from taking the medication he urged me to be patient, to keep my spirits up. And to go to a sanatorium. I subjected myself to all kinds of procedures, massages, baths. I tried to do it all as conscientiously as I could. But how effective could it be when all you're thinking about is the fact that you're no longer playing, and may never play again. If your thoughts are going one way and your treatment the other, you're not going to see any effects. I even avoided getting to know anyone there, it was good morning, good morning, nothing beyond that. I never went anywhere except on walks. The only thing I did was before or after a walk, I'd sometimes stop in at a cafe for coffee or tea. Other than that I didn't go anyplace. Not to concerts, though there were some pretty good orchestras that played there, opera singers and popular singers, often really fine ones. The spa park was large so there were plenty of places to walk. There were avenues and paths, you could easily turn off if someone was coming towards you and you wanted to avoid them. There were benches everywhere, sometimes I'd sit down, but even if someone else so much as sat down at the other end of the bench I'd walk away at once. I didn't feel good around people. Truth be told, I didn't feel good around myself.

It was only when the squirrels would scamper up to me for nuts that I'd forget about myself for a moment. I always carried a bag of hazelnuts. It was like they knew. The moment I sat down they'd come hopping. Can you imagine? Why were the squirrels so trusting with people? You think people in a sanatorium are different? If that's the case, everyone should be sent to a sanatorium. Except that even there it happened that someone for example left a dog behind. There were quite a few dogs like that, wandering in search of their owner.

Not at that sanatorium but at another one a long time before – I don't recall if I told you about my beginnings abroad? Well, so back then, at one sanatorium I picked a spot on the main avenue, put a basket next to me on the ground, and started to play. As people passed by they threw money into the basket. Sometimes they'd sit on the nearby benches to listen. Occasionally someone would request a particular tune, those kinds of people generally gave more. It wasn't easy to begin with, not at all. But I had good luck.

One time one of the convalescents, a guy on crutches, took a seat by me on a bench. He listened and listened, then he got up and threw a bill into my basket. Then he asked me to play something else for him, then something else again, then he asked me to move the basket closer, because it was hard for him to bend down, and he tossed in an even bigger banknote. From that time on he came almost every day. He'd sit down, listen, request this or that, then ask me to pass him the basket, and throw in a banknote.

At some point he told me to come sit by him and he started asking me where I'd learned to play, whether I had any qualifications. No, I didn't lie to him. I told him the whole truth, that I'd gone to such and such a school, then that I'd been taught by the warehouse keeper on the building site, and of course that I'd played in the works band. He nodded, but I had the impression he didn't really believe me. I still didn't know the language properly, I could barely express myself, but he seemed to understand everything.

Some time later he asked me again to sit by him. He didn't ask me any questions, he just started complaining that the sanatoria weren't doing much good, and it was looking like he might end up in a wheelchair. He'd been a dancer, he loved dancing. Now he owned a club. He gave the name, said where it was, and he asked if I wouldn't be interested in playing in the band at his club. He was leaving, he'd come to say goodbye. He left me the exact address, gave me money for the ticket, and we agreed when I should come. And that was how it all began.

So you can imagine how I felt now. At one time I'd played for money thrown into a basket, but still I'd been playing. Now I was throwing money into other people's baskets, while I myself had no hope. Plus, I could see him before me, inching along on his crutches, facing the prospect of being in a wheelchair. Yes, he was already in a wheelchair when I played in his club. Let me tell you, I felt like I was waiting for a sentence to be passed, especially since for the longest time there was no improvement. I even seemed to be worse. So you can understand that I had to forget about the saxophone. It goes without saying that I kept visiting the sanatorium just as the doctor had instructed, but by then I was afraid to drive a car, so I used to take the train.

One year I was traveling to the sanatorium, the train pulled up at some small station, and a moment later a woman appeared in the doorway. Normally it made no difference to me who sat in my compartment, but she riveted my attention from the first. I jumped up to help her put her suitcase on the shelf, though at that time, with those hands of mine that had no strength in them, I might not have managed. I myself had to get other people to help me. Luckily someone closer to the door beat me to it. She was more or less middle-aged, though as you know, that age is the hardest to pin down. She was dressed smartly and with good taste. She radiated a mature beauty that was beginning to wane. Or the impression may have come from an intensity of being that suffused her beauty and drew out its depths. Faces, even young ones, that are merely good-looking are only so on the outside as it were, till the intensity of being reveals that extra something in them. But that wasn't what took possession of me, though it wouldn't have been surprising if it had been that alone. The thing was, the longer I looked at her, surreptitiously of course, the more certain I was that we'd met once before. But where and when – I racked my brains. It even occurred to me that she might have been the woman in the black veil covered in tiny knots of lace like little flies, as we were standing around the pile of dry potato stalks in the dream. I spent the whole of the rest of the journey trying to remember.

She got off at the same station as me. On the platform I nodded goodbye, investing the gesture with all of my feeling of regret that we'd probably never meet again. I doubt she read it that way. She nodded back without the faintest smile. So I was all the more certain that was the last time I'd see her.

Then one day, would you believe it, I was sitting on a bench in the park smoking a cigarette, I look up and all of a sudden I see her coming towards me. She was dressed differently, more the way you do at a sanatorium, more casually, but with equally good taste. I recognized her from far off. She'd been constantly in my thoughts since the time we'd shared a compartment on the train. Often, in between procedures I found myself wondering where we could have met and when, that I should know her at once like that. She came up to the bench I was sitting on. She didn't so much as smile to show she remembered me. She simply asked if she could sit down, because she felt like a cigarette, and she saw I was smoking.

"No one else is smoking on any of the other benches," she said. After she finished her cigarette, as she was about to leave she said: "Thank you."

That was all. Again I tried to figure out where I knew her from. Because by now I had no doubt it had been a long, long time before the train. In the park, in the sunshine you could see a lot more clearly, you could see as if from the most distant time. But how long ago it could have been, I strained to recall. I smoked one cigarette after another. One by one, as if looking through a photo album I went through all the women I'd ever known, but I didn't find her. Perhaps she'd been much younger then, perhaps she'd changed a lot. Yet that intensity of being must have marked her beauty even back then, because that must have been how I remembered her.

A few days later, after my walk I stopped by a cafe. I was sitting there drinking my coffee and reading a newspaper when something made me glance up.

The cafe was packed, all the tables were taken, and here I see her coming into the place the way she'd come into the compartment in the train. She took a few steps, looking around for a free table. Without thinking I followed her gaze, but it didn't seem as if any table would be available for a while. It didn't occur to me to invite her to sit at my table. I was probably afraid she'd say no, since on the bench in the park she hadn't seen fit to even smile, let alone ask if we hadn't once shared a train compartment. That's right, I remember you, she could have said. I buried myself in my newspaper again. All at once I heard her voice right next to me:

"Would you mind if I sat at your table? All the other seats are taken. One might free up soon, so it won't be for long."

"You're welcome to," I said, perhaps a little too stiffly. It was just that I resented the fact that back then, on the bench, she hadn't recognized me as the person she'd shared a compartment with. Now it would have been easier to start a conversation. Yet I couldn't for the life of me think of anything to talk about with her, while it would have been wrong to continue reading my paper. As you know, though, women have a preternatural gift for seeing through things, even when you hide it deep down. Before sitting she hesitated and asked:

"Or perhaps you're expecting someone? If that's the case . . ."

"You're welcome to sit," I repeated, much more warmly this time. And in the way of the few words one has to utter at such moments, and which as it happened she'd already put in my mouth, once she took her seat I added half-jokingly: "Though the truth is, we may always be expecting someone, even if we're not always fully aware of it."

She was visibly embarrassed.

"Oh, I'm terribly sorry." She was all set to jump up again.

"Please, sit here," I said to stop her. "I was just talking in generalities."

"In that case, I'll have some cake and be going," she said. "Sometimes I can't help myself, though I shouldn't," she added apologetically.

In order to set her completely at ease, I said:

"In any case please don't pay any attention to what I said, because you might not enjoy the cake, and I wouldn't want that to be my doing. I was just talking."

"That's how I took it," she said.

She still seemed uneasy, though. It showed in the nervous way she looked for the waitress, who a moment ago had disappeared into the back.

"Don't worry, she'll be out any minute."

"I'm not worried," she replied abruptly. "Why would I be . . ."

I had the feeling I'd touched a nerve, though I'd only meant to talk about the waitress. It may have been in an effort to make up for my faux pas, or for some other reason, that I said:

"Though we can never be sure in any situation that chance isn't making use of us."

"What do you mean, chance?" she asked with a start.

"For example, the fact that when you came into the cafe there weren't any free places. Thanks to which, we're sitting together at the same table."

"Chance?" she repeated, as if pondering.

"Years ago, another man and I nodded to each other on the street by mistake, he took me for someone he knew and I did the same, but it turned out we didn't know one another. I apologized to him, saying it had just been by chance. But he disagreed, and invited me to have a coffee with him."

"Can it be that cafes turn chance into destiny? Is that what you mean?" Her tone was bantering.

"It's possible," I replied, giving my own voice a hint of irony, though I had no intention of being ironic. "It all depends on what we take things to be. So why should we not take it that you came here because I was expecting you."

"Really?" She feigned surprise, but a certain wariness had appeared in her eyes.

"Would that be so impossible? So much against common sense? All the more since we actually already know one another."

"Really?" Her eyes widened. I thought she'd burst out laughing. Yet instead she quieted down a little, as if she were thinking about it. "You must have me confused with someone else," she said after a moment. "I don't remember you at all."

"Surely you must. We traveled together in the same train, in the same compartment. You got on, wait a moment, what station was that . . ."

"That can't be. I came here by car."

"By car?" I wasn't exactly surprised so much as troubled. "But you were sitting opposite me, in the seat next to the door. You had a large black suitcase. I was going to help you put it up on the shelf, but somebody else got there first."

"I'm sorry. I never travel by train. I can't stand trains. Coming here by train would have been too much for me. That hopeless space rushing past outside the window. Besides, I have unpleasant associations with trains."

She had shaken my confidence a little. Yet I didn't believe her. I sensed that she recognized me, that she was sure it was me. Perhaps she was only playing a game, the rules of which I didn't know. Or protecting herself from something. What, though?

"But you remember that a few days ago I was sitting on a bench in the park smoking a cigarette. You came up and asked if you could join me because you also felt like smoking."

She burst out laughing:

"I don't smoke! Never did. You really do have me mixed up with someone else."

"What? You mean you don't remember?" I refused to give up. "You said that no one else on any of the benches was smoking. As you left you thanked me."

"Perhaps after all you'd be so kind as to ask the waitress to come over," she said with a hint of impatience. "I'd like to have my cake, then take myself off your hands."

She gave me no hope. I wondered if I shouldn't turn the whole thing into a joke, say, I'm sorry, I was just kidding. Sometimes I like to see how someone will react in certain situations. But there was no doubt in my mind that it was her. I beckoned the waitress, who had just reappeared. She came up to the table.

"We'd like to see what cakes you have."

She returned a moment later with a tray of cakes. As she held it in front of us, I asked:

"Which one would you like?"

Her eyes filled with an almost childlike delight at the sight of the cakes.

"Which do you recommend?"

I suggested the one that I usually took.

"You won't hold it against me if I pick a different one?"

And she did. So I asked for the same one she selected. At that point she seemed to get it, a moment of musing flashed in her eyes. She smiled, though her smile seemed artificial. With a similarly artificial nonchalance, as she ate her cake with relish, she said casually:

"I'm so grateful you let me sit at your table. I had such a craving for cake today."

"And that particular kind," I added.

"How did you know? You couldn't know, since you suggested a different one."

"Out of contrariness," I said. "Just like out of contrariness you refuse to remember that we shared a train compartment, that you sat down next to me on a bench in the park to have a cigarette. And wherever else we might have met before, you'd deny it, I know. Even if I told you you'd appeared to me in a dream, you'd deny that too, you'd say it wasn't possible."

"Now that, that's possible, though it's corny."

"But *how* is it possible, since you claim we've never met before?"

"Maybe that's the only way you could have remembered me." She looked at me with a fixed gaze, as if the life had suddenly gone out of her eyes. For a moment we stared at one another in this way, till her smile began to return.

"You know, I think that today of all days I'll allow myself another cake." She signaled to the waitress. When the latter came back with the tray of cakes, she first had me choose. Then she asked for the same kind that I picked. "You see what a pig I'm being?" she said. "I really shouldn't. I never let myself have more than one . . . It's all because of you. You're awful. If only I'd known . . ." She glared at me in a mock sulk, and I saw something like a hint of alarm in her eyes. But she immediately said: "Whenever I can't resist something, I always regret it later. I'll have to punish myself for the second cake."

"Punish yourself? What will your punishment be?"

"I haven't decided yet. I'll think of something. Oh, I know. If I come here again I'll just order tea or coffee, I won't have any cake at all. I'll teach myself a lesson so I remember in the future." She began almost savoring her self-imposed punishment. "Or no, I won't have tea or coffee either. I'll have them bring me a glass of water. Or I'll be even harsher. I'll order a cake, but I won't eat it. I'll leave it. Or two cakes. Yes, that's it, two cakes, as if I were expecting someone else. And since the other person won't come, I'll leave both cakes uneaten." She started to laugh, as if the punishment she was going to inflict on herself amused her greatly. "I mean, you yourself said a moment ago that we're always expecting someone, we just don't always know it. This way I'll at least know. Two cakes, and I'll leave both of them."

I was on the point of telling her that she shouldn't punish herself at all, what was one extra cake, it wasn't going to hurt her. She was slim. When she came into the cafe and was standing there looking for a free table, it even struck me that she looked like an Easter palm branch. But I realized she might not know what an Easter palm branch is, and I asked if she wouldn't like some tea or coffee, apologizing for not having thought of it before.

"No, no thank you," she said, still laughing. "It'd spoil the taste of the cake. I never drink tea or coffee with cake, not ever." Laughing all the time, she reached for a paper napkin. As she did so, the sleeve of her blouse pulled back and under the hem of her cuff, above the wrist, about here or a bit higher, I caught a glimpse of numbers written on her skin as if in ink or indelible pencil. It lasted a split second. She snatched a napkin from the stand on the table and pulled down her sleeve before she put the napkin to her lips.

I ought not to have noticed it, because you shouldn't notice everything, especially a man looking at a woman. Even in themselves people don't always like everything. There are many things we'd like to change in ourselves. We're at odds with many things in ourselves. We'd like to improve things in ourselves, as we would in others. But since that isn't possible, you must admit that at least it's less troublesome when we don't notice it. But she evidently saw that I'd noticed, and felt obliged to say:

"Oh, that's from when I was just a child." She was embarrassed, or perhaps unsettled, because her eyes turned away to look around the cafe. Only after a moment did she return to her cake, taking a tiny piece on the tip of her spoon. "You know what I used to dream of most often as a child?" she said, holding the spoon at her mouth. "Of one day eating my fill of cake."

I laughed. It must have seemed insincere, because no shadow of a smile appeared on her face.

"I never imagined that when my dream could come true, I'd have to deny myself the pleasure." Once again her eyes drifted away to the cafe, she stared at something or other, and when she went back to eating her cake, or rather picking at it, her gaze seemed buried in her plate. All at once she livened up and, clearly looking for a fight, she declared: "I have to say the first cake, the one I chose, was better."

We began to argue about which was the better cake, the one she'd selected or my one. And you know what it means to argue about cake. It was like we were debating something of the utmost importance. Like it was ourselves we were submitting to a test, not just some cake. In this way we got onto the topic of the best cake we'd ever eaten in our lives. It was mostly her who remembered which cake and when and where, and each one was the most delicious. Even though the previous one had been the most delicious, the next one was even better, and the one after that was so delicious it canceled out all the preceding ones. I even tried to picture her as the child whose dream was being fulfilled, because she was thoroughly engrossed in remembering all those best cakes.

Myself, I didn't really have much to recall as far as cake was concerned. At any rate I couldn't have said which was the best one I ever ate. In response to all those best cakes of hers, I said that at Eastertime my grandmother used to make a babka that to this day I could taste in my mouth. Though I couldn't say if it was actually the best cake I'd ever had. That didn't matter. Sometimes I buy a babka for Easter, in one cake shop then in another for comparison, but so far I've never found one that tasted the same as my grandmother's. Not to mention that babkas from the store go dry after two or three days, whereas the ones my grandmother baked could sit there for months, then when you cut it it would still be moist with butter. Plus, they were so plump. Have you ever had a babka like that? Then you've missed out on one of the best things there is. You should have come at Eastertime. Or right after, or even a few days later. We used to take the babka up to the attic and leave it there. We wouldn't eat more than a slice each a day. You could have tried it.

When I was married my wife decided to find a recipe for babka like that, because at Easter she was sick of hearing about how my grandmother baked babkas and all that. She even wrote to some well-known pastry chef. He actually sent her a recipe and she made it, but it wasn't the same. Grandmother would usually make a dozen or more babkas at a time. The kneading trough would be brimming with dough. She'd fill the earthenware baking dishes about half full, then when the cakes rose, they virtually bubbled. They looked like mushrooms. We'd usually each have a piece for afternoon tea. Grandmother would divide it up so it lasted as long as possible. Thanks to that, it felt like Easter went on and on.

No, she hadn't had Eastertime babka. She asked me to tell her about it. But how can you tell someone about babka. You can describe the shape, say that it had notches in it from the earthenware dishes it was baked in, that it was broader at the top and narrower at the bottom. But none of that amounts to anything.

It's the taste that matters, not the shape. And how can you describe a taste? You tell me. Any taste. Let's say, something sweet. What does sweet mean? There can be a million kinds of sweetness. As many kinds as there are people. One person puts a spoonful of sugar in their coffee and it's already sweet enough for them, someone else needs two or three spoonfuls for it to be sweet. During the war for example there was no sugar, so people would boil up a syrup out of sugar beets, you'd have been disgusted if you'd tried it, but everyone found it sweet like before the war. There's sweet and sweet, no two sweetnesses are alike. Sweet today, sweet once upon a time, sweet here or there – each one is a different kind of sweetness.

So I told her it was made of flour and eggs and cream, because that was all I knew, the rest my grandmother took with her to the grave. She may have taken the whole mystery of those babkas with her. All that remained was the fact that they melted in your mouth.

She grew sad when I told her that. To cheer her up I said that all the cakes she'd told me about were for sure the best. I asked if she'd like to have one more. I'd give her a free pass. She smiled through her sadness and said the only thing she would have been tempted by would be a piece of the Eastertime babka. In that case, perhaps she'd have a glass of wine, I asked. She said yes at once. As we were drinking our wine, lifting the glass to our lips over and again, she gave me a look as if she finally remembered me. For myself, I no longer had any doubts that it was her. I don't mean from the train, or the park bench, or anywhere in particular. By then, none of that was of any significance.

You probably think that you have to meet a person first to be able to remember them later. Have you ever thought that sometimes it's the opposite? So you think it all depends on the memory, yes? In other words, first something has to happen, and then, even if it's years later, memory can bring it all back? If you ask me, though, there are things that it's best for memory not to meddle with. I agree with you that in the cases you're talking about, that's how it is. But we don't always need help from our memory. There are times when our greater need is to forget. It'd be hard to live perpetually in thrall to memory. So sometimes we have to mislead it, trick it, run away from it. I mean, when it comes down to it we don't even need to remember the fact that we're here on this earth. Despite what you think, not everything has to happen according to how it's organized by memory.

Why was it that when she came into the cafe and looked around for a free place, I was certain that even if someone had vacated a table at that moment, she still would have come up to mine and asked:

"Would you mind if I sat at your table? All the other seats are taken."

"You're welcome to," I would have said, as I actually did say.

And the rest you know. I'm not hiding anything. Why would I? I've not brought happiness to women. I don't know a whole lot more than that. Besides, you can read a book, watch a film and it'd be the same. It's always the same. There aren't any words that would make it different. Yes, if you ask me, everything depends on words. Words determine things, events, thoughts, imaginings, dreams, everything that's hidden deepest inside a person. If the words are second-rate the person is second-rate, and the world, even God is second-rate.

If I tell you that I loved her, it still won't tell you anything, because it doesn't tell me anything. Today I only know as much as I knew back then. Or rather, it'd be better to say that I don't know now just as much as I didn't know then. Because what does it mean to love? Please, tell me if you know. And since I loved her like I loved no one else on earth, why didn't we know how to be with one another? Actually, to say I loved her isn't enough. I sometimes felt that she was the one who had finally given me life. As if it wasn't that she was made from my rib but that I was made from her rib, the opposite of how it is in the Bible. When I'm dying I'll see her coming into the cafe, looking around for a free table, then coming up to mine and asking:

"Would you mind . . . ?"

"You're welcome to."

She sits down, but we don't feel like talking anymore. Not even about cakes.

Not because we've said everything already to each other, since we've hardly said anything. We'd have needed an eternity to say everything to one another, not just the short moment we've lived through. I don't know, maybe by now we're afraid of words, even words about cake. Maybe there are no more words for us. And without words there's no telling what any of the cakes were like, and all the more which one was the best.

We weren't good together the way you might have expected. But we were even worse without each other. We split up, came back together, split up again, came back together again. Each time we swore we'd never part. After which it was the same thing. Then when we got back together, every time it was like we were back in the cafe that first day.

I can't remember if I told you that one time I happened to go back to the same sanatorium, and after taking a walk one day I dropped by the cafe. I was sitting there drinking my coffee and reading the newspaper. At a certain moment I look up over the paper and I see her coming in. By then we'd separated for good. There were free tables, but she came up to me and asked:

"Would you mind . . . ?"

"You're welcome to."

"Oh no, your hands don't look good."

"How's your heart?"

And once again we decided never to part. But soon we did. Tell me, was that love? If you ask me, love is an unsatisfied hunger for existence. Whereas the two of us had been hurt by existence. Neither of us was young anymore. She was a few years younger than me, it's true, but it was a long time since she'd been young. I often had to ask her not to be ashamed of her body. She'd always look over anxiously to check I wasn't watching when she undressed. It was always:

"Turn the light off."

"Why?"

"Please, turn it off."

"But why?"

"Don't you get it?"

I didn't get it. She probably never suspected that as I watched her undressing I had the feeling I was being enriched by all her hurt, all her pain, by the way time was passing her by. I'd lived through a great deal myself, but it wasn't as important to me as what she had been marked by. No, it wasn't that I felt sympathy for her. Besides, does love require sympathy? What I'm trying to say is that I experienced her existence as my own existence. You ask what that means? It's like you desire to take the entire burden of someone else's existence upon yourself. As if you wished to relieve that person entirely of the necessity of existing. As if you wanted to die in their place too, so they wouldn't have to experience their own dying. That's something different than sympathy the way it's usually understood. At the very possibility of such a thing, even if I was only imagining it, I felt a renewed desire for life. You say that isn't possible. It's possible that it isn't possible. But in that case, what should be the measure of love? If you and I understand the same thing by this word that has no meaning? In accordance with what do we supposedly experience it? The appetites of the flesh? The flesh has its limits, and they're reached much, much sooner than death.

Do you know if she's still alive? Did I take you by surprise? Who on earth else other than you could tell me? I thought I'd at least learn that much from you. Because if I knew she was no longer alive, I'd not want to live anymore either.

Sometimes I think to myself that maybe if I could still have played. Or perhaps I was afraid to involve her in my life. Or I no longer had the strength to take on that love on top of everything else. You have no idea what it means to love when you're not young anymore. It's the hardest challenge. When you're young, ceasing to exist doesn't seem so terrifying. But you see, me, I always lived on the boundary between existing and not existing. Even when I seemed to be there, it was like I was only passing through, only there for a short while, visiting someone, though I don't know who, because I have no one.

You think that's why I came back here? But this isn't my place either. So what if you came to buy beans? You could have gone anywhere, and not necessarily for beans. If you hadn't found me you'd always have found someone. What difference does it make? For you none at all, I don't think. I'm not mixing you up with someone else. Though for a long time I kept thinking about where and when it had been. At one point, right at the beginning, I even wondered if you might be him. Oh, no one. It just occurred to me. But no. If you'd been him, you wouldn't have come to me for beans. How would you have known that someone like me exists.

What time is it? Ah, I have to be getting along. I've got to make my rounds of the cabins. Like I told you, I always go around at least once every night, often twice when I can't sleep. See, the dogs are awake too. What is it, Rex? Eh, Paws? Sit! You've already sniffed the gentleman. No, they're not hungry. They ate earlier in the evening. Maybe they had a dream. I'll leave them with you. Don't be afraid of them. Just keep shelling the beans.